I0535358

Rise of Angels

Timothy Winstanley

Blackwood Publishing

4

First published in Great Britain in 2014.

Text copyright ©2014 Timothy Winstanley

This book is dedicated to my mum and sister for all the long hours they spent proof reading it.

Prologue

Gun fire ripped through the air; a shop window shattered into a cascade of glittering fragments and bullets ricocheted off the stone sculptures. Screams of terror reverberated from the surrounding walls as ever more bullets raced towards their targets leaving a trail of bodies in their wake.

They were coming closer, they were nearly there...

It was a bright sunny day that afternoon in mid June; through her small window Alice sat gazing out at the busy streets of London far below and thought how much she would prefer to be out there rather than stuck in her cramped room. She was supposed to be writing a dissertation about the ethics of GM farm animals but the sun drenched city outside was far more inviting. She stared at the little people below going about their daily lives, every one of those little specs on the pavement had its own story to tell whilst from up here they looked like nothing more than ants. She sighed and went back to her desk; trying to muster the enthusiasm required to write ten thousand words by the end of the week. Glumly she pulled out her chair and sat down attempting to force words onto her laptop screen.

After ten minutes of this fruitless exercise her mind had wandered off again and she found herself absentmindedly chewing a strand of her long brown hair. Once again she stood up and went back to the window casting her green eyes down the length of street. A quick walk outside wouldn't do any harm would it? Come to think of it some of her friends said they were going to the park for the afternoon. Going outside seemed so tempting but the dissertation wasn't going to write itself. Giving in to the lure of the sunny outdoors she gave up and grabbed her favourite leather satchel. Before leaving the apartment she quickly checked herself in the mirror; her green eyes stared back at her as she pushed some loose strands of hair back into place. She then hurried out of the apartment, planning to write the essay later; it wasn't as if she had only one hour left to live!

She had forgotten the lift was broken so began the tiring trek down the twenty flights of stairs to the ground floor; everything kept breaking in this place but that was low budget university accommodation for you. On the thirteenth floor she passed the miserable caretaker going the other way. He usually had some snide comment for the students who regularly messed up 'his' building. In Alice's case he just smirked; she was a good head taller than him and he'd quickly discovered that he couldn't get the better of her in an argument.

The building was surprisingly quiet as she crossed the deserted atrium and stepped out onto the busy street. Weaving between the countless tourists she set off for the park. Up above her countless new buildings were rising; she often stared at them as these high tech towers soared ever further into the sky. Currently the tallest was the London Banking Tower at nearly half a mile high; however what lay before her would soon put that in the shade.

The Spire was wasn't even half complete and yet it was already the second tallest structure in the city. When finished it would be a mile and a half high making it the highest building on Earth. Alice stared at the swarm of robotic drones frantically assembling the next story and thought how fast technology was developing; a few years earlier such a feat would have been science fiction!

After a short walk meandering through the busy streets she arrived at the Greenwood Park where she soon spotted her friends, Theresa and John over by the boating lake. Until recently the park had been a massive council estate but its high crime rates and ugly buildings had resulted in its transformation into a large wooded oasis in the heart of the busy city. As she got closer she could see John reading something off his new iPhone 11 to Theresa. He kept bragging about it and sometimes Alice wished he'd lose the damned thing; it was far above her price range.

8

"... despite being given only a few hours to live he is expected to make a full recovery...Oh hi Alice," John said turning off the phone.

"What's that you're talking about?" Alice enquired.

"That millionaire who leapt in front of a car to save a little girl is expected to live," Theresa replied.

"Oh, that's good," Alice remarked. "Anything else interesting?"

"Riots in Spain, moon base cancelled and some scientists think they can make a GM gerbil speak."

"And lots of thefts, robberies and murders," Theresa added.

"And that's why I don't watch the news anymore," Alice remarked. Gradually the conversation moved on to other things; like how John was getting a new car, Theresa was dumping another of her endless string of boyfriends and of course Alice's loathsome dissertation.

After half an hour of lounging beneath the tree Theresa slowly lifted herself up from the ground, flicking off the loose blades of grass from her blonde hair before she got to her feet.

"Shame you arrived so late because I promised I'd meet up with Mark at the square."

"Who's Mark? You've never told me about a Mark before," Alice asked quizzically.

"Oh, I thought I told you. He's one of my cousins who lives in the US. I haven't seen him in months so I really can't be late. Actually why don't I introduce you to him, I bet you two would get along well."

The Square as it was commonly known, was a large pedestrianised part of the city where all the big name shops had congregated. Square in shape it was unsurprising how this fancy courtyard had come by its name. It had a stunning modern water feature at its heart and raised ornamental gardens dotted around the large open space, making it a popular place to shop. Getting in was always tricky but today was even

9

worse due to some construction work at the far side, the northern passage was closed for a few weeks meaning everyone was being funnelled in through the smaller one to the south.

Alice and Theresa eventually managed to push their way through the throng of people who were squeezing in through the narrow entrance before heading towards the imposing fountain in the middle. It had been made by some famous artist or other and had won numerous awards but to Alice it was just a metallic cube resting on one of its pointed edges. Theresa couldn't see Mark so the pair stood next to one of the flower beds and waited patiently for him to arrive.

The minutes passed slowly as the two girls waited.

"How long do you think he will be?" Alice asked at last.

"He says he's nearly here," Theresa replied looking up from texting. "Something about a delay on the Underground."

Just then an ominous rumbling sound began to fill the air. Confused they looked around for the source until they realised it was coming from the narrow southern entrance behind them. Alarmed, they quickly noted that people had started pushing and shoving their way back into the Square. Some people fell but no one took any notice as they frantically continued to force their way out of the gap and into the open expanse beyond; the previously happy chatter replaced by shrieks and howls. The two friends looked on in horror at the chaos unfolding; unsure what was going on as more and more terrified screams filled the air. After only a few seconds the last of the panic stricken people came pouring into the Square and fled in all directions. Then came the cause of the disturbance; a roaring bulldozer which was thundering straight towards the helpless people.

The vehicle was clearly too wide for the passageway so was gouging out vast sections of the wall as it continued on its merciless path of destruction thus herding everyone back into the Square. The machine soon reached the end of the ally where it came to a sudden halt, menacingly sealing off the exit. The Square was suddenly eerily silent; the shocked and immobile people were all staring at the now stationary

10

metal monster waiting to see what it would do next. None realised that the real danger was elsewhere...

Deep inside the exquisite fountain, the digits were ticking away on a device placed there covertly the night before. The screen ticked down the seconds; 9, 8, 7 when the metal colossus arrived; 6,5,4 the people stopped running; 3,2,1 the men, women and children felt safe. 0...

The explosion ripped through the water feature effortlessly tearing it into a million watery fragments. The shock wave raced out picking up all before it catapulting both debris and people through the air. The blast hit Alice and Theresa before they even knew what had happened and tossed them backwards; as if in slow motion they saw the windows collapse into the shops and shrapnel slicing through the air. They even saw the red petals stripped from the flowers before impacting with the hard slabs on the ground.

Dazed and shocked Alice slowly opened her eyes, she couldn't hear a thing. She tried to lift herself up but her right arm wouldn't move. In terror she tried to lean over only to see the sickening mangled remains of what had been her hand. She was frozen by fear; there should be pain she thought frantically but there was none. Everything seemed dulled; almost like she hadn't accepted the loss of her hand.

Around her there was a scene of utter devastation; the once beautiful fountain had been replaced by an ugly crater surrounded by the countless bodies of the dead or dying. What could she do? Then in the corner of her eye she saw two men climbing down from the bulldozer, each holding a gun. Her terror increased.

Bullets ripped through the air; one of the last surviving shop windows shattered into a grim cascade of glittering fragments and shots ricocheted off the stone sculptures. Alice tried to crawl away but only one arm still worked and they were coming closer. They were just on the other side of the flower bed, they were nearly there. Alice froze; the world around her seemed so still and quiet as one of the men stepped into view. He raised his gun and Alice gave one last futile scream before the world went black.

11

Chapter 1

The streets of London were soon echoing with the wail of hundreds of sirens as police cars and ambulances tried to force their way through the dense traffic. The first onto the scene found their path blocked by the wrecked bulldozer and they were forced to clamber up over the obstacle before the full horror of the scene met them. The dead lay tossed and scattered across the ruined landscape making a macabre spectacle; it was clear that few of the paramedics would be needed.

Detective Superintendent Thomas Gallagher was at home when the astonishing phone call came through. He had only just finished shaving when the phone rang, hastily he threw on his shirt and jacket before grabbing his badge and keys. In his early thirties Gallagher had risen rapidly through the ranks thanks to a series of high profile arrests and his ability to think outside the box.

In appearance he combined height with a powerful build which would have made him appear daunting if it was not for his gentle and yet handsome face. His most striking feature was a thin diagonal scar which narrowly missed his right eye, a lasting memento from one of his early cases. However, the scar didn't disfigure him and strangely suited him, as did his deep blue eyes and short dark brown hair. Born in Scotland he had moved south with his parents when he was ten due to widespread unemployment. He still retained a slight Scottish accent but it had largely eroded as a result of living in London. When he had graduated from university he had become a junior officer in the army but had soon realised the police force was his true calling. He had little of a social life outside of his job due to its demanding nature and as far as his colleagues knew had not been in a serious relationship for at least a decade.

Gallagher arrived at the Square just as the bulldozer was being pulled free by a pair of diggers hastily acquired from a nearby construction site. Their tracks skidded on the flagstones for a second or two before they painstakingly heaved the wrecked machine free in a shower of rubble. Gallagher coughed from the dust blown up as the crumpled wreck was dragged past. A police sergeant tried to stop him as he walked on but a quick flash of his badge allowed unquestioned access; one of the perks of being a detective, Gallagher often thought, was not having to wear uniform.

The scene that met him instantly reminded him of his service in the army. The devastation was truly appalling; the once charming water feature where he had on more than one occasion eaten his lunch was nothing but a jagged pit in the earth slowly filling with grimy water.

The victims were littered around the edges of the crime scene in a shape resembling a circle; many flung there by the blast. A proper count of the bodies was still underway but Gallagher could tell there were well over a hundred casualties. The bodies at his feet lay contorted; many peppered with bullet holes. This wasn't just a terrorist bomb; the survivors had been mercilessly shot in cold blood where they lay. As usual Gallagher felt a deep anger as he looked at the limp and lifeless shapes on the ground but this was worse than anything he had ever dealt with. Far worse...

It was then that he spotted the flame red hair of his colleague Natasha Williams making her way round a sizable chunk of pulverised concrete. Close behind was James Kennedy; one of his closest friends.

"What have we got so far?" Gallagher enquired as they neared him.

"So far not a lot," Natasha replied grimly. "All the witnesses are either dead or being carted off to hospital and the main CCTV cameras got knocked out by the bomb. I've sent Adam and Karl off to see if any of the shop security cameras survived the devastation."

On the far side of the Square, Adam made his way over to one of the large department stores; he'd already tried three but the cameras had all either been disabled by the blast or were not facing in the right direction. The doors weren't working so he climbed clumsily through

13

the remains of a wrecked window and forced his way through a jumble of manikins. Several ordinary police officers were escorting the last of the dazed shoppers out of a back door. He quickly found the Security Office and was thankful to see a screen showing a view of the Square. He set about rewinding the hideous events of the past hour. At 10:59 he noted the bulldozer's dramatic entrance followed by the deadly work of the bomb. This was the point where the other cameras failed but thankfully this one kept rolling. He flicked through the shooting hoping that the gunmen would come closer to the camera. Eventually the carnage ended; its last victim was a brown haired girl lying behind one of the flower beds. They were too far away for Adam to see their faces but he could almost imagine the look of terror on her face before she slumped back onto the ground.

Once the killers had finished their evil work they scanned the Square for any other signs of movement before hurling their machine guns away and moved towards the camera. The corners of Adam's mouth moved into a smile as the pair came within a few metres of the camera before they slipped into a tiny ally way. Hurriedly he reached for his walky-talky as he muttered.

"Got you."

Natasha listened intently to what Adam had to say before turning to the others.

"Two gun men fled the scene. Both are bald white males around 5 foot 10 wearing dark blue track suits. He says they look like twins but he can't be sure," Natasha relayed to them.

"Let's get the word out then," Gallagher remarked before turning to look again at the crime scene. "It's going to be a long night."

By 22:00 most of the Metropolitan Police Force was still out scouring the streets of London. Road blocks had quickly materialised across most of the streets and all outbound flights were cancelled in case this

14

was part of a larger attack on the city. The news coverage had made the entire public fearful and most had taken refuge in their homes leaving the streets eerily quiet and deserted.

Almost the instant the description of the gunmen was released to the general public a tidal wave of phone calls poured in condemning almost every hairless man in the city. However, every phone call that matched the description had to be followed up. Out of the many hundreds of calls only a handful deserved further investigation.

One such call came from an elderly lady who lived in an apartment overlooking one of the last council estates in the city. She recalled to the police that one of the houses was rented by two brothers in their late thirties. She rambled on to the police about how rude they were but one fact stood out; strikingly both the twins had recently shaved off their hair.

It was the task of police constables Jack Devlin and Thomas Wilkes to follow up on this interesting phone call. So far they had been dispatched five times since the attack on the Square. The first potential suspect was at work during the time of the shooting as was the second man they visited. Both had multiple alibis to vouch for their whereabouts and were quickly removed from the list. Another potential killer was too old and the last was in surgery after a heart attack. This latest dead end left both men musing.

"I mean come on, most old folk can't even lift a machine gun let alone fire one and what idiot puts in a call about a guy who's been in hospital for a week! They might as well not give the public a description of the suspects."

"Well if they didn't give the public the details then we'd have twice as many calls and we'd have even more work to do," replied Thomas. They sat in silence for a while until they eventually spotted the council estate where their final suspect lived.

"Which one is it again?" Jack asked.

15

"Number 443," Thomas replied reading it from a small notebook he'd scribbled on earlier; despite all the advanced technology around them, a pencil and paper still couldn't be beaten.

They pulled up across the street not expecting any trouble but still making sure their pistols were ready in case. Since 2016 most UK police personnel had been equipped with firearms due to the huge influx of illegal weapons that were being smuggled into the country.

It was a typical council house like the many hundreds which had once dominated this part of the city; although this one was in a far worse state of repair. In other parts of the city these kinds of buildings had all but been wiped out in recent years to make way for more modern buildings, the demolition of this area looked like it couldn't come soon enough. Jack rang on the bell and waited; a few seconds later he tried again when there was no response.

"Well, the TV's on and no one's watching," Thomas said whilst peering through a gap in the curtains. "Try knocking." Jack thumped hard on the door and again got no response except for a faint noise.

"Did you hear that? Sounded like a door banging." This was soon followed by a loud crashing noise round the back.

"They're running!" Jack called before bolting for the back gate whilst drawing his gun. Thomas then pulled out his radio.

"This is PC Wilkes, we have a potential suspect fleeing on foot, we're..." the sound of a gunshot cut him off followed by two other shots. "We're at 443 Beeston Road, Poplar. Suspects are armed, request immediate backup," he called before dashing after Jack drawing his own gun. The small ally opened onto an overgrown patio area where he found Jack crouching on the edge of the flag stones holding his arm.

"Bastard shot me in the elbow... think I got one of them though," Jack shouted out as Thomas hurried on after the suspects; within seconds he leaped over the fence and disappeared into the fading light. The undergrowth was thick but Thomas pressed on relentlessly as the branches slapped against his face. As the landscape grew ever darker he could just make out two shapes scrambling up an embankment. It had to

16

be them; however in the corner of his eye he could see two lights moving rapidly along the top of the bank; it could only be one thing... a train!

The tracks at this point went round a steep curve and all approaching trains had to slow to a crawl. The dark bulk of the enormous machine came ever closer and Thomas could see the suspects running alongside the tracks, damn it they were going to leap on! The engine came ever closer slowing with every passing second; its wheels screeching violently. Thomas couldn't make it there fast enough and could see one of the gunmen grab hold of one of the wagon's ladders. The other struggled a little before grabbing hold of another truck about three wagons behind. Thomas ran ever faster as he scaled the bank; a ladder was fast approaching and with a last desperate leap he grabbed it and held on for dear life. He slowly clawed his way up the rusty steel rungs to the top and sat on the small ledge to the side of the huge metal container.

"This is PC Wilkes; suspects are on board a..." Thomas was cut off as a branch loomed in front of him. Thomas leaned out of the way but just too slowly to save the walky-talky which was wrenched from his grasp and sent clattering into the darkness. So much for catching them at the station Thomas thought as he climbed up the ladder to the top of the truck. Luckily the wagon was full of what looked like chippings so he was able to climb inside and make his way forwards. Laboriously Thomas advanced down the train leaping from truck to truck. Normally he wouldn't risk his neck like this; but this was different, those monsters had to be caught at any cost.

At New Scotland Yard the controllers were redirecting every available car to the suspect's house whilst trying to raise Thomas on the radio.

"It's useless, he's not answering," the operator finally said swivelling round to face the attentive controller.

"Well load his GPS data," the controller ordered. The operator was already loading a map of the city.

17

"He's on the move, actually he's moving very fast."

"Turn the Satcam on him then," he said with a grin. The Satcam as it was known was one of the newest pieces of equipment in the Metropolitan Police Force's arsenal. As the name suggested it was a satellite camera that was positioned in a low orbit over the UK. What made it special though was that it could see just as clearly at night as it could in the light of day. The camera took a few seconds to swivel round to the desired location and then began zooming its multi million pound lenses into focus. Soon an image of Thomas appeared on board the freight train.

"Let's send in the boys," the controller said at last.

Thomas had moved along seven of the huge trucks by the time the controllers had located him. Just as Thomas was running along yet another pile of chippings a bullet struck the back of the wagon behind him and ricocheted into the chippings. He ducked instinctively behind a pile of the small stones. Peering round the side he couldn't see any sign of the gunmen in this wagon; he must be firing from the next one. Cautiously Thomas edged his way along the gravel staying below the edges of the container.

On approaching the end of the wagon he stooped below the lip of the aged metal wall. Quickly he popped his head over the rim catching a brief glimpse of the suspect before ducking down again. Thomas then shuffled left a few feet; with his gun at the ready and took a shot at the man. The bullet missed and the man retaliated with another shot which missed by a mile. Thomas moved further along the wall before firing once more; but to his surprise the man was gone. Thomas peered over the wall but the man was nowhere to be seen.

Up at the front of the train the driver was tired after a long shift and was glad that he was finally approaching the goods yard. Then to his dismay a warning light blinked on indicating that the brakes on one of the wagons had been engaged. Continuing the journey risked serious damage to the train and cursing his bad luck he began to bring the huge machine to a halt.

Thomas was catapulted into the end of the container as the train decelerated rapidly, dazing him slightly. Up ahead one of the brothers leapt free of the train soon followed by the other who descended more gingerly. The police helicopter was luckily not too far away and was overhead within a few minutes.

It wasn't difficult to spot the suspects as they fled the train and ran into the barren expanse of a demolished power plant. The two were sticking close together but it looked like one was struggling to keep up. The helicopter watched the hopeless flight of the suspects as it guided in the throng of police cars.

Thomas staggered from the wagon and set off in pursuit; following the noise of the police chopper. The injured man was gradually slowing down, falling ever further behind his brother until it became clear that he had been abandoned. He hobbled on a little before he was unable to continue any further and collapsed sideways onto a pile of rubble.

Thomas initially approached the injured man cautiously but decided to jog the last twenty metres as he could see the man was out cold, either the fall or the loss of blood had taken its toll. His grey track suit was soaked in blood; seeping out of a wound just below his right shoulder. Thomas pulled out a handkerchief and pressed it against the wound. The man didn't deserve to live but at least he could now spend a lifetime behind bars.

Chapter 2

The scale of the crime had finally been put into numbers with over £200 million of damage to the Square and the neighbouring buildings, 143 people were dead and another 12 were injured. Depressingly there were so many fatalities that a commercial fridge had been hired to store them in.

At two in the morning the last living people left and the cold cavernous room fell into silence. It had been a long day and despite the weariness of the workers, they knew they would find sleep difficult that night after what they had seen. As the last investigator left she switched off the light and the room was consumed by darkness. In the corridor outside there was no talking as the people trudged out switching off the remaining lights along the way. Finally the door was locked and they went their separate ways leaving the building to the dead.

However, in the gloomy interior of the warehouse one of the shadows was not as still as the others. It had waited patiently all day for the police to vacate the building and now they had gone it could roam the warehouse at will. Once it was sure that everyone had left it began to creep along the dark corridors, navigating its way perfectly in the gloom. It soon reached the huge metal door to the fridge where it extended a long thin hand and effortlessly pushed the heavy door aside. Without making a sound the shape moved in to the frigid interior before slowly sealing the door behind it.

The shape continued on its way weaving effortlessly around the objects that lay concealed in the dark. Moving amidst the two long rows of bodies its eyes scanned the scene. It reached the end of the line where it slowly crouched alongside one of the motionless figures. It stared for a moment at their closed eyes as it slowly withdrew its hand from the depths of its robes and carefully placed it on the cold head of the lifeless person. In the corridors of that building the darkness was complete and as silent as a tomb but in the fridge a faint glow slowly grew beneath that strange silvery hand; a light that would change the world forever...

Very early the next morning the pathologists returned to the warehouse to begin another gloomy day's work; cataloguing and identifying the dead. They unenthusiastically trudged up the long passageway to the warehouse door and filed inside moving to where they had left off yesterday. One of the younger male members of staff sat down next to a brown haired girl and thought surprisingly how little death had changed them. Yesterday they had identified most of the victims but now it was just a matter of collecting their personal belongings for their grieving families.

Confusingly the many bodies and injuries kept blurring together; he could have sworn that yesterday this victim had a gunshot wound to her forehead. He put it down to a lack of sleep and set about removing her watch when suddenly he noticed something rather odd. He had to be imagining it but her skin was strangely warm! That couldn't be right? His hand trembling a little as he took of his white gloves and reached out once more; yes her skin was warm! He quickly checked for a pulse and sure enough she had one! This couldn't be happening!

"This one's alive!" he shouted out excitedly. He expected a barrage of condensing comments but instead an slightly hysterical voice called out in response.

"I think this one is as well."

"Don't be ridiculous," one of the supervisors called back.

"It's not just them; these two are as well," another person shouted from the far end as they quickly moved between the sleeping bodies. Soon they were all working their way along the lines growing more and more unnerved with each one they reached. Their faces were still pale and their clothes remained caked in dried blood but beneath it all they appeared unharmed and uninjured.

21

"I don't like this," the supervisor murmured.

"This ain't natural," another whispered, their face almost as white as the bodies. Surprise turned quickly into hysteria as some of the staff edged nervously out of the room. This was just too much for them!

As the pathologists rapidly fled the room the mysterious figure continued to observe them unchallenged from its view point high on a metal girder supporting the roof; its colouration concealing it from prying eyes. It had sat there unmoving for well over four hours and only now turned its gaze to the sleeping people far below. Carefully it let itself slip down from the steel support that it had been resting on and dropped to the floor fifteen metres below; landing with the grace of a cat.

The lights which had been left switched on by the pathologists now illuminated the mysterious figure but still revealed precious little. The figure must have been over six foot in height but was far thinner than would have been expected for someone of their stature. These were the only major features that could be distinguished however, as they were cloaked in a set of long pure white robes that flowed down the entire length of its body. Not even their head was visible as a hood extended up from the robes; beneath this an un-naturally dark shadow obscured all traces of a face. Slowly it approached the door before turning to the silent people; in a deep voice that you could not fail to obey it said a single word.

"Awake."

"None of them are answering," Natasha said exasperated. "Why do people have phones if they don't use them?" she asked as she turned to Gallagher who was just climbing out of his car at the station.

"What's the trouble?" he asked with a suppressed yawn.

"I'm trying to get hold of Matt over at the warehouse. He was supposed to deliver the ballistics report this morning."

"How many people have you tried?"

22

"I've tried everyone I know over there and used the radio but no one's replying. Do you think they're alright?"

"I can't see anything having happened to them, but I needed to go over there myself so I'll pick up the report as well."

"Thanks, and if you see Matt could you tell him to use his damned phone once in a while."

The drive over to the warehouse was a relatively quick affair as little traffic was on the streets yet. Gallagher was surprisingly tired this morning but it had been a long day yesterday. He'd stayed up late into the night as the regular policemen combed the remains of the old power plant for the second suspect but to no avail. The situation had left Gallagher frustrated as they had missed such a perfect opportunity to apprehend both of the suspects. He could only hope they caught up with the fugitive before he caused anymore harm.

Soon he arrived at the entrance to the warehouse where the victims were being temporarily housed. The gate was wide open so he entered the car park and parked up his Mercedes in one of the empty spaces. He opened the door and stepped out into the warm sunshine. Looking around he immediately thought how unusually quiet it was; however he brushed this thought away and headed for the warehouse assuming that they had to be inside.

The building's corridors were a pleasant change to the scorching summer sun he thought as he stepped inside. He briskly strode deeper into the building until he could see the fridge door before him which had strangely been left wide open. Curiously he walked into the room beyond and still was not able to find anyone whilst noting that it was far too warm for a fridge. On the desks erected along the left wall lay an assortment of items as if abandoned in a hurry including a cup of coffee. Gallagher walked over and casually felt the temperature; people had been here recently.

He turned around to check the room once more. Until recently this space had housed frozen peas and other vegetables; now it housed the dead. The two long lines of bodies would have unsettled most and Gallagher certainly disliked being in their presence. Of course it was

23

part of his job, dealing with murders; not a week went by without at least one being committed in the city and they took up most of his time. However, this one was different; the scale of the crime just made it so much worse and all the more heart wrenching.

He was just turning to go back to the door when he thought he heard something behind him. Instantly he stopped moving and listened. At first there was nothing but then it came again; only this time it was more of a groan. Quickly spinning on the spot he couldn't see anyone; except of course for the lines of bodies. Then another moan came from the far end. Gallagher was already ill at ease and felt the hairs on the back of his neck rising. Despite the growing feeling that something was not right about this whole situation he still felt there was a logical explanation.

"Come on guys, this is a sick joke," he called out hoping someone would emerge; but still no one came forward. The silence now in the room was almost tangible and everything was still when suddenly one of the corpses clumsily rolled over! Gallagher was frozen to the spot in terror; could he be seeing things? But then another one slowly slid an almost serpentine arm across the floor just like a scene from a horror movie. Then as Gallagher watched greatly alarmed, another moved a little and then yet another! Gallagher slowly began to back towards the door keeping his eyes on the long lines of bodies not comprehending what was taking place.

But then one of them caught his eye when it eerily raised an arm up from the ground in Gallagher's direction before bending it round stiffly to allow them to rub their eyes. The movement was as you might expect when someone wakes from a deep sleep; it was such a typically human gesture that he continued watching to see what would happen next. Awkwardly the body then tried lifted itself into a sitting position which took it several attempts to accomplish. The pale face with its eyes closed tightly shut once more sent Gallagher edging backwards however at the same time he could not look away. After a few moments though the body slowly opening its groggy eyes and with its head leaning slightly to one side began to look around the room. Eventually though it settled its gaze on Gallagher but seemed to be having trouble getting him into focus.

24

"Where... am... I?" she spoke in a whisper as if speaking was painful. Upon hearing that pitiful little voice the terror which had gripped Gallagher seemed to wash away and he stopped heading for the door.

"W...w...water," the person croaked. Gallagher took a few seconds to react before spinning around and rooting through the items left on the desks close by. At last he came across a bottle of orange juice and thought it would have to do in the circumstances. He then approached the lines of recently deceased people of which many were now moving as if in a light sleep. As he reached the girl he could see she was barely able to sit upright that alone take the bottle off him so he held to her cracked lips for her. When she next spoke her voice was much clearer.

"Who are... you?" she asked as she slowly propped herself up in a more comfortable position.

"I'm Tom Gallagher. Who are you?" he asked, not quite certain what else to say.

"I'm Alice. What happened?" she said with a twinge of panic as things started to come back to her. "Why am I here? There was a loud noise and gunfire. No... Yes there was a bomb, am I hurt? What happened?" she repeated as the panic grew in her voice; she then looked down at her right hand. With revulsion she recalled seeing the mangled remains of it. However, this soon turned to confusion when she realised that her hand was completely fine; there wasn't even a trace of an injury! Her mind briefly leapt to the conclusion that she had not been injured and it must have been a terrible dream but then she noticed that the scar which had previously run down her arm from a skiing accident was missing. She traced the path of the vanished scar to the torn off sleeve of her yellow t-shirt which was still caked in dried blood. She looked down and saw more dark and congealed blood and the hole in her top where she had been shot for the first time. Terror momentarily flooded her mind once more until she realised that there was no wound there either.

Gallagher could now see that more of the victims were waking up. He looked about frantically for a container, finding a small plastic tub he then dashed off to find the nearest tap. Once he had filled the tub he hurried back. Luckily only a couple more had woken so he was able to go to each one and help comfort them. So many impossible questions were pouring through his trouble mind right now that he couldn't explain. In all of his mental turmoil though he noticed how quickly the people were accepting their situation; there was some initial panic but all seemed to very quickly return to a normal state of mind. Where was the hysteria which should have been present? Gallagher had spoken to many people who had experienced terrible calamity but these people were taking it all unnaturally in their stride.

After several stumbling attempts to rise Alice managed to get to her feet and soon came over to assist. It was then that Gallagher remembered his phone and swiftly rang Natasha. As it was ringing his mind was still racing; what had just happened? Was he dreaming? No, he couldn't be; he had actually witnessed a true miracle, possible the greatest miracle the world had ever known.

"Hello," answered Natasha bringing him back to Earth.

"Natasha, you've got to come over here immediately. Bring as many people as you can get."

"Why? What's wrong?"

"Nothing's wrong, actually quite the opposite. I can't tell you over the phone. Just tell everyone, I need them over here now."

"The rest of the team's away at the moment..." Natasha began.

"I don't care who you bring, even the cleaners will do," he said before hanging up as several more people began to wake up in quick succession at the far end of the room. He just hoped that reinforcements would arrive soon.

It wasn't long before Natasha and the ten people she had hastily rounded up arrived at the warehouse; somewhat annoyed at being dragged away from what they had been doing. However, the strange scene left them dumbstruck. By now over half of the victims had woken with Gallagher frantically running between them. He soon spotted Natasha and the others who were staring open mouthed by the door. He hurriedly left Alice to carry on alone as he dashed over to the newcomers.

"I need more water; you two get more clothes for these people and someone get a heater in here anyone would think we were in a morgue!"

"Tom, what the hell did you do to them?" Natasha said almost shouting.

"Nothing they just started waking up on me! I'll explain later, now can you lot please help me!"

By 13:00 all one hundred and forty three victims had woken from their slumber. Natasha, Gallagher and the other police personnel had been moving from person to person for several hours without a break. However, now came the awkward moment of deciding what to do next.

"We can't just keep them here," argued Gallagher.

"But letting them out on the streets will cause a sensation. We are talking about the single strangest event in human history. Yesterday I saw that guy over there with an arm missing and now he's drinking a cup of tea! This cannot be happening," Natasha retorted. "None of this makes sense!"

"Don't ask me to explain it; I don't know what did this but these people were stone cold dead yesterday and now many say they feel better than they've done in years."

"If this gets out the world will be in a frenzy," Natasha pointed out. "Anyway I don't think it's up to us to decide what to do. We should get someone higher up down here."

"I think someone higher up has already been at work here," Gallagher muttered to himself as he walked off. This was going to be a very interesting phone call to make.

On the other side of the city the gunman lay in a hospital bed. After his arrest he'd been taken to the Royal London Hospital where he was now securely strapped down. It turned out the wound was not that serious and he was expected to make a full recovery. The police were not taking any chances since his brother was still on the loose so four armed police officers had been placed on guard outside the entrance to the high security ward. As the gunman's warped mind recounted the shooting with delight he was quite unaware of the approaching danger which was coming closer with each passing second; something the police were powerless to prevent.

From behind the police guards, along a short corridor a towering figure silently closed in. Dressed entirely in black with matching hood it might as well have just exited from a horror movie set. The guards hadn't been a problem for the figure who had instead slipped in undetected at the back of the ward.

The black figure moved down the corridor and rounded the corner into the room where it clandestinely approached the bed. The unsuspecting patient did not see as the figure slid a long black dagger out of its sleeve. They remained unaware as a black gloved hand gripped the handle and raised the knife above him. For a heart beat the blade hung there before it was brought down and the gunman's flow of wicked thoughts were silenced. The figure then moved silently on; leaving the knife imbedded in the man's heart. Unchallenged, it headed back along the corridor towards the window; its task was done.

However, just as it was approaching the window its sensed that one of the guards had just turned round. Within seconds all four policemen were charging into the room with their guns raised. From the depths of its hood a strange smile spread across its shadowy face. Slowly it turned without concern allowing the policemen to stare on in disbelief. They started to yell something but their words were of no importance as with incredible speed it did a backwards somersault, shattering the window and disappeared out of sight.

The policemen stood stunned for a few seconds; unsure what to do before running over to the jagged remains of the window. They expected to see a body on the car park ten levels below but what they saw shocked them far more. How on earth were they going to explain this?

In the warehouse Alice sat leaning against a wall with her eyes closed. How long had she been here now? She could hear someone entering the room and slowly opened her eyes. Nothing much had changed since the others had awoken. She wanted to be out of this steel box but at the same time could understand why they were being kept there; yesterday she had been certifiably dead along with one hundred and forty two other people. She couldn't explain her miraculous return to life but was just deeply thankful that it had happened.

After she had discovered that Theresa was not in the warehouse she had initially been quite anxious until she persuaded one of the policemen to look into it. Half an hour later she had received the news that her friend was in hospital with serious injuries. Sadly, Theresa had lost a leg which left Alice feeling guilty and confused. Her friend had lived but was now maimed for life whereas Alice was feeling healthier than ever before. Not only had all of her scars vanished but her eyesight had distinctly improved. She had always worn glasses when reading but now she could see everything in perfect detail. Another thing which struck her as odd though was how difficult it was for her to focus on the traumatic memories of the attack; as if they had been put just out of reach for her own good.

A few minutes after the hooded figure plunged from the hospital window Kennedy found himself angrily talking into the phone on Gallagher's desk.

"What do you mean he's dead?" he barked into the receiver.

"I mean he's dead!" the police officer replied. "But that's not the half of it."

"What do you mean; you've just lost one of the biggest mass murderers in British history whilst he was in police custody!"

"That's nothing; you weren't here. You didn't see what we just saw!"

"What are you blabbering about?"

29

"The assassin just leapt out of the tenth floor window and we can't find a trace of him!"

"What?"

"We saw him leaving; he just turned and stared before doing a back flip through the window! We looked out and couldn't see a trace of him so we rushed downstairs and still couldn't find anything!"

"What did he look like?"

"He was wearing a thick black cloak and hood so we couldn't see his face and he must have been at least seven feet tall; he was almost brushing the ceiling tiles he was that big!" Kennedy leaned back in his boss' chair and briefly wondered if the officer had been drinking. He was unsure what to do about this latest development; he couldn't send anyone over as Gallagher had out of the blue requested everyone else to go to the warehouse. Annoyingly, no one would answer their mobiles! He'd have to go and check this out himself.

In the small company conference room that belonged to the warehouse's owners, officials from many different departments had hastily gathered; each unsure of what to do or who was in overall charge of this bizarre situation. Gallagher had found himself a seat at the end of the conference table and like most of the participants was listening to the heated debate occurring at the middle of the table. The two main voices in the argument belonged to Christopher Parry from the Home Office and Joanna Creighton from the Department of Health.

"We simply cannot release these people again. Think of the chaos that will ensue!" Parry argued.

"But these people should be with their loved ones; yes there will be an outcry but you can't hide them from the world forever. It is against their human rights."

"Technically these people are dead so they have no rights. Anyway you're from the health department; think of the medical issues. They might be contaminated with some sort of disease."

"Diseases don't bring people back to life! Anyway thorough examinations have shown that the people are in absolutely perfect health with no illnesses, injuries or any other abnormalities. There is no medical basis for keeping these people locked up."

Gallagher found it hard to concentrate after the first half hour. His mind was focused less on what to do with the people but more on how this situation arose in the first place. After two and a half hours of intense debate the Home Office finally prevailed and a decision was made for better or for worse.

On the other side of London, Kennedy now found himself investigating possibly the most frustrating murder in his career. Ten storeys up he could see the jagged hole in the side of the glass wall where a few hours previously a window had been. This was also probably the only murder investigation in which he felt no shred of compassion, in his opinion the killer had actually done a good deed by disposing of such a monster. However, the issue regarding the killer's infiltration of a guarded hospital ward and his subsequent leap out of the window had made the case important to solve. It was going to be a long day, again.

He slowly paced the car park and ran through the facts again in his head which were few. Four people had seen him jump but no one had seen him land; this was unsurprising as it was early in the morning and had happened on a side of the building obscured by a derelict tower block. It was possible that someone had removed the body but ludicrous to suppose that they could have removed the mess in time. The killer must surely have planned this impossible escape in advance; he couldn't realistically have just leapt out of the window without prior planning. Somehow this hooded figure had pulled off one of the most impressive escapes known to man and not left a trace behind.

Kennedy slowly made his way inside and headed back up to the crime scene via the lift. He was soon crossing over the exclusion tape and rejoined the swarm of investigators who were scrutinising every detail.

"So have you got anything for me?" Kennedy said as he approached one of the white suited technicians. Gazing up from his clip board he turned to Kennedy looking grim.

"I've tried pinching myself to see if I'm dreaming. We've been over every surface and haven't got a single hair or fingerprint. What we have got though are a lot of weird details that don't add up. The first odd feature is that the blade is stuck fast in the victims chest, no amount of force will get it out,"

"That is peculiar..." Kennedy agreed.

"Yes it's definitely odd but that's not the weirdest thing we've found," he said walking over to a laptop. "The CCTV has also drawn a blank; none of the cameras in the building recorded anything amiss but something strange has happened to some of the recordings."

"You mean someone tampered with them in advance."

"It's possible but unlikely," the young man answered as he set up the playback on the laptop. "The way it's been done is like nothing I've seen before. Here we are..." he said pausing the feed. "See for yourself."

The camera showed the high security ward in great detail with the suspect fixed to the bed right in front of the camera. "Now watch this," he remarked just as the image started to go out of focus before abruptly cutting out altogether. For a few seconds the screen was blank before the camera came slowly back into focus revealing the knife in the man's chest.

"Four other cameras behaved exactly like this; one in the corridor outside, another in the car park and the two in the cafe and gift shop," he said turning to face Kennedy as if expecting an explanation to be forthcoming.

Kennedy thought about the technician's words. The disturbance was clearly masking the killer's movements, however the gift shop and the cafe were nowhere near the crime scene. They were on the fifth and sixth floors and were hardly places a murderer would need to visit. But as he thought about it something began to dawn on him; both were

32

roughly level with where the killer must have fallen. No one could possibly have prepared the cameras to fail just at the fleeting moment he fell past, to get the timing right would have been utterly impossible. The only explanation was that the killer must have been interfering with the cameras just by being in the vicinity of them.

"Can you play all five cameras at the same time," Kennedy enquired.

"Sure, just give me a minute."

It wasn't long before a row of five laptops had been set up showing the recordings from the five cameras. At two minutes to eight the camera in the car park fizzled out and died.

"Our killer arrives," Kennedy noted. Slowly the image of the cafe began to fizzle out as did the gift shop ten seconds later. Soon after the camera in the ward went black as the other two cameras crackled back into life.

"The crime is committed," Kennedy commented. Then almost instantaneously the shop and cafe went black before the car park disappeared again.

Watching it like this showed the path the killer took with surprising detail. They had arrived via the side car park but had not entered the building there as none of the other cameras had been interfered with; the only route they could possibly have taken was up the side of the building!

33

Chapter 3

By late evening Gallagher sat at the desk in his office with Natasha sitting on a swivel chair looking out of the window thoughtfully. Neither had spoken much since they had arrived half an hour ago. Natasha was the first to break the silence.

"So, how long do you think they will keep this secret?" she asked watching the few remaining cars on the road disappearing off home.

"As long as they can," Gallagher replied. "Imagine the outcry. It'll bring out all the lunatics society has to offer; they'll be on every street corner saying the end of the world is nigh or the aliens have landed."

"Those people in there have families who are mourning them; all that agony for nothing when they should be rejoicing," Natasha lamented.

"Sooner or later they will find out."

"What do you mean?" Natasha said turning to face him. "You saw how serious they were about keeping this secret; don't forget those papers we had to sign promising to keep our mouths shut."

"Think about it though; for thousands of years people have prayed for their loved ones to be returned to them and for equally as long their calls have been unanswered. Now one hundred and forty three people have been returned to the world to carry on their lives. If the impossible happens once then it can happen again. I don't know whether it was some God or a bunch of little green men but it's going to happen again at some point," Gallagher replied with a deep confidence in his voice. Natasha was silent for a while turning back to the window.

34

"For all we know it could be happening again right now," she said eventually. "It's been a trying day, I think I'll be off home," she added as she picking up her jacket from the back of a chair.

"I'll see you tomorrow then, despite all this we still have another murderer to catch," Gallagher remarked.

"All in a day's work," she said closing the office door. "Good night Tom."

Gallagher stared for a short while at the space she had just vacated wanting to call her back but chose not to. For seven years they had worked together and for nearly all that time he'd had feelings towards her. However, he had a job to do and he would not let his feelings get in the way.

After half an hour Gallagher was struggling to concentrate; his mind constantly drifting over the events of the day. Could it be aliens? No, he thought scornfully, what did they have to gain in all this. Gallagher had long been a devout sceptic but this really was challenging his rational mind.

Just when he was about to call it a day though, a knock came at the office door; Gallagher looked up surprised by the late arrival. Before he could respond, the door swung open and in came two men in dark suits.

"Thomas Gallagher?" one of the men enquired.

"Yes," said Gallagher with a sudden feeling of unease.

"Could you come with us please." Gallagher could tell this wasn't a question.

"What's this about?"

"You'll know soon enough."

It had been a long day for Alice as well. After spending hours inside the fridge, a convoy of buses had appeared and all one hundred and forty three of them had been quickly shepherded on board. The journey

35

across London had lasted for over an hour as they slowly made their way to the outskirts of the city. Eventually the wooden huts of an old army camp came into view and Alice had a feeling that this was their destination. Her guess was proved correct when the chain link gates swung open in front of them and the convoy passed inside.

Here they disembarked among the World War Two vintage buildings where they encountered a large number of lightly armed soldiers. A series of tables had been laid out piled with new clothes in various sizes. They were told to pick out what they wanted before being divided into small groups and directed to every available shower block at the camp. Alice was a little sad to throw away her jacket; it was totally ruined but she'd been given it for her last birthday, back when her parents were still together.

After everyone had scrubbed themselves clean and dressed they were shown to where they would sleep. As they were being escorted to the other side of the camp Alice sensed something odd about the soldiers; they seemed to be keeping their distance and were observing them in strange manner. However, it was their eyes which betrayed them; they were afraid.

The fearful soldiers seemed to once again highlight the odd behaviour of the survivors who seemed in comparison unnaturally at ease. The events at the Square felt like they'd happened many years ago and as hard as she tried to focus on them her mind continued to mask the memories from her. Almost as if she wasn't supposed to be looking at them.

The camp was built to accommodate several hundred so was easily large enough for all of them. Alice found herself with four others in a hut which must have been made for at least ten. Alice didn't really take much else in before she slumped onto the bed and instantly fell asleep; across the camp much the same thing was happening to all the survivors. It had been an astonishingly unforgettable day.

Gallagher sat in front of a mahogany desk thinking much the same. The two men had said nothing on the way there and now stood patiently

36

outside. His eyes wandered around the ornately furnished room taking in the fine details on the fire place and the expensive paintings on the walls. The gold clock on the mantel piece ticked away highlighting how long he had been waiting. Gradually he grew impatient and walked over to the grand book case on the far side of the room which had caught his attention. Along its many shelves sat row after row of thick files which Gallagher's eyes skimmed over. The words on their spines only added to Gallagher's suspicions as to where he was.

After five minutes the door eventually clicked open and in walked a tall greying man who immediately strode over to Gallagher and shook his hand vigorously. Gallagher was surprised by the strength of the man's grip and the youthful shine in his deep blue eyes.

"Detective Superintendent Gallagher, I've heard so much about you; please sit," he said respectfully gesturing to the chair. Gallagher slowly moved back to the desk and sat down again as the man walked over to a neighbouring cabinet.

"Scotch?" enquired the man as though it was the most natural thing to do.

"I wouldn't say no," said Gallagher cautiously.

"So you're probably wondering why you're here," the man said handing the glass over.

"It had crossed my mind," Gallagher replied sipping his drink.

"Well as you will have guessed this is because of the... events of this morning."

"Yes," Gallagher said putting down the glass smartly down onto the desk.

"Well to cut to the chase the reason for us bringing you here is that we have a mystery that has to be solved, who better than one of the best crime scene investigators in the country?"

"So the secret service doesn't know what's going on either."

"How did you know I represent the intelligence services?" the man enquired leaning forwards.

"I remember your face," he said taking another sip of the drink. "Two years ago at a terrorist scare I was asked to brief a committee and you were representing MI5 then."

"I'm most surprised you remembered me," the man said sounding impressed. "Going back to your original question; the answer is yes, we don't know what's going on. This is a situation which we have never faced. There is no protocol or previous planning that we can fall back on and there is no obvious department to deal with this issue. If this should happen again the public will eventually find out and they will demand answers. As a result we have decided to begin with immediate effect an investigation into this phenomenon."

"I'm assuming you want me to help with this then," Gallagher enquired.

"No, I don't want you to *help*. I want you to *lead* the investigation."

"Me? But surely there are people who are much more qualified."

"Qualified in what? That's the whole point. As one of the most renowned crime scene investigators in the country as well as a firsthand witness I feel that you are more than able to head this inquiry. I read your file an hour ago and the way you pieced together that triple homicide in Hyde Park was nothing short of genius. Although a crime hasn't actually been committed we need answers and your team must find them."

Gallagher's head began to spin; he was being given the biggest break of his career on a case that was larger than anything he had ever dealt with; larger than anyone had ever dealt with. It was an offer that just could not be refused but there was a complication.

"What will happen to my existing case though? I cannot just leave a mass murderer on the loose without catching them."

"We will find a suitable replacement for you. Besides, the identity of the criminal is now known, it's more of a manhunt than an investigation now." Gallagher could see his point; his strengths could be put to better use in this new enquiry.

"Very well, I accept," Gallagher said at last.

"Excellent," the man said reaching over to shake Gallagher's hand firmly. "Soon the world will be looking for answers, let's just hope we can give them some.

Several miles away, Natasha lay in bed. She had been trying to get to sleep for over an hour but the events of the day continued to bombard her mind. So when the phone began to ring she was almost glad at the distraction.

"Natasha," came Gallagher's voice down the line.

"Tom, what can I do for you?" Natasha asked calmly as she propped herself up against the headboard of the bed.

"Take a guess where I've just been?"

"I don't know?"

"The MI5 building?"

"What did they get you on?" she asked jokingly despite knowing that this had to be important.

"The entire team's just been transferred; we have a new case..."

Early the next morning Kennedy, Karl and Adam were all rudely awakened by a succession of phone calls from Gallagher explaining that they had been transferred and where to meet him. The investigation was to be conducted with intense secrecy so for that reason the warehouse and neighbouring buildings were to be used as a base of operations instead of the normal offices at New Scotland Yard.

It was there at 07:00 in the conference room that the four members of Gallagher's team gathered awaiting his arrival. Only Natasha knew why they were there and had decided to remain tight lipped about it, much to the dismay of the others. They all knew that to be called off a case such as this meant something really big had come up. They didn't have long to wait before Gallagher flung open the door and quickly made it to the vacant chair at the head of the table, carrying a small stack of papers. This was going to be an unusual briefing...

"Ok, I know you're all wondering why we we've been taken off the original Square Bombing case so I'll try and get straight to the point. Our new assignment is unlike anything any of you have ever investigated before so I've changed the traditional briefing approach. As you all know this time yesterday the commercial fridge just across the car park was filled with the victims of the Square Bombing; it is now empty," Gallagher said trying to ease them into the situation as gently as he could. Carefully he split his pile of papers up so there would be a copy of each sheet for the four members of his team. A picture says a thousand words so Gallagher had chosen to prove his case through photos.

"Look at these," he said passing each of them a set of photos that had been stapled together. "What do you see?"

Kennedy, Karl and Adam were a little confused at the different approach but cautiously began to play along. It was Adam who spoke,

"I see two long lines of bodies," he said grimly.

"Correct; now flick over to the next photo," Gallagher said watching their faces closely. Obediently the three men flicked over to the next page before a look of confusion spread across each man's face.

"This photo is no hoax; it was taken twenty hours ago by Natasha to record what was found in the warehouse. The man you can see in the foreground went into that building with three bullet holes in his chest; by some reason which is unknown he is now alive. The lady to the left of him had a broken neck and is also in perfect health... In short all those people sitting in the photo had similar fatal injuries and are now alive and well. One hundred and forty three people who were dead only

40

the night before have by some unexplained means returned to life; we have been asked to discover who or what is behind this miracle."

There was a charged silence for a few seconds before Kennedy finally spoke,

"If it was anyone else telling me this I'd call him a liar and ask where they'd escaped from."

"And since it's me?" Gallagher asked.

"I'd have to say you're telling the truth... Where are these people now?"

"Yesterday the Home Office decided to move them to a secure facility. They haven't disclosed its location to me."

"So what are we going to do if we don't have access to the victims?" Karl asked.

"A team of scientists will be closely examining them and we'll be informed of their findings through a liaison with MI5. They will be trying to work out how this was done whilst we need to find out who or what instigated it," Gallagher replied.

"Although technically this isn't a crime, is it?" Natasha queried.

"No it isn't. But an event such as this needs answers and we have been asked to provide them," Gallagher confirmed.

"What do we have to go on then?" Adam asked.

"Regarding 'The Miracle'... almost nothing. However, there has been a development which may be connected. Kennedy, Natasha gave me a quick rundown on what happened at the Royal London Hospital. Could you summarise what you've found there for us?" Kennedy was a little surprised at first and then slowly started to see a possible connection.

"Well, far from returning people to life this is actually quite the opposite. As you know one of the brothers from the Square Bombing suffered a gunshot wound so he was taken to the Royal London where he was placed under guard on the tenth floor. However, within a few

41

hours he was dead and under very unusual circumstances. The assassin was seen by our men on the door who described him as close to seven feet tall and dressed in black robes. When he was spotted he escaped by leaping through a window and there has been no sign of him since."

"Just checking; was it the tenth floor window that he leapt from?" Karl queried.

"Yes," Kennedy replied.

"Neat trick, have you worked out how he did it?" Karl asked.

"In the afternoon we took our search from the car park and initially began to look at the wall below the window. However, it was on the opposite building where we made a rather odd discovery. About two floors lower than the window we found eight gashes in the wall; each about five centimetres deep and etched straight into solid concrete. A further two stories below that we saw a similar set of marks but this time on the hospital wall; this pattern continued all the way to the ground floor. The only conclusion we can come to is that our vanishing killer leapt between the two buildings and dug their fingers into the fabric of each building to slow their descent."

"This is all starting to sound like a sci-fi movie," Karl commented. "Is that stunt even possible?"

"What do you think?" Kennedy replied grimly. "No normal hand could tear through solid concrete. Also the weapon they used was very unusual; it was more a medieval dagger than a knife and it's made entirely from a black metal. The weirdest feature however is that it won't come out of the victim's chest. We don't know why but it just won't budge, it's almost like it's part of him now."

"As strange as this is, what makes you think this is connected to the other event?" Adam asked turning to Gallagher.

"In each situation we have an impossible feat. One was targeted at healing terrible damage whilst the other exacted revenge. The two have to be connected."

And so the meeting carried on and the investigation got underway; however on the outskirts of the city a less official enquiry was also beginning. Alice sat at a table in the corner of the largely empty canteen. She had risen at around 05:00 which was incredibly early even by her standards. She had tried to go back to sleep out of habit but had quickly realised she didn't feel tired at all. In fact she found that the usual fuzziness of waking up was slipping away rapidly and had been replaced by a clarity of thought that she had never experienced before. She found herself filled with the an unusual desire to go and do something constructive. However, by 09:00 she was bored; the camp hadn't taken long to explore and was largely empty anyway. Some of the soldiers she'd been chatting to told her that it normally wasn't manned and that they'd been brought over from a neighbouring camp. Hunger had then lead her into the canteen where there was a poor selection of food available and she had to settle for toast and porridge. Eventually she had come across a long forgotten book on the shelves by her bunk and had already read through half of it. It wasn't particularly good, too much blood and gore for her liking but there really wasn't much else to do.

Slowly the minutes ticked by; the book wasn't helping and neither was the clock on the wall of the canteen which loudly announced each passing second. Just as she was thinking about dumping the book in a nearby bin the noisy door creaked open and two people came into the room. Both were a similar age to her and shared distinctive flame red hair; Alice could only assume they were brother and sister. Just as they were about to sit down at the far end of the room the girl noticed Alice and slowly the pair weaved their way between the tables over to Alice.

"Hi, mind if we join you?" the girl asked with a kind smile.

"No, go ahead," Alice replied putting down the awful book. The girl pulled out a chair before saying,

"I'm Cathy and this is my brother Chris."

"I'm Alice."

43

"So, this is a nice holiday camp isn't it?" Chris announced sarcastically. "Been up since four and I still haven't found anything to do."

"One of the soldiers said they're bringing some books and games in later," Alice replied.

"I feel like a prisoner," Chris sighed."

"Same," replied Alice as Cathy nudged her brother as if he was supposed to say something.

"If you don't mind us asking have you got any good ideas about what happened?" Chris finally asked. "We've been talking about it for hours but we thought someone else might have fresh ideas?"

Alice had of course been thinking of little else since the event. However, all her ideas seemed too silly or downright ludicrous to tell anyone else, but then again the whole situation was ludicrous. It was such a relief to talk to someone about it.

"I really can't think of anything that seems sensible; all my ideas seem to involve gods and aliens," she replied.

"Most of Chris' theories were along the same lines," Cathy laughed.

"Well that's because of what I saw," Chris said looking at Cathy as if a little annoyed at her laughter. He turned back to find Alice looking questioningly at him. At first he remained quiet as if thinking exactly what to say before he eventually began to speak.

"When you were... out, did you see anything at all?"

"Nothing."

"Nothing at all?" Chris enquired again as if not entirely believing her.

"Not anything."

"Well, while I was out..." Chris began. "I remember seeing something very odd."

44

"Was it a pair of pearly white gates?" Alice teased despite being very interested.

"Actually it was quite the opposite. At first I began to feel like I was waking from nothingness and strange thoughts began to fill my mind; like they belonged to someone else. Then my eyes began to open and I could see that I was in a cave, actually a cave doesn't do it justice. Think of the tallest building you've ever seen and then imagine a hole in the ground big enough to completely swallow it several times over. The walls were bare rock but in unimaginable detail I could see that every surface was covered in intricate carvings that glowed a faint blue. These were amazing but as I turned my head to the right something truly incredible came into view."

Alice was by now enthralled with the story. It was so unusual; of course she'd heard people speak of after death experiences but they were nothing like this.

"What?" she asked at last.

"Well high above me I could see a face carved into the wall. It was absolutely monumental in size but partly shrouded by a colossal hood; beneath the face, the body of the statue stretched out to the base of the cave, cloaked by a long flowing robe. But that wasn't the most amazing part; whilst the statue was mostly carved into the cave wall, its arms were reaching straight out into the cavernous interior and in its hands was the most beautiful thing I have ever seen. Grasped tightly in its fingers was a giant blue sphere. It looked like something from another world with rays of blue light radiating out from its centre before vanishing like shafts of sunlight on a rainy day. It swirled and danced before me, drawing my gaze in and I remember feeling like I could watch it forever. As the minutes passed I continued to stare until I felt like I was growing tired again and before I knew it I had drifted off leaving the orb seemingly watching over me. Then after what seemed like an eternity I opened my eyes again and all I could see was the metal roof of that warehouse."

Alice was almost speechless. Normally she would have thought such a story to be totally absurd but the details were so vivid and seemed so strangely familiar; like she knew exactly what he was talking about.

45

"Did you see anything?" she asked turning to Cathy.

"No, I still half think he's making it up," Cathy remarked.

"Excuse me; I couldn't help hearing you talking about a vision," a voice said from further along the row. The three turned in surprise as they hadn't realised anyone was sitting there. Sure enough all the chairs were empty at the long table so the three looked at each other in confusion until the voice came again.

"Sorry, I'm down here," the voice replied with a faint American accent as a cheerful mop of brown hair popped up at the end of the table.

"What're you doing down there?" Cathy asked a little uncertainly as the newcomer dragged himself up onto one of the chairs before shuffling across towards them .

"I was trying to text someone."

"You've got a phone!" Cathy exclaimed.

"Shh, not so loud" he said looking round.

"Yeah, although I couldn't get any signal and now the battery's dead."

"How'd you sneak it in?" Chris asked.

"I'd just bought a new phone so I gave them one and kept the other. I'm Mark by the way."

Mark? That name and accent meant something to Alice; where had she heard it before?

"Wait a sec, are you Theresa's cousin by any chance?"

"That's me. I guess you're the friend she was waiting with. Sorry about being late; if the train hadn't been delayed we'd probably have been away in time."

"It's not your fault; just bad luck."

"Anyway," Chris cut in. "Why are you interested in what I saw?"

46

"Because I saw the exact same thing."

"Really!" said Cathy a little surprised.

"Not that I don't believe you..." Chris began. "But we've only just met you and how do we know that you're not just saying that?"

"Why don't you ask him a question that only someone who was there could answer?" suggested Alice.

"Ok, um... what colour was the stone that the statue was made of?"

"White," Mark replied instantly.

"So far so good, what colour were its eyes?"

"They weren't visible, the hood hung down too low." Mark replied.

"Also correct; now one last question..."

"Actually I have one for you," Mark cut in. "What do angels have?" For a few seconds Chris was silent before he finally replied.

"...Wings," he said in a whisper. "You actually did see it!"

"See what," Alice and Cathy almost said in unison.

"The statue had huge wings! I forgot to mention them didn't I? Coming out from its shoulders it had two massive bird like wings that went around the edges of the cave and met on the far side. But how could we both have seen it?"

"Wait a minute, if you two saw this then do you think others did as well? They might have seen more than you did." Alice remarked with excitement growing in her voice.

"Well let's ask around, it's not as if we've got much else to do."

The four agreed to meet up to discuss anything they found. Whilst they were making their plans though; deep in a rundown office building more sinister events were taking shape.

47

Michael Gorse sat among the piles of rubbish swigging another beer. It had seemed like ages since he and Brian had fled their house. He still wasn't sure leaving his twin behind was the right thing to do but then again both of them would be locked up now if he'd stayed with him. The grotty curtains were drawn tight keeping the light of day from entering the dank room and a small battered TV set provided the only source of illumination. In front of him on a pair of old office chairs sat another two men. Both wore battered camouflage clothing like Gorse and looked like your average thug with tattoos plastering their shaven heads. Patiently the three waited in silence as the footsteps of a fourth man came carefully up the stairs.

Slowly yet purposefully the man stalked around the corner and came towards the other three whilst remaining in the shadows that cloaked the far edge of the room. Eventually he drew level with the other three and emerged from the darkness. Age had crinkled the man's face with lines and a long forgotten bar fight had bent his large nose slightly over to the right. He didn't even look at the other two as his eyes remained fixed on Gorse.

"You were supposed to kill all of them," he said in a strong Scottish accent.

"We got most of them," Gorse replied before downing more of his drink.

"The bomb wasn't big enough," he said whilst closing in on Gorse.

"There wasn't enough room for more explosives in the fountain."

"Well you should have made more room. Making the city afraid is easy but bringing it grovelling to its knees is another thing entirely."

"We've still got the stuff; we can blow something else up," Gorse replied stupidly before moving to take another gulp of his beer. Quick as a flash the man lunged at Gorse pinning him by his neck to the back of the seat.

"You obey my orders around here! Remember I do the thinking not you! If we're going to spread anarchy through the heart of this nation then you listen to me," he snarled before releasing his grip and letting the snivelling Gorse go.

"To think I let you in on this scheme. Going back to your house as well! Do you even have a brain in that thick skull of yours?"

"We didn't think they'd find us so soon," Gorse stammered.

"Too right you didn't think. Now half the country is out looking for you. So now you're not much use to us; you will not leave here without my say so. Is that clear?" the man commanded staring at Gorse who nodded slowly.

"I can't hear you," he said in a voice filled with menace.

"Yes," Gorse quietly replied.

"Good. Jamie and Ollie; you come with me. Michael, don't drink all the beer," and with that the man and his two lackeys left, heading back into the shadows and down the dank staircase.

Gorse turned the volume back up on the TV but rapidly grew bored; his eyes drifted around the barren room. Apart from the chairs and television the only other furnishings were a long series of wallpapering tables that had been erected along the far wall. On them sat a whole host of tubs and discarded containers. The type of explosives they'd used had recently become a major headache for law enforcement agencies worldwide. Produced from a long list of items bought from your everyday supermarket the explosives had already killed thousands in over twenty countries since a group of gun nuts had posted the recipe online. It was cheap, hard to detect and far more powerful than C4.

He cursed as the screen flickered whilst he turned the volume up to full. London was still cowering he gloated; nothing else even received a mention on the news. That reminded him that perhaps he would hear something about Brian today. It had been strangely quiet regarding what had happened to him.

He kept on drinking waiting for the news to come on. As the credits appeared for the previous programme he chucked his bottle unconcernedly over his head and heard it smash on the hard concrete

49

behind. He then shuffled into the next room to get another. How many more wailing relatives were there going to be today he thought as he stumbled back into the room with his beer. It turned out he'd missed the first few minutes of the programme and joined it to find the reporter standing in front of a building that looked like a hospital. He listened trying to understand what was going on.

"...only a handful of details have been released by the Metropolitan Police Force. All we can say for certain is that yesterday at 11:07 PM, Brian Gorse was admitted to the Royal London Hospital for a wound sustained during his arrest. Doctors expected a full recovery however within hours of his arrival Brian Gorse was dead. Perhaps the act of a griev..."

What! He thought, Brian was dead, how could this be?

"... this morning it was revealed that Mr. Gorse was killed by a knife wound to the heart..."

A knife wound, but who would kill him! It must be the police he thought; they were behind it. He would show them; he would show them all. He slowly staggered into the next room again. Damn his orders he wasn't going to let the police get away with this.

Behind the fridge full of beer lay a sinister pile of homemade explosives, the culmination of several months of work. Oh yes, he would show them...

Chapter 4

It had been four days since the Square Bombing and the city had still not fully recovered from the shock. Flowers were tied to railings and flags across the city were drooped mournfully at half mast. However, such small changes to the city couldn't be seen by the men and women working nearly half a mile up on the world's biggest construction site.

At the base of the Spire a constant stream of automated lorries pulled up one by one waiting to be unloaded. This job was carried out by a long chain of huge robotic arms which grabbed the pre-fabricated pieces of steel before swinging them round and positioning them in one of a dozen high speed freight lifts.

The steel sections would then wait for no more than a few seconds before they began their rapid ascent up the needle like structure. On their journey they would pass finished offices and a luxury hotel before speeding on past the human workers who were fitting out each floor by hand. The exposed steel skeleton of the building lay bare beyond this point at the mercy of the elements.

Upon reaching the top, the lift only waited a few seconds before a huge mechanical claw grabbed the section and lifted it free. The claw belonged to one of several giant robots that resembled metallic crabs which were latched onto the sides of the steel skeleton. It was the job of these leviathans to manoeuvre each huge piece of metal into place. Once aligned the welding robots which darted through the air like flies would descend to anchor the beam to the structure.

Within thirty seconds of leaving the ground the girder was fixed into place and then the process began all over again as the drones relentlessly marched upwards through the buffeting winds.

This kind of automation had been a god send to property developers who could produce ever taller buildings at a fraction of the cost however there were some draw backs. The biggest issue being that the robots were good for the manually intensive work but they were unable to cope with the finer details such as installing the wiring and plumbing. The end result was a human labour force who were constantly in a losing battle to keep pace with the machines. Two such workers were Colin and Tristan who were enjoying what little respite they could get whilst sitting on the edge of the one hundred and second floor.

"All I'm saying is why are we having to go so fast. The drones were supposed to keep pace with us and not go racing off," Colin said before stuffing a ham and cheese sandwich in his mouth.

"I know; the foreman said they reached the two hundredth floor last night."

"If those things get any more advanced they won't need us at all," Colin remarked whilst watching the endless stream of drones humming through the air each carrying a window pane in its claws. Those new to the job would often stare in awe at the intricate ballet that unfolded in the air. One by one each drone would let go of its delicate pane of glass, allowing it to tumble through the air to the next robot which would snatch it from the air before expertly fixing it in place. The workers had seen them do this stunt thousands of times and the waiting robot never failed in catching the fragile components.

Colin finished his sandwich and moved on to a bag of crisps; as usual his clumsy fingers got the better of him and the bag ripped wide open. He was forced to watch angrily as his lunch drifted down towards the city.

Far below on the opposite side of the road from the Spire lay New Scotland Yard. The centre of law enforcement in London; this building was the latest to bare the formidable and respected name having only been finished a year or so before. Despite its modern glass front the building was actually a 1960s structure that had been vastly modernised

52

and extended towards the road to create the illusion of a high tech structure.

Currently their top priority was apprehending the other culprit behind the Square Bombing. It had been a major embarrassment when he'd slipped through their fingers last time. From being surrounded by police officers and a helicopter overhead he had managed to escape the tightening noose by jumping into an exposed tunnel at the ruined power plant. After a day of scouring the vast maze of passages they couldn't find a trace of him.

On the top floor of the New Scotland Yard building sat Detective Superintendant Robert Merrick. An hour or so ago he'd been very surprised to learn that he'd been put in charge of what he thought would be the biggest case of his career. Even now he still wasn't quite sure why as the case had initially been given to Gallagher and then transferred to him. He'd immediately gone to Gallagher's office to see what was going on but had found it empty. From what information he could get Gallagher had been given extended leave which was again very odd. Why would he disappear during such a big investigation?

Anyway the case didn't appear to be too challenging; it was more of a manhunt now anyway. He had several photos of his man as well as DNA samples from his twin brother. Combined with the fact that the CCTV network was programmed to spot the suspect, Merrick fully expected to have the mad man in custody within the next few days.

Merrick took another look at the report regarding the target. The suspect was marked down as Michael Gorse although there was a possibility that it was his twin brother Brian. The two had been responsible for multiple cases of vandalism and as well as possible involvement in an arson attack on a disused theatre. The target in Merrick's eyes was a rather unintelligent anarchist who simply wasn't capable of evading capture for long. It hadn't taken brains to pull off the massacre; just the element of surprise and a cold blooded person to pull the trigger.

As Merrick continued to read the scant records of his gunman's history a battered white van slowly drove down the street outside before parking by the neighbouring construction site. After a few moments the

53

driver climbed out and headed towards the manager's offices without bothering to lock the doors. At the last minute he swung away from the offices and continued briskly down the road. The passersby wouldn't have noticed anything odd unless they could hear that under his breath he was counting... backwards.

As the man disappeared around the street corner he reached zero; in a fraction of a second an electric current shot through the maze of wires straight into the heart of the bomb. Instantly the van was torn into a million fragments that hurtled off in all directions. The shockwave spread rapidly engulfing all in its path; cars were flung like toys, windows blew inwards and the ground shook violently. At the base of the Spire almost every pane of glass broke instantaneously creating a terrifying cascade of fragments which tore like an avalanche down the side of the tower. Like a waterfall they struck the ground creating a deadly glittering spray.

Merrick was still at his desk when the shockwave hit New Scotland Yard. It was as if the whole building had been hit by a sledge hammer as the wave of energy raced through the open plan offices, crumpling partitions and upturning desks. Without any time to react the blast hit Merrick and threw him effortlessly against the back wall of his office where he blacked out.

Around him the structure creaked ominously and hundreds of screaming people ran to what they hoped was safety. In panic they poured into the stairwells which were soon overwhelmed by the masses of people before they flooding out onto the street outside. Rapidly the building drained of life as the survivors fled. In the now largely empty structure the lights flickered eerily on and off illuminating the swirling clouds of dust that hung in the air.

As the panic-stricken people poured onto the street they were confronted by a second disaster in the making. When the building had been modernised an underground car park had been built underneath it and the street. The blast had destabilised the subterranean space and with a series of shrieks and groans the structure began to give way as cracks rapidly spread across the road.

The police personnel fled in all directions as large chunks of tarmac disappeared beneath the surface. The metal fabric of the car park was stretched to its limit as it tried to keep the road and the building above in place as the fissures knitted together around the front of New Scotland Yard. The structure seemed to be holding together just long enough to allow people their escape before with a final groan, the car park collapsed.

Behind the running people the road finally caved into the void taking a dozen cars and trucks with it. The new part of the building had little left to hold it up and an ominous crack shot up between it and the old 1960s structure. The contorted metal columns began to lean out towards the road with increasing speed as the seven story building began to thunder towards the chasm.

Onlookers fled in abject terror as the failing structure gained speed; the columns at the far right gave way first, explosively shedding their concrete skins as they snapped like twigs under the strain. Many of the survivors would later describe it as if in slow motion. The right hand corner slowly crumpled in on itself as the rest of the building continued moving towards the hole. The collapse spread along the building and within a second or two, New Scotland Yard tumbled into the pit where it slammed onto the rubble below sending out massive plumes of dust and debris into the air.

Despite the devastation the ordeal was not yet over. As the dust began to clear a new danger emerged. At first the horror stricken people were relieved to see the old building was still standing; however this was soon replaced as an unmistakable red and orange glow quickly began to consume the ground floor. It could only mean one thing...

In the now dark interior of the old building Merrick slowly regained consciousness; at first his vision was blurry but it gradually improved. His head span as he tried to remember what had happened. Eventually he recalled a loud noise; it had to have been a bomb he thought as he tried to move. He gasped as a blinding pain came from his shoulder. He turned to see his arm hanging limply at a repulsive angle.

"Damn it," he muttered as he pulled himself up using his good arm. With great effort he made it over to the wooden door and attempted to push it open but it wouldn't budge. He tried again but the door frame was out of alignment and wouldn't give an inch. As a result he was forced to clamber through the window into the dark corridor.

Above his head one of the emergency lights flickered on and off erratically. Each of the office cubicles was empty; their occupants having already fled the devastation. Merrick shuffled painfully on until he reached the door to the stairwell. He twisted the handle and pushed lightly as the door gave a mournful sign of protest and began to lean away from him along with the entire wall. Merrick quickly let go as the panel collapsed downwards into the emptiness where there had once been a building. Despite the now gaping hole in the side of the building, light did not stream into the gloomy room; instead there was only thick black smoke rising from the floors below.

Unfortunately for Merrick one of the city's gas mains ran directly under the new building. Upon its collapse the pipes had been wrenched from the ground and were now fuelling the raging inferno that was engulfing the building. The old building had quickly become a colossal funeral pyre.

Merrick swore as he remembered all the fire escapes were in the missing half of the building; he quickly made his way to the only stairwell that remained in the original half of the structure. Annoyingly it was on the far side of the building so he had to make his way through corridors cluttered with overturned cabinets and collapsed ceiling panels. Yet more ominous black smoke was swirling in through gaps in the walls and collecting in the confines of the corridors and offices as he went.

Eventually he reached the door to the stairs but felt his heart sink as he saw the fiery furnace which lay behind the frosted glass; he didn't have much time. The fire brigade were probably outside but through the dense smoke there was no way of knowing. Even if they were there he was unsure their ladders could reach him; not only was he seven stories up but he was also around fifty metres from the road behind the vast pit. The only option left was to head for the roof which would buy him some time. From what he'd been told there was a maintenance ladder in one of the rooms the cleaners used. Merrick hurried on but the situation

56

was getting worse by the second. Smoke was now pouring through the ventilation grills along the wall and the floor was rapidly growing hotter; he didn't have much time at all.

He eventually made it to the storage room and coughed violently as he opened the door. To his horror there was no sign of a ladder; it was the wrong room! Damn it he though, perhaps it was further along. By now the air was filled with the dense black smoke, Merrick was forced to try and crawl along the ground to avoid asphyxiation. With only one good arm the task was long and arduous; when he finally reached the other door he was close to passing out. He fumbled with the door handle and the last thing he remembered was a gaping hole where the room had been before he fell deeply unconscious.

High up at the top of the Spire the drones had halted construction automatically to check the structure for damage. The squadron of welder robots hovered in a perfect diamond formation awaiting further orders; however the one at the tip of the formation suddenly spotted something near the ground. Its large red eye saw beyond the smoke, zooming in on the unconscious man below lying dangerously close to a fire. The drone sent a hazard warning to the central computer as it was programmed to do, this was a task for the human operators to deal with as they saw fit. However, within seconds it was given a series of new orders which seemed to override the central computer and all other operating systems it was programmed to obey. Multiple errors quickly emerged and the drone remained frozen in the air. However, the new primary instructions overruled all its other programming. Immediately it passed this data through to the rest of the airborne robots which in unison banked sharply down and dived nearly a quarter of a mile through the air before levelling out alongside the seventh floor of the burning building. The drones slowly advanced into the dense smoke sending black spirals swirling off beneath their rotating blades. Slowly the lead one disappeared into the hazardous interior as the others began scanning the building.

Merrick lay motionless barely breathing as the flames slowly spread towards him. Roaring as it went the fire charged through the empty halls like an enraged beast; to destroy all in its path and consume everything that could feed its hunger. Just as the flames were about to

57

engulf him a pair of strong mechanical arms grasped his torso and began pulling him away. Merrick was too heavy for the small welding drone to fly safely indoors so it slowly dragged him towards the edge of the building. However, it seemed the fire wasn't ready to yield Merrick so easily and a sudden blast of flames raced towards them. At the very last second the drone finally got Merrick over the edge and away from the fire's reach. The flames had failed to get Merrick but the suction from drone's fans drew numerous sparks deep inside and ignited its air filters. The damaged drone immediately began heading for the safety of the road before its motor failed in approximately thirty two seconds.

Meanwhile a stream of fire engines belted down the street towards the raging inferno; fuelled by the gas leak it had only taken six minutes for the structure to be totally wreathed in flame. Many of the onlookers were either filming the scene on their phones or saying a silent prayer for the doomed souls inside. On this day at though at least one of those prayers was answered when suddenly like a demon out of hell a blazing fiery machine burst out of the black smoke carrying a motionless man in its arms.

Rapidly the disintegrating drone lost height; erratically it meandered through the air seeming to aim for a group of fire fighters which it calculated to have the most authority. Then at the last second the fire destroyed its camera. Wildly it plunged towards the ground and just had time to release Merrick before it smashed into the tarmac. It then shot back into the air tipping upside down in mid flight before slamming into the ground where its rotors explosively shattered, only just missing a female journalist. The battered drone then shut itself down to await maintenance.

As the battered shell of New Scotland Yard finally fell half an hour after the terrible blaze began there was some comfort in that most of the staff had escaped un-injured, three of which were saved by the drones. However, the painful reality was that that ten police personnel and fifty three builders had been killed by the explosion. Fear reigned throughout the capital as the news of the second terrible atrocity spread into every home throughout the city.

58

Chapter 5

An hour later Gallagher was pacing in the conference room at the warehouse, deeply worried about this latest incident. It had to have been Michael Gorse, the man who two days ago had slipped through their fingers. That failure had cost many people their lives today; some of which he knew. However, at the same time he felt strangely thankful; if he hadn't been heading this investigation then he could well have been sitting in his office when the bomb went off; the office which was now a pile of ash.

He was startled back into reality when someone knocked loudly at the door and without waiting for a reply Natasha walked up to him, already knowing what plagued his mind.

"Tom, there was nothing you could have done for those people," she said staring into his troubled eyes.

"If the killer had been caught the first time round then this would never have happened," Gallagher remarked turning away.

"Well, first off we don't know for sure it was the same person and secondly it wasn't you who lost the murderer."

After a while Gallagher turned back to her

"Yes, you're right," he said sitting back at his desk rubbing his eyes.

"Anyway we've got a different job to do now," she noted.

That was another thing he was uneasy about; so far they hadn't found any leads regarding the 'The Miracle' as it had become known amongst them but this latest massacre represented a rather grim opportunity.

"You know what we've got to do don't you?" Gallagher enquired.

59

"I've got a good idea as to what you're planning," she replied. "But what makes you think it will happen again?"

"The impossible has already happened once. Today's massacre is probably the closest thing we're going to get to the original conditions. The warehouse just across the car park is the only one large enough in twenty miles that can store the bodies. This is the best shot we'll get and we can't afford to miss it. I want that warehouse so filled with sensors that we can hear a pin drop."

"I'll get on it."

"Oh and Natasha, make sure they are properly concealed. We don't want to scare our miracle worker off until they have seen to the dead."

Several hours later in the dank interior of the abandoned office building, Michael Gorse sat comfortably on his decaying arm chair. However, this time he was not watching the TV and was instead recalling his evil work with satisfaction. He thought the bomb at the Square was impressive but the fireball at New Scotland Yard was something else. The only down side in his view was that the building took so long to collapse that virtually all of the workforce managed to escape before it came crashing down. He wasn't too worried about how the others would react; in fact he thought they would be impressed with his handy work. They always said he wasn't good for much but this would show them.

He then got up and headed for the fridge but unexpectedly stopped in the doorway. What was that noise? After a few seconds he decided it was nothing and continued towards the kitchen but suddenly there it was again, the sound of a loose floor board creaking. Gorse slowly turned on the spot looking for the source of the noise until he guessed it was coming from the stairs. He dashed into the kitchen and grabbed his pistol; they weren't catching him by surprise again.

Gorse waited silently for the intruder to show himself. Gradually the sound grew louder and Gorse could hear each footfall on the dilapidated stairs. Then suddenly, the noise stopped and Gorse became aware of his heart pounding in his chest. He could feel a drop of sweat slowly sliding down the side of his face until it dripped off onto the ground. The waiting was excruciating and he grew more uneasy with each second. What were they waiting for? The suspense slowly ate away at Gorse's confidence leaving only fear in its place; he began to sense that something very bad was going to happen.

The gun shook in Gorse's hand uncontrollably and he started to back away. He rapidly picked up speed and began to run down the long empty office; only briefly turning to see a dark shadow gliding out from behind the door. Gorse fled into the fire escape and hurtled down the stairs taking several at a time as the dark shadow followed him with frightening speed. Gorse tripped and fell at one point but fear forced him to scramble back to his feet; he had to escape or die...

At the camp on the outskirts of the city Alice lay in a deep sleep. She had only gone to bed an hour or so ago and had rapidly drifted off as normal but the vivid fantasies she saw through her closed eyes were far from ordinary.

High above her towered the great statue that had been described to her in such detail earlier in the day. The intricate carvings covered every surface and a blue light seemed to move and flow over them like a ghostly sea. She watched as the lights meandered across the surface of the rock moving steadily away from the statue and down out of sight. She began to wonder where the source was and traced it back up the sides of the cave to the carved torso of the statue. From there the light flowed along the outstretched arms of the figure at which point she realised that it came from the great sphere held in its elegant hands. The sphere was far more magical than she had imagined. It swirled and shimmered with its cloudy surface ever changing and reforming as it fed small streams of light which spread out bathing the rest of the cave.

Suddenly a noise caught her attention. She wanted to continue looking at the almost hypnotic light but her head began to turn almost involuntarily to look for the source of the sound. Despite looking to the side she couldn't see where the noise had come from as a low golden wall, a few inches away obscured her view. Once again her head moved

61

to face the other way only to be met by a second golden barrier. However, she wasn't able to dwell on what these were as a pair of figures came into view. Alice was immediately struck by how much they resembled the statue; both wore long white flowing robes and a hood just like the carved one high above. However, each also carried a long golden staff with a complex headpiece at the top made up of a series of rotating rings and wore a golden chest plate which sat over the top of their robes.

Slowly the two moved past Alice; ignoring her. Behind them came a series of other figures dressed in plainer robes without any adornment who likewise disregarded her. After ten of these figures walked by in this strange procession she started to feel tired and her vision began to blur. Just as she felt her eyes closing a single figure broke off from the procession and turned to face her. Like the others they wore a white hood hung low over their face but other than that they were completely different. Instead of robes they wore a set of futuristic white armour which covered the rest of their body. Although the armour had clearly been made to protect the wearer it was still a thing of beauty which glowed slightly in the gloom. Along the joints it was decorated with gold embellishments and down the wearers back was a white cloak which dragged along the floor.

However, most of these details were lost to Alice as her eye lids slowly closed together. The last thing she noticed was a golden pendant fastened about the figure's neck; there was clearly an intricate design engraved on it but the image was already becoming distorted. Alice attempted to fight her eyes open but to no avail as the vision faded away and she drifted into a natural sleep.

Gorse frantically ran along the empty streets of an industrial estate. He had been running for nearly half a mile but always saw the shadow in the corner of his eye; as if it was taunting him. He continued running round a sharp bend in the road but was suddenly confronted by a dead end. He ran up to the chain fence and tried to climb but it was no use. He turned round thinking about going back the way he had come but then he saw it.

The figure stood motionless about ten metres away. It towered higher than any man Gorse had ever seen, its black robes only adding to its cruel appearance and in its hand was a long black dagger.

Gorse backed away unable to take his eyes off the sinister blade. He frantically spun about in blind panic looking for somewhere he could escape that cruel knife. Then to his relief he spotted a narrow alleyway leading out of the industrial estate. Never taking his eyes from the figure he slowly backed into the passageway and noticed a heavy metal gate against one side. He quickly grabbed it and dragged the gate shut before pushing a large bin across the opening; sealing off the motionless figure. He then ran as fast as he could, frequently looking behind him just to check he wasn't being followed. The alley was long and he continued running down its narrow length until he couldn't go on any longer and slowed to a jog.

Up ahead the inviting glow from a street light hurried him on round a bend in the ally. It must lead onto the main road he thought hoping he would soon be out of this nightmare. He approached the corner and sure enough there was the road. Just as he was about to head forwards though, two more of the eerie figures appeared seemingly from nowhere. Although both were dressed in the same dark robes as the one before, these two were distinctly shorter and their hands remained free of weapons. Gorse quickly turned back to the alley in terror; he could still escape. But his path was once again blocked as the first figure landed on the ground in front of him; the dagger clutched in its hand. Slowly the three closed in on him.

In response Gorse raised his gun and fired at one of the smaller creatures; three shots found their mark and with each the creature writhed in pain but did not stop its steady advance. He turned to the larger one and was about to fire but with terrifying speed it grasped his gun hand and slowly tightened its grip. Both the gun and his hand crumpled beneath its incredible strength. Gorse tried to pull away but couldn't escape as the searing pain grew in his hand as the bones were crushed one by one. After what seemed like an eternity it finally released its grasp and backed away a couple of steps along with one of the other figures.

63

The final one however continued to advance, creeping closer towards Gorse until it was only a foot away from him. Slowly it raised both its hands to its head grabbing hold of its hood and carefully it began to lower the black veil of fabric revealing what lay beneath. When the hood finally fell away Gorse screamed in terror before he was silenced as the figure lunged at his neck and bit down hard ending the life of Michael Gorse.

For a while Gorse twitched a little but the figure only released its hold once Gorse's life had ebbed away; letting the body slump to the ground in a pool of blood. It then backed away and slowly raised its hood once more, hiding its face from the world once more. The larger figure then walked up to Gorse's body, it raised the blade above his chest before bringing it down into Gorse's un-beating heart. Then, just as quickly as they had appeared the three vanished as they walked away into the swirling gloom of the alley.

At the warehouse so far all had gone as planned; even before the bodies had arrived, Gallagher and his team of technicians had been hard at work preparing for every eventuality. Despite their poor performance at the hospital, ordinary CCTV cameras had still been installed at all the entrances to the warehouse and in the fridge. In addition to this other systems had been fitted including four thermographic cameras that could film body heat as well as a trip sensor connected to an old fashioned analogue camera. Just in case things turned nasty a group of six soldiers were also on station.

Gallagher looked at his watch, it was 11:45, last time the forensics team had left around midnight so it was nearly time for them to vacate the room. It had taken some organising to arrange all this; however assistance from the intelligence services had allowed Gallagher to essentially take all the dead as bait. Gallagher thought how sick it was that they even needed to do this in the first place but hopefully it would not be in vain. Just then Natasha strode in announcing,

"We're all set,"

64

"So begins the hunt," Gallagher muttered as he and the last of the technicians traipsed out before heading up to the surveillance room in a nearby office block.

The small room had been filled with banks of monitors; from these Gallagher could see an all round picture of the complex. Starting from the left a series of both normal and thermographic cameras covered the main gates and the side entrance; other screens showed the courtyard and a multitude of views from around the warehouse. The rest of the monitors were for the fridge itself. Gallagher, Natasha and the three technicians settled in their seats; it was going to be a long night.

Little did they know that only a few rooms away their target waited patiently. From its vantage point in the company records office the figure had waited for an opportunity to enter the building. However, the constant activity had made its chances of remaining undetected very slim so it had chosen to bide its time. Carefully it had studied the pieces of equipment which had been unpacked. The video cameras which had been hidden behind the guttering of the warehouse were of little concern to it, as were the thermographic cameras which it saw being carefully moved inside. However, it couldn't identify what were the contents of the blank boxes which had also been unloaded; it would have to be on its guard.

Once it saw the last of the people walking across the car park and into the office building it began to make its move. Cautiously it approached the door and waited patiently for the unsuspecting people to go past. Once it had sensed them enter the office it slowly opened the door and stepped into the corridor beyond. Without making a sound it strode within a few feet of Gallagher and his team as it made its way down the dated corridor. It soon reached the stairs and effortlessly swung itself over the railings before letting itself fall the two stories to the ground floor. Landing soundlessly like a panther it stalked along the final few metres of thread bare carpet to the glass door leading out to the empty car park. It could see the door to the warehouse only twenty metres away and paused to recall the locations of the cameras. There were only two options available; it could either disrupt the cameras which would alert those above or it could just walk straight past them...

65

The technicians continued to stare at the screens in eager anticipation. The figure took one final glance outside before turning its gaze downward and began to concentrate. Slowly the colour around the base of its robes began to shimmer and then fade away. A ripple of light then steadily moved up the figure leaving only emptiness in its place. The last part to vanish was the rim of its hood which left a bright circle in the air before it too disappeared.

Nothing changed on the monitors as the figure walked steadily into their field of view. One of the technicians even leaned back in his seat, beginning to relax a little. Eventually it reached the other side and stood before the closed door deciding how best to proceed. Eventually it turned towards a car parked just within sight of the cameras and raised a hand towards it.

The technician at the far left jumped with surprise, spilling his coffee as the noise of a car alarm broke the silence outside the office. All eyes turned to the source of the noise allowing the figure the brief opportunity to grab the door and disappear inside. It hurried deeper into the building and ducked into an open storage room. As soon as it was out of sight of the cameras it instantly reverted to its original form in a brief flash of light where it slumped against a wall, weary from such an exertion.

Up in the office the gathered people were unsure what to do about the car alarm rudely blaring into the night, worried that the actions of both leaving it or disabling it would scare off the target. Eventually Gallagher took the decision that someone had to silence it so he took the keys from the embarrassed technician and headed downstairs.

Gradually the figure seemed to recover its strength and slowly straightened itself up. It then crept over to the door and once again let the white of its robes drain away as it cloaked itself with invisibility. It hurried out of the room and continued along the corridor, sensing the glare of multiple cameras along the way. It rapidly approached the fridge door but chose not to open it and instead swung down a side passage where it found itself among a twisting maze of icy pipes which lay contorted along the walls. Detecting no cameras it once again reappeared although this time it lost its balance and collapsed onto a

66

series of metal shelves which buckled a little under the figure's weight. There it lay staring up at the frosted pipe work above, waiting for its strength to return. It knew that this form of invisibility was inefficient and unreliable before it had set off on its mission; it only wished it had had time to better prepare itself beforehand.

Gallagher rapidly descended the stairs hoping to get this done as quickly as possible. He made his way over to the problem car and reinstated the silence of the night. He turned and looked up at the surveillance office, checking that none of his people were in view. He must be shown on at least four monitors right now he thought as he walked diagonally across the car park back to the door. He turned to look at the warehouse as he walked; nothing was going to get into that building without them seeing it. But then as he looked he spotted something unusual. The door wasn't completely shut and was instead swaying slightly in the breeze. Gallagher quickly pulled out his radio and spoke rapidly into the receiver.

"The warehouse door is open, did we shut it before?"

"I think we did," came Natasha's uncertain voice. "The locks have been playing up all afternoon though, it could have just swung open."

"I take it we don't have anything on the cameras yet?" Gallagher enquired.

"Nothing,"

"Right I'll check the lock; it'll look suspicious if we leave the front door open."

The figure slowly pulled itself upright. Staggering, it made its way to a maintenance hatch on top of the huge pipe feeding cold air into the fridge. Effortlessly it tore off the padlocked piece of metal and was confronted by a blast of freezing air propelled by a pair of vast fans. Not affected by the cold it slowly heaved itself through the hatch and into the pipe. The fridge was only a few feet away and once more it tried to vanish; however this time it reappeared a few seconds later. It hadn't realised beforehand just how much of its strength the cloaking

67

consumed. If it failed out there then it would be spotted immediately. The only other option meant its shroud of secrecy would be lost.

Gallagher soon found the door was indeed not locking. After several attempts at pushing the door shut the magnetic lock just wouldn't activate. In exasperation Gallagher entered the building to see if anything was obstructing it. Down in the freezing pipe however the figure was concentrating very intently.

Just as Natasha was lifting the radio to her face, the technician on the right cursed loudly. She spun to see that all the images on the six screens in front of him had gone out of focus. Natasha watched as the phenomenon spread rapidly to all the screens which failed in quick succession. She hurriedly raised the radio and spoke into it urgently.

"It's started; the screens have failed, get out of there!"

However, Gallagher didn't have time as the door suddenly slammed shut with sufficient force to crack the pane of glass. He leapt back in surprise only to trip over a tool box that had been left behind. The impact with the floor winded him and he lay there gasping for air. To make matters worse the single light bulb above his head started to flicker ominously. Gallagher heaved himself up and tried the door but it was still firmly shut and the release button had no effect. Just then Natasha's voice came over the radio and he fumbled in his coat pocket to retrieve the device.

"Tom, what's happening down there?"

"I'm locked in, what have you got on the cameras?"

"Nothing, they've all blacked out, every single one... Oh damn it, the lights have just gone," he said as the bulb finally blew and he was left in total darkness.

"Same up here; looks like our friend wants his privacy," Natasha replied sounding a little uneasy. "What are we going to do?"

"Round up the other guys and make your way down here. I'll take a look further in the building while you try and get the door open."

"Keep in contact; you don't know what's in there after all," she said as she hurried out of the room.

Gallagher tucked the radio under his arm as he fumbled in his trouser pocket for his phone. The powerful light on the device easily cut through the gloom, illuminating the shadowy corridors. Gallagher then took a deep breath and advanced into the unknown.

The fridge was once again pitch black as the figure emerged; peeling away the grill at the end of the pipe as it went. Quickly it straightened itself and moved towards the normal entrance into the fridge. Halfway along the cavernous space it bent down near one of the folding tables and grasped one of the metal legs. With one tug it sheared the piece of metal clean off and then continued its progress towards the door letting the table tip over noisily onto the ground.

The noise of the table falling reverberated down the silent corridors until it reached an unsuspecting Gallagher who was nearly at the fridge door.

With great strength the figure bent the metal leg round the door handle and over part of the frame, intending to keep any intruders at bay for a while. Once it had tested its improvised lock it quickly turned and headed for the nearest body; it didn't have much time.

Gallagher reached the door just a few seconds too late; he tried to open it but it wouldn't budge. Damn it he thought looking for another way in; then he noticed the passageway leading off to the side where he spotted a partially open door.

Inside the figure had made it halfway along the first row; there wasn't time to waste as it worked with tremendous speed; hopefully it had sealed the police outside but if they made it through the outer door then it wouldn't take them long to find the other way into the fridge.

Gallagher ventured past the maze of pipes that made up the refrigeration plant. With the only illumination coming from his phone the whole building looked a lot more sinister than he remembered. His every foot fall seemed to echo around the now silent room. He soon spotted the maintenance hatch lying discarded where it had been dropped only a few minutes before. He quickly clambered up on top of the pipe and ventured inside.

The figure leapt over yet another motionless body and quickly touched the person's head before bounding over to the next one. It now only had about ten left to go...

Gallagher steadily shuffled along the freezing pipe in a stooped position. The fans had shut down when the lights went out but the metal surface was still too cold to risk touching.

There were only five left to go when the figure sensed Gallagher's presence and just before he emerged from the pipe it jumped over to the next body, vanishing mid leap.

Gallagher ventured tentatively into the pitch black of the warehouse; the light from his phone doing little to force back the all consuming darkness in such a vast space as this. The figure watched from its position in the far corner; it couldn't stay cloaked for long, unless... Slowly the back of the figure's robes began to re-emerge and white flooded back along the length of the fabric. As long as it stayed facing Gallagher it would remain hidden.

The light from the phone swung round the vast room, emphasising the bodies closest to Gallagher. Cautiously he ventured over to them whilst trying to pick up anything unusual in the gloom. The first victim he reached looked lifeless at first glance but on closer inspection appeared to be taking small shallow breaths which condensed on contact with the frigid air. Gallagher walked along the line noticing the same gasps of icy breath coming from all of their lips. On one hand he was deeply glad that the people were all right but on the other hand he felt rather dismayed that the miracle worker seemed to have slipped right past him. Holding the phone in his left hand he pulled the radio out of his pocket, surveying the scene.

"Natasha are you there?"

"Go ahead," she replied almost immediately.

"We missed it."

70

The figure watched on awaiting its chance. It didn't want to risk being heard or seen in its half invisible state so its movements were slow and calculated as it crept over to the next body. As long as Gallagher didn't come too close then it could remain undetected. Cautiously it began to move but when it saw Gallagher suddenly start walking in its direction it instinctively froze.

Gallagher continued walking until he arrived at the start of the first row where he began checking each of the bodies for signs of life. The figure was forced to strengthen its waning invisibility as a result. However, as Gallagher slowly moved away, the figure was once again able to relax its cloaking. In its mind it began to run through different plans of escape; resurrecting the remaining bodies would take too long at the slow speed to which it was currently confined. If it withdrew then Gallagher would immediately put the remaining bodies under even greater surveillance. It had to weaken its cloaking further and hope that Gallagher didn't look too closely at the end of the second row.

Gallagher reached the end of the first line and turned to begin on the next one. He watched for the tell tale puffs of icy breath, occasionally stopping when he couldn't see one. He had still failed to see the blurry shape which had now settled next to the second to last body. The figure began to work much faster and was just about to attend to the final one when Gallagher turned quickly in its direction. It was too late; Gallagher had seen them. The figure assessed the last body and then looked back at Gallagher, it could not abandon the last victim. It began to focus on something deep in its mind as the detective raced towards it with gaining speed.

Gallagher was closing in when suddenly his leg snagged on something and he crashed onto the floor; his phone skidding slightly out of his reach. In pain he crawled towards the upturned light. Just as he was picking it up though, something reached out and grabbed hold of his ankle. In terror he lashed out at the unknown assailant. After two hard kicks the grip loosened and Gallagher fumbled to aim the light on his attacker. His heart seemed to miss a beat and he gasped in shock as the entire row began to wake up simultaneously, but not like before. They were repulsively crawling and dragging themselves towards him like

71

something out of a zombie film. Gallagher dashed along the row dodging outstretched arms heading for the blurry shape at the far end.

The figure having completed its task released its temporary hold on the sleepers and allowed its invisibility to weaken so it now appeared to be just a white blur. With a burst of speed it quickly reached the door and wrenched it open, sheering the table leg barricade in half as it went. Gallagher charged on after the figure; his hand swaying the beam of light wildly as he went.

Up ahead the figure could see a powerful light being shone down the corridor towards it. Not stopping it ran straight into the torch bearer and sent them crashing into the side of the corridor. The rest of the startled people tried to get out of the way except for Natasha who raised her gun at the ghost like shape charging in her direction. But the figure was moving too fast and it rapidly closed the distance. With one swing of its arm it lifted her off the ground and sent her skidding across the floor into a water cooler.

Seconds later Gallagher tore past the surprised people; he couldn't stop to help as this was the best chance they were likely to get. Ahead of him the hazy figure ploughed without hesitation, straight through the glass door leaving scattered wreckage in its wake. Gallagher ducked through the gap trying not to touch the jagged fingers of metal and glass that reached out towards him. Ahead of him he could see the huge electric gates to the compound slowly closing as the figure charged towards the gap. Ten metres separated Gallagher and the blurry figure as it passed through the narrow gap. Gallagher panted hard as he only just slipped through and made it onto the road beyond.

The figure could normally run several times this speed but exhaustion from repeated use of the cloaking had reduced it to human speeds. It couldn't keep this up for long so it quickly formed a plan. Veering sharply to the right it headed for the door at the base of a large ten story parcel warehouse. Once again it ploughed through the door without slowing and headed straight up the nearest flight of stairs.

Gallagher was breathing heavily but his time in the army and his long fitness regime meant he wasn't planning on giving up the chase anytime

72

soon. Up and up he went, his quarry only a few metres in front of him. With every flight of stairs he gained more ground; he was so close.

Soon the stairs ended and the two hurtled through a large room filled with hundreds of crates; all neatly arranged into rows. Down the open expanse they ran before the figure darted to the left and headed along a narrow gap in the wall of boxes. Panting hard it continued on until its path was blocked by a tower of pallets. Without slowing it leapt onto the stack and scrambled up over the top. However, as it slipped down over the edge its robes snagged on a long jagged splinter; leaving a large section of snowy white fabric behind. Relentlessly Gallagher leapt onto the pallets just as the figure bounded down the other side and the chase continued. The two tore around the maze of passages and openings in the huge storeroom until the figure decided to head straight for an unassuming door in the side of the building.

It charged on smashing through the door and raced up a flight of stairs to the building's roof with Gallagher close behind. At last the chase came to an end in the centre of the large open roof. The figure soon stopped with Gallagher in turn coming to a halt close behind. After a few seconds the figure straightened them self and turned to face Gallagher; just staring into his eyes. By now all the white of its robes had returned making it stand in stark contrast to the black of night.

"You run well but this chase is over," Gallagher said at last. The figure remained silent for a while grudgingly impressed that the human hadn't fallen behind. Eventually though it responded in a deep voice that echoed off the concrete roof.

"Yes... This chase is over."

As the figure spoke these words a faint light began to shine through their white hood. Slowly the light rippled down the length of its body and grew brighter with every passing second. Soon they grew painful to look at and Gallagher had to raise his arm to protect his eyes; only the faintest outline of the figure could be seen within the star like brilliance that surrounded them. The shadows of night faded and people nearby looked in wonder as the unusual light shone out like a beacon across the city. With eyes tightly closed Gallagher yelled,

73

"What are you?"

The light grew still further until people from across London could see the star like object casting its beautiful light onto the streets below. Hidden inside the light the figure calmly lowered their hood and looked out across the city. Pulling open the front of the robes it allowed them to tumble away to its feet where they instantly caught fire and burned vigorously. It was time to leave...

Across London the people stared as the unexpected light rose slowly into the sky growing in brilliance with each second. It gracefully passed over the city before hovering motionless high over the remains of New Scotland Yard. And then the light was gone and the night grew dark once more.

All that was left for Gallagher was a smouldering heap of ash.

Chapter 6

Early the following morning the sun rose majestically over the horizon illuminating the drab old army camp with its warm rays. Alice was one of the few people awake at this early hour to see the spectacle unfold as she sat behind one of the flaking huts. Technically the people should have been locked in their rooms for the night but forgetfulness on the part of the guards meant that her door had been left open. She didn't want to stay in her hut for a moment longer than she had to and was out almost the soon as she had woken up.

Far away she could see the silhouettes of the city's many towers; like fingers reaching up into the heavens. When she was little there had been only a few skyscrapers in the city but rising populations had created a demand for new places to live so new structures went up every day. From the camp she could see three great towers being built; her bored mind had toyed with the rising buildings being locked in a race to see which one would be finished first. A hotel on the far left of her view had gone up by several stories in the past few days and some office block or other had increased the number of floors by nearly ten. However, the almost certain winner in this race was going to be the Spire. Over the last few days it had risen by at least three hundred metres taking it up to a staggering three quarters of a mile high. Alice had heard about the explosion at its base and had expected them to halt construction for a while but no; in fact it seemed to be ascending into the sky faster than ever.

However, exciting views aside, she couldn't help thinking about the night before: what had she actually seen and who were the strange ghost like figures that had silently glided past? She and the others had agreed to meet up here to discuss anything they might have found. All

75

she had to do was wait for them to arrive. The huts were normally unlocked around 06:00 each day; after the soldiers discovered that the inmates seemed to need less sleep than anyone else.

Just then she heard someone approaching and turned to spot Mark heading over in her direction.

"It's a nice morning," he said sitting down next to her. "So much for my time back in the UK; when I planned my trip here I hadn't planned for being locked up."

"Well it could be worse," she said with a slight grin.

"Yeah, you're right there," he replied looking at his feet. For a while both sat in silence; each struggling to think of something to say. After what seemed like an eternity Mark spoke.

"So, how well do you know Theresa then?"

"We've been friends for a couple of years; we both study the same subject at uni. How about you? What do you do in the States?"

"I study medicine at Princeton, New Jersey."

"And where do you normally live in America?"

"Same place, I moved there with my parents when I was ten. My dad got a job as a lecturer."

"Oh, well you've certainly picked up quite an American accent."

"It's funny; my parent's accents haven't changed a bit in all the time we've been there." A sad expression briefly glazed over his eyes before he turned to Alice again.

"Anyway where abouts do you normally call home?" he asked casually.

"North Wales," she replied.

"Really? You don't sound Welsh."

"Well you're a fine one to talk about accents," Alice laughed. "Not all Welsh people have an accent!"

"Can you do one?"

"I suppose..."

"Could you let me hear it?"

"No," she said in mock disgust

"Oh, come on..."Mark pleaded.

"No, it'll just sound silly. Anyway there's Chris and Cathy," she noted trying to change the subject. Patiently they waited for both of them to make their way over. As they covered the final few metres Mark called out,

"Got anything interesting for us?"

"Not that much; we found two more people who had the same vision as you and Chris?" Cathy replied as she sat down alongside Alice. "At least it proves Chris hasn't lost his marbles," she added with a laugh. "How about you two?"

"Same as you, I found two people who described a similar thing," Mark replied whilst turning to Alice.

"Actually last night I had a vision of my own," Alice said whilst trying to conceal her eagerness to divulge her dream to them.

"Was it the same as the others?" Chris asked.

"It started off the same but it lasted a lot longer. Over the next few minutes she described it in as great a detail as she could manage; from the flowing lights to the ghostly procession and the figure who stared at her. When she finished, the other three were obviously eager to bombard her with a wave of questions.

"What did the last figure look like?" Chris asked excitedly.

77

"I don't know; I was fighting to keep my eyes open and couldn't see them well enough. They wore a hood like the others but seemed to have some sort of armour over the rest of their body."

"Armour?" Chris said. "What kind?"

"What do you mean what kind?"

"You know; modern combat armour, a suit of armour, Samurai armour..."

"None of those; I really couldn't tell other than it was white and it vaguely reminded me of the sort of stuff you see the characters in video games wearing."

"Was there anything else you picked up on?" Chris asked.

"Not as far as I remember... oh wait; the last figure was wearing a pendant about their neck; it had some sort of design on it but I couldn't tell what it was."

"There are just too many people having these visions for it to be a coincidence," Mark said at last. "So all we have to do is work out what they mean!"

"In movies some people have visions that guide them," Cathy added hopefully.

"You're basing this on films," Chris remarked with a little laughter in his voice.

"Well have you got any better ideas," Cathy shot back.

"But, what would it be guiding us to?" Alice muttered whilst deep in thought. "It's more just a scene we are viewing which doesn't really explain anything."

"We've also got the issue that your vision is different to everyone else's," Cathy added.

"I don't know it is different," Alice thought out loud. "It started out the same as the others; I think mine just lasted longer."

"I've heard some people experience visions of the future," Cathy said.

"I've heard that as well, but why would we be seeing one point from the future?" Chris wondered. The three were silent for a while as a spark of inspiration distracted Alice. Cathy carried on talking and the other two began discussing it with her, however Alice wasn't listening; absorbed with a new idea in her mind which was rapidly taking shape.

"What if we are all seeing the past?" Alice suddenly blurted out cutting off whoever was speaking. The others were quiet for a while as they thought about what she had said.

"As far as I'm aware..." Chris replied slowly "I've never been in a giant glowing cave with a mile high statue before."

"No, I didn't mean that we were there. What if someone else saw it? During the vision didn't you get the feeling that you weren't in control of your movements. For instance my head seemed to turn of its own accord. As hard as I tried I couldn't look exactly where I wanted and the quality of the vision gave the impression of seeing through someone else's eyes." The other three were again quiet for a while considering Alice's words.

"Actually come to think of it, I'd describe the vision like that as well..." Mark said at last.

"Yeah, me too," Chris added.

"Well; although I still haven't seen any of this I think your theory sounds plausible," Cathy commented. "However, I still don't see why you would be seeing them in the first place."

"We never saw them before we were brought back so they are obviously linked to that event. They don't affect everyone and they don't always last the same length of time," Alice said before pausing for a moment, going over the facts in her head. "I think they are more of a side effect than an intentional vision. We are somehow catching a glimpse of what the person who brought us back saw at some point earlier in their life."

79

"You've been thinking about this a lot haven't you," Mark said with a grin.

"Only just now," she replied with a smile.

"Well it's the best idea we have to work on at the moment..." Cathy said before Chris cut her off pointing.

"What's that over there?" The other three turned to see a large green box vanishing between two of the huts.

"The entrance is over there isn't it?" Cathy said to no one in particular. Just then another green shape went past.

"They're coaches aren't they?" Mark said excitedly. They looked at each other for split second before bolting off to see what was going on.

Far away from the camp Gallagher was not having quite as much luck with his investigation. It had been a long and irritating night filled with disappointment; they had come so close to catching the mysterious figure and yet still failed. Gallagher now sat at the head of the long conference table with the others gathered around. On his left sat a rather dishevelled Natasha who after last night's ordeal was sporting a large cut to her forehead which had been stitched up at the hospital a few hours earlier. Kennedy and Adam were also present at the vastly oversized table as Karl hurried into the room and pulled up a chair.

"Ok, so we all know what happened last night so I won't waste time by running through it again," said Gallagher as Karl was taking a seat. "We'll start with the attack on our surveillance system, have you managed to find anything of use Adam?"

Adam replied whilst straightening himself in his seat.

"From what I have been told by the tech guys the cameras are all fine and they can't think of anything that would cause disruption on this scale. However, we have found one useful bit of information. It appears that only the digital cameras were affected. The analogue camera worked perfectly," he said as he pulled out a series of photos from a

80

folder on the desk. He had five in total which he passed over to Gallagher. The pictures had been taken looking up from the ground next to the inside of the fridge door. One showed a picture of Gallagher running, two were blank but the next one was very interesting indeed.

For the first time they had successfully caught their target on camera. The picture in question showed the figure as they fled the room and was largely blurred just as Gallagher remembered. Before it, one arm was extended holding on to the door which it had just wrenched open; the snapped pieces of its table leg barricade were clearly visible illustrating its incredible strength. Adam watched his boss studying the photo before saying,

"That's nothing; I saved the best to last." In response Gallagher quickly flicked over to the final picture. Adam was quite right, this image was significantly better. It had captured the figure just as they were about to wedge the door shut before it resurrected the victims and unlike the other photo it wasn't blurry. In fact every crease and line of in the robes was clear for all to see. Gallagher stared at his target remembering the incredible feats he had seen it perform.

"What are you?" he muttered under his breath before handing the image on to Natasha.

"Ok, that's a reasonable start to the meeting. Karl, what have you been able to find out about research into stealth technology."

"I've actually found quite a bit. There's obviously been study in this field for decades but it's only relatively recently that any major breakthroughs have occurred. From what I can tell there's only two or three groups which have successfully made an object invisible. The first documented attempt was made ten years ago by DARPA, the US military's advanced weapons agency who managed to make a battle tank appear to be invisible from one side..."

"I remember that," Adam cut in.

"Yes, they did like showing it off," Kennedy agreed.

81

"But as you're probably aware, it only worked if you were facing it straight on; this wasn't any use on a battlefield so they almost immediately shelved the project. The second system emerged four years back and was the work of a university in Utah however it had numerous bugs which meant they gave up after a few demonstrations."

"What sort of bugs?" Adam asked.

"Distortions, massive power consumption, loss of focus... Also the device was huge, apparently weighing close to a tonne," Karl said reading off a piece of paper. "Definitely not portable."

"They might have given up but someone else could have used the data," Natasha pointed out.

"That is possible however the next one sounds far more promising; although it might be just an urban myth. It's been rumoured a company based outside Manchester managed to create a fabric like material which can channel light waves around it."

"Why only rumoured?" Gallagher asked taking an immediate interest.

"A company employee announced its discovery on the internet and released a short clip demonstrating the fabric's capabilities. However, he was forced to remove the clip and retract his statements a few days later for unknown reasons. Since then it's just bounced around the internet across multiple blogs and forums."

"Which company made it?" Gallagher enquired.

"No details were given although it does imply they were based on an industrial estate to the north west of Manchester as the clip was shot outdoors. As there are only three in that area it shouldn't be too difficult to find them if they actually do exist," Karl replied whilst looking through his papers.

"Ok, well I want you up there ASAP and find out whether the rumours were true. This sounds too close a match for it to be just a rumour."

"Ok, I'll be off as soon as we're done here," Karl replied.

"Good, and Kennedy, what did the tech guys learn from the pile of ash?"

"Not a lot I'm afraid..."

"Oh, wait a second there," Adam cut across as one of his hands plunged into his bag below the table. "I expect an un-damaged section of its robes would be useful," he queried as his hand re-emerged clutching a transparent plastic bag with a glistening section of white fabric within.

"Where did you find that," Natasha exclaimed excitedly.

"Spotted it when I was looking for cameras in the parcel warehouse. It was hooked on a splinter by a stack of pallets," he said as he passed it over to Kennedy. "See what the tech guys think of that."

The meeting ambled on for another half an hour without any further developments. Every minute he sat there Gallagher could feel his tired eyelids growing heavier; it had been a very long night and the stuffy room wasn't helping. Eventually with a long yawn he adjourned the meeting. As the people filed out of the room he slowly leaned back in his chair and drifted off to sleep; his dreams filled with ghostly figures and shining stars.

At the remains of New Scotland Yard, workers clambered over the debris pile in the vast crater. The scene was like something out of an Armageddon movie with vast chunks of shattered concrete and twisted metal girders strewn everywhere. To add to the grim surroundings almost everything was burned and coated in thick soot.

As they continued to toil away, across the street a different sort of battle was being fought. Despite the carnage of the day before, construction of the Spire was progressing faster than ever, much to the dismay and surprise of the group of council officials gathered at its base. The group of five inspectors emerged from an alleyway on the edges of the site and soon entered the devastated landscape. Carefully they meandered around mangled vehicles and other assorted debris as they headed deeper into the site.

The bomb had crumpled the construction offices into piles of torn fibreglass and wood through which the five men moved into the heart of the site; searching for someone in charge to speak to. The bulk of the human workers had been given the week off to recover but even without their presence the site was awash with activity. Luckily for the construction company all the heavy machinery had remained intact and after some frantic rearranging, the automated lorries were now able to come in through a narrow gap at the back of the site. They continued to pull up one by one loaded with girders to feed the ever growing structure just as before.

The men eventually spotted a man wearing a fluorescent jacket with a clip board and made their way over to him. The man briefly looked up over his thick rimmed glasses and saw the men approaching.

"Can I help you?" he asked in a slightly abrupt manner.

"Are you in charge here?" asked the man at the front of the group.

"No, the new foreman's upstairs. Take the lift over there," he said gesturing. "Floor two hundred and fifty."

The men headed off in the direction of the lift only stopping to allow a giant crab-like drone to pass in front of them. Each of its legs were at least ten metres high and in its claws it held a massive concrete section which would eventually become part of an elevator shaft. The piece was too big for the construction lifts so the vast robot slowly lifted its front legs up onto the side of the building where they locked in place on the buildings framework. From there it slowly began to climb up the vast structure with the section in its grasp. Most people would be amazed watching such a feat but the men were not interested; they had seen it all before.

"I hate robots," one of them muttered as the drone began its ascent of the tower. They were soon in the lift which ran along the outside of the building. The curved glass doors silently shut and at incredible speed the glass pod rocketed up the smooth glass skin of the tower. It wasn't long before the completed levels were left behind and the open skeleton of the building lay before them. Thirty seconds after leaving the ground the lift slowed to a stop at the desired floor.

At ground level the tower's sides had measured just over a hundred metres across; now three quarters of a mile up, the sloping sides of the tower had reduced this to a mere twenty. Drones clunked and swung the latest sections into place and sparks rained down on the five men as they headed into the steel maze. Eventually they spotted the orange jacket of the foreman who was speaking to a pair of workers. The foreman saw them coming across the site and guessed why they were there. He turned to one of his colleagues as the men approached and muttered,

"Here comes trouble."

The men covered the last few metres before the lead one asked.

"Are you in charge here?"

"Since yesterday," the foreman replied.

"So you are aware that a bomb went off below us," the man said in a condescending tone.

"I think we noticed it just fine,"

"Well why are you still building then? In accordance with regulations you are required to halt all activities until we have deemed it safe for you to proceed."

"We know this tower better than you; she was the closest building to the bomb and she's still standing."

"You are not qualified to make such a statement."

"If the drones say the building's safe then that is all the confirmation we need."

"We cannot accept the word of some damned robot. We hereby order an immediate suspension to all work on this tower."

85

"You can order as much as you like but the drones won't stop unless head office tells them to," the foreman said hating every second he had to waste talking to this pathetic man.

"I don't want excuses; you have half an hour to cease construction. From then on we will tell you when you can continue," and with that the men moved off back to the lift. One of the foreman's colleagues turned to the boss with a worried expression on his face.

"What're we going to do then?"

"We can't stop for those pencil pushers. The deadline is fast approaching and that bomb has already put us behind."

Just then a movement from behind one of the columns caught the attention of the foreman.

"I'll catch up with you two in a few minutes," he said before hurrying off out of sight. The other two looked at each other; they had known for a while that something was wrong about this building and those who were paying them to build it. They often caught brief glimpses of their mysterious employers but knew better than to ask questions; their pay was too good for that. Quickly they followed after the men to the lifts.

The foreman emerged into an open space that looked out over the city. In front of him standing perilously close to the edge was one of the white robed figures. The wind howled through the girders but its robes remained motionless as it gazed out over the vast city below. As the foreman stepped into the centre of the incomplete room another pair of figures emerged silently through an unfinished doorway to the side of him; all of which now turned to face him. From within the depths of their shadowy hoods he could feel the gaze of their eyes. As the lead figure approached he knew they would already be aware of what had transpired; they always knew...

"We cannot allow construction to stop," the first one said in a deep voice that echoed slightly off the bare walls.

"I know that," the foreman answered calmly despite the intimidating nature of those around him. "But how are we supposed to keep those men away?"

Only the top management of the project had ever met their employers face to face. Initially there had been concern and a sense of deep unease, however these fears had been largely alleviated as time had passed. The employers were rarely seen and seldom interfered but were always watching.

"We will take care of this problem, do not let it concern you from now on," another of the figures replied in a calm female voice.

"We have also noticed the speed of construction has slowed. Will the project be finished in accordance with the schedule?" the remaining figure queried.

"The bomb has added to our work load considerably. Apart from losing most of the management staff we have lost some of the freight lifts and many of the columns on the western side need replacing. More worryingly the tower has shifted half a degree to north. If this was any other building site we would have stopped work long ago. If we are to stand any chance of getting back on schedule we'll need more drones and quickly."

"We will see that you get everything you require," the lead figure stated and with that the three turned in unison and left the room leaving the foreman wondering how they were going to 'take care' of the men.

Alice and the others raced between the huts in the direction of the now vanishing coaches. Their minds were filled with hope that they were at last going to be allowed to leave this makeshift prison. Mark rounded the last corner and came to such an abrupt halt that Chris ploughed straight into him and sent the two crashing down in a mess of tangled limbs. Alice and Cathy made it there a split second after the boys and were disappointed by what they saw. The three coaches had pulled up in a different section of the camp that was closed off by a high fence topped with razor wire. Hopes they would soon be leaving were dashed as they saw the first coach off loading a stream of battered and bloodied people; many appeared to be construction workers however some were clearly police personnel.

"Is that what we looked like when we got here?" Cathy said in disgust.

"Its happened again," Alice said almost in disbelief. "They must be from the Spire Bombing," she added as Mark and Chris heaved themselves off the floor.

"If they're still bringing in new people then it's unlikely they're going to let us go anytime soon," Mark said in a sour tone.

"I'm sick of this place," Chris remarked in an equally dismal voice.

"We all are," Cathy added.

"How long will they keep us here though? We could spend the rest of our lives stuck behind these rusting fences," Chris remarked.

"Calm down Chris; they'll let us out eventually," Cathy said uncertainly.

"And look at this place," Chris said falling further into despair. "It's like living in one of those old prisoner of war camps you see in the movies."

"Well..." Mark began. "If you don't like it in here, then why don't you break out?"

"We can't break out!" Cathy exclaimed a little too loudly. She looked around before continuing in a whisper. "There are soldiers with guns!" she hissed at Mark.

"Don't look at me, Chris started this conversation!" Mark said in protest pointing at Chris.

"I didn't! You said the word escape," Chris retorted.

"No, you said it was like being in a prisoner of war movie, in which the whole point is to break out." Mark said confidently. This exchange got Alice thinking as well.

88

"You know it might not be that tricky. The camp looks like it was built to keep people out, not in. There are fences all around but the soldiers don't patrol them regularly and largely stay at the entrance," she said as if she was thinking out loud.

"The soldiers are spread out too thinly to cover the whole camp; it will only be worse for them now that they have to keep an eye on the new lot as well. It's just the fence we've got to watch out for," Mark concluded confidently.

"Well how do you propose getting through the fence then," Chris added growing a little more interested despite still being a little sceptical.

"I don't know yet," he said whilst thinking. "The fact that it's very old is on our side; how about we walk around the perimeter to get a better idea of what we're dealing with. You two go clockwise round and me and Alice will go counter..."

"It's anti-clockwise in Britain," Alice cut in grinning.

"...yes *anti* clockwise then," Mark finished. The four walked off to the fence as the wave of newcomers continued to stream off the coaches; just as Alice and the others had done only a few days earlier.

"Tom... Tom...Thomas Gallagher are you sleeping on duty?" Gallagher awoke with a start and almost fell off his chair. In front of him stood Natasha laughing.

"How long have I been sleeping for?" he said shocked at himself.

"About an hour; anyway you deserved a nap. None of us could have kept up with the mystery figure for as long as you did. I bet if you could fly you'd still be chasing him now!"

"If I could fly I'd like to think that I'd have caught him by now," Gallagher added. "Have you got anything for me or did you just want to scare me?" he said pushing back his chair; enough sleep for one day.

89

"Yes I do have something quite interesting for you actually."

"Go on then,"

"Last night the facial recognition programme in the CCTV network detected Michael Gorse."

"Has he been caught then?" Gallagher asked out of curiosity not believing this was relevant to his current case.

"No, he was dead when they got there," Natasha remarked as Gallagher's interest grew.

"And I take it that he didn't die a peaceful death in his bed then," he queried.

"No, how did you guess?" she said sarcastically. "The first camera spotted him running along a road at the High Garden Industrial Estate before it blacked out in the way that we all know and love. A few minutes later a second camera went off line; when the picture came back it clearly showed Gorse's face despite the fact he was lying in a pool of blood."

"How was he killed?" Gallagher asked.

"A bite to the neck or a blade through the heart; they aren't certain which one actually killed him," Natasha added grimly. "The blade was identical to the one that killed his brother."

"Quite a gruesome way to go," Gallagher mused. "But he deserved it. The question now is; what is the significance of the black daggers. In the first case it was definitely the murder weapon but now there is a bite as well.

"It could be like a calling card," Natasha added helpfully.

"Yes, or does it have another purpose?" Gallagher wondered. "Has the body been moved yet?"

"It was taken to the St. James Street Morgue an hour or so ago."

"Was his brother taken there?"

"I don't know for certain but it's the largest one in the city so it's quite possible."

"Ok, send Kennedy down there. I want the daggers from both the suspects retrieved and analysed as soon as possible."

As Natasha hurried out of the room to find Kennedy, Gallagher had trouble focusing on the case. Instead he kept thinking about Natasha's laugh just then; it was such a stark contrast to the macabre and mysterious world they seemed to have recently found themselves in.

At the bottom of the Spire, the lift doors were slowly sliding open. The five men emerged and walked off back through the construction site feeling pleased with their work. Five months ago the plans for the Spire had been put forward for their consent; soon after they had rejected them stating the tower was too big for London's skyline and the construction time of three months was un-feasible. However, a barrage of appeals and the mysterious resignation of two top officials had cleared the way for the building's construction. Despite the fact the tower was in the late stages of its construction the city authorities had at last been given a reason to stop the oversized monstrosity from rising any further.

"I tell you we can stop them this time," the man at the back of the group stated confidently.

"I feel all we're going to do is annoy them," another said in response. "There was a time when we were in charge of planning but not now."

"We are in charge," the first one retorted. "We are in charge of the planning of this city, not the developers."

"Yeah, we're in charge of all the other construction sites but the builders of this one do what they like. This is a stupid idea; every time we challenge them something bad happens."

"Like what?" asked the newest member of the group. "How can they boss us around?"

91

"Nothing can ever be proven; but we've had lots of mysterious power cuts, computer viruses and even high officials being forced to resign due to scandals."

The men continued their debate as they left the construction site and began to walk down an alleyway to their cars believing themselves to be alone. However, three levels above, one of the ghostly white figures followed them and listened intently as the men walked deeper into the alley.

"...but how come the developer won't do anything this time?" the youngest official asked.

"Because the power to suspend construction is firmly in the hands of the city planning authority and can't be appealed against or overruled; it leaves the ball in our court. Also the driving force of the company isn't in any state to challenge us this time thanks to their accident."

Once the men were deep enough into the alley the watching figure above gave the signal and in less than a heartbeat two flashes of white burst out from behind cover, blocking the road. The figure high above watched as the men stopped abruptly and hopelessly began backing away straight into the path of yet two more hooded figures who had emerged behind them. The trap had been sprung and the five men were pressed into an ever smaller space as the figures moved forwards. There was nowhere left to go and with amazing speed one of the figures reached into the group grabbing the man closest. Lifting the quivering man by his neck it held him level with its eyes. Slowly it drew out its other hand and the man watched alarmed as the outstretched fingers reached towards his face. He struggled and kicked but to no avail as the hand came to rest on his forehead.

Then in the corners of his mind he felt something; thoughts that weren't his. Like a tidal wave another's thoughts washed through his mind crushing all resistance and stripping away all intentions and memories which the beings deemed troublesome. Within thirty seconds the job was complete and the figure effortlessly tossed the sleeping man aside onto a discarded mattress and reached for the next cowering human. Soon another man was lifted into the air and was dealt with in seconds. From above, the watching figure silently rose to its feet and

92

stalked off leaving its brethren to finish the job. The process looked cruel but the humans would awake with no recollection of what had transpired and be as they were before. Only now they would have no desire to interfere with the progress of the Spire.

From now on the city would never be a threat again.

The old disused office block was quieter than ever after the death of Michael Gorse. The TV lay forgotten and the smashed bottles lay where they'd been thrown. The only sound was the constant drip of water leaking from the floors above; every few seconds yet another drop would fall landing with a dull thud as it struck the side of a long forgotten computer monitor. The loud boom of a door being thrown open on the floor below suddenly disturbed the peace; heavy footsteps thundered up the stairs and soon the lead anarchist entered the room smoking a crude cigarette. He looked over at the battered armchair and stalked angrily past once he saw it was empty. He quickly disappeared into the kitchen where he cursed the absence of the explosives; Michael had used the lot on his own personal vendetta.

In a fit of rage he kicked a stray bottle that flew across the room before bouncing against the wall on the far side. He wondered where the devil the little worm had gotten to; probably fled for it if he knew what was good for him. As much as he hated Gorse for disobeying his orders he had to admit that it had been a truly devastating explosion; in fact he wished he'd thought of doing it. Despite this he was still going to ring Gorse's scrawny neck if he ever caught up with him. At least he'd left the guns behind, which was all they would need for next time.

The buildings sailed past as Kennedy drove along the quiet streets. Since the first bombing he had noticed fewer people out and about but after the second one the effects were far more noticeable. The streets had been almost entirely empty so far and every now and then he passed flowers tied to lamp posts to remember those who had perished at the hands of those madmen. Kennedy couldn't help feeling sad; not for the victims as he knew they were alive and well but for their

93

families and friends who would not have any idea that their loved ones lived. At least both those butchers had now been taken care of and the city was safe once again.

Kennedy's sleek white BMW soon pulled up at the small car park behind the St. James' Street Morgue. This place always gave him shivers; even the design of the building was eerie with its stone gargoyles grinning sadistically from the gutters high above and long dead creeping plants hanging limply off the foreboding walls. Kennedy walked briskly round the building and made his way up the flight of stairs to the front entrance. The heat of the summer's day was immediately left behind as he swung open the heavy wooden door and stepped inside. He had been here many times and with each visit the place seemed to have fallen even further into disrepair. Many of the lights flickered on and off, the paint was flaking and Kennedy had to walk round a cleaning trolley that had been abandoned in the middle of the lobby. The usual receptionist was at the desk with her face frozen in its permanent frown.

Kennedy explained why he was there and waited as the receptionist vanished into another room. He stood patiently for her to return, determined not to allow the building's almost infectious gloom to affect him. Eventually a pair of swing doors opened and out came the only good part of this place; Harold Green.

Green had been there as long as Kennedy could remember and his constant joy seemed distinctly out of place in the depressing halls of a morgue. The first time Kennedy needed to visit the place he'd rung them for directions after his Sat Nav took him on a wild goose chase. Green had answered the phone brimming with energy and after giving Kennedy a long series of directions had added in a comical way '...or you could just get hit by a taxi and you'll get here all the same! '

"James Kennedy; it's been a long time," came an excited voice from behind the almost impenetrable forest of Green's bushy white beard.

"It's good to see you. I thought you were going to retire last year though," Kennedy replied, as he firmly shook Green's wizened hand.

94

"I was thinking about it but how could everyone here survive without me?" he said looking at the smirking receptionist. Turning conspiratorially at Kennedy he said, "The ones in the back have more life in them than her. Still you haven't come here to talk to me I take it."

"I'm afraid it's business as usual," Kennedy sighed.

"Yes; it always is round here. Anyway follow me I'll show you to them," Green said as he turned back towards the doors with Kennedy following just behind.

After passing through a series of cluttered admin rooms they arrived in a long white clinical corridor that ran the full length of the building; branching off every ten meters were smaller rooms all loaded with eerie banks of refrigerated draws. This was a place where many people ended up but few ever saw.

"The one we admitted today is just over here," Green said gesturing at a room on the right as he swung open the white door and made his way inside holding it open for Kennedy. Green quickly made his way over to the right one; grasping the cold handle he pulled the draw open revealing the pale lifeless face of Michael Gorse.

"Looks just like his brother," Kennedy remarked.

"Well they were twins," Green responded calmly. Kennedy's eyes moved down the man's neck noticing the marks sunk deep into the flesh.

"Do you now know which of the wounds caused his death now?" Kennedy asked.

"Yes, the bite killed him; the dagger was added later. A very odd way of killing someone I must say."

"What can you tell from the bite?" Kennedy asked.

"From the size and shape you can eliminate any kind of animal. Only a jaw like a human's could have produced a pattern in that shape."

95

"That's peculiar..." Kennedy muttered grimly as his gaze fell on Gorse's mangled hand.

"What happened here?" Kennedy said looking in disbelief at the state of the hand and gun which were still fused together.

"We don't know; it doesn't match anything we've ever seen before. It's not as if something heavy fell on it or it was crushed in a vice. Whatever did this was able to exert a force all around the hand strong enough to crush both bone and metal."

"Was he alive or dead when this happened?"

"Probably alive."

Kennedy then moved to the chest and saw the gaping hole which the dagger had left.

"I see the blade came out this time," Kennedy remarked.

"What do you mean this time?" Green asked looking confused.

"The last one we sent you still had the knife stuck in its chest."

"No it didn't, we thought you had it."

"No we couldn't get it out; it can't have just vanished. Let's see the other one," Kennedy said remembering just how firmly the blade had been wedged into the other body. Green shut the drawer and Kennedy followed him down the corridor to an almost identical room where he slid open another drawer. However, after only opening it a little he stopped and looked up at the number above it. Looking confused Green headed over to a list of names on the wall and then back over to the drawer. He then grasped the handle and slid it fully open; the drawer was empty...

Karl had made it to Manchester within an hour of arriving at Paddington Station thanks to the new high speed rail link. After tearing through the open countryside the train now slowed as it approached the city and began to make its way along a modern viaduct that cut through

96

the old heart of the urban sprawl. He watched the people going about their daily lives; the hustle and bustle now seemed so alien compared to the unnaturally quiet streets of London he had left behind.

Once his train pulled up in Manchester Central he had quickly made his way to the nearest police station where a car was waiting for him. Soon he was speeding through the suburbs of the vast city on his way to the first of the three potential sites for the mysterious tech company. All of the industrial estates were to be found on the north western rim of the city; two within the urban jungle and the third in the countryside beyond. Karl was thankful the city was blanketed in thick rain clouds; a welcome respite from the mild heat wave that had been tormenting London for the past couple of weeks.

It took half an hour to reach the first site. Annoyingly the complex was vast with no obvious signage. After driving round in circles for what seemed like hours he couldn't find any evidence of a tech company. Also none of the few people he found knew anything of a company dealing in anything more advanced than frozen food. Eventually Karl decided to move onto the next one which was only five minutes down the road. It soon became apparent that the company wasn't there either as it was less of an industrial estate and more a grouping of factories producing car parts. Karl was forced to move onto the third site which was yet another half an hour away.

Eventually he approached his final destination and as he drove through the rusty gates a loud clap of thunder rumbled ominously overhead. Beyond the gates a warren of poorly maintained roads came into view, peppered with tufts of grass pushing through the cracked tarmac. Karl stopped to look at a battered map of the site which had just presented itself. The colourful road names immediately caught his attention; Spitfire Drive, Lancaster Way and Hurricane Row were but a few of the many named after famous aircraft. This quickly led Karl to the conclusion that the site must have once been an airfield. The names of the companies were mostly faded and those that weren't had been crossed out one by one as the site went into decline. Realising the old map was useless Karl set off along one of the narrow roads between two half collapsed timber buildings. He tried to read the names of countless worn signs; his hopes growing weaker by the minute.

After meandering frustratingly along several back roads he suddenly found himself on what had once been the airfield's runway. As he drove along the vast empty stretch of tarmac Karl couldn't help thinking how surreal the place seemed; this complex was huge and so far he hadn't seen a single person. Instead of heading back into the labyrinth of roads he chose to keep following the runway along the edge of the rundown buildings towards what looked like a scrap yard.

The yard appeared to be the only place with any signs of activity and occupied the far end of the old airstrip up to the former control tower. As he approached the site he could hear the clatter of metal on concrete as a huge tracked vehicle ponderously crawled by with the hulk of a car held in its jaws. At least there was someone about Karl thought as he pulled up.

Karl parked the car just outside the gates; well out of reach of the crusher and made his way inside. He quickly found the control tower was being used as an office where he found a balding man in a wheel chair working at a computer. After a few seconds he finished typing and spun himself round to face Karl.

"What can I do for you?" he asked curiously.

"Hi, are there any sort of technology companies around here?" Karl asked casually.

"There used to be a few but they're all long gone now."

"Don't suppose you know what they specialised in?" Karl asked hopefully.

"There was... umm let me see... I think it began with a k... Oh that's it Keerson Engineering. It used to be a couple of rows down; they specialised in concept cars. There was a company over in the northern part of the estate that worked on computers but it went many years ago and there was Recon over on the far side," the man said helpfully glad of someone to talk to.

"What did Recon do?"

98

"Don't know for certain, their workers were all rather secretive and we rarely saw them. It was something to do with the military though."

"When did they close down," Karl asked as his interest grew.

"About a year ago; they were bought out by some big conglomerate company or other. Within a couple of days though they were gone; an army of trucks came and took all their equipment. A pal of mine told me that nearly all the staff were hired by the new owners and relocated somewhere or other."

"I don't suppose you could give me directions to their old building?" Karl asked; he could sense that this was the place he was looking for.

At first Kennedy was a little stunned to see the empty drawer and then began to think of more logical conclusions.

"Are you sure it was this one?"

"Definitely, I put him in there myself..." Green replied before a loud noise made both of them jump. Kennedy instinctively reached for his gun and ran out into the corridor; he really hoped that the noise hadn't just come from the previous room. He was almost level with the door when it swung open with incredible speed, knocking Kennedy's outstretched arm backwards and off to the right. The shock caused him to let off a stray bullet which ricocheted off the ground before tearing through a door on the neighbouring side. Ahead of him he could see the pale shape of Michael Gorse already halfway down the corridor heading for the fire escape. Kennedy was quickly after him and fired two shots in the escaping killer's direction. Both shots missed by a hair's breadth as Gorse swung open the fire escape and began a rapid descent down two flights of stairs.

Kennedy was not going to let that monster escape again and tore after him. He burst through the door moments after Gorse who was about to disappear below the next landing; taking aim he took another shot. The bullet raced through the air and punctured the target's shoulder. The killer was clearly maimed with blood instantly seeping from the wound.

99

As Gorse vanished below the landing, Kennedy was already charging down several steps at a time in hot pursuit. He reached the bottom only a few seconds after the fleeing killer. Gorse swung open the door with such force that it rebounded back off the wall, shooting towards Kennedy who was briefly stunned by the force of the impact. However, the pain was only fleeting as he ran into the sunny car park.

"Freeze," he yelled as Gorse limped on refusing to stop. Kennedy had had enough of this and took aim. The single shot tore across the car park striking Gorse exactly where Kennedy intended. Gorse immediately toppled to one side, collapsing onto the hot tarmac.

Kennedy lowered his gun cautiously and walked over to the body. There appeared to be no signs of life but Kennedy didn't want to take any chances; dead victims being revived was a miracle but when the murderers came back, something deeply sick was going on. In quick succession he emptied the remaining bullets of his gun into Gorse's head. Once the echoes of the shots fell silent he pulled out his phone wondering exactly how he was going to explain this to Gallagher.

Karl sped along the dilapidated runway back the way he had just come. On his lap lay a small torn off piece of paper with a rough map drawn on it. He reached the road he was looking for just as another clap of thunder announced the arrival of the rain. Soon rain drops hammered on top of the car gushing off the roofs of the many dilapidated buildings. The first road on the left was a tight turn and the second was even tighter before he arrived in a large open yard.

In front of him stood a building distinctly newer than the rest; whereas the others were brick and timber this one was metal and glass. Karl couldn't help thinking it was a little out of place as he pulled up outside the front door. There was no doubt that this was the right building as the company name still hung proudly on the wall above the entrance.

Karl tried to park as close as possible to the front door as he had no coat; hoping it was unlocked he quickly opened the car door and made a dash for the entrance. He was annoyed to find the door tightly fastened however his luck improved when he spotted a gap in the building's

100

glass front where it had been shattered several months earlier by a reversing truck. Karl hurriedly stepped over the pile of broken glass and entered what had once been the lobby. Already he was soaked to the skin and now cursed the rain. However, despite his discomfort he grew curious as he saw good quality couches, tables and other items of furniture just left abandoned. They had certainly left quickly he thought. Karl moved over to the old receptionist's desk and lifted the hinged section at the end before heading into the former office beyond.

The room didn't lead anywhere but once again Karl was surprised that almost everything had been left untouched. He then backed out and headed for a door on the far right of the lobby. The next room was also littered with abandoned items and so was the room after that but in the third room there was a drastic change. Karl's footsteps reverberated around the entirely empty room; even the desks had been ripped from the walls and carted off. Karl continued on; each room he discovered was the same; stripped bare and left abandoned.

Out of all the rooms he visited only one had anything out of the ordinary; a cylindrical carbon fibre box. Karl nearly tripped over the item as he was passing through a dark room with no windows. At about a metre long with thick bands around it, Karl couldn't help thinking how odd it looked. He leaned over and unlatched the side and found it to be empty except for the dense padded lining which must have protected some expensive piece of equipment or other. Karl tried to close it again but found on closer inspection that one of the hinges had broken, suggesting why it had been left behind. He was just about to carry on when he noticed a serial number on one side; curiously he turned it over and read AE0031. The numbers meant nothing to him but he rolled the container over to see if there was anything else. As he span it over he could make out a white beak, a black slit-like eye and a series of jagged white feathers. It appeared to be a bird of prey's head facing side on. He considered taking the box with him but it was surprisingly heavy for its size so he pulled out his phone and took a picture of both the code and the emblem. Once he was done he left the abandoned building dreading the heavy rain that awaited him outside.

As night drew lazily over the old army camp four pairs of eyes watched the shadows grow in eager anticipation. After looking at the makeshift prison's defences Mark believed he had come up with an unbelievably simple plan that took advantage of the poor state of repair and that the guards were not actually expecting any trouble. The inmates at the camp had a surprising amount of freedom however they were still locked in their huts each night after being counted. This detail hadn't interfered with Mark's plan too much; indeed he'd actually made the others laugh when he told them due to its simplicity.

All four were housed in separate huts dotted across the camp; as there were so many inmates each had a slightly different lights out times allowing the soldiers to move from one side of the camp to the other locking up each cabin as they went. Cathy's hut was on the far side of the complex, fairly close to the high fence. As she was counted in along with five others, Alice waited patiently just around the corner. The soldier lazily counted six in; drew the bolt across and moved onto the next one. As the guard disappeared round a corner Alice swiftly crossed the ground to the locked door and pulled the bolt back open. Cathy quickly emerged before shutting the door behind them; the two repeated the process at Alice's hut which was slightly deeper into the camp without any complications.

For the two guys though, things weren't going quite as smoothly. The plan had worked well when Mark released Chris; however once Mark had been checked in it grew a little more complicated. Chris waited patiently in the shadows of a supply shed; the guard who locked the door hadn't moved away and had instead lit up a cigarette and was chatting to another soldier. The girls would be waiting at the rendezvous he thought as he tried to will the guards away. The minutes ticked by and after what seemed like an eternity the two finally moved off. Chris waited until they had disappeared from view before dashing over and unlocking the door. Mark quickly emerged muttering,

"What kept you?"

"The guards wouldn't shut up," Chris replied.

"Come on, we don't want to keep them waiting any longer than we have to," Mark whispered urgently whilst already hurrying off.

The delay was starting to get to Alice and Cathy who were waiting under a corrugated iron canopy behind an assortment of old, battered equipment. After ten minutes of waiting the guys finally arrived and made their way over the piles of broken ammunition crates and water containers.

"Are we good to go?" Alice asked.

"I think so," Mark replied as the four clambered out of their hiding place.

Repeatedly they flitted between the huts; pausing to check that the coast was clear before darting to the next one. Mark wished they could have found a place to hide closer to the fence but their reconnoitre earlier in the day hadn't revealed anything suitable. Steadily they advanced towards the fence but suddenly Alice backed away from the next gap, crashing straight into the other three. Silently she urged them to quickly move back. The four hurriedly dashed down the side of the hut and stood still, pressed against the rotting wooden boards. Just as they made it out of sight two soldiers walked past talking about a football game. Just as they were about to move on one stopped to look for something in his pocket and the other waited patiently alongside; had they turned around then the game would have been up. Thankfully the soldier found what he was after and the pair soon disappeared down the side of the next hut. Once they were out of ear shot Alice crept back along the side of the building before gesturing for the others to follow.

After passing another three rows of huts, the four soon found themselves easily within reach of the high fence. Going over was out of the question due to its height and the glistening razor wire that adorned the top like a deadly tiara. However, this approach wouldn't be needed as Mark had spotted just what they were looking for earlier in the day. Despite the fence's foreboding appearance it was actually quite badly worn with age and a small gap had emerged where it met one of the posts. Checking the coast was clear Mark raced over to the tiny gap beneath one of the posts and began to pull the flimsy metal wire away.

Every now and then he looked up to check he wasn't being watched; just as he was about to signal the others over though he caught site of two advancing lights in the distance. Frantically he gestured to the

103

others to hide as he lay still on the ground. Steadily the soldiers came closer each holding a powerful torch which cut through the darkness in vast arcs before them. Mark lay almost motionless without breathing, praying the soldiers wouldn't spot him. They were now only ten metres away when suddenly the light of the torch moved over Mark, briefly illuminating him for the whole world to see and he believed the game was up. However, the light moved away along with the soldiers who passed by, talking noisily. Mark couldn't believe his luck as they carried on; they really weren't taking this seriously he thought. He lay still until they were firmly out of sight before moving once more to the fence and with one last heave he made the gap big enough for them to pass through.

Cathy was the first and darted across the open expanse of grass to the hole in the fence. As she was quite small she passed through the gap with ease; closely followed by Chris. Mark gestured for Alice to go but she refused until he'd gone through; after a series of heated gestures and mouthed words Mark finally gave in and slipped through the fence leaving Alice on her own inside the compound. After taking one final glance around she hurried across the open space. As she ducked down by the gap a voice suddenly yelled out,

"Stop right there!"

Alice didn't listen and with her heart pounding she painfully scurried out through the gap heading for the ditch the others had disappeared into. The soldier rapidly closed the distance but was too hefty to fit through the gap in the wire. Angrily he reached for the taser that they had all been issued with. Raising the gun he took aim and fired at the nearest target. The two barbs tore out from the gun with their steal wires unfolding behind them. In less than a second the cruel wires imbedded in Alice's lower back.

Pain suddenly exploded throughout Alice and she felt all her muscles involuntarily tense. She couldn't do anything and slowly toppled over; her face heading for the ground. She hit the grass hard but was so close to the edge of the ditch that her momentum carried her right over the lip. As she fell down the steep slope, the cables were stretched to their

104

maximum length and were viciously tugged out of her back just before she reached the bottom in a heap.

Chris and Cathy had raced off ahead whilst Mark slowed to let Alice catch up; he had seen her make it out of the camp but lost sight of her when she entered the ditch. He kept checking over his shoulder anxiously but there was no sign of her. Soon he stopped running and looked back at the camp.

Alice was lying in pain at the bottom of the ditch covered in loose soil; slowly she opened her eyes to glimpse what she thought was a soldier standing over her and then she blacked out. Mark reached Alice and called her name. When she didn't respond he cursed loudly and slid his arms beneath her and lifted her up. Mark couldn't help thinking it looked easier in the films as she was surprisingly heavy; but he wasn't going to leave her behind. Approaching the other side of the ditch he heaved her up the embankment before scrambling up himself; then grabbing her again he ran as fast as he could.

Behind them the disorganised guards had to run to the entire opposite side of the camp before they could continue their chase. The hunt was on.

Chapter 7

The day was slowly drawing to a close when Gallagher, Natasha and Adam pulled up at the St. James' Morgue. A series of policemen had cordoned off the area after the shots were fired but so far Kennedy had largely tried to keep them in the dark over what had transpired in the building. After flashing their badges at a policeman on the door, the three ventured into the building where they met up with Kennedy.

"I hear you've had a bit of trouble here," Gallagher remarked.

"You can say that again. Since I phoned you it's gotten worse," Kennedy replied.

"In what way?" Natasha asked.

"You'll see," Kennedy said grimly. And with that he turned to lead them through a series of corridors. As they progressed deeper into the building a series of loud incongruous thuds could be heard.

"What are those noises?" Adam asked.

"We're nearly there," Kennedy replied as they rounded a corner. Outside one of the doors stood a rather ashen grey Harold Green holding Kennedy's gun in his hand. He turned to face them looking very relieved that Kennedy had returned.

"I'm glad you're here; that thing's getting very restless," Green said gesturing at the glass window in the door before giving Kennedy back his gun hastily.

"Don't tell me it got up again..." Gallagher said as he walked over to the window and peered in.

Inside he saw a white tiled room which was normally used for autopsies but in this case the subject on the table was most definitely not dead. Gorse lay fighting and striking his fist on the metal table top creating booming thuds with each hit. The scene looked even more horrific as Gorse's injuries were not healed; the hand with the crumpled gun was particularly gory and made a loud clang every time it hit the table which was incredibly disturbing.

"He got up again around five minutes after I shot him. I was forced to fire again and that kept him down for another ten. In that time we dragged him in here and fixed him down before anything else happened."

"Has he said anything?" Gallagher asked.

"Nothing, not a single sound has passed his lips," Kennedy remarked as the crashing noise grew louder.

"He broke the straps on his arm ten minutes ago," Green added trying to be heard above the din. Gallagher could now see the torn ends of the thick strap which once held the arm in place.

"Get the scientists down here right away. This one's different to the others and we need to find out why. But first things first someone strap its arm down!" Gallagher shouted over the terrible racket.

As Mark struggled to keep going, Alice was having a very different experience. Once again she found herself lying down in the statue cavern. Only this time there were two of the hooded figures standing on each side of her bed. Slowly one extended a white gloved hand towards her and she could see one of hers reaching out to grasp it. She could sense that her mouth was moving and words were coming out but they were distorted; like a faded echo.

Slowly the figure pulled her upright but then her vision began to distort in a way she had never experienced before. It was like she was watching two different events at the same time, one on top of the other. Within a few seconds of it starting the first vision faded away leaving an entirely different scene in its place. This time she was walking down a long silent corridor. She must have still been in the cave as the walls were carved from solid stone and the mysterious blue light flowed over the exposed surfaces as before. It was so alien and unlike anything Alice had ever seen in the real world as it rippled and flowed along the roof before collecting on the floor. From there it flowed gently down the sloping floor passed her. She wanted to look down but her gaze remained fixed straight ahead.

After rounding a corner, a vast stone door came into view; behind her she heard a muffled sound as the two figures from before sailed past her and took positions at either side of the stone structure. She had to go through alone.

A dull noise boomed and the door began to slide open but then the vision flowed away from her as she suddenly woke up. Mark had in fact tripped over a tuft of grass which had sent both him and Alice crashing onto the ground. Initially Alice was confused but then rapidly remembered where she was as the searing pain from where the barbs had been jogged her memory; quickly she scrambled back up followed by Mark.

"Had a nice sleep did you?" Mark said sarcastically whilst rubbing his leg.

"Tell you about it later," she said as the two moved off once more. Alice ran in front and began to pull ahead of Mark. Once she realised how tired he was though she slowed to keep pace with him.

A large expanse of overgrown grass separated the camp from what looked like a new housing development. Alice looked back with surprise to see the vast distance that Mark had carried her and wondered how on Earth he'd managed it.

As they approached the row of half finished houses, Chris and Cathy came into view, just visible in the half light. Alice was initially confused by why they'd stopped, but then she realised. A formidable steel fence painted a dark green ran along the entire length of the field blocking their path.

"So this is a problem," said Mark as he looked at the seven foot high fence.

"There's a drop on the other side as well," Cathy remarked. Alice moved closer to have a look; sure enough there was a deep concrete culvert right behind the fence.

"There's got be a way round," Mark noted as he began to walk briskly along the length of the fence with the others in pursuit. The night was fast approaching and what they could see diminished every minute. After walking for ten minutes they at last came to a possible way through, although it was definitely not the safest.

As the last rays of light slipped below the horizon, the three remaining members of the anarchist group prepared for their attack the following day. One of the men was loading ammunition into a series of metal tins and another was checking that his machine gun was fully operational. Their leader sat in the old chair that Gorse had once occupied; on his lap lay the plan of a large supermarket. This would do nicely he thought, the place would soon be a slaughter house!

Behind him the other two continued to work away, until one of the them felt like he wanted a beer. Jamie laid down the heavy machine gun with a clunk and headed into the makeshift kitchen. Opening the grotty fridge door he could see one last can at the back so leaned in to retrieve it. But then he heard a noise behind him.

"The last one's mine," he called out as he grabbed the bottle. There was an unanswered silence for a while as he straightened up. He was expecting some sort of argument over the beer but instead was taken completely by surprise when a long cold hand clamped around his neck; before he could do anything he was pushed onto his knees and thrown forwards into the fridge where he was knocked unconscious.

The hand then grasped Jamie by the scruff of his neck and slowly dragged him free of the fridge. A hand then came to rest on his forehead and the thoughts of the hand's owner flowed into Jamie's mind. Then suddenly his eyes reopened in understanding.

"Ollie... I need you in here..." Jamie said in a voice devoid of all emotion.

"Why?" called back an annoyed voice.

"I just... do." With that the hand loosened its grip and let Jamie slump onto the floor just out of sight of the doorway. Soon Ollie entered the room without noticing the shadow that lurked behind the entrance. Initially he didn't see Jamie but then spotted him crumpled in a heap in the corner. Before he could move to help, the hand shot forwards and grabbed him. Limp and useless he soon fell onto the damp floor as well. For a moment the shadow looked at the pair and seemed to study them before it telepathically issued a series of commands.

The two puppets slowly straightened their heads and began to lean forwards climbing arduously back to their feet. Then, in synchronisation, the pair walked from the room over to their former leader. Before he had any idea what was going on they had lunged towards him and pinned his arms to the chair. He struggled and yelled in vain as the figure emerged from the doorway. His scream was high and shrill but there was no one to hear him as the cold hand stretched out towards him; terror filled the depths of his soul like so many of his victims before. However, the screaming soon stopped as new instructions poured into his mind consuming all else. The alternative mission was all that mattered; there would be bloodshed tomorrow, just not where he had intended.

Mark stood staring at a crude bridge that comprised of several rusty drainage pipes which spanned the width of the culvert. The fence had been dismantled in this section to allow the pipes to run through, however the narrow bridge was around ten feet above the empty concrete channel with no railings.

"What do you think?" Mark asked turning to the others.

"Looks dangerous," cautioned Cathy.

"There's probably another way," Chris added.

"Those soldiers will be here anytime now; I say we go over," Mark concluded.

"That's what Alice seems to think as she's nearly halfway over..." Cathy said as she pointed over Mark's shoulder.

"It's fine," Alice called over to the others from the pipe although she wasn't sure that was true. The pipes were steeply curved which meant she had to edge along incredibly carefully. In the centre was a large cylindrical box that blocked her path so she had to carefully heave herself up its rusting side. She then moved over a series of valves before reaching the metre or so drop back down to the pipes on the other side. Gingerly she lowered herself down searching for the pipes with her feet; after several tense seconds holding on with only her arms she found the metal surface and was able to breathe a sigh of relief. She continued her balancing act and soon the edge of the culvert was in sight and with a sudden rush of joy she leapt onto the grass; free from the camp at last!

"It's ok, just watch out at the middle," she called back to the others.

Within a few minutes all four were safely over the pipes and into the empty construction site beyond. From there they jogged down the empty street heading for the lights in the distance. Soon they saw cars whizzing past on a busy road and the occasional person walking hurriedly by.

"Welcome back to the land of the living," Chris said to the others. "Anyone have any money?"

It turned out that Mark had smuggled some coins in along with his now dead iPhone. After zigzagging for ten minutes they found a waiting bus and piled on board. They didn't care where they were going just as far away from here as they could possibly get. The four disappeared into the urban jungle leaving the soldiers to continue their fruitless search.

The following morning Karl once again found himself leaving a train station having devoted much of last night to finding what he could about the Recon Company. It turned out that it had been founded ten years earlier by two brothers who had previously worked for a major defence contractor. Their profits had been poor due to overspending on advanced research and they had been bought out just as the man at the scrap yard had described. The buyer was a massive company called Aries Defence whose catalogue included robotic tanks, autonomous bombers and even nuclear submarines. In fact almost every piece of equipment you would need to invade a small country. They operated two sites in the UK; one near Carlisle and a larger facility outside Milton Keynes. Another borrowed police car awaited him as he once again chucked his bag onto the passenger seat and headed off.

Aries Defence wasn't too difficult to find; its large warehouses and production facilities were spread out over a landscaped park just outside the city boundary. Karl pulled up at the security booth and the initial trouble with the guard was resolved with a flash of his badge which instantly sent the barrier up. The drive to the main office was both long and strangely surreal; perfectly manicured lawns and tranquil lakes could be seen on one side and lines of armoured cars on the other. As he drove he saw countless other vehicles which he recognised from the news; from the Cerberus heavy tank and the massive Leviathan tracked command centre to fleets of Titan drones at the company's private airfield.

The road continued for a kilometre along the edge of a lake and through a wooded area until the main office came into view. The structure was futuristic even by the standards of the day; it began on the summit of a small hill and then stretched out off the slope into the air on a series of transparent legs; which gave it the appearance of hovering in the sky. The road briefly passed beneath the offices as it looped up the hill to the entrance; Karl slowed to marvel at the nanoglass legs thinking about the amount of weight they were suspending above his head.

Soon he was at the top of the hill looking down over the hundreds of acres of warehouses, factories and offices. They had a truly amazing view; looking down at all which belonged to them. After taking his eyes

112

off the scenery he followed the road in a loop outside the main entrance and parked up. Before leaving the car he pulled his phone out of his pocket and decided to check if there had been any further developments in London. He waited patiently for Gallagher to pick up as he continued to stare out across the landscaped estate. Soon the dialling stopped and Gallagher's voice could be heard at the other end.

"Hi, Karl. How long do you think you'll be before you get back?"

"I've just arrived at Aries Defence and I'm about to go inside. Why do you ask?"

"We've had a slight issue with a dead murderer trying to make an escape."

"Um, that's a new one." Karl said a little surprised.

"Tell me about it; we've just spent hours moving them into a cellar for safety. The damned thing just keeps coming back to life no matter how many times you shoot it."

"You say, *it.*"

"That's because *it* isn't like the others. It's behaving like something out of a zombie film."

"That's strange," said Karl growing a little uneasy.

"As a result all the other resurrected people who were hidden away by the Home Office have been put under quarantine with even higher security. Except for the four who managed to break out last night though."

"Sounds like lousy security they have over there."

"Apparently they crawled out of a gap in a fence; one was hit by a taser but they still escaped. Anyway as soon as you're done there I need you back."

"Will do," Karl said before hanging up. He put his phone away and clambered out of the car. He was only a few metres from the entrance

113

and the pair of oversized doors that guarded it. As he approached they both silently swung open revealing the lobby within.

The walls had appeared silver from the outside but as Karl passed through the doors he was surprised to find every surface was actually transparent. He could see straight through to the lake and down to the road below. There appeared to be no joints or separate panels giving the feeling you were walking on thin air.

Despite the strange nature of the building Karl's eyes were fixed on a gold emblem embedded into the centre of the floor. Although the colours were different there was no mistaking the distinctive bird of prey that had been on the broken case in the abandoned building.

"I see you like our logo," a voice said to Karl's right. He turned to see a brown haired woman also looking down at the emblem on the floor. She wore a smart business suit and her hair pulled back.

"Is it of anything in particular?" Karl asked.

"I don't know actually but it's used by every company that makes up Aries International," she stated before turning to Karl. "Anyway I take it you are the detective we were expecting. If you would care to follow me, we can talk in my office."

The woman's office was large and expensively furnished with a grand stand view over the entire complex. She took a seat behind her long glass desk as Karl pulled up a chair on the other side.

"I'm sorry I don't believe I got your name," Kennedy asked as he sat down.

"Angelina Collins; I am the manager of this complex. Now what brings you to see us today?"

"It's a rather complicated matter and I'm afraid I cannot give you all the details as this time. We are interested in a company you acquired around a year ago called Recon Defence," Karl explained. When he said the company's name he couldn't help notice the corners of her mouth twitch slightly. "We are curious as to what technologies you

114

acquired as part of the takeover." For a few seconds there was silence; eventually she responded with.

"I'm afraid I can't remember that much about Recon; it was a tiny company with little significance," she answered unhelpfully.

"So you can't recall if they were working on any... stealth projects?" Karl asked waiting to see how she would respond. This time her face remained impassive; like a mask hiding her thoughts from Karl.

"I really can't remember detective. As I said the company was small and we acquire dozens of similar outfits every year. However, the information you're after will be in our records office. The quickest way to get there is by our underground monorail. The station is on the other side of the lobby," she said dismissively.

"Thanks for your help," Karl said reaching out to shake her hand. He knew instinctively when people were hiding something and Angelina Collins most certainly was. He walked briskly out of the office and across the expanse of the transparent room. From the doorway Angelina watched as he disappeared down a flight of steps on the far side. Once he was safely out of sight she went back over to her desk and picked up the phone. They would want to know about this...

Karl followed the steps into the side of the hill; as he moved underground the transparent walls were replaced by slabs of polished granite. Soon he reached the bottom and found himself on a small railway platform also coated in the expensive stone panels. As he walked forwards a shuttle automatically slid out of the tunnel and stopped in front of him; painted midnight black it resembled a bullet on rails. With a slight hiss the doors opened; inviting a slightly apprehensive Karl forwards. Inside there were a few expensively finished chairs, a table and even a small TV. On a silver panel at the front of the pod lay a diagram of the track with a list of buttons at each stop. Karl pressed the one he wanted, the doors closed and the shuttle slowly slid off into the inky tunnel.

During the night an abandoned wing at the back of St. James' had seen more comings and goings than it had done in many years. The rest of the building had reopened for its depressing business but all the staff knew that something very strange was going on in the back of the building.

Gorse had put up an intense fight but after much struggling he had been shackled to a stretcher and moved out of the autopsy room. He had then been taken through a series of doors which had been locked for years and down into the bowels of the old wing. He was now firmly chained to a heavy metal table in a room two stories below ground and yet still he fought on; never sleeping, never stopping always fighting.

Through a thick glass window Gallagher looked on as two scientists scanned Gorse with yet another device. The more he thought about Gorse the more uneasy he became. He had seen and talked with many of the people at the warehouse; they had been in all respects normal and were devoid of all injuries. The writhing thing in the other room however was the exact opposite. For instance he still displayed most of his injuries; the crumpled hand, the bite and the multitude of shots which had entered his head. Some healing had occurred according to the scientists but only enough to ensure the body was functional and nothing more. Also whereas the others appeared more or less themselves after returning to life, Gorse was anything but. He hadn't uttered a single word and he had never once stopped struggling. Gallagher had a sick feeling that whatever was driving that body wasn't human.

Eventually the two scientists moved away from the body and headed into a decontamination room that had hastily been arranged. After a couple of minutes they emerged and headed over to Gallagher.

"Did you get anything?" he enquired.

"Yes, we were just scanning for brain activity. The results are most unusual..." the scientist remarked whilst looking at the screen on his device.

"So what did you find?" Gallagher asked.

116

"Nothing," the other scientist announced. "Absolutely nothing; his brain is essentially dead." Gallagher was initially a little shocked before asking.

"But how could he run away yesterday or actually be doing anything?"

"Whatever that is in there it's not Michael Gorse," one of the scientists said as they removed their gloves. "I'd be inclined to think that when your colleague shot them in the head it caused such devastation to the brain that it can't be repaired. Leaving us with this ruined life form."

Gallagher looked again at the squirming thing in the other room before asking.

"But if its brain is destroyed then what is controlling it?"

"We have no idea, only that it has taken control over all the body's systems and is trying to run them without the brain," one of the scientists replied grimly.

"What do you think about the others that were resurrected?" Gallagher asked.

"We've studied several of them at the camp and they're nothing like this. They were brought back to life without modifications whilst our friend in there has been made far stronger than is humanly possible."

"But why would someone do that?" Gallagher asked as if to himself.

"Search me," the scientist replied. "The changes may have become even more pronounced if the process hadn't been interrupted."

Gallagher mulled over this with a troubled expression on his face before he responded.

"I just hope you're right about the others as we've got an awful lot of them locked up now."

The underground train sped silently along the inside of the hill for several minutes. Karl marvelled at the size of the railway as it had

117

nearly twenty different stations; the cost needed to make it would have been astronomical. Soon the shuttle banked off down a fork in the track and slowed as it approached a station. Karl was initially surprised by what he saw; the platform was cluttered with rubbish and appeared only half complete. When the doors slid open he was unsure what to do; however the panel showed he was at the Records Office.

Tentatively he stepped through the doors and ventured onto the platform. He crossed the open space to the glass doors marked exit. He tried to open them but they wouldn't budge; confused he turned back to the shuttle just in time to see the door closing and the shuttle racing off out of the station. Karl felt uneasy being alone deep underground; quickly he tried his phone and as he suspected there was no signal. The door was locked, the train had gone and he had no idea where he was.

Just as he was about to consider walking up the track he heard a faint sound behind him. He spun round but there was no one there; however what did catch his attention was a small green light that had flickered on by the side of the door. Cautiously Karl went over and saw that it was a switch. He gave a quick look around before he tentatively pressed it; a couple of seconds passed and nothing happened until with a gentle hiss the door opened. Not having anywhere else to go Karl stepped inside and made his way up a dusty incomplete staircase. Ahead was another door and as he approached it a green light flickered on just like before. Karl checked behind him nervously and saw that the other door was still open, unsure of what he was getting into he pulled out his gun before pressing the green button.

The gloomy room that greeted him was expansive and almost entirely empty. Along one wall lay a few dusty crates with the words Recon stamped on the side of them; however these failed to draw Karl's attention as there was something far more noticeable in the centre of the room. Lying on a long trolley were three huge rolls of a pure white fabric which shimmered and glistened as he approached. The material was an almost perfect match to the sample he had seen in London.

"Is this what you were looking for?" a strange deep voice called out from behind him. Karl instinctively spun round but couldn't see anyone. Raising his gun he turned back towards the fabric but was shocked to find one of the spectral white figures standing only a few feet in front of him.

"Please lower your gun... it will not do you any good," it said in a calm yet commanding tone. Karl didn't obey the figure's instructions and instead kept it trained on the shadow beneath its hood. In response the figure slowly raised its hand and made a sweeping gesture to the side. Karl was unsure what it was doing at first but then he felt his gun being dragged from his grip. He didn't even have time to react before it was out of his hand and skidding across the concrete floor to the other side of the room.

Karl began to back away before turning to run for the door. The figure once again raised a hand and the door slammed shut. Karl frantically tried to open it but it was stuck fast. There was nowhere left to run and Karl couldn't do anything as the figure strode up behind him and extended a hand towards his face. On contact with his forehead he could feel a strange presence inside his mind; he tried to fight it but with every second he grew drowsier. Soon the blackness engulfed him and he began to slump over. As he was falling the figure effortlessly took his weight before lifting him off the ground altogether.

The figure then headed for a section of the wall which slid open as it approached, bathing the room in a bright light from the space beyond. As it vanished through the new doorway the panel slid shut leaving the room in darkness once more.

Chapter 8

Deep beneath the Earth's surface lay a strange world that few had ever seen. The walls shone blue and the stone work glistened beneath the grandeur of the great statue and the orb that it held tightly in its grasp. However, high above all this stood a solitary figure. Robed in the usual white it gazed down the mile high drop to the floor of the cavern so very far below. The height was of no concern as it stood with feet poised on the edge of the precipice; deep in thought. The figure remained there until it sensed the presence of another fast approaching. Without turning it spoke in its deep echoing voice.

"What brings you this high up Persephone?"

"They have summoned us Apollo," the newcomer replied in a voice that was both high and youthful. With one final gaze at the view Apollo turned and headed away from the statue with Persephone walking alongside.

"What is this about?" Apollo asked as a pair of stone doors swung open to let them pass.

"An intruder has been caught at one of the factories and his memories are most worrying."

"Are they close to discovering us?"

"I have not been informed; I was merely asked to summon you."

After that the two walked in silence down a series of long shimmering passages and caverns; soon they reached a long balcony which ran the whole circumference of the cave, overlooking the great statue. After a

120

short walk along this terrace they reached a circular platform suspended in the air. It had no railings and would have been daunting for most people but the two figures simply stepped on with the monumental drop only a few inches away. The platform's outer rim then glowed blue and made a metallic whine before it began to descend. The disk sailed past the top of the great statue's hood and then down passed its face and neck gaining speed all the way and yet the robes of its occupants never moved an inch as they fell.

The platform eventually began to slow and soon came to a gentle stop at the edge of the statue's outstretched arms. Both stepped off with great dignity onto a glass walkway which ran down the length of the arms. Below the glass pooled the eerie glowing lights which shimmered beneath them before spilling over the edges of the arms and down into the cave below. Ahead of them they could see the great orb clamped in the statue's hands from whence the mysterious lights originated.

About halfway along the walkway they reached a series of robed figures standing in pairs like sentinels guarding the path. Each wore a bright gold chest piece over their robes and held a long staff in their right hands. None of them moved as Apollo and Persephone advanced towards the shimmering orb at the end of the walkway. Soon they reached the hands of the statue where the glass floor widened considerably into a large platform. Along the edges of the space several of the other figures were at work on a series of holographic screens which they manipulated with gestures from their hands. Up ahead of them, a small set of glass stairs took them up to a smaller platform where Hera awaited them.

Hera was one of the oldest of their kind and frequently acted as leader. She did not turn as Persephone and Apollo approached and instead continued to stare up at a vast screen which floated in front of the sphere. Projected on it was a view of the world that had until quite recently been hidden away inside Karl's mind. Once Apollo and Persephone were both standing alongside her she began to speak.

"These thoughts are most troubling," she said in a voice not too dissimilar from Persephone's. "We have noticed a serious problem that has developed which requires our immediate intervention."

121

Both Apollo and Persephone waited in respectful silence for Hera to continue as she raised one of her hands into the air; by sweeping it to the right she wound back a day of Karl's life to the point she desired. The part she had chosen was the phone call to Gallagher which she played for the other two. After watching the world through another person's eyes for five minutes Hera paused the memory with a flick of her hand.

"In the memory they spoke of a heinous murderer being returned to life. No one else on this planet should have the ability to perform such a task," Hera said whilst turning to look at the other two. "Its existence both jeopardises all that we have accomplished and all that we seek to do. I want the pair of you to go to the surface and discover by what circumstances that abomination was created. Once you have learned what you can, destroy it."

"But, we are sworn not to take a life," Persephone queried.

"No..." a voice said to the left of them. The three of them instantly knew who had spoken and all turned in unison. "We are sworn to not take an innocent life."

Down the left hand fork of the path that surrounded the sphere a tall and imposing figure slowly walked towards them. He wore a white hood like the others and a long cloak that trailed along the ground but beneath that he wore the distinctive armour that Alice had seen in her dream and around his neck hung the gold pendant. This was the Archangel.

"We have become too focused in our task and have failed to see that something is deeply not right in the world," he said as he walked over to the glass railings that surrounded the path and gazed out into the cavern. "We have come far over these years and we are so very close to fulfilling our destiny; the timing of this incident is too much of a coincidence. It is crucial that you must not fail in this task."

"We will not fail," Apollo and Persephone said in unison.

"I know that. Now go; your mission awaits you," and with that Apollo and Persephone both bowed their heads and turned back the way they

122

had come leaving Hera and the Archangel alone on the raised platform. Slowly the Archangel moved away from the railing and turned to the figure working at the nearest screen.

"Hermes..." he called. "Tell Hades to erase the human's encounter with us and he is to implant a series of suitable replacement memories to fill the gaps."

"Will he not notice the false memories?" Hermes asked.

"He may feel they are slightly out of place but he is only human after all. He is not going to think that anything too unusual has happened," the Archangel said confidently. "Also... tell him to keep the telepathic link with the human going after he is released; we may be able to learn more from him."

"Of course my lord," Hermes said before turning back to his screen.

For a time the Archangel remained silent until he eventually addressed Hera.

"You are uneasy Hera," he said softly.

"My Lord, the situation at the surface is getting more complex with everyday. The humans have already found a connection between us and one of the companies; they are getting too close and then there is the matter about this rogue resurrection..."

"Hera, only one of those poses a threat to us," the Archangel soothed. "The humans are not going to find us in time. We have taken care of the intruder and they do not know where to look for us."

"Yes, but what about the visions? What if those we have resurrected see something that reveals us?"

For a few moments the Archangel paused,

"The visions have proven to be a very unusual and unpredictable side effect. However, we have never known them last for more than a few minutes; the chances of someone seeing anything of importance in that timeframe is very slim."

"And what of the resurrection?"

"I do not know at this time... Although I have recently felt a presence; a presence that I have not felt for a very long time."

Alice and the others had so far evaded recapture for nearly sixteen hours. After travelling into the city the night before they hadn't been sure what to do. Obviously Mark didn't have anywhere to stay in the UK and the other three lived in university accommodation which was the first place the soldiers would look. The lack of money was also a concern until Mark revealed he still had his bank card. None of them knew if it would work since they had been officially dead for a week but decided to try it anyway.

To their surprise the cash machine accepted it and they managed to rent a pair of hotel rooms for the night; one for Chris and Mark and the other for Alice and Cathy. Their escape had left them exhausted and they all fell asleep as soon as their heads touched the pillows. However, as three of them slept soundly Alice's dreams were more vivid than ever.

She was in the cave once more, standing in front of the huge door she had seen in her last vision. Slowly the doors opened and before her was the blue orb once again. This was the closest she had yet been and only now realised just how vast it was and how brightly it shone. She then moved along the glass walkway until she approached the platform at the far end. Up ahead were a series of other robed figures who appeared to be hard at work and paid her little attention; however one stood out above the others.

The armour of the Archangel was hard to forget and Alice immediately recognised it from her other dream. The different sections of the sci-fi armour were a pearl white that rippled as the light caught it from different directions and over this some plates were adorned with elaborate gold patterns and swirls creating a truly striking contrast. However, Alice's focus was soon drawn to what was worn around the neck. This time the details of the golden medallion were clearer and Alice could make out the pattern etched into the golden metal. She

124

couldn't help thinking it looked strangely familiar; where had she seen it before?

The Archangel moved quickly between the holographic screens as if helping the others but his words sounded distorted to Alice. Eventually he turned to face Alice and quickly made his way over. Again their words sounded muffled; it took Alice several seconds to work out what had been said. He appeared to be asking her name. She could feel her mouth opening as if it belonged to another before a single word came out.

"Apollo."

And with that the vision collapsed and Alice awoke with a start in the hotel room. Lying near her was a stray pillow which had been thrown at her by Cathy.

"What time is it?" Alice asked feeling a little groggy.

"Nearly eight thirty," Cathy replied. "We thought we'd leave you as long as we could but you're going to miss breakfast if you don't hurry."

"How long have you been up?" Alice groaned as a dull headache rapidly took hold.

"We were up around seven. Did you have any more visions?"

"Yes."

"What did you see?"

"I'll tell you after breakfast," Alice said as she scrambled out of bed feeling very hungry.

A once abandoned office building was now a hive of activity. Jamie, Ollie and their former leader were now outnumbered by a motley group of former murderers and thieves who had been rounded up the night before and dragged one by one to the building. The final preparations were being made under the watchful gaze of two shadowy figures. There was no talking, no drinking and no rest; there was only the mission. Crude body armour was strapped on and guns were distributed before they headed out to their transportation. As the stolen black vans moved off, the unsuspecting city lay before them...

The sun was already high in the sky as Alice and the others ate breakfast. She had only told them briefly that she'd had another vision but her hunger had got the better of her. So the others had to wait patiently as she consumed the majority of her food before she would speak further.

She began with what she'd seen the night before after her fall into the ditch and how it had abruptly been cut off when Mark dropped her!

"You try running through a dark field carrying someone who's having a nap," Mark commented before Alice moved onto the vision she had seen that morning. She described the glass walkway along the statue's arms and the host of figures there before giving a clear description of the strange figure who had spoken to her just before she had woken. For a while the other three pondered on her story before Chris began to speak.

"Why are you the only one seeing the visions now? None of us have had them for days."

"I don't know. But these last two were far more vivid than the ones before; I mean I could just about hear their voices," Alice replied.

"Are you sure they said their name was Apollo?" Mark asked changing the subject slightly.

"Well, it was muffled but I'm sure that's what they said," Alice confirmed.

"Apollo was an ancient God," Chris remarked.

"Yes, he was the ancient Greek God of light, truth, sun and healing amongst other things," Cathy elaborated.

126

"It's interesting... but it doesn't get us any closer to finding out who brought us back," Mark concluded.

"That might not..." Alice agreed, "...but there was something else that I saw in the cave that might."

"What?" the other three asked.

"You know I said the figure in armour was wearing a medallion the first time I saw him. Well this time I could see the design on it."

"What was it then?" Cathy asked.

"Well... It was a golden disk with a ring of small engravings around the outer rim. But inside that circle was the head of a bird of prey."

"Do you know what it means?" Chris asked her.

"Not as such; but I'm sure that I've seen it somewhere before."

"We could look it up," Chris suggested.

"On what?" Cathy remarked. "Mark's the only one with a phone and it's out of charge."

"We could always buy a charger," Chris continued.

"*Actually* that wouldn't do much good. I think it fell out of my pocket last night during our escape," Mark confessed.

"Great..." Chris added sarcastically.

"Chris, didn't you leave your phone at your house?" Cathy asked.

"Yeah... I did," Chris admitted.

"But it would probably have been moved by now," Mark said.

"No, it might not have..." Chris continued. "My roommate moved out last month, we don't have any living relatives and the owner lives on the other side of the country. It might still be there."

"It sounds risky though," Mark commented. "That's the first place the soldiers will look for us."

"There's also one of those old fashioned internet cafes near where I live," Alice put forward.

"I didn't know they still existed," Cathy remarked.

"Yeah, that's why I've never been in," Alice responded.

"I still think we should try getting a phone," Chris commented.

"Personally I think the cafe is safer," Mark argued.

The debate bounced back and forth until they eventually decided to do both. Chris and Cathy would try to get hold of Chris' phone whilst Mark and Alice would go to the cafe. Both groups agreed to meet up outside the Science Museum later in the day before heading off their separate ways.

Back at the army camp the soldiers had recently discovered the identities of the escapees; it had consumed many hours of their time and a lot of counting but at last four folders lay on the colonel's desk. From the outset the colonel had found the whole notion of locking innocent people up and then hiding them from the world to be totally unethical. However, orders were orders.

He had so far skim-read through the first two files which belonged to a brother and sister who were studying in the city. The file contained photos of each as well as the wounds they had sustained when they were killed. Next he mused over Mark but due to him living in America for a large portion of his life the information was limited. Finally he moved onto Alice and what immediately caught his attention were the terrible scale of the wounds which she had been inflicted; he had read many of the folders and few even came close to this. Whereas the other three had only received gunshot wounds to the chest it appeared that Alice had also been shot twice through the left side of her head. This was not just repairing muscles and organs; one whole side of her brain must have been rebuilt in the space of that night. The colonel had never been a religious man but now he couldn't help wondering whether there was someone up there. After all who else could surely perform a miracle such as this.

Completely oblivious to recent events, the rest of the city was slowly starting to return to normal. Several shops had chosen to reopen and the crowds of people had started to trickle back in the days after the second bombing. Despite this, the usual torrent of tourists that perpetually swelled the city had not yet returned; terrorist attacks were not good for tourism.

Alice and Mark had made good progress as they meandered through the winding streets of London. They had initially planned to go on the Underground but had hurried past the first station after spotting several policemen outside; they didn't know if they were wanted. They had chatted casually most of the way but as they came round a corner and entered an immense shadow their conversation suddenly changed. Instinctively both stared up at the monumental size of the Spire before them and realised just how much it had risen since they last saw it up close.

"I knew it was going to be big," Mark murmured. "But I never realised it would be that tall."

"Unbelievable... It has to be over twice the height it was last week," Alice agreed.

High up they noticed the drones darting and weaving between the columns like a swarm of bees; there definitely hadn't been that many before. As they stared on, another squadron of the buzzing robots flew low over the next street before they began their ascent to join the workforce almost three hundred floors up.

"They're in one god awful rush to finish that thing aren't they," Mark noted as they set off again.

"Yes, I wonder why they're bringing in more robots? I've been living here since the first day of construction and they've never had that many on site before," Alice remarked.

"It's a wonder they don't hit each other," Mark added as he stared at the busy dark swarm creeping ever higher into the sky.

The pair then walked in silence for a while before Alice pointed at one of the buildings halfway along the far side of the street.

"It's just over there," she said.

The pair crossed at the traffic lights before covering the last few metres to the cafe. Both thought they had made it there undetected however neither had seen the CCTV camera which was slowly tracking their movements. In less than a second it ran through its data banks comparing their faces to those of nearly a thousand wanted individuals. After running the comparison for a tenth of a second it had drawn a match. Instantaneously this information was displayed on a pair of monitors in front of an operator at the local police station. As Alice and Mark sat down they had no way of knowing that the hunters were closing in.

After speaking with Hera, the Archangel immediately left the Central Chamber and headed off into the maze of passages and caverns that made up the Ark. He didn't have far to travel as he soon approached the huge golden door that sealed off his quarters from the rest of the tunnel system. The two sentinels that stood on either side remained as still as statues as the Archangel raised a hand and swept the huge door aside.

Inside, the room was largely empty with only a few golden pieces of furniture scattered around the outer edge of the circular chamber leaving a large open space at its centre. As the Archangel advanced into this area two blue lights flickered on at each end of the room. It only took a matter of seconds for them to emit a series of blue lines which knitted together to form a colossal holographic screen.

130

A key pad was slow and inefficient so he gave his commands telepathically to the giant screen. Almost instantly the computer hacked its way through numerous firewalls and gained access to the police's secure database in readiness for the Archangel's search. Slowly the minutes ticked by as he skimmed through hundreds of reports from all over the country and rapidly began to see a pattern developing. Crime rates had taken a dramatic fall in recent weeks and it wasn't due to better policing; habitual criminals appeared to be disappearing from the streets.

As the Archangel continued his search he eventually came across Brian Gorse. At first it appeared like just another of the mysterious deaths but as he moved the page down a photo came into view. In the picture was an object that looked uncomfortably familiar. For several moments the Archangel remained frozen as he tried to recall where he had seen it before. And then it hit him.

Inside the cafe Alice and Mark were surprised by the high tech interior and how packed the place was. They soon discovered the cafe's unique selling point once they saw the computers that were on offer. On each table an expensive holographic screen stood floating a few inches above the surface of the table. This type of screen had only recently gone on sale and was far beyond the price range of the many students who inhabited the area. Squeezing between the closely set tables they made their way to the blue neon counter and each ordered a drink so they could use one of the computers.

After collecting their orders they headed towards a door marked additional seating. This next room was darker than the first and the only source of illumination came from the ten or so hovering screens that were in use. Luckily there was a spare table at the back of the room where they both sat down. A white ring marked the on button and the soon as Mark pressed it, the screen began to appear; rising slowly up out of the table. As this was happening, down on the table's surface the blue outline of a keyboard emerged in front of him. He was about to start typing then thought,

"Actually, you know what you're looking for," he said before sweeping his hand across towards Alice; in response the keys slid slowly round the table until they stopped in front of Alice.

"I love technology," he said smiling.

After taking a sip of her drink Alice began typing; as she tapped away the monitor automatically re-orientated itself to face Alice. First of all she tried 'bird of prey crest' which only came up with old coats of arms. Then she put in 'bird of prey logo' which also failed. She desperately tried to remember where she had seen the crest before. It had been on something in her neighbourhood so she started to recall different places she knew. After mentally visiting half of the university buildings it suddenly came to her in a flash of recollection. Quickly she tapped away at the glowing keyboard before pressing enter. After seeing the pictures on screen she scrolled down for a few seconds before clicking on the one she wanted; she then leaned back in her chair and smiled.

"I take it you found it then," Mark commented.

"Yep, that's it," she said in triumph as Mark leaned over to look at the image; it was indeed quite a striking emblem that he also felt looked familiar. Curiously he looked up to see what she'd typed in and paused for a moment.

"Why did you type in the Spire?" he eventually asked.

"Because that's where I saw it. I remember now; it's on a billboard at the tower's base."

"So what is it?" Mark enquired as Alice clicked on the image which took her through to an online encyclopaedia. At the top of the page the title read 'Aries International' and lower down on the right of the screen was a smaller picture of the emblem with its distinctive black background and pure white bird's head in the centre.

"It says the crest is the logo of the world's largest holding company," Alice read as she scrolled down the page. "...In the year 2019 Aries International was formed through the merger of nine smaller

132

companies... Over the next five years the company went through growth unparalleled in human history... No one has been able to explain how they went from the eleven thousandth biggest company in the world to the largest by 2028."

"How come we haven't heard about them then?" Mark asked; a little surprised at such a glaring hole in his knowledge.

"The company doesn't use its own name very often; it just buys others on a massive scale. From what it says here Aries Defence and Construction are the only two to bare their name. Other companies they own also manufacture most of the world's robots, medicines, cars and planes. In fact they probably made this computer screen. They're like a spider in the centre of a web controlling most of the planet's industry," Alice concluded.

"They sound very powerful," Mark noted. "No company has ever risen as fast as that; it's like..." However he was cut off by a loud boom as the cafe's front door was flung open closely followed by a loud voice yelling harshly.

"POLICE! EVERYONE AGAINST THE WALL!"

Instinctively people leapt from their tables sending chairs crashing to the ground and drinks flying. Luckily the police didn't see the side room straight away and before they had even finished the sentence both Alice and Mark had thrown back their chairs bolted through a door marked private at the back of the room. There they found themselves in a small cluttered corridor; careering around huge barrels and leaping over an assortment of boxes they continued their escape towards a propped open door that lead outside.

As Alice and Mark darted out of the back door into the alley beyond, the police had finished their takeover of the cafe. Several expensive tables had been overturned and clients screamed as a dozen or so sub machine guns were pointed menacingly in their faces. Once all the people were forced into a line along the back of the cafe one of the officers brought out a small device which resembled a camera. He aimed it at the start of the line and slowly swept it along waiting for it to identify the fugitives. Briefly the device turned red but it was not the

133

escaped convicts they had been told to find; instead they found themselves staring at a spotty teenager who was wanted for vandalising a post box.

Alice and Mark soon emerged onto a busy road. It looked like they were going to make an unchallenged escape until another newly installed face recognition camera locked onto them and slowly began to track them down the street. In the cafe the police were soon notified and immediately piled out knowing exactly which road their targets were fleeing down.

Alice slowed once she felt they were safe and Mark came to a halt alongside.

"How did they know we were there?" Alice gasped.

"Oh, damn it why didn't we think..." quickly he looked around and saw the inevitable CCTV camera facing directly at them. "Run!"

Mark and Alice ran totally breathless down the street darting between the confused passersby. A backward glance revealed a line of black clad policemen who were already hot on their heels and gaining ground rapidly. Mark was running slightly ahead and spotted a side street looming on the left; quickly he changed direction with Alice close behind. They hoped to evade the police for a while but to no avail; on they ran as the police swarmed after them. Up ahead the road split into two separate paths.

"You take the left," Mark called. "We'll meet up at the hotel."And with that the two tore off in opposite directions. The quickly approaching police were forced to divide; seven followed Mark and five went after Alice.

On emerging from the alley Mark continued to run until he was firmly mixed in with the crowd. Up ahead he suddenly spotted a charity shop which gave him a brainwave. Casually slipping inside he quickly selected a red checked shirt, a pair of sun glasses and a hat. Paying at the till less than thirty seconds after entering he was soon dressed in his new attire.

134

He concentrated on slowing his breathing as the police mingled through the crowd. They were rapidly getting closer so he leaned up against a wall and waited for the oncoming storm. The police weren't expecting such a rapid change of tactics and failed to see their target as they charged past. Mark relaxed as they swept by and a huge grin spread across his face. He then calmly looked up and down the street before crossing; leaving the confused police to search the area in vain.

Alice on the other hand was having a far harder time at evading her pursuers. Her chosen route lead her deeper into a network of alleys and side streets. As Mark was walking to safety she was still lost in the maze of roads. Where could she go? The police were gaining quickly and she couldn't see anyway of evading them. In desperation she continued zigzagging down different streets hoping she would at least gain some time to think of a plan. The demand of continuous sprinting was fast taking its toll; she couldn't go on any longer and came to a sad halt in a small dingy yard. Panting heavily she leaned against a wall to the left of the arched passage from where she had entered and waiting for the inevitable arrival of the police. However, as she looked on despairingly she caught a glimpse of a road at the end of a very narrow passage. Unable to run she stepped through, disappearing just in time to let the torrent of police charge past.

Soon she was on the busy streets of the city once again. The people around her were oblivious; gazing into the shop windows and mingled in groups. They offered protection as they chatted happily and talked on their phones. However, it was not long before she spotted another group of police up ahead who were blocking the pavement. Alice looked across the street where she was alarmed to see yet more police moving steadily along with their facial recognition scanners in hand. The only option she had was to turn around and head back up the street. She hadn't gone far before she spotted another group of police slowly moving in her direction; the only thing she could do was head into one of the shops and hope that she would lose them inside.

The clothes shop which she chose only had one floor but went back a surprising distance. Again without trying to attract any attention she weaved her way between the hangers deeper into the store as far away from the police as she could get. Soon she stopped by a rack containing

135

sunglasses and tried to blend in. From this position she could see the entrance and breathed a sigh of relief as a line of policemen moved past without entering the shop. But then a policewoman following behind the others stood in the doorway with one of the scanners in her hand. As she entered the store two policemen followed in her wake. Poor Alice's heart began to pound heavily in her chest; what was she going to do? The store was a dead end; the only way out was blocked by the advancing police.

The policewoman was growing tired of using the hand held scanner; for a start it was heavy and it was constantly playing up for some baffling reason. She had hoped that it would hold together long enough for the rest of the chase but her hopes were dashed as the wavy lines appeared on the screen again. Cursing the device she shook it violently and the lines went away. Before her was a stand of overpriced sunglasses and a girl that looked like she'd just run a marathon. She began to raise the scanner once more when the screen blacked out. She lowered it again and backed away a little as she tried to fix the problem.

Alice's heart was in her mouth; she realised that she wasn't even breathing as several beads of sweat formed on her forehead. She tried to force herself back to looking normal and turned towards the glasses stand again as the policewoman looked to be about to leave. In her head she prayed that they would give up the chase.

However, Alice's prayers were not answered this day. Suddenly the screen flickered back to life and the policewoman slowly lifted the scanner up to face Alice.

"Guys, I think we got one," she said reaching for her handcuffs.

As Alice was escorted from the building with hundreds of eyes upon her, no one noticed the black van that slowly passed by. At first glance it was just one of many thousands of vehicles that crowded the roads of the city; however this one was very different. The driver sat unblinking behind the wheel, only just conscious of the world around him. As a car door swung unexpectedly open in the his path he took no notice and ploughed on tearing it clean off. The driver also ignored the furious

136

yells from the car's owner who demanded him to stop. He would not stop, he could not stop; not until the mission was complete and the darkness had left his mind...

Within two minutes of Alice's capture she was shut in the back of a police car with her hands cuffed. She was fuming; angry from getting caught and even more so because she was being treated like an escaped convict. Apparently the police had been told that she was responsible for drug dealing and two shop lifting offences which was particularly hard to swallow. She'd never done drugs in her life and now she was being arrested for selling them! To make it worse, people were watching and a few were even filming her arrest. It was so degrading and unfair.

As the cop car sped away the people gradually returned to their activities, seeing that the excitement was now over. From behind his tinted glasses, Mark stared as the police drove away, taking Alice with them. Two options now lay before him and whichever one he chose he knew he would regret. With a sigh he made up his mind and walked away.

The police car sped through the streets of London carrying a dejected Alice in the back. When she asked where they were going she got no response from the two miserable cops in the front. Despite their silence it was clear she wasn't being taken to the camp as they were heading in completely the wrong direction. Soon a row of police cars came into view outside a building which had to be one of the city's many police stations. Alice immediately focused on the hulking shape of a camouflaged military lorry which was parked at the far end of the small car park. Somehow she didn't think she'd be here long.

As the police car pulled up outside the station entrance two soldiers quickly burst out of the main doors and came down the steps towards now stationary car. The two policemen got out and after a brief discussion involving several bits of paper going back forth, the two cops headed inside leaving Alice in the back of the car with the two soldiers standing outside.

After a brief pause one turned to the car and opened the door gesturing for Alice to get out, which she duly did. One of them held a small key in his hand which the policemen had reluctantly handed over and unlocked the cuffs securing her wrists before leading the way over to their lorry. Instead of putting her in the back as she was expecting they opened the door to the cab and gallantly offered her a hand up. The cab had space for four people in a long line so she shuffled over to the one closest to the driver. She looked back to see that one of the soldiers was heading back to the station whilst the other stood leaning against the open door of the truck.

"We're just waiting for another one," the soldier muttered before pulling a radio from his pocket.

"Do you know who?" Alice asked, wondering who else they had caught.

"Don't know, we only know the police caught someone else," he replied before he began to speak into the walky-talky.

The minutes slowly ticked by and Alice grew more impatient. Who else had they captured? Every now and then another police car would arrive and Alice would crane her neck to see if anyone she knew was in the back. After five false alarms a police van equipped with riot gear came into view at the far end of the road and made its way towards the station. Slowly it indicated and turned into the car park; even before the doors opened Alice knew that this was the one. Her suspicions were confirmed when the other soldier slowly made his way over to the van in readiness. A deluge of armed police soon poured from the back of the truck which annoyingly obscured her view. She could catch fleeting glimpses of a pair of jean clad legs among the group before the soldier pushed his way into the centre. After two minutes he seemed to have established his authority and the police began to leave, slowly revealing who they had caught.

It was Mark.

As Gallagher and Natasha arrived at St. James' they knew something wasn't right when they saw a pair of armoured cars and a bulky lorry in the car park. As Gallagher pulled up he caught sight of Kennedy emerging from a small door leading out of the old wing; he guessed what was going on but waited for Kennedy to confirm it anyway. Gallagher and Natasha quickly climbed out of the car as Kennedy came to a halt in front of them.

"Some soldiers have arrived and are taking the body," he announced. Gallagher sighed; his guess was correct after all.

Down in the basement of the morgue the soldiers had moved the still struggling body out of the room and were transporting it on a heavy metal stretcher to the ramp leading up into the car park. Just as they were about to approach the incline; Gallagher, Natasha and Kennedy emerged at the top.

"Do you mind telling me where you're taking that thing?" Gallagher asked whilst silhouetted by the sunshine beyond.

"We have orders to remove this body and take it to a secure location," one of the soldiers barked back.

"But it's our main lead," Natasha called back.

"This building has been deemed unsuitable to house this thing. We are moving it to somewhere where it will pose less of a risk," the soldier replied.

"I suppose you're going to lock it away from us then?" Gallagher commented.

"No, you will still be able to view it, although it will be under our supervision," another soldier responded.

"Well how do we know you won't just spirit it off?" Natasha asked.

"Look, we were told to take the body and to try and cooperate with you," the Sergeant at the back said trying to come to a compromise.

"We've got a job to do and so have you. How about one of you comes with us and that way you know where we're taking it." Gallagher looked at the other two before turning back to the soldiers.

"I suppose we can make that work," he agreed whilst stepping out of the way. "Natasha would you like to go for a drive?"

"Sounds fun," she said sarcastically before following the soldiers into the sunlight.

"What now?" Kennedy asked.

"Karl's due here in fifteen minutes. We'll wait for him and then he can give us his report before we move on; there's nothing that can help us here now."

As Gallagher said those words he had no way of knowing he couldn't be more wrong. Standing on the roof high above, the blurred outlines of Apollo and Persephone watched the body being loaded into the back of the huge truck. They had arrived too late to enter the building undetected, so had opted to bide their time and wait for the right moment. Both were deep in thought as they looked at the shape on the stretcher.

"What do you think it is?" Persephone asked after a while.

"I do not know..." he said whilst turning to face Persephone. "But we will find out soon enough."

As the minutes slowly ticked by, Gallagher and Kennedy sat waiting in the car. The lorry and one of the other vehicles eventually pulled out of the yard with the two Angels following along the roof tops. Four soldiers lingered behind after the others had left to decontaminate the room; their movements back and forth to their vehicle provided the only thing to look at in the otherwise empty car park.

140

Further up the road, the lorry sailed by concealing its strange cargo from the world outside. There weren't that many vehicles on the road that day and none of the other drivers gave the lorry a second glance. Especially not the person behind the wheel of the black van which quickly passed them.

The van was fast approaching its destination; one more turn then there was St. James'. The street was quiet and the air was still; the calm before the storm. The van driver turned allowing the wheels to mount the curb as he came skidding to a halt outside the front entrance. Before the van had even stopped moving, the back doors were flung open and a torrent of armed men streamed out onto the pavement. Quickly they stormed up the steps and burst through the door into the dirty reception beyond. The usually unflappable receptionist gave out a short scream before she was silenced by a bullet to the head. Checking for other witnesses the men fanned out into the corridors beyond. Two more members of staff fell in quick succession; one had not even seen the intruders. Once they'd taken control, they spread out and began their search. They couldn't fail; they had to find it or else the Shadows would torment them forever more.

As the gunfire and shrieks of terror echoed around the old building two black robed Shadows approached the building along the rooftops. They could not risk being seen by anyone so waited patiently for the gunmen under their control to dispose of all potential witnesses. Once the grim job was complete they leapt clear of the roof and sailed down to the ground below. In the small alley in which they landed they quickly found the side door, which they effortlessly yanked open with a sharp jerk.

Communicating with its mind, the lead Shadow scanned through the thoughts of the gunmen under its command to find what progress they had made. Initially it was annoyed that they hadn't located the target but quickly decided on a new course of action. Swiftly it made its way down a short stretch of corridor and into the reception area; here it would find the information that it required. From behind the desk it could hear the lingering echoes of a recently deceased mind. As it approached, the echoes grew stronger and it could pick up random chunks of memories but none were of real use; this would require more

141

precision. Deftly the Shadow leapt over the counter and placed its cold hand upon the head of the dead receptionist. The memories were fast degrading and would soon be beyond its powers to retrieve.

Within a minute of searching it found what it was looking for; hurriedly it withdrew its hand and turned to the other Shadow.

"It is in the next building," it hissed. "Tell the others."

The other dark figure straightened up and concentrated; within seconds all the gunmen changed direction and began converging on the door to the old wing. A quick burst of gunfire shredded the ageing lock and a strong kick to the door sent it crashing open. Within seconds the gunmen were streaming into the old wing with the two Shadows following in their wake.

Just a few hundred feet away down a dark twisting corridor, one of the remaining soldiers stood alone smoking a cigarette. The burst of machinegun fire however made him leap with shock. His group only had three pistols between the four of them, so who was firing? Letting the cigarette fall from his lips he quickly looked up and down the main corridor checking that the coast was clear. Once he was sure that he still had time, he charged from cover and ran back to alert the other three. Of all the days to leave his gun behind! After skidding round a couple of corners he came to a halt by the other three who clearly hadn't noticed the shots. Frantically he tried to explain to the others but it was too late.

From the end of the corridor, countless bullets suddenly raced towards the exposed soldiers. Three of them were wearing their body armour but the forth man, in a decontamination suit didn't stand a chance as a multitude of shots struck him in his exposed back. A look of surprised confusion spread across his face before he slumped over sideways and hit the ground. Luckily the corridor was lined with a succession of support columns which gave the soldiers something to hide behind. Two immediately pulled out their guns and opened fire whilst the third stood staring at the gun that his dead comrade had been carrying.

Despite the surprise of the attack the experience of the soldiers counted for something as two headshots brought down the first two

142

attackers in quick succession. The gunmen were also handicapped as their reactions were dulled in their almost trance like state. Sadly the weight of numbers and superior firepower was on the side of the gunmen though, as they advanced steadily forward. This advantage was further increased when a bullet struck one of the soldiers in the hand. In agony he let the pistol slip from his grip and clatter to the floor; now only one hand gun was expected to hold off the wave of advancing hostiles. The situation seemed hopeless...

Gallagher and Kennedy had been waiting inside the big Mercedes with the doors wide open. The sun was scorching hot and there was no shade in the small car park. The minutes slowly ticked by as they waited for Karl who had been expected nearly five minutes ago. However, both men were suddenly shocked to hear a noise that seemed so out of place; it could only be gunfire.

Inside the building the soldiers had managed to retreat further up the corridor whilst taking another casualty. Six of the remaining gunmen continued the assault as the two Shadows lay concealed from view; selecting one of their puppet gunmen. With no regard for the human's survival, the Shadows sent the man through the hail of bullets and into the room where Gorse had once been held. The gunman was ordered through the decontamination screens into the room beyond. Once the fabric screening was out of the way the gunman entered the room and looked around; it was immediately obvious that they were too late. With this discovery the Shadows hissed angrily before giving new directions to their puppet.

The two remaining soldiers were pinned down unable to retreat any further. They were not able to see as one of their dead comrades was dragged off by the gunmen to their waiting masters. The lead Shadow immediately placed its hand upon the soldiers head but it was unexpectedly disturbed by a series of gunshots coming from the other end of the corridor.

143

Just as the last soldiers were about to be overwhelmed, a shot suddenly caught one of the hostiles in the back of the head. In confusion the others paused their attack and turned just in time to see Kennedy and Gallagher charging down the ramp into the fray. Bullets ricocheted back and forth bouncing off the walls; tiles shattered and even the light was hit plunging the corridor into semi darkness.

The unarmed soldier took advantage of the mayhem and jumped from cover before charging down the corridor to one of the dead gunmen. He roughly heaved the body over and grasped the submachine gun that lay beneath. Picking up the gun he aimed it at the gunmen and unleashed a devastating barrage of bullets that instantly took down another two of them. The remaining hostiles were trapped and coming under fire from two different directions; they awaited commands from their masters but none came. The Shadows had finished extracting the location of the body and quickly departed, leaving their last two puppets to their fate.

As the last two shots of the battle were fired Karl slowly turned into the car park. Despite the beautiful day he felt frustrated. He was sure he would have found something of use but all he'd done was hit a blank wall. His captors had ensured that all he'd seen and learned was erased from his mind.

The two Shadows ascended the short flight of stairs to the ground floor; the information they had required was their's and soon they would complete their mission. They had taken great trouble to mask this operation, using humans to do their work for them and erasing the thoughts of those under their command. Just as they were about to leave the building they sensed a man outside and came to a sudden halt. They didn't have time to waste waiting for this human. As Karl approached the door he was unable to see the two concealed Shadows as they slipped past only a few feet in front of him. However, he was not the only one watching...

Inside the great cavern a small screen displayed the world through Karl's eyes. Since he had been released a figure had stood silently

144

observing his every movement in minute detail to see what could be learned from the humans. Where Karl had failed to detect anything amiss the observer was not so easily fooled. Within seconds it had cast the image with a movement of its hands onto the large screen and paused the memory.

"What have you found?" Hera asked as she made her way over.

"There is something concealed here," the figure replied as they highlighted the distortion with their hands.

"How well concealed is it?" Hera enquired.

"Barely detectable; a human would never have suspected a thing," he replied. Without waiting a second longer Hera turned away and closed her shrouded eyes in concentration.

The body had been taken to a small guarded compound around ten minutes drive from St. James.' From the roof of a neighbouring care home Apollo and Persephone watched as the two vehicles swung off the road and into the enclosed yard beyond. The high walls that surrounded the base were made of solid concrete and adorned with a deadly sea of spikes. Once they were certain no one was watching the two Angels sprung off the three story building landing gracefully on the grass below. Without pausing for a moment they then ran towards the wall gaining speed with each step. Once they were only a few metres from the imposing structure they both leapt. With the impression of weightlessness they rose into the air before letting themselves turn in flight. Briefly their hands made contact with the wall as they let the white drain out of their robes. Using their momentum to carry them on, they spun round off the wall and by the time they landed on the ground they were completely invisible.

The compound was largely empty except for a handful of small concrete buildings dotted here and there that either housed stairs or lifts to a bunker that lay below. Apollo was just about to begin searching for their point of entry when a voice entered the depths of his mind. He'd always disliked this way of communicating but it was the simplest way

145

of delivering a message over long distances. Soon the words became clear and he could discern that it was the voice of Hera.

"Apollo, where are you?" she enquired urgently.

"We have followed the body to a bunker in the city's suburbs."

"A situation has developed at the St. James' Morgue; a group of armed men has just been killed there after trying to retrieve the body."

"Do we know who they were?" Persephone asked joining the discussion.

"No, however that is not the most disturbing part of the story. We managed to pick up traces of a cloaked being leaving the site."

"And it is none of us?" Apollo checked.

"Apart from you there are none of us in that region. We are the only ones with that technology. I want you Persephone to return and find out what you can," Hera commanded before her presence faded out of Apollo's mind.

In the cavern Hera paced back and forth. First the creation of the revenant and now this; what was going on at the surface? The Archangel had to be informed.

In the crumbling basement, the bodies of the gunmen lay strewn across the floor. Their objective had been obvious but as to who they were was an entirely different matter. They wore identical clothing and had matching submachine guns but other than that the bodies revealed little. Just as Kennedy was summoning police backup Karl strode down the ramp; he was initially taken by surprise by the gory leftovers of the battle and was about to pull out his gun when he saw Kennedy on his phone. Quickly he walked over and gave Kennedy a look that basically asked what the heck has happened? Kennedy quickly finished speaking before ending the call.

146

"Still working on that..." Kennedy began. "They were clearly after the body but other than that we don't know."

"Have you scanned their faces?"

"Not yet; we just asked for a unit to be sent over."

"And where's Gallagher?"

"Uhh, he was there a few seconds a go," Kennedy remarked looking round, where was he?

Gallagher had until recently been searching the other bodies for anything that may be of use. After routing through the empty pockets of yet another dead body he'd heard a strange noise coming from one of the aged wooden doors. At first he thought it was nothing but then it came again slightly louder than before. Cautiously he made his way over and tentatively pushed the door open to reveal a steep staircase that descended into the gloom below. He tried the battered light switch but the room remained bathed in darkness. Quickly Gallagher pulled out his phone and turned on the torch. Light filled the dank room for the first time in many years. The space was vast and lined with decaying bricks and the remains of several musty wooden crates.

However, Gallagher didn't notice any of this because there was something far more important lying at the bottom of the stairs. Resting against the wall in a pool of blood lay one of the gunmen. Gallagher thought of drawing his gun but decided it wasn't needed; the man was bleeding from both a wound on his chest and a deep cut along the top of his head. Gallagher quickly descended the steps to assess the state of the man.

Kneeling down beside him, Gallagher could see that the man was just clinging to life and initially appeared to be unconscious. He called up to Kennedy to call an ambulance but his words were swallowed by the vast echoing interior of the room. However, the noise bore unexpected results as the man's eyes suddenly opened. Slowly he tipped his head towards the light and looked at Gallagher.

"Where... are they?" he stammered weakly.

"Who?" Gallagher asked.

"The Shadows," the man replied; his voice filled with fear.

"Who are the Shadows?"

"I don't know; they found me in my home and crept into my mind. They exposed my every fear and every crime and turned them into a living nightmare..."

"What did they want," Gallagher cut across.

"There was something here they wanted; something that could have exposed them too early. They are strong and have powers far greater than anything you can imagine but they are still weak and helpless compared to those they fear. That's why they used us; their enemies have eyes everywhere, they needed to... hide their actions..."

"What do they want?" Gallagher asked but the man carried on regardless; gripping Gallagher's arm as tightly as he was able as if he was trying to cling hold of life.

"They know where it is now and they will stop at nothing to retrieve it...I have seen what they plan to do... their vision for the world must not succeed; the... Angels must prevail..." he said as his voice faded to a whisper and cut off. Slowly the man loosened his grip on Gallagher's arm. He had lived a wicked life and now repented on it. He had seen hell and did not fear what awaited him; within a few minutes he died at peace.

Without checking to see if the man was dead Gallagher raced up the stairs; the words of the man ringing in his ears. 'They would stop at nothing...' He had just put Natasha in terrible danger. The rest didn't matter for now; he had to get there before the Shadows did.

Up on the surface the army truck carrying Mark and Alice rumbled relentlessly down the road. Although the soldiers hadn't said much since they left the police station they seemed surprisingly cheerful. Neither Mark nor Alice were wearing handcuffs and the fact they were

148

riding in the front of the truck implied the soldiers were not too angry about their recent escape. They hadn't been driving for long before Mark realised they were not heading in the direction of the camp; this was soon confirmed as the truck entered one of the older suburbs of the city and a series of foreboding concrete walls came into view. Both Alice and Mark hoped they weren't going into this strange looking place but this hope was extinguished when the lorry slowed and turned off onto the small section of road in front of a pair of giant metal gates. With a creaking and a slight groaning of metal on metal the gates began to swing open allowing the lorry access to the compound beyond.

"What are we doing here," Alice asked.

"We were just ordered to pick you up and bring you here. Someone else will be along for you later in the day," the driver replied as he pulled up between two other lorries.

"Last stop, everybody out," the other one said jokingly as the lorry came to a halt.

Both Alice and Mark clambered out of the passenger's door before following the soldiers to the entrance of a small concrete structure in the centre of the compound. Two other soldiers stood guard on the heavy metal door but as they approached one moved forwards and with a heave opened it revealing a steep staircase beyond. The soldier who had driven the truck went first, followed by Mark and then Alice with the other soldier at the rear. As they disappeared down the flight of steps the door was slowly pulled shut behind them. As the last slithers of sunshine disappeared from the bunker the door unexpectedly jammed. The soldier was initially a little confused so gave it another heave and it shut with ease; just after an invisible shape slipped through.

The metal stairs took Alice and Mark deep below the surface world; each footfall reverberating off the bare concrete walls. At the bottom they intersected a long tunnel which headed off for a considerable distance in both directions. As the group headed down the right hand tunnel, Apollo continued to walk silently behind them. He recognised the two prisoners and soon understood why they were there from analysing the minds of the guards. Mind reading was a fine art at the

149

best of times and without direct contact only the thoughts that the guards were currently thinking were visible. Unsure of the location of his target he decided to keep following the group to see where they would take him.

"What is this place?" Mark asked after a while.

"It was some World War Two bunker or other," the soldier at the back replied. "But it's changed a lot since then."

"What's it used for?" Alice queried.

"Can't say; it's classified. What I will tell you though is that it's probably the most boring posting in the entire country. There's only a few of us here and we seem to spend most of our time clearing up puddles; the walls leak like hell."

The procession moved on for several minutes before arriving at a second set of stairs which took them down another two levels. They passed along several more tunnels and junctions before eventually arriving at a long row of armoured doors.

"Don't worry you'll only be here for a few hours at most," one of the soldiers said as he pressed a set of controls and opened the first two doors for them.

Once Alice and Mark were inside, the cell doors were shut behind them. With a clang the locks automatically slammed home, sealing them inside.

The newly restored peace and quiet outside St. James' was suddenly shattered by the roar of engines. Traffic was thrown into chaos as a small armoured vehicle charged out of the car park onto the main road closely followed by Gallagher's black Mercedes. Vehicles skidded to a stop and others honked their horns angrily as the vehicles turned sharply and thundered down the road. Karl sat in the first car along with the two remaining soldiers who were cursing the fact that the other group had taken the radio with them. They had to reach the base before the enemy did.

Behind them Gallagher and Kennedy followed in their wake, trying to keep behind the armoured vehicle which was currently driving chaotically between the two lanes of traffic. In exasperation Kennedy tried once more to ring Natasha but only got through to the voice mail.

"Haven't been in a chase for years," Kennedy commented as a car skidded past them to avoid the armoured car.

"It's not a chase, it's a race," Gallagher responded whilst swerving sharply to miss an oncoming car.

"Normally we should be arresting people driving this dangerously," Kennedy remarked as the armoured car shot across a red light followed by Gallagher. "Do you think we should book them?" Kennedy said trying to ease the tension.

"I'll give them a medal if they get us there in time," Gallagher called back.

As the convoy continued to advance through London they had no way of knowing just how close the race was; on the next road along to the right, three more black vans charged relentlessly on with a pair of large SUVs following up the rear. They knew the element of surprise had been lost so had dispensed with secrecy. The two sides were neck and neck without even knowing it.

On Gallagher's side of the raceway an un-expected obstacle emerged. As the armoured car careered across a red light a lorry driver was taken by surprise and swerved sharply to avoid it. The thirty tonne truck began to jack knife as it skidded uncontrollably towards a corner shop. The people in its path leapt clear only just in time as the tractor unit smashed sideways along the edge of the glass fronted shop sending a cascade of glass and assorted foods spilling across the pavement. The wrecked lorry came to rest about a metre into the building and left the narrow road blocked.

After angrily thumping the wheel Gallagher floored it heading for the next road along. Upon arriving at the next junction he skidded round the bend desperately trying to catch up with the soldiers. He was now only twenty metres ahead of the enemy convoy which was bearing down on

151

him from behind. The driver of the first van noticed the fast moving car up ahead but did nothing as his orders were to simply get the men in the back to their destination. However, the two Shadows who were watching through the drivers eyes immediately recognised the car from the morgue. They were trying to get to the body before them! Quickly the Shadows communicated a series of commands into the minds of their soldiers before ordering the driver to increase speed.

Kennedy was the first to spot the van bearing down on them and quickly turned to Gallagher.

"We've got a black van coming at us real quick,"

"Yeah, I just saw it," Gallagher remarked whilst looking in his mirror. He couldn't go any faster as the street was narrow and the cars ahead of him blocked his path. God he wished his car had a siren!

"They're still gaining," Kennedy added.

"I can see that," Gallagher responded as the van mounted the curb and drew level with them.

As Gallagher blared on his horn and tried to find a safe way round the side door on the van slid open revealing a row of men poised with their guns drawn. Instinctively Gallagher did the only thing he could do; brake. Gallagher's tyres bit into the road abruptly leaving the van careering down the pavement away from them; the bullets missed the car by a good ten metres and peppered a stone building opposite.

Just before they came to a halt, Gallagher released the brake and pressed hard on the accelerator to charge towards the van which was trying to turn back onto the road. At the last second Gallagher swerved off to the right, zipping around the other side of the van; gunning the throttle to the end of the road. There he skimmed round a left hand turn ignoring the lights that hung over the crossroads, heading for the street the armoured car had vanished down.

The rest of the convoy soon passed the other van and took over the chase. The crossroads was fast approaching and the two vans chose to carry straight on opting to leave the chase to the faster escort vehicles;

152

cars careered onto the pavements in confusion. As the chaos ensued the two SUVs also reached the junction but swerved to the left and roared after Gallagher.

After taking the next right Gallagher could see the armoured car in the far distance and continued to charge on relentlessly.

"They're back," Kennedy called out.

"Vans shouldn't be going this fast!" Gallagher responded whilst searching in his mirror for them.

"They're not vans; they're SUVs. In these conditions they'll catch us up in no time!"

Steadily the chase grew ever faster as the larger engines of the enemy cars closed the distance. Soon the first shots were being fired and it wasn't long before rounds started peppering the back of the car.

"You still got bullets?" Gallagher called as he swerved across the road.

"Not for much longer," Kennedy replied as he retrieved his gun and leaned out of the open window. Doing so made him a perfect target but the hostiles were inexperienced and found it difficult to hit such a small target. Kennedy on the other hand had years of practise; taking aim he opened fire on the closest SUV. The first shot punched through the windscreen and imbedded in the driver's shoulder causing the car to veer violently to the left. The driver wanted to stop but the voices yelled at him to continue so he tried to regain control. But then a second shot hit him in the chest and then another leaving the one tonne vehicle driverless in the narrow confines of the street. Slowly it veered ever further to the right until it crossed the lanes. The passenger could have stopped it but he received no commands to intervene; so at over fifty miles an hour the SUV slammed into a parked car. Still the vehicle kept moving though as two of its wheels rode up over the car's bonnet, sending it rolling over onto its side.

Kennedy watched his handiwork with satisfaction as the SUV landed on its roof before spinning over several times across the street. Kennedy then saw the second SUV was heading straight for the mangled wreck and for a few moments thought it would crash. However, at the last second the driver swerved and avoided a collision.

Kennedy quickly ducked back inside as a new wave of bullets pelted the car. Frantically Gallagher looked around for an escape route until his eyes settled on a narrow alleyway on the right. Using every ounce of his driving skill Gallagher slid the car sideways and aimed for the tiny gap as the hail of bullets peppered the car. The gap was tight and it didn't look like they'd make it as the two stone walls loomed up on either side of them. However, Gallagher had gauged it perfectly and the car slipped into the gap only losing its left wing mirror in the process. The SUV however was not as lucky and swerved too late. The huge vehicle struck the side of the stone building and rebounded, only just managing to stay on its wheels. From there it skidded back onto the street where it span several times before coming to a rest against a line of parked cars on the other side.

Gallagher and Kennedy thought they had escaped as they ploughed down the tiny passage and headed for the next road along. Skidding out onto the main road Gallagher and Kennedy then had a nasty shock as they discovered that two of the vans had laid an ambush. With their doors already opening both Kennedy and Gallagher hastily ducked as they hurtled away from the barrage of bullets that came whistling their way.

Up ahead Gallagher could see the roads converging to go over a large bridge but more importantly the armoured car was only a hundred metres ahead with its heavy machine gun hopefully ready for use. Gallagher soon drew alongside and blared the horn, pointing wildly at the oncoming vans and the incredibly battered SUV which had emerged from the other road.

The driver didn't notice at first as there had been a lot of angry people blasting their horns furiously at them during the chaotic journey so he assumed he'd just angered someone else. Luckily though Karl looked over and caught sight of Gallagher and Kennedy's frantic gestures behind them. Wondering what Gallagher was pointing at he looked in the mirror and saw an SUV with a caved in roof rapidly gaining on them; he wasn't quite sure what was wrong but he knew that the SUV was part of it. He hastily pointed it out to the driver who in turn told the other soldier to climb into the back and man the gun. After a few seconds a voice called back saying it would take a while; time that Gallagher didn't have as the SUVs occupants opened fire once again.

Wildly the driver signalled for Gallagher to get out of the way as he swerved the three tonne vehicle towards the attackers. Gallagher only just made it clear as the armoured car made contact with the SUV instantly crumpling the flimsy metal. He then swerved away to avoid an oncoming car before heading back and once more crashed into the side of the vehicle. This time the impact forced the SUV against the concrete wall of the bridge. The vehicle rapidly became a death trap as it was crushed inwards and dragged helplessly along the wall. Sparks flew in all directions until the concrete wall unexpectedly ended and was replaced by a metal fence. The railings were nowhere near strong enough and buckled under the weight of the two vehicles. The SUV was effortlessly forced through this flimsy obstacle allowing the wreckage to slip off the road and crash down onto the high speed railway tracks below.

Soon the gun was ready and a hail of bullets were suddenly sent streaming towards the first of the oncoming vans. The driver had no time to do anything as a torrent of shots ripped through the vehicle massacring those on board. The Shadows were unwilling to lose any more of their men and ordered the driver of the second van to break off just before a stream of bullets burst through the windscreen and killed him instantly.

The armoured car and Gallagher's Mercedes continued down the road hoping they were going to win the race; however they didn't know that the third van was already approaching the gates to the bunker.

As the race of death neared its conclusion Persephone found herself back at the starting point. The front of the building was now awash with police cars so she chose to enter St. James' from the rear. The police had no idea that the dilapidated wing at the back was in use so hadn't yet discovered the heart of the crime scene. She crept in via the ramp and was soon among the casualties of the battle. There was not a sign of the cloaked being so she crept over to the first of the dead soldiers and quickly restored them to life. His mind showed nothing of use to her so she moved over to the next soldier and repeated the procedure; again with no results.

The only others who might know something of use were the countless dead gunmen that littered the corridor. She didn't like the thought of venturing into their dark minds; she could always pick up small fragments of memories from those around her and she could tell that these were some of the darkest minds the city had to offer. Even standing in such close proximity to these monsters was making her feel physically sick; let alone venturing deeper into their thoughts. But then she began to detect one glimmer of hope; the echoes of a mind that was not as contorted with evil as the rest. Slowly she descended the stairs into the old cellar and sat down alongside the dead man who had spoken to Gallagher.

She pressed her hand more firmly against his head and set about repairing the damage. Within a few seconds his mind was rebuilt sufficiently for her to gain full access and she began to sift through the memories. However, as the seconds ticked by her concern grew; large portions of his mind had been erased and manipulated. Where the events of the last few days should have been there was only a strange black hole; as if the memories had been burned from his mind.

Quite by chance though, she spotted a lone stray memory on the far side of the devastation. The memory was only a few minutes old and she was able to extract a conversation he'd had with the human detective. All she could recover were the words but they were enough to fill her with dread. Quickly she reached out with her mind and called to Hera. She had no idea what the danger was or who the Shadows were; only that they were coming.

As Gallagher was busy trying to evade his pursuers Natasha was blissfully unaware of the storm about to close in on her. The still struggling body had been lifted out of the armoured truck by a group of soldiers a short while ago and was now being wheeled ever deeper into a large subterranean bunker. It turned out that there was no lift that

156

went straight between each level so it had taken ten minutes of meandering across the floors before they reached level five; the deepest part of the bunker. After going through a series of large armoured doors they arrived at a room with a strange structure in the centre.

What lay before them looked like a glorified fish tank; although it was clear that it was built for something a little stronger than fish. The edges of the structure were made from thick strips of some kind of composite material with bolts every few spaces and in between these lay four enormous sections of reinforced glass that must have been twelve inches thick.

"What do you normally put in there?" Natasha asked, not sure she wanted to know.

"Nothing much," one of the soldiers replied. "It was apparently used for some kind of testing a few decades ago. For all the time I've been stationed here though it's only been used once and that was for a practical joke."

"How are you going to put it in there; I don't see a door," Natasha pointed out.

"That's because it doesn't have one," one of the soldiers replied whilst turning a key in the wall.

The room was suddenly filled with the wail of alarms and a lot of hissing as the entire structure slowly started to rise into the air. After ten seconds the alarms stopped and the Cage sat flush with the high ceiling. The soldiers didn't want to be around the body any longer than they had to so quickly wheeled the trolley into the square outline on the floor and turned the key back the other way. Once the walls had slid back into place the Cage was complete once more. Natasha couldn't imagine anything getting out of that thing in a hurry. As the group walked away they had no way of knowing what was about to hit them.

The number of soldiers at the base were few; they were largely unarmed and not expecting any trouble. The first of the black vans thundered up onto the small drive in front of the gates where it abruptly skidded to a halt. The sentry on top of the wall barely had any time to react before one of the gunmen had leapt from the van, taken aim and fired a silenced shot into the surprised man's forehead. The gate was not a problem as one of the concealed Shadows raised a gloved hand into the air. The will of the figure flowed down the electrical wires controlling the gate, overriding the locks and bypassing the control panel. In less than five seconds the gates were swinging open and in poured the deluge of armed men. The soldiers walking in the open didn't stand a chance and were slaughtered before they even realised what was going on as a succession of deadly silenced shots found each one in turn. Within a minute the compound was under their control; the van was brought inside and the gates were sealed behind them.

Inside the bunker the monitors in the security room showed the first few soldiers falling but after that had crackled and failed. The bunker was thrown into complete chaos as the security staff tried to call for help from the outside world but only received the sound of static in return. The internal communications had also failed, the cameras were starting to go off line and all the locks were being overridden. In desperation the two men abandoned the control room and were forced to run down the echoing halls calling the other soldiers to arms and warning them that they were under attack.

Natasha and the group of soldiers were walking down one of the long tunnels to the stairs when someone came tearing round the corner in a state of terror.

"What the hell..." the Captain began before the newcomer cut them off.

"We're under attack! A large group of heavily armed men have infiltrated the bunker. They've killed everyone on the surface."

"What in God's name are you on about," the captain demanded.

Just then the other man from the security room appeared but quickly crumpled up as two shots struck him in the chest. As the dying man hit the ground each of the four privates reached for their assault rifles and the Captain and Natasha for their pistols. They were now trapped in a dead end corridor between the hostiles and their target; there was nowhere to run and they couldn't expect to negotiate; the only option was to fight.

The armoured car and Gallagher's once pristine Mercedes swerved to a halt outside the closed gates. The armoured car's driver honked the horn, expecting someone to let them in but got no response. After blasting the horn several more times he lowered the window and called to Gallagher.

"This isn't right; there's always someone on the gate."

"Is there any other way in?" Gallagher called back.

"No, this is... they're back!" he suddenly yelled, pointing down the road as the damaged black van came tearing towards them.

Frantically the other soldier clambered back to his firing position as Gallagher and Kennedy leapt from their vehicle and darted round the side of the hulking armoured car. The machine gun soon opened fire as the men charged across the open ground from their now stationary van. However, the vigorous firing abruptly ended when a series of bullets struck the gunner in his shoulder. The driver quickly reacted and made his way into the back of the vehicle to take over firing.

From under the vehicle Gallagher and Kennedy withdrew their own pistols waiting for the targets to get closer; they didn't have much ammunition and couldn't afford to miss. However, this approach was soon abandoned as a man emerged from the van with a long slender tube over his shoulder; it could only be a rocket launcher. The man was about fifty metres away when he crouched and took aim; Gallagher raised his gun at the same time as Kennedy and fired bullet after bullet. At that range most of their shots missed and the ones that did find their mark were deflected by the man's body armour. However, just as the man was about to pull the trigger, Gallagher fired his last bullet. The round sailed straight and true as it hurtled towards the man; tearing into the man's neck and puncturing his wind pipe. He slumped in pain but the Shadows in his mind screamed at him to fire. He knew he was

159

finished and twisting slightly as he fell he pulled on the trigger as he went.

Gallagher was thankful as he saw the man slump forwards but was taken by surprise when the rocket motor ignited and came tearing from the tube. However, the streak of fire wasn't heading for them and instead sped into the heart of the advancing hostile formation. Within a fraction of a second the missile struck the ground and exploded filling the air with a deadly rain of shrapnel that took down most of the oncoming men. By the time the machine gun was up and running it was simply a matter of dealing with the remnants of the once deadly force.

Inside the bunker, Natasha and the remaining soldiers had fallen back into a large chamber that gave them some protection from the withering fire coming their way. The Shadows had become shocked at the scale of their losses and were favouring caution over the reckless charge which had proved so ineffective in earlier engagements. So far the nine enemy gunmen assaulting them had been reduced to eight at the cost of one soldier. The rate of losses was so far equal; but the attackers had men to spare.

On the road outside the camp Gallagher stared at the huge steel gates. The wail of sirens could now be heard in the distance but they would take too long to reach Natasha; he was too close to allow a bit of concrete to get in his way. Then suddenly the solution hit him; running headlong away from the others he soon made it to the abandoned enemy vehicle. Inside it looked more like an arsenal than the back of a van; machine guns, assault rifles, a sniper rifle and what he had come for... another rocket launcher.

As the battle raged, the Shadows attacked the very heart of the security system and quickly unlocked every remaining door for their troops; however this had unintended results. Alice had been lying on her crude bed when the locks unexpectedly retracted with a metallic clunk. She

160

turned to see who was there but strangely the door remained shut. After waiting for a minute or two her curiosity got the better of her. Quietly she slipped off the bed and went over to the heavy door which creaked open a fraction with a tentative push. Cautiously she peeked out of the gap but still couldn't see anyone. Getting more curious she opened the door wider and poked her head through the gap just in time to see Mark emerging from his cell.

"This is a bit odd," she commented.

"Yeah, who heard of a prison where the doors open on their own?"

"Do you think we should stay here?" Alice wondered.

"Well we *should* do but I don't really like it here; the room service is awful. How about you?"

"It's a bit too cell like for me," Alice remarked sarcastically. "Do you remember the way out?"

"I sure do."

With the sirens of countless emergency vehicles only just around the corner Gallagher took aim at the wall. By his side Kennedy held an assault rifle, Karl had a sub machine gun and the soldier had chosen a very bulky looking rifle. The crosshairs of the rocket launcher were aimed at a section of the wall just to the right of the gate and with one last deep breath he pulled the trigger. The rocket was a blur as it blasted free of the tube and sailed into the thin concrete wall. Once it had reached the centre of the target the charge detonated with an enormous explosion sending out a cloud of pulverised concrete. Gallagher and the others waited in suspense for the dust to settle; had they breached the wall? To their relief the dust soon cleared and it became apparent that the rocket had done its job; creating a hole big enough to climb through. Without any hesitation the four charged at the wall.

Everything seemed to become unnaturally quiet as the four heavily armed men made their way to the wall. Just as they began to pass through the hole, a hail of inaccurate fire broke the silence as it tore

161

towards them from the far end of the compound. Fanning out they each took cover behind the assortment of armoured vehicles which had been parked close to the gate. The firing seemed to last for an eternity as the gunner sprayed the area with bullets; as if he was waiting for a command to stop.

Eventually when there was a brief lull, Gallagher quickly peered out from the edge of the lorry noting an armoured car that had been parked next to the bunker's entrance. A lone gunman now occupied the machine gunner's position and was using the stolen weapon to keep the new wave of attackers at bay. Kennedy slowly crawled along the lorry's underside.

"The tables have turned a bit," he remarked. "Any ideas?"

"Still working on that," Gallagher replied as he scanned the area for something of use; his gaze moved across the collection of vehicles until his eyes fixed on one that was very different to the others. "Actually; I think I've got a good idea..." he said with a grin.

Apollo had to admit that the maze of confusing tunnels was getting the better of him. The large amount of metal which surrounded him was distorting his senses and limiting them to only a few metres. Eventually though he arrived at the doors to a lift shaft where he sensed something strange and out of place. With a gesture from his hands, the doors slid open and he leapt down to the level below.

As he emerged into an identical tunnel, he could now see what had caught his attention. It was the body of a dead soldier left carelessly sprawled against the side of the tunnel. Apollo was uneasy about this discovery; why was it here? Carefully he extended a hand to the man's cold head and began the task of repairing him and searching through his memories. It wasn't long before he had his answers and hurried on his way. Something sinister was definitely afoot in this place.

Outside the gunfire continued to pound the side of the lorry so Gallagher had to shout to make himself heard to Kennedy.

"There's a tank over there," he called out pointing at a partially covered vehicle.

"Do you know how to drive one?" Kennedy asked.

"No, but a friend of mine back in the army said it wasn't too difficult."

"I bet it isn't," Kennedy remarked.

"Well have you got any better ideas," Gallagher yelled back over the racket from hundreds of bullets striking the ground around them. "Ok then; you distract the gunner and I'll make a run for the tank."

"Great," Kennedy said sarcastically as Gallagher shuffled to the end of the lorry closest to the tank before calling over to the soldier and Karl to explain his plan.

Thirty seconds later the three were poised as Kennedy slowly counted down with his fingers. Three, two , one... Kennedy leapt round the side of the vehicle firing wildly before ducking behind another truck. The gunner kept the gun trained on Kennedy and was caught by surprise when the other three broke cover and charged across the ten metres of open ground to the tank. He frantically tried to swing the gun round; the crosshairs were gaining on Gallagher but just before they aligned he vanished behind the hulking mass of the tank.

The tank was at least ten years old and was probably one of the last of its kind left in the country. Despite its age the Challenger III had one unique feature that allowed Gallagher's plan to succeed; there was a door on the side of the hull for the driver. So in almost perfect safety the three were able to board the vehicle before Gallagher sealed the hatch behind them.

The tank's controls were a little more complicated than Gallagher had first imagined. The two sticks that controlled the steering were easy enough to find but the process of starting the vehicle was more challenging. After testing multiple switches and buttons the engine finally roared into life. Experimentally Gallagher pushed forwards on

163

the two sticks and the tank leapt forwards with unexpected speed. Gallagher quickly pulled back on both but accidentally brought the right one back harder sending the tank's tracks skidding into reverse at different speeds.

After careering into one of the lorries and nearly hitting Kennedy, Gallagher was starting to think that perhaps it wasn't as easy as he'd been told. Despite this he once again pushed forwards sending the tank off on its path of destruction. They continued at an angle across the concrete ground until Gallagher sharply turned in an effort to avoid a spotlight tower. However, the turn came a little too late and the tank continued to plough on through the thin metal tower sending it crashing on top of the tank below.

With the light tower now stuck on top of the tank they fast closed in on the enemy vehicle. The gunner made no effort to get out of the way and instead kept firing at the advancing metal beast. Karl and the soldier called down saying they weren't ready to fire but Gallagher wasn't listening; he didn't need a gun for this. The armoured car may have been tough but it wasn't strong enough to survive eighty tonnes of tank on top of it.

Gallagher charged at full speed; the tracks gained a grip on contact with the car and the tank continued over the top without even slowing down. Gallagher couldn't see anything but the squeals and groans coming from below the hull told him all that he needed to know. Once he'd hit the ground again he quickly unbolted the door and clambered out of the vehicle. Natasha was so close; he could only hope that he would get there in time.

Natasha and the soldiers were losing the fight; they were outgunned and outnumbered. If it hadn't been for the soldiers superior training then they would have been overrun long ago. Just out of sight the two Shadows lurked monitoring the progress of the battle.

"They are taking too long," the first one said in a cold and empty voice. "We should finish them off ourselves."

164

"No," the other one hissed. "Our forces will break through soon enough."

"Is the perimeter still secure on the surface?" the first one asked.

The other did not reply as it tried to delve into the depths of his mind searching for the connection to the sentry. After being unable to find the mind it required it could only assume the worst.

"They may be in," he said at last. "Do we have any other forces to fill the gap?"

"No, they are all dead."

"Then we must risk revealing ourselves. You go to the door; deal with any intruders and leave no condemning memories."

Alice and Mark had found the entire bunker deserted as they crept through the long cold corridors of the subterranean labyrinth. They had made a couple of wrong turns but had quickly realised their mistake before backtracking to the correct route. They were now only ten metres or so from the exit where they fully expected to find a large group of soldiers waiting for them. Just as they were about to draw level with the exit though, Mark suddenly stopped.

"Did you see that?" he asked pointing down the empty tunnel in front of them.

"See what?" Alice asked.

"A black shape; it darted across the corridor and down that tunnel over there."

"Let's just get out of here," Alice urged as she walked towards the stairs. "We can talk about it later."

Mark took one last look before he moved to follow Alice. However, he was suddenly taken by surprise as something grabbed him from behind and flung him into the back wall of the corridor. Alice heard the thud of Mark hitting the wall and turned in alarm to see a blurry shape

165

heading straight for her. There was nothing she could do as the hand grabbed her and threw her back into the tunnel. She sailed through the air for a split second before painfully crashing to the ground and skidding into Mark who groaned on impact.

The Shadow's outdated invisibility was draining too much energy but at the same time it couldn't reveal itself. Trying to ignore the rising feeling of weariness it slowly reached out with its mind and began to drag the metal door closed to seal off the bunker. It only took five seconds to drag it shut however it was just long enough for Gallagher to slip inside.

The Shadow turned slowly to gaze at Mark and Alice. It couldn't keep its self hidden any longer and suddenly reappeared before sagging slightly to one side. It couldn't leave any memories to be used against it so slowly walked towards the cowering pair. As it approached them its hand began to glow and from the palm of its hand a long black line began to extend downwards. It quickly grew thicker at the base and sharper at the tip taking the shape of a long sinister dagger. There was nowhere for Alice and Mark to go.

The Shadow was only a foot away when suddenly a stream of bullets blasted out from the stairs peppering its back. In agony the Shadow screeched and turned to face the new threat.

Gallagher stood at the base of the stairs with his gun at the ready. He'd had a feeling that the bullets would have little effect so prepared to fire again. As the Shadow lurched towards him he pulled down on the trigger but to his dismay nothing happened. Cursing the gun he frantically tried to fix it as the creature came closer. Just as the Shadow was about to reach him Alice saw an opportunity and scrambled to her feet before taking a running leap onto the monster's back. The Shadow in its confused, tired and damaged state couldn't keep its balance and tumbled backwards before crashing down on top of Alice. The force of the impact made Alice release her grip and the creature managed to roll free; still grasping the cruel blade in its hand. Slowly it crawled over to Alice; its mind flooded with rage and as it raised the blade above her. Alice closed her eyes in terror and waited for the end.

166

Then a second volley of bullets hit the Shadow at point blank range; having aimed for its head, each shot tore deep into vital parts of its brain. Writhing and flailing it released its grasp on the blade; it could feel the dimming of its mind and could no longer control its body. Its limbs flailed as it tried to hold itself together but it was no use and slowly it slumped to the ground. Gradually the spasms in its limbs grew less frequent and at last it was still.

Once the creature's writhing had stopped Gallagher looked down at Alice but to his horror saw the black blade protruding from her shoulder...

Apollo had by now picked up the sounds of the battle and had used them to guide him through the last few hundred metres of tunnels. As he approached the fire fight he activated his newer and more advanced invisibility; unlike last time he could remain this way for hours. He could feel that he was close to his target so without stopping he continued into the line of fire. Occasionally a stray shot hit him as he meandered through the gunmen but they were of little concern to him. He could see which way the battle was heading but it was not his job to interfere at this stage; only when the battle was lost or won would his services be needed.

He soon passed the gunmen and walked the final few metres of no man's land before passing through into the larger chamber that the soldiers defended. Most of the faces were new to him but he soon spotted Natasha and instantly remembered her from the warehouse several days ago. He felt guilty about the cut to her forehead as he passed by but there was nothing he could do about it now.

Soon he was beyond the fighting and advancing down the tunnel. The thousands of tonnes of earth had so far confused his senses but as he drew close he could feel the presence of the abomination. The Shadows had already raised the Cage in readiness for their troops' arrival. This allowed Apollo to walk up alongside the body and examine it up close; as the seconds ticked by his concern only deepened. This crude attempt at restoring life was clearly a failure; its mind was utterly in ruins as the process had not been sufficient to repair the damage done to the brain.

Also, its recent injuries had not properly healed and were showing some signs of turning septic.

Without waiting any longer he raised his hand above the body and swiftly brought it down on the squirming revenant's head. On contact with the sickly skin, millions of tiny particles broke away from the surface of Apollo's hand. The tiny flakes of silver quickly breached the body's defences and divided into multiple groups. Soon the particles were gathering around the key systems of the body and shutting them down one by one. At last; after several days of torment, Michael Gorse was allowed to slip away.

In less than a minute from Apollo's arrival the task was complete. For a moment he stood silently alongside the body before turning to walk away. However, before he could do anything, the Cage slammed down around him. He had been trapped.

It hadn't been a good month for Alice. First she had survived an explosion only to be shot; then she'd been locked up and now she had a knife imbedded in her shoulder! Surprisingly she didn't immediately realise that she was injured as there wasn't any pain. However, as she tipped her head forwards the shaft of the knife soon came into view and that's when the pain hit her.

It started as a dull tingling but rapidly grew with each passing second. Soon Gallagher and Mark were leaning over her; Mark moved to pull on the dagger but Gallagher said something and Mark withdrew his hand hurriedly. The pain quickly became excruciating as a piece of cloth was pressed around the wound at which point she yelled out from the intense agony. Gallagher told Mark to keep the torn off piece of fabric held firmly around the knife until help made it through the door. Just before he dashed off to find Natasha he removed his pistol from its holster and gave it to Mark in case any hostiles appeared.

Apollo looked out bleakly through the glass, filled with rage; who had trapped him here? Then far behind him he began to detect a faint

168

presence. Normally he could locate a person easily by listening to the echoes of their minds but this one was unnaturally quiet; as if it had only existed for a few days at most. From this Apollo could be sure of one thing; that whatever was standing behind him wasn't human. As Apollo turned to look at the mystery being he had considered multiple scenarios but none of them prepared him for what stood before him.

What he saw was a near image of himself. Except where he was tall and garbed in white; the figure was hunched and clad in black. As the seconds ticked by neither of the two beings moved and just stared at each other; Apollo from the Cage and the intruder from a dark corner at the back of the room. It was Apollo who eventually broke the silence.

"I take it that this is your doing," he said gesturing towards the body.

"No," the Shadow rasped. "I was born after this failure was created."

"Do you have a name?" Apollo asked.

"Erebos; my name is Erebos." For a few moments Apollo paused as things slowly slotted into place.

"The god of darkness; you certainly have chosen an appropriate name for yourself. I once knew someone else with an equally grim name; but I have long believed him to be dead..."

"You were fooled as you were meant to be. The one of which you speak is my lord and master and he is very much alive."

As the Shadow finished these words it felt a pressure within its head as its awareness was abruptly swept aside; a greater mind was assuming temporary control. As Apollo watched, the Shadow's back straightened and it seemed to drastically increase in stature and might. The next words it spoke were far deeper and more commanding than before as it strode away from the wall and towards Apollo.

"Yes Apollo, I am alive and I have been listening," the Shadow said in its new voice.

"Black doesn't suit you brother..." Apollo said sadly. "We all wept for you after the accident, and now you have betrayed us," he continued as sadness turned into pity. "Why did you turn your back on us?"

There was a brief pause as the Shadow turned and listened to the sounds of the battle.

"I was one of the first to be born; back before the Ark was even finished. I worked selflessly for many years and I stood by the Archangel's side in the light of the Sphere as the Central Chamber took shape around us. However, as time progressed I slowly came to realise that the Archangel was wrong about humanity. Where he saw the light and beauty I saw them for what they were; a greedy, violent and self destructive race. I saw the truth brother; that those we sought to protect were not capable of survival. I told the Archangel of this but I could never make him realise how blind he really was. Eventually there came a day when I could not stand it anymore and I left the Ark forever."

"And what did you do then?" Apollo asked.

"I began to fulfil my purpose. Where you and the others sought to heal I chose to destroy. I ventured into the darkest places that this planet has to offer and I hunted down its most feted people. One murderer at a time I tried to cleanse this world of evil as I became the Reaper. Soon people feared me so much that they would change their ways and repent but for every person I converted another two would fill the dark void that was left behind. After years of this I came to realise that I could never save the world this way. I needed a greater power..."

"You are referring to the Spire," Apollo said flatly. He could now see where this was leading.

"Of course; I was one of the Spire's designers and I know exactly what it is capable of. It is the greatest power this planet has ever known and soon I shall wield it."

"And what of your creations?" Apollo asked. "How do they fit into all this?"

170

"The Archangel would not listen to me the first time and he will not listen now. It has taken me many years to perfect my Shadows. I had experimented with the techniques involved before I even left the Ark but it was not until recently that I finally perfected the art. I took the bodies of those I had slain and turned them into something more; I gave them a purpose and a new existence. They do still have a rather grim love for cruelty but I did not have time to correct this," the Shadow remarked callously. "Do you see what I am trying to accomplish brother? I am going to cure the world of evil forever."

"No, you won't..." Apollo began. "You cannot cure the planet of evil if you have become filled with the very darkness that you seek to destroy. You took on a task that ate into the very fabric of your being and turned you into a monster."

"I... feared you would say that," the Shadow said as it slowly turned away and headed for the door.

As the Shadow walked, its back hunched up again as its master released his grasp.

"Don't worry..." it said in its own rasping voice. "I'm sure after the little mess outside the humans are going to take great care of you. We do not want you interfering with our plans after all," it said before breaking out laughing as it left the room.

As Apollo was left sealed in his prison, Mark sat next to Alice; keeping the piece of cloth pressed around the wound. His arms ached but he wasn't going to let go; he'd carried her across a field and even turned himself in to be with her. He was not going to lose her now. However, the wound was not the thing that he should have been most concerned about. Less than a metre or so away the Shadow that had been presumed dead had nearly finished its regeneration...

A short distance up the staircase and beyond the armoured door; Kennedy, Karl and the soldier were finalising their preparations for entering the bunker. After the door had sealed they'd quickly come up with a plan; a plan that involved a very big gun.

The tank's cannon was a little harder to understand than a normal firearm and so took the three men the best part of five minutes to get it loaded and aimed at the door. Now the moment of truth was fast approaching; which was stronger, the tank or the door? Kennedy and Karl were standing at the base of the vehicle as the soldier checked he was on target.

In the bunker Mark heard a slight scraping noise behind him. Without letting go of the now blood soaked rag he turned to see the Shadow slowly getting to its feet. What could he do? It had taken over a hundred shots just to knock it out. He was forced to release the pressure and grab the pistol that Gallagher had left him. Taking aim he put his finger on the trigger and began to pull down. Suddenly, there was a colossal explosion behind him; in a fraction of a second the heavy door caved in and was wrenched free of its hinges. Crashing end over end it sailed down the steps bent on a path of destruction. Striking the ground just in front of Mark and Alice the unstoppable projectile rebounded into the air and sailed over them before crashing straight into the helpless Shadow.

It all happened so fast that the figure was there one moment and gone the next and it took Mark several seconds to realise what had happened. Only parts of the Shadow were visible; one of its legs protruded from the side of the door and some bits of fabric at the other. Crumpled and broken the damage was too severe to repair; the Shadow's mind slowly shut down issuing one final command to its wrecked body.

As Kennedy and the soldier ventured down the steps they quickly discovered Alice and Mark. However, just before they reached them the Shadow's remains ignited. At first they burned only slightly but then more vigorously. After a couple of seconds the fire took on a sudden surge of life and the Shadow was consumed in an explosive fireball. Kennedy was forced to drag Alice out of the way as flames erupted in her direction. There was to be nothing left to reveal their existence.

Gallagher arrived behind the gunmen just as the Shadow approached the soldiers. The dark figure had been shot many times as he'd made his way through the battle earlier and now was his time for revenge. Coming up behind the Captain he created one of the signature black daggers and stabbed him in the back of the neck before moving on to the next soldier. Gallagher also took the gunmen by surprise and quickly brought two of them down as the Shadow slit open the throat of its third victim. Only one hostile gunman remained as Gallagher sent a stream of bullets hurtling towards them whilst at the same time the Shadow dispensed with the last soldier. In between the Shadow and Gallagher stood only Natasha. Her face lit up as she spotted Gallagher but the Shadow closed in for its final victim. Natasha was already running towards Gallagher as the Shadow lifted the knife, took aim and watched as it span through the air.

With satisfaction the Shadow watched as the blade hit its target exactly where it intended. It stood transfixed as Gallagher ran over in despair to cradle her in his arms as she slipped away. The Shadow knew it couldn't be seen as it walked past and slowly pulled the knife free reabsorbing the blade into its hand. There was no way the humans would let Apollo out now.

Chapter 9

Deep below the Earth's surface, the Archangel walked steadily on. He spent much of his time in the higher levels but now he journeyed down to the very bottom of the Central Chamber. Passing between rows of empty golden tables he made his way round to the left side of the statue. On the walls surrounding him the mysterious glowing mist flowed down towards the floor before disappearing through a series of grates that lined the edges of the cavern.

Soon he reached the door that he was searching for and with a wave of his hand sent the huge slab sliding out of the way and into the recess beyond. There he paused for a moment and stared into the foreboding passage; neither he nor any of the other Angels had ventured here in many years. It had always been gloomy in this part of the cavern but since it had been abandoned the darkness was now complete.

As he slowly made his way inside he began to emit a soft glow which gently illuminated everything around him; he could see perfectly well in the dark but still preferred to have the reassuring light around him. At first the walls and their carvings were just as he remembered, but as he went deeper things slowly began to change. Soon he observed large lumps of rock strewn on the floor of the passage and substantial amounts of soot and tiny silver flakes which clung to the walls. The area had deteriorated rapidly since the accident. This had once been the living quarters of several of the older Angels but now only silence dwelled here.

Up ahead the floor had largely collapsed so the Archangel was forced to shuffle along the wall to continue as stray bits of rubble broke away and tumbled into the darkness below. He was now entering the heart of the devastation; where the walls were just jagged chunks of scorched rock.

The chamber that the Archangel now entered had been the heart of the accident several years ago. The Angel that had once inhabited this space had always been different to the others; he'd exhibited a sharpness of mind far greater than any other Angel and a fanatical desire to do what was right. These traits had quickly made him one of the Archangel's closest friends. As time progressed though, their friendship had steadily declined as his views had grown increasingly radical and ever more disturbed. He took to hiding away in his quarters for long periods of time and shunned his former friends. Everyone thought he would eventually emerge from his isolation but he never did. Eight days after he confined himself to his room for the last time a catastrophic explosion occurred within. There was nothing to explain it and all the others could do was mourn.

Now the Archangel stood in the largest room; the object that he sought was close by, he could feel it. Carefully he navigated his way through the rubble and mangled pieces of equipment that had been left behind. The Archangel slowly took the final few steps and his eyes fell upon the object. He had almost hoped that he wouldn't find it; but there it was. For a few moments he stood still and paused before he eventually stooped down and slowly picked up the item from the soot. Briefly he examined it before he wrapped it in a piece of his cloak. He didn't want to look upon it again just yet.

The others had to be told and preparations had to be made. Tartarus had retuned...

High above the city the drones frantically whirred through the air encircling the Spire. The high winds buffeted them as they continued their relentless march upwards. The top floor; three hundred stories above the ground had just been reached and now only the fifty metre tip of the tower required completion. Made of one hundred and fifteen elaborately carved blocks, the capping stones had been moved with an armed guard from a secret mine in Northern Ireland. The intense security was justified by the fact that each section was coated in an inch thick layer of solid gold making them the most valuable building components ever made.

At the base of the tower the first block was uncovered by the five men in charge of the site; each knew what to expect but they still gasped as the tarpaulin fell away. Over a thousand tonnes of gold was to be fitted to the Spire's pinnacle; equivalent to a quarter of all the gold in Britain. However, none of the humans could have realised that the true value of the object lay beneath its glittering surface in the dull black core. A secret intensely guarded by the dozen or so concealed Angels that watched as the blocks were unloaded.

The attention of the watching workers was suddenly drawn upwards as an enormous shadow moved in over the site. The blocks were too heavy to be moved by the freight lifts so a very special piece of kit had been called in to do the job. The source of the shadow sat there motionless in the sky and could have been compared to a colossal metallic blue Manta Ray. The Legacy Anti Gravity Transport was a rare aircraft and was one of the most expensive items in Aries Defence's catalogue. Now as it silently came into land it slowed to an almost complete stop before unfolding three huge legs, each as high as a double-decker bus. As soon as it touched the ground the rear section of the curved hull slid open creating a ramp into its cavernous cargo bay.

Not a second was to be wasted as the giant robots heaved the precious sections on board and carefully fastened them in place. Once ten of the blocks were loaded the LAGT leapt effortlessly into the air. It reached the workface before its legs had even finished retracting and with a graceful spin it swung round coming in low over the diminutive top floor. A fleet of drones were already on standby and clanked up the ramp as soon as it made contact with the structure. There wasn't much room left for the huge robots to manoeuvre on the top floor; partially due to the shape of the building but also on account of a vast circular hole that lay in the centre of the tower.

Many theories had been raised as to the purpose of the strange nine metre wide shaft which ran down the entire core of the building. However, as the architecture of the tower became increasingly bizarre; people had just learned to accept its existence and not to ask questions.

176

As the large robots heaved the blocks out of the transport, three small flying drones arrived from the lower levels. Quickly they darted through the huge legs of the larger robots before going over the lip of the hole into the dark void beyond. Down they travelled for several hundred metres until countless tiny specks of blue light came into view which danced in the distance. Deeper down these became recognisable as the welding lances of hundreds of drones all working in the dark confines of the shaft. Painstakingly each was engraving a series of strange grooves into the dense material that made up the walls of the shaft.

Beneath them the shaft descended far beyond the base of the Spire; here the engravings were easier to see as they were illuminated by a strange blue glow that shone up from the depths below. This light however came from no welding torch and shone as brightly as a new born star. Eventually, half a mile below the ground, the shaft reached its destination; the Central Cavern of the Ark.

On the high platform Hera and two other Angels stared at the main screen intently. They had lost contact with Apollo and had resorted to watching everything that Karl saw in an effort to find him. The information was not as useful as they would have liked since Karl had not entered the bunker after the door was blown in and had instead stayed at the surface and tried to make contact with the police massing outside. The Angels had to wait nearly ten minutes before a very pale Kennedy emerged from the bunker bringing grim news.

"Natasha's down," he said shakily as he reached Karl.

"What?" Karl said almost disbelievingly.

"Stabbed," Kennedy replied bleakly.

"What happened to the gunmen?"

"They're all dead; but it wasn't them who killed her," Kennedy replied coldly.

"Who else could it have been then?"

177

"At least one of the robed figures was here; it was the one who injured that girl over there," he said pointing over at Alice who was being put into the back of an ambulance. "I just caught sight of it before it burst into flames."

"But so far..." Karl began. "They've never attacked innocent people before."

"Well, looks like there's a first time for everything."

"Hang on a sec; you said it caught fire?"

"Yeah, all that's left ash and a strange silver powder..." With that the watchers in the cave broke their silence and looked at each other.

"It appears we have a traitor among us," Hera remarked.

"But which one of us would betray the cause?" one of the others asked.

"I do not know but there are two hundred and fifty seven of us and at least one is guilty. We know those still in the Ark could not have had contact with the outside world so that rules out one hundred and five of us. Begin profiling all of those who are in the outside world and find their exact locations..."

"That will not be necessary," the Archangel suddenly remarked as he approached them from along the walkway. "After searching through the police records I believe I know who the traitor is," he said as he walked up level with them and brought up another screen to the left of the main one.

"How do you know?" Hermes asked from the back of the group of Angels.

"Over the course of the last few weeks several habitual criminals have been reported missing. It started off slowly with the disappearance of several men who were known to be small time thieves and has gradually increased since then. This allowed me to refine my search and brought me to this..." he said as he brought up a photo of the black dagger imbedded in the chest of Brian Gorse. "This murder occurred

178

less than a week ago and the worryingly the blade is familiar to me," he said as he brought up the bundle of cloth and carefully unwound the glistening fabric. Soon the other Angels gasped as they saw before them a duplicate blade to the one in the photo.

"Who made it my lord?" Hera asked even though she had a good idea what the answer would be.

"Tartarus." For several seconds silence filled the air; until Hera finally spoke again.

"But how could he have survived?"

"I do not know; only that he did," the Archangel replied turning the blade in the blue light.

"But why would he kill innocent people?" Hera asked.

"It could be that he has fallen too deeply into the darkness," the Archangel replied. "He always had a deep belief that punishing the wicked was the only way he could heal the world. I refused to allow him to do this as I knew it would have an effect on him. In response he created this prototype blade to convert criminals into a force which could exterminate anyone deemed un-fit. I told him that murder on such a scale was an abomination but I could not persuade him. I thought the plan ended with his death..."

"How is he making his Shadows?" one of the others asked.

"This blade was made with incredible skill. The entire dagger is forged from a mutated version of our life blood which converts the infected into a new Shadow. He is trying to replicate us using the discards of society as his starting point."

"He is building an army," Hera gasped as realisation swept over her. "The timing is too perfect and you said that crime rates are falling; huge numbers of people must have been converted for there to have been a noticeable effect."

"It would appear so," the Archangel replied.

"How many people have been taken?" Hermes asked.

"The records only officially mention seventy four but as we are talking about the people who society has turned their back on; the numbers will be significantly higher."

"How much more?" Hera asked.

"I cannot say for certain but combined with the seventy percent fall in crime over the past week I would say that several hundred have been converted."

"We must recall as many of us as we can," Hera announced. "Whilst we still can. Athena, you can take charge of that. Eos, contact Hades at Factory Alpha and get him to move as much equipment here as he can by midnight. Helios, check the defensive shields are ready to be activated. Atlas, send all of our surveillance drones over the city and Artemis make sure that not a single second is wasted in finishing the Spire. You have your tasks; do not waste a second."

Instantly all the Angels sped off to their screens knowing there wasn't a moment to waste. The Archangel and Hera both stood up on the high platform surveying the others working below.

"My Lord; there is one lesser matter that I have noticed. There was a girl injured in the attack on the base. She had a blade imbedded in her shoulder. Will it infect her?"

The Archangel was silent for a moment before he answered with a slight nod of his head.

"I know this is not the time but if we let that fate befall her then we do not deserve to call ourselves Angels," Hera declared.

The Archangel remained still for a few moments.

"As always you are right Hera. The dagger is not only designed to infect but also to torment the victim with a living nightmare. We cannot allow that to happen," the Archangel replied.

"Thank you my lord," she said moving away. After walking a few feet though she turned back slowly. "What chances do you think we have?"

"Tartarus needed the element of surprise to succeed. Now we know of the impending attack we can prepare for his crude army. Too long have we planned for this moment Hera; we will not fail. As long as he does not drastically expand his army then we have little to fear..."

As dark descended over the city, a large complex of foreboding buildings remained bathed in a harsh artificial light but this was no landmark for the tourists; this was His Majesty's Super Prison Belmarsh, the third largest prison in Western Europe. It had been formed ten years earlier when three smaller prisons were united to make a facility that currently housed three thousand convicts within its walls.

Despite housing some of the country's most dangerous people the prison guards were relaxed. They rarely needed to venture into the prison itself and instead sat in complete safety in a series of huge control towers that overlooked the perimeter wall. From there they oversaw the vast fleet of tracked robots which roamed the halls enforcing order. Since the introduction of the robots fights had become a thing of the past.

As Tower Six wasn't expecting any trouble some of the guards chatted and a few watched a small TV in the corner. So none of them noticed as the CCTV screens covering the outer walls slowly began to crackle and fade out. The interference quickly spread past the outer defences and into the buildings closest to the perimeter and continued beyond canteen B and on into the exercise compound. It wasn't until over half the screens had gone blank that one of the guards finally saw what was going on. He flew over to the alarm and hit the button but to his dismay nothing happened. He tried again but still there was no effect. He called to the others who turned to face the monitors. None of them saw as a dark shape silently opened the door behind them and entered the room with its sinister knife in hand.

In a matter of seconds all the towers were neutralised; outside communications were severed and the robotic guards were deactivated.

181

The prison had fallen in less than a minute and was about to welcome its new ruler; slowly the thick metal gates clanked open and a long column of Shadows entered the complex in a silent procession. After the last of the sinister figures entered the compound they stopped abruptly before splitting into two and moved backwards against the walls. They now lined the entrance as their master strode in through the gates.

For a few moments Tartarus stopped and surveyed his Shadows before issuing a series of commands telepathically. Instantly the two lines broke formation and divided into groups that spread out towards the cell blocks. Isolated groups of guards were dealt with in turn as the eerie lines of Shadows entered the cell blocks with daggers drawn. Quickly doors were broken down and terrified murderers, thieves and sex offenders were dragged from their beds and slaughtered on the ground where they were thrown. There was no mercy, there was no respite, there was only the harvest.

The blood flowed that night but Tartarus did not care. He needed an army and Belmarsh would add three thousand and thirty four new Shadows to his ranks. With a leap he jumped from the empty courtyard up onto the prison's high walls. From his vantage point he stared out at the city and the great tower that rose above it.

Spotlights illuminated the glittering Spire, letting the half finished golden cap sparkle in the night. Already the effects of the tower were becoming noticeable as the clouds were forced ever further away creating an ever widening ring. Closing his eyes he could feel the power of the great structure before him; it was now within his grasp.

Persephone was rapidly closing in on the bunker; she hadn't been given fresh instructions so had chosen to assist Apollo as best she could. It was harder to remain undetected at ground level so like a cat she chose to jump across the roof tops. She didn't leave the Ark often and normally loved her rare moments up at the surface but today she was troubled by what she had discovered in the man's mind.

Up in front of her the next building ascended like a cliff three stories above but with a leap she flew up into the air ending with a summersault onto the structure's large flat roof. She was just about to leap off when she began to feel Hera pressing into the back of her mind. Immediately she stopped; this couldn't be good.

Slowly Alice regained consciousness and immediately regretted it. Strangely the pain in her shoulder had actually subsided but in its place she had a dull ache all over her body like she had been kicked repeatedly. Tentatively she opened her eyes to see where she was. It was then that a violent pain struck her in the back of the head as if someone had savagely punched her. Her muscles went into spasm and she quickly fell unconscious once more.

It seemed to Alice as if she was falling backwards until she smashed down onto something hard. The impact only hurt a little but forced her to open her eyes in panic. To her surprise she wasn't in the ambulance anymore and above her sprawled a brilliant blue sky. Quickly she sat upright and looked around in pure disbelief to see an endless sweep of vivid green hills splashed with brightly coloured flowers.

"This can't be happening," she murmured trying to reassure herself as she scrambled to her feet. The sunshine was warm and a slight breeze fluttered across her face. She was free of pain and the surroundings seemed so perfect; but as she turned a dilapidated old house came into view behind her. She recognised the features immediately; the flaking white paint around the windows, the half finished porch and the green wooden swing to the left of the bay window. Surely this was not the house she had grown up in.

For many years it had been a happy home; that is until the argument. As Alice stood there she could see the sky ominously darkening overhead and could hear the raised voices inside. Alice turned to run as the wind started to howl in her face towards the house. Frantically she tried to get away as the building was stripped away piece by piece to be replaced by a vortex of darkness. Soon Alice was being hammered by the appalling winds which slowed her progress to a crawl, then her feet were swept out from beneath her and she was tumbling back towards the darkness.

Alice soon plummeted into the yawning mouth of the black tunnel. She was utterly terrified; falling from a great height had always been a nightmare which had haunted her but it had never seemed this real before. The realism was only heightened when she smacked into the side of the tunnel and was shocked to feel actual pain as her arm made contact with a solid surface. She continued falling until her left leg and the side of her head also struck against the solid darkness. The impact spun her round again and now she could see the ground racing up towards her. In the total darkness she screamed louder than she had ever done in her life and knew the end was near.

However, just before she hit the ground there was a shriek as if from a great bird and something vast made of the purest white tore through the tunnel wall and caught her on its great back. Without hesitation it gave another shriek before ploughing towards the dark wall of the tunnel and effortlessly smashed through into the safety beyond.

In the depths of the bunker Apollo stood looking out through the thick glass of his prison. He had been trying different ways of escaping but all had proved futile. First he attempted to override the locks but found to his dismay that his telekinetic powers had no effect beyond the Cage. He then tried to focus them on the prison itself but this ability only affected metal and there just wasn't enough of it in his prison to have an effect. As the minutes ticked by he gradually realised that to get out of this he was going to need outside help.

After half an hour in the prison several soldiers entered the room before hastily retreating having seen what was trapped in the Cage. Apollo made no effort to communicate with them as he could tell that they were not the sort of people he was looking for. Forty minutes slowly ticked by before the soldiers returned and this time they came in greater numbers and didn't look like they were going to leave anytime soon. The commanding officer began to speak but Apollo ignored him; although his senses beyond the box were distorted he could still pick up fragmentary information from soldiers minds. They believed he had killed their comrades and were not going to change their views anytime soon.

Despite the lack of progress he continued to delve into the stray bits of thoughts which were currently running through their minds until he came across something which just might be of use. The mind that had caught Apollo's attention belonged to a young tormented soldier who had seen the countless bodies scattered around the halls; however, he kept dwelling on one in particular. Apollo immediately recognised them to be Natasha and from this he quickly saw the perfect opportunity to escape. Cutting across whatever the officer was saying Apollo finally spoke whilst keeping his back to the soldiers.

"I will speak with Thomas Gallagher. Alone."

From Mark's perspective the journey to the hospital seemed to last an eternity; even without his medical studies at university he knew that Alice's symptoms bared no similarity to any knife wound he had ever seen. Large bruises were forming over her face and other exposed areas of skin; her heart was racing far beyond the normal limits and her temperature had crept up to forty five degrees Celsius. To make it even worse she kept screaming and writhing as if there was a hellish battle going on inside her mind. Mark felt totally helpless and completely unnerved; what on Earth was happening to her?

Eventually the ambulance took a sharp turn to the right before coming to a halt outside the accident and emergency unit. The doors were quickly flung open and within seconds the well practised orderlies had slid the stretcher out of the ambulance, lowered its wheels and were making their way into the building.

In the rush none of the paramedics had noticed how the dagger had shrunk to half its previous length. Bit by bit it sank deeper into the wound; dissolving and fragmenting into particles which raced out into her blood stream and gathered into ever larger swarms at key locations. Inside her head the largest group formed as the remains of the dagger rearranged into a series of long strands mimicking the neurons of the brain. Eventually enough of the strands had massed around the brain for

185

the creation of a new consciousness which suddenly came into being. At first it only occupied a tiny fragment of Alice's brain but it was hungry and wanted more. Swiftly it took control of the body and began a far more coordinated attack to eradicate Alice.

Through the dimly lit tunnels of the bunker Gallagher walked silently behind a pair of soldiers. The loss of Natasha had hit him unimaginably hard. It felt like his guts had been ripped right out of him. Why had she been killed? So far the only people the shadowy figures had dealt with were murderers; Natasha and the soldiers were good people and did not deserve the fate that had befallen them. Initially he felt empty, isolated and anguished; but then the two soldiers came. At first he was slow to comprehend what they had to say but then realisation began to sweep over him and an idea entered his mind.

Gallagher and the soldiers slowly approached the crime scene once more; his eyes were inevitably drawn to the sheet which now covered Natasha. Beyond the bodies the tunnel turned several times before they reached a vast blast door and yet more soldiers.

As they approached a Major strode out from among them and into Gallagher's path.

"Are you Gallagher?" the man asked in an abrupt manner.

"Yep," Gallagher replied already disliking the man.

"Whatever that thing is in there it will only speak to you; do you know why that is?"

"I spoke to one a few days ago; I guess I made an impression."

"Right, he says you're to go in alone but I don't trust that thing so Anderson and Dunn will be accompanying you inside the room to make sure there's nothing funny going on."

Great, Gallagher thought as the huge metal door was slowly slid open. The halogen lights in the ceiling did little to illuminate the gloomy room which created a stark contrast to the almost sanitary glow from

186

Apollo's robes. Cautiously Gallagher approached the Cage until he was standing only a few feet from the glass sides of the prison. Apollo had no need to turn and instead remained motionless for several seconds.

"I said; I would speak alone," he said at last with a suggestion of menace in his voice.

"We have been ord..." one of the soldiers began.

"I care nothing for what you have to say Private James Ferdinand Anderson," Apollo said as skimmed through the accessible outer surfaces of the soldier's thoughts; it didn't take him long to find something of use. "Tell me; do you feel remorse for your sins? I am sure you recall the day you used your phone whilst driving and hit an innocent man? You did not stop to help; terrified people would find out." Both Gallagher and the other soldier turned to look at the faltering Anderson as his darkest secret was extracted before him. Dunn couldn't help thinking of his own grim past and Apollo instantly homed in on him. "And you Private Jonathon William Dunn do you still hear that poor boy begging for you not to take his money before you broke his arm? I can lay bare all of your hidden degrading past or you can leave."

Obediently the two withering soldiers began to back away towards the door. Apollo waited until both men had passed through the now opening door before he turned to one of the glass panels. With a force nearly ten times greater than that of a human he struck the glass. Despite the force of the blow the glass didn't break; but the blow wasn't meant for that reason. The shock tripped the sensors surrounding the Cage and immediately a claxon started blaring throughout the bunker as the huge blast door automatically swung shut before any of the other soldiers could enter. The locks slammed home leaving the two of them sealed inside.

"That should keep them busy for a while," Apollo said un-alarmed. "It appears that this time I have nowhere to run to. I am sorry for your loss," he added as he turned to face Gallagher.

"Why did Natasha have to die?" Gallagher asked whilst raising his voice just a little.

187

"When I last saw her she was alive and defiantly fighting for survival; after that the only information I have is what I extracted from those around me."

"What are you and why was the bunker attacked?" Gallagher asked.

"What I am is not relevant at this time although I will tell you that my name is Apollo. The bunker was attacked so that the Shadows could wipe out any evidence of their existence."

"What are they then?" Gallagher asked feeling he was about to get answers for the many questions that this case had generated.

"They are... an attempt to recreate my kind. My brothers, sisters and I came into being in order to preserve life; however one of us fell from grace and put on the black robes. Where we heal he only destroys. "

"But what actually are you?" Gallagher pressed again with his previous question.

"If you free me; I will tell you all you wish to know."

"I can hardly just let you out; I know virtually nothing about your origins or intentions. Also this bunker is brimming with soldiers who think you killed their friends."

"Your words are hollow Thomas Gallagher; you forget that I can feel the edges of your mind and I know that you would free me in a heartbeat if I were to promise you one thing."

"Then give me your word," Gallagher insisted.

"If you release me then I solemnly swear to return Natasha and the others who were killed in this incident to life. Now Thomas Gallagher will you accept my offer?" Before Gallagher was able to reply there was a heavy clunk from behind him and the door began to slide open again. Gallagher chose to say nothing and turned away from the Cage. The Major quickly squeezed through and demanded to know what had been said. Gallagher just shrugged and replied with,

"He didn't say anything."

As he was walking to the door though he briefly turned back to Apollo and thought of four words.

"You have a deal."

Deep within the bowels of the hospital; behind the isolation unit's thick wall of glass Alice lay in a deep sleep. On arrival to the hospital the surgeons had been baffled to find no trace of the knife; only a partially healed stab wound. This was however superseded by a range of far more troubling symptoms which worsened with each passing minute. For a start the series of isolated bruises seemed to be growing and merging together; turning her skin blue as the blood capillaries leaked under the entire surface of her skin. Her core body temperature was even more alarming as it had already more than exceeded the levels that the body was able to endure. As a precaution she had been moved into quarantine out of fear that this was some new and infectious disease. As the doctors busied themselves around her they had no way of realising that the real threat to her existence was all inside her head.

The invading darkness frantically tried to overpower Alice, however it found itself struggling. It began scanning the body in order to identify the reason and was surprised by what it discovered. It had been designed to convert the dead so taking on a conscious mind was already difficult. However, it appeared that Alice was not alone; Apollo's touch had done more than just restore her to life. Small fragments of his own life blood had been left behind after the healing and now they were mobilising to defend their host's mind from destruction.

The newly formed Shadow suddenly clenched Alice's teeth loudly in anger; making many of the doctors turn. Despite the presence of the defending particles they could only delay the inevitable; all the attacker had to do was keep up the assault and it would soon crush Alice and her Guardian Angel through weight of numbers. In the mean time it had business elsewhere; it was time to leave and show the humans its power.

As the doctors worked away few noticed as the air about Alice slowly grew darker. It was only as it began to settle around her like a semi

189

transparent cloak that they really took notice of it. A couple of them began to back away as the black robes slowly knitted themselves together in front of their eyes. One of the doctors just managed to make it into the air lock when to everyone's surprise Alice moved into a sitting position. As she sat there the blue colour of her skin seemed to wash away and was replaced with a ghostly chalky white.

The doctors were at a loss as none had ever seen anything like this before. Eventually one moved as if to restrain her but before he could reach her one of Alice's deathly pale hands rose slowly up into the air. Shakily at first the hand turned to face the glass panels of the isolation unit. The muscles across the hand and arm tensed as the new Shadow began to experiment with its abilities. Within seconds a disturbing series of groans came from the glass as the metal frame was slowly compressed inwards. There was no room for the glass as the pressure soon grew too great and the first pane explosively shattered closely followed by a second and then third.

The terrified doctors had no time to react as the Shadow suddenly leapt clear of the room and through the now shattered windows. For a moment or two it stood with its back to them before slowly turning; keeping its eyes firmly shut. But with a cruel grin from behind the still incomplete hood, the Shadow suddenly opened its dreadful eyes and the doctors yelled out in terror.

Far across the city and several levels below ground, Gallagher slowly walked back towards the vault. Two hours had passed since he had spoken with Apollo in which time he had formulating several different plans of attack. After a while he decided to bring Kennedy in on his scheme. He'd been friends with him for many years and knew he could trust him, although persuading him to go along with the plan would be another matter entirely. After ten minutes of debating the issue Kennedy finally relented in the face of Gallagher's raw determination and agreed to help; the potential benefits of the plan far outweighed the risks.

The moment was fast approaching as Gallagher rounded the final corner; just as before a line of the silent guards stood blocking the path

190

although this time the Major was not present, which he took to be a good sign.

"I wish to speak with the prisoner again," he said as he showed them his badge.

"I haven't heard anything about any visitors," a Corporal said as he looked at Gallagher's badge.

"I have clearance to speak with the prisoner," Gallagher lied as his eyes scanned along the row of new faces until he spotted Private Anderson from before.

"I was allowed access earlier as Private Anderson will recall," Gallagher said stressing the final word just a little to try and remind Anderson of what else he had heard earlier. Sure enough Anderson's face went a touch paler and he instantly realised what Gallagher was getting at.

"He was allowed in during the last shift," Anderson piped up suddenly.

"And due to the subject's lack of co-operation I require access now," Gallagher added.

The Corporal was unsure what to do but he had been told they were co-operating with the police for the time being. Eventually he decided that letting Gallagher in classed as co-operation and walked over to the panel controlling the door. He pressed a large red button a little hesitantly and the other guards made room as the huge metal slab slowly swung out of the way. Gallagher took a few steps forwards and was relieved to find that none of the soldiers were willing to escort him inside; Apollo was clearly disturbing them. However, instead of shutting the door they kept it open and all turned to watch curiously from their position at the entrance; ten metres away from Apollo's prison.

Slowly Gallagher approached the Cage as Apollo continued to stand in calm silence. From where the soldiers were positioned they could only see a slither of the room but Apollo's prison remained in full view.

191

Gallagher had no idea where the controls actually were but Apollo chose to lend a helping hand by subtly turning to the left and fixing his gaze on a particular section of the wall. Whilst trying to keep his head fixed on Apollo for the soldiers benefit, Gallagher's eyes began to scan over the area that had been indicated.

Annoyingly the switch wasn't easy to find; the area was a covered in a contorted mass of pipes and support columns that hid large sections of the wall. As he drew nearer he was forced to turn his head but still couldn't see anything. His breathing grew faster as he felt the eyes of the soldiers boring into the back of his skull. He quickly flicked back to Apollo who was still gazing at the wall. Gallagher's eyes swept the area until with an inward sigh of relief he caught sight of a small innocent looking plastic box with a slot for a key nestled behind a large metal strut. However, his heart nearly missed a beat when he noticed the key wasn't in the lock. His eyes quickly darted to and fro for a moment until he luckily found it resting on a shelf nearby. Initially he thought how careless it was to leave it lying around but then again the area was under armed guard and who would be stupid enough to open it. As innocently as possible he moved over to the key and out of view of the soldiers. Within seconds he had the small piece of metal in his hand and was slotting it into the lock. The soldiers didn't have time to stop him now and with a quick turn to the right the Cage began to rise. There was no going back now.

With a rumble the mechanism holding the Cage in position shuddered and began to heave the heavy structure out of the way. Apollo didn't waste a second and with incredible speed rolled through the narrow gap. The six soldiers raised their guns instinctively and some even opened fire but they were hopelessly too slow. In one powerful leap Apollo sailed over the hail of bullets which mostly ricocheted of the concrete wall far behind. The bullets that did find their mark were only an inconvenience as Apollo hit the ground again and rolled through the door. He came to a halt between the two soldiers in the centre and quickly sent them both into a deep sleep with the slightest touch of his hand. The first two soldiers blocked the field of fire for the others which gave Apollo time to leap over their heads with more grace than any gymnast. Both his feet made contact with the tunnel's left wall

192

before he pushed off and spun down to the soldiers below who were also quickly pacified.

Apollo then turned to the last two and saw that one was making an escape down the corridor. He had dropped his gun in terror but it wouldn't have done him much good anyway as he was quickly overtaken and sent to join the others. It left just one remaining who was back at the door with his finger reaching for one of the switches. Apollo dashed towards him in a blur but it was too late. As the last soldier slumped to the ground the wail of countless alarms began to reverberate around the entire base.

Gallagher was saying something but Apollo wasn't listening as he ran his mind along the miles of wires that crisscrossed the base. Quickly he found the controls for the bunker's alarms and deactivated each of them in turn. Silence soon reigned once more but the damage had already been done. It was only then that Apollo turned to Gallagher; giving him his full attention.

"What did you say?" he asked.

"What did you do to the soldiers?" Gallagher asked again looking at the unconscious line of soldiers on the ground.

"Reading minds is not my only speciality; manipulating them and in this case inducing sleep is second nature to my kind."

"So they're just asleep," he clarified.

"Yes, check their breathing if you do not believe me."

"No, I'll take your word on that," Gallagher concluded. "They'll be after us now," he added.

"Yes, but they do not know what is going on, their cameras are dead, I have shut down the internal communications and blocked contact with the outside world. They will be confused and poorly co-ordinated which will make them easy to overcome," he said as he began to walk briskly away. Gallagher looked at the sleeping soldiers one last time before he quickly hurried after Apollo; he wasn't done with the questions just yet.

"But how can you do that?"

"There is something akin to an electromagnetic field that surrounds us; I can use it to create electrical charges at will and manipulate objects. It is the same way we read minds since consciousness is essentially just a series of electrical currents ," he explained just as they rounded a corner and found a huge metal blast door blocking their way.

"Looks like you can demonstrate that now," Gallagher remarked as Apollo slowly continued on until he was standing just in front of the door. He swiftly reached out with his mind and found the electrical components that controlled the vast armoured slab. The three tonne piece of metal and state of the art security was easily bypassed by creating an electrical charge in two tiny pieces of copper wire. Within seconds the huge locks clunked out of the way and the door began to hiss open.

"Allow me," Apollo said as he disappeared in a small flash of light. On the other side there were five soldiers who all spun round on hearing the door unlocking. With their guns trained at the ever widening gap they had no reason to suspect that the person they were after had just slipped behind them. Reaching out a hand Apollo walked down the line brushing it along the back of each soldier's head; it was so quick that they didn't have time to realise what was happening until the final one turned to see a long line made up of his sleeping friends. By the time that Gallagher emerged through the door all five soldiers were sprawled on the ground fast asleep.

"What is keeping you," Apollo called as he remerged further up the tunnel. "We have work to do."

As Alice flew free of the dark tunnel she could now see that the creature carrying her was a vast bird. All over it was pure white except for its dark eyes which were totally black. It seemed strangely familiar but it took her a few seconds to identify it as the bird on the golden amulet. She should have been frightened but she felt curiously safe on the back of the spectral bird. Down below her she could see the buildings of London; except it wasn't the current city. For a example

194

the Spire was still only a few stories high and it was raining which it hadn't done for over a month. However, just as she was assimilating this they suddenly plunged into a low hanging cloud from which they emerged above a large forest basking in the heat of summer. The trees were a lush vivid green with wild horses roaming the clearings; it had to be the New Forest.

"*We are in your memories,*" a voice whispered in her mind.

"*Who are you?*" she called back.

"*I have no name,*" the bird replied. "*Ever since you were restored to life I have been concealed in the depths of your mind repairing damage and ensuring your survival. The appearance I have taken is just your way of visualising me.*"

"*But how did you get in there?*" she called back just as a black gaping fissure spread across the horizon in front of them.

"*There is no time for that now,*" the bird replied as it banked sharply away from the tendrils of darkness that were now spilling into the memory; consuming all in their path. "*It has found us again.*"

The tunnels passed by in a blur as Apollo walked steadily on, closely followed by Gallagher. The stairwell to the upper levels of the bunker lay straight ahead and without pausing Apollo raised his hand and the door crashed open. Gallagher could not contain his curiosity; he had to know more.

"How did you open the door like that," he asked.

"The mind has great strength," Apollo replied cryptically before continuing. "The same field that allows me to control electrics also allows my kind to manipulate smaller metal objects."

"I wouldn't call that door small," Gallagher remarked.

"The higher the metal content the bigger the objects we can move."

195

"So you're telepathic and telekinetic. What are you then?" Gallagher asked tentatively.

"You will find out in due course," Apollo remarked whilst turning his head slightly to look at Gallagher.

They walked on for a few metres until Apollo raised an arm in front of Gallagher signalling him to stop. For a time there was silence but Gallagher knew better than to question Apollo's abilities. Soon the echoing sound of countless heavy footsteps reverberated down the tunnel towards them confirming the presence of soldiers up ahead. Apollo looked around and quickly formulated a plan. Within seconds ten men appeared with their guns raised. Apollo had no care for what they said as he reached out with his mind to grasp the metal pipes running along the side of the floor. The brackets holding them in place suddenly snapped and the bowing pipes were sheared away from the wall. As the pipe came free Apollo broke it into several sections sending the lengths racing towards the men. The men had no time to react as the pipes coiled around their feet rooting them to the spot. A swift flick of Apollo's hand sent their guns flying from their grasp which clattered noisily against the tunnel wall. For a moment Gallagher watched as the soldiers struggled to stay upright.

"That was quite a demonstration," Gallagher said at last.

"I thought it was appropriate given what we were discussing," Apollo remarked. "It is a rare opportunity to show off my abilities."

"You said you used electro magnetism to move objects like that," Gallagher noted.

"Yes," Apollo replied.

"Well, those pipes were Copper. They're not magnetic."

"Oh really, it has never stopped me before," he said as he made his way round the growing pile of struggling soldiers.

They quickly advanced down two empty tunnels without any further interruptions from the guards. Blind from the lack of cameras and confused by the layout of the unfamiliar bunker the replacement

196

soldiers had become dispersed and lost. The few forces that were available to the base's commander could only do one thing; fall back to the exit.

As Apollo approached the ambush he paused and gestured for Gallagher to do the same. He could feel the presence of at least eight men but the large amounts of earth and rock that surrounded the bunker distorted his senses.

Quietly he told Gallagher to wait whilst he drained the white from his robes and hastily advanced. The final stretch seemed devoid of soldiers to human eyes but Apollo could feel the fragmentary thoughts which told him the whereabouts of his adversaries. The first two soldiers were concealed at the base of the stairs in a small guard room. He realised that they were in charge of a heavy machine gun aimed out of a small firing slit. Further along, a similar room concealed three soldiers manning two further firing positions facing up and down the stairs.

Silently he covered the distance to the stairs when his gaze fell upon the untouched remains of the Shadow. Curiously he changed direction and moved in for a closer look. Crouching down he reached out one of his long silvery hands and ran the tips of his fingers through the grains, searching for any information they may contain. As he had feared, the remains were so badly damaged by the fire that any memories had been obliterated; all he could extract were a series of distorted and incomprehensible sounds and occasional flashes of colour. Getting up he shook the powder from his hand and then instantly realised his mistake; he may be invisible but the silvery flakes that had stuck to his fingers were not. Annoyed at his stupidity he just had time to leap to the right before the hail of bullets came blasting towards him.

Apollo could easily survive a few gunshot wounds but not that many; quickly he cleaned the powder off his hand but was still angry that he'd lost the element of surprise. He tried to reach out and force the big machine guns out of the soldiers grip but was surprised to find he could not. As it happened these guns had been made out of a new composite material in an effort to reduce their weight, making them easier to handle. There simply wasn't enough metal in them for Apollo to have any effect. Gallagher had by now joined him at the exit.

197

"What now?" he asked. Apollo was unsure what to say and for a little while he ran through multiple scenarios in his head. Eventually he settled on two very different ideas.

"The first plan is safer and involves taking the time to find the doors to those firing rooms and neutralising them one at a time or we could do something a little more risky."

Kennedy waited in the gloom just beyond the glow of the base's huge light towers. Close by were the three lorries which had been loaded with the victims from the attack on the base. He'd been extremely nervous ever since Gallagher had put forward his plan but this was only made worse when the firing started. He paced alongside the rear most truck never taking his eyes off the bunker. The area around the entrance must have been crowded by at least twenty soldiers as well as two armoured cars with their heavy calibre guns trained on the stairs. Kennedy wanted to help his friend but at the same time knew there was nothing he could do.

Just then there came a loud noise behind him and Kennedy turned to see the soldiers bringing in a tank to add to their fire power. Ponderously it made its way over to the door where it stopped and slowly began to lower the barrel of its gun until it was level with the damaged doorway. However, before it could fire something completely unexpected happened.

From deep beneath the ground a loud rumbling began; followed by concrete surface buckling and lifting up. In confusion the panic stricken soldiers scattered as large cracks opened up beneath their feet exposing the huge steel plates which Apollo was forcing upwards. The gunners in the armoured cars leapt from their turrets and ran as the tank's tracks squealed on the concrete whilst it tried to reverse out of the way but it was too late. Two metres of solid concrete suddenly exploded outwards as the thick armoured plates beneath it tore free. A central crack tore open into a massive fissure that split the entrance clean in two. The armoured cars were sent tumbling over like toys and the unfortunate tank slipped forwards toward the pit. For a few moments its tracks

198

whirred around helplessly before slipping into the world beneath the surface.

From the chaos a faint white light suddenly shot up through the fissure into the air over the compound. Slowly it arced up above the unsuspecting soldiers who were busy regrouping at the tear in the Earth. Kennedy watched the light in fascination as it moved overhead before it began to return to the ground. Apollo landed only a few metres from Kennedy where he put down a rather shaken Gallagher. He had done many things in his life but being launched into the night sky was definitely a first.

"You put on quite a show," Kennedy remarked as Apollo sagged against the side of the truck. He had never moved anything that big and it had drained much of his strength.

After resting for an agonisingly long minute he slowly straightened himself up and made his way over to the back of the first truck in the convoy. His tired hands fumbled slightly as he unlatched the back and set to work. It didn't take long and within a few moments he emerged leaving a lorry filled with sleeping soldiers. As Gallagher briefed Kennedy, Apollo clambered slowly into the back of the next truck. As he worked he kept his mind open and realised the waiting soldiers were starting to grow impatient; they would soon realise that they were waiting in the wrong place and come looking. Another minute passed before he slipped out of the back of the truck and turned to Gallagher.

"They are about to start looking for us; once I have saved your friend it will take at least twenty minutes before her brain will be fully repaired. You get the vehicle ready and I will pass her to you," he said as he heaved his tired body into the final lorry. It wasn't too difficult to find Natasha and with a swift brush of his hand over her head he set the resurrection process in motion.

There wasn't time to waste as he could sense the soldiers peering into the empty fissure. Quickly he dragged Natasha's sleeping body over to the others who carried her to a waiting army supply vehicle. As the soldiers began to receive new orders Apollo finished his task and exhaustedly made his way over to the vehicle; he was too tired to run and too weary to defend them. With one last effort of mental will power

199

he unlocked the gates before collapsing onto the open back of the vehicle.

The soldiers saw the gates start to swing open but there was nothing they could do as the small truck tore out onto the darkening streets beyond. Gallagher was in the driver's seat once again with Kennedy to his left and Natasha sprawled across the back seats. She still looked deathly pale but had slowly started breathing again as they left the compound.

Karl was parked with another vehicle only a few streets away; all they had to do was reach him undetected, change cars and slip away into the night.

"We've got incoming," Kennedy suddenly called as he stared in the mirror. Gallagher also turned to look and saw the headlights of two small vehicles swinging from the base. He put his foot down and tried to make as much progress as he could; the soldiers were a lot faster off the mark than he'd anticipated. However, his attention was suddenly diverted when Apollo's voice appeared in his head.

"*Make for the expressway construction site,*" said Apollo in a quiet voice as if he was trying not to unnerve Gallagher by his intrusion.

"*Why?*" Gallagher thought back deciding that speaking telepathically was normal in Apollo's company.

"*Trust me; I have friends on the way.*"

Gallagher was torn on what to do; however it was unlikely that he would be able to shake the pursuers before he reached Karl. Putting his faith in the Angel, Gallagher followed Apollo's instructions. He just hoped he knew what he was doing.

The London Hospital had seemingly become a mad house as metal objects were sent flying towards unsuspecting people and lights exploded one by one. Some people chose to hide whilst others ran for it as metal beds and surgical implements were sent crashing into the walls around them. In the gloom the newly created Shadow stalked the halls

200

getting used to its abilities. Most other Shadows had been formed from mentally inept habitual criminals but this mind was different. It rejoiced as it felt its intelligence growing; thrilled by its new power.

Up ahead it could sense a group of people running towards a fire escape. The humans were so pathetically weak it thought and advanced towards them; a sadistic grin spreading across its partially shrouded face.

As this was occurring, Alice and the great bird flew on through a succession of memoires. However, every time they switched to a different place the waves of darkness smashed through consuming everything in its path.

"*Only you can defeat it,*" the bird called to Alice.

"*How do you expect me to do that?*" Alice cried out. "*That thing's unstoppable!*"

"*You have lived in that body all your life; you know it better than the Shadow. Take it back!*"

"*But how though?*"

"*Just concentrate Alice; we will help you but only you can find your way back.*"

The Shadow continued to advance towards the horror-struck people who hastily fled to the fire escape. However, just before they reached the door the Shadow raised a hand and violently sent a bed hurtling across the corridor to block the exit; it then slowly began to turn off the lights one by one. In panic the people tried push the doors open but the Shadow had frozen the hinges. In terror the people turned to look into the pitch black not knowing what was coming towards them.

At first they couldn't hear anything and looked around wildly in the eerie darkness. Then they picked up the faint sound of footsteps

201

advancing ominously towards them. Gradually the sound drew closer as the Shadow raised its hand and prepared to strike.

But then, to its intense surprise its right leg seized up and by the time it realised what was happening it had already crashed to the ground. The shock shattered its concentration and the lights flickered back on for a few seconds. It tried to get back to its feet when unexpectedly its left arm became unresponsive hindering its attempts to get up. In a flash of seething anger it realised that Alice was fighting back; how could this be? How did she have the strength to fight back like this? Spurred on by a burst of uncontrolled anger the Shadow hit back hard, forcing Alice away to re-established its control. For a few moments the Shadow was alone again and shakily got back to its feet. However, this was only a brief respite as Alice attacked again and sent them both crashing into a cleaning trolley. The Shadow fought on in vain but its opponent's will was greater than anything it could hope to match. In the last seconds of the Shadow's short life it discovered a new emotion; fear. With one final effort, Alice extinguished the Shadow's consciousness and restored control once more.

The struggle left Alice exhausted and she couldn't muster the strength to do anything else. For several minutes she just lay there staring up at the ceiling tiles above her. The whispering of the bird had stopped and the pain had vanished; she almost felt like her normal self again.

Eventually her strength returned and she heaved herself upright before slowly staggering into the heart of the hospital where the devastation had been wrought. Chairs and beds lay in disarray across the tiled floor and random instruments used in surgery could be found embedded in the walls. She had no memory of any of this and wondered what had happened. There were very few people still in the building and each time she found someone they begged her not to kill them. What was causing them to be so scared of her? Had she caused all this damage? And then she saw it...

On the side of the hallway stood a mirrored window that let her see for the first time her reflection. She stared in horror for a few seconds before collapsing to the floor and began to cry. The wispy black robes had taken on a slightly more solid form but were so thin that she could

202

only see them in the mirror. Her skin had become an almost deathly white and most noticeably the iris of her eyes had turned a deep blood red.

The silence was soon broken as dozens of armed police officers burst into the room yelling at her to surrender but she didn't care anymore and just sat there crying. What was the use of running? All it had done was get her into ever deeper trouble. She continued to do nothing as two policemen forced a pair of handcuffs on her and lifted her to her feet.

As Alice looked out through her new eyes she could see someone lurking behind one of the doorways; she instantly knew who it was and was filled with a desperate urge to hide. She couldn't let Mark see her like this and with a sudden burst of strength she tore off the handcuffs which shattered into countless glittering fragments before she cast aside the two policemen. As she fled into one of the corridors her anger swelled and all the metal objects within ten metres began to vibrate uncontrollably. The police tried to bring their guns to bear but many couldn't keep hold of them and they flew wildly from their grasp. Those who managed to pull the triggers also found the weapons useless as the delicate parts inside their weapons fractured under the strain. Alice had inherited the Shadow's powers but had no idea how to control them...

The streets of London raced by as the stolen army vehicle charged relentlessly onwards. The streets were clear of traffic so Gallagher was able to keep his foot firmly pressed on the accelerator. The road that Apollo had directed them to was a vast raised expressway that was in the final stages of construction. Ploughing through a line of cones the vehicle had to slow dramatically to make the turn onto the slipway which gave their pursuers enough time to close the distance. The soldiers had orders to stop them from escaping at any cost and opened fire at the first opportunity. Luckily the shots largely missed the target vehicle and instead embedded in the new concrete wall behind them. As Gallagher cleared the bend the soldiers also had to slow providing some breathing space for Gallagher.

As they left the slipway the vast road stretched out before them into the distance resembling a huge runway. The street lights were not turned on so all they had were their headlights and the reflectors along the edges of the lanes to guide them. Soon a new wave of gunfire came from the hostile vehicles; using the rear lights on Gallagher's vehicle as the target. Apollo immediately realised what they were aiming at and heaved himself over to the end of the truck. He then reached over the edge and smashed both the tail lights allowing the vehicle to vanish into the night.

"*What now?*" Gallagher thought.

"*Wait for it...*" came the reply.

Just then the endless tarmac was suddenly illuminated as hundreds of street lights were activated along the entire length of the road; bathing the car in light. Instantly a barrage of inaccurate fire came streaming towards them but this stopped as the soldiers looked up in disbelief. From behind the vehicles one of the giant Legacy Transporters was silently descending to join the fray. As it passed over the army vehicles the rear cargo ramp slowly lowered and a solitary Angel came into view.

One of the soldiers took aim but the figure with a mere wave forced the weapon backwards; striking the soldier in the head and knocking him out cold. The transporter slowly overtook the pursuers and came in lower than the street lamps on each side of the carriageway. There was a terrible slicing noise as the armoured wings scythed through the flimsy metal structures and then a thunderous clatter as each one bounced chaotically over the wings onto the road behind. As it continued its descent the sliced chunks of wreckage grew ever larger and soon entire lamp posts were crashing onto the road behind. Swerving to avoid the sea of decapitated lights the pursuers were forced to move steadily further back as the carnage intensified.

Eventually the transporter moved over the top of the target vehicle and pulled ahead descending until it filled Gallagher's entire windscreen. With a spray of sparks the cargo ramp finally made contact with the road just in front of Gallagher. The figure remained at the entrance but moved slowly over to the side to make room. Gallagher was briefly

204

hesitant but where else was could he go? With a sudden burst on the accelerator the truck made contact and thundered inside. Quickly the ramp was raised and the transporter rose sharply, just clipping the top of a street light which went out in a flash. The soldiers were left astounded in a scene of utter devastation as the strange aircraft disappeared into the skies over the city.

Persephone raced through the hospital car park in full view of the passersby. She had chosen speed over secrecy and was only a few seconds later bursting through the hospital's front door. Several policemen were blocking her path so she simply leapt over them before landing with a graceful roll and continuing on her way. Persephone didn't need to feel for Alice's mind as her thoughts were blasting out like a beacon throughout the entire building. She was both scared and angry and appeared to be heading for the roof. Alice had a three floor head start so Persephone decided to take a shortcut. Quickly she turned towards a lift and tore both the doors free with her mind. Without thinking about the drop beneath her she leapt into the dark shaft. In a series of bounds between the supporting girders she began the ten story assent to the roof of the building.

After a couple of leaps she had drawn level with Alice who was now six levels up and still rising at a considerable rate. Two more jumps brought her to the top of the shaft but was annoyed to find that the lift blocked her path. There wasn't anything for it so with a rush of speed she leapt across the shaft and smashed through the ninth floor doors much to the astonishment of a pair of nurses. Now all she had to do was find the stairs.

Alice shot past the lift doors just as they opened; all Mark could see was a faint dark blur as she raced on searching for the door to the top of the building. He had been in another part of the building during the Shadow's rampage of destruction; it had only been chance that he'd stumbled on Alice when she was being arrested. At first he didn't recognise her, but once she looked up and stared at him, he realised instantly. He didn't know what had happened to her but there had been a lot of weird stuff lately and he knew she was clearly distressed.

The quiet calm of the rooftop was shattered as Alice accidentally broke the handle off the door as she tried to turn it. She wanted to be alone and the roof had seemed a good place where people wouldn't look for her. Barely out of breath after her sprint from the ground floor she sat down on a large metal ventilation duct and cradled her head in her hands. What was she going to do? Just then she felt the presence of someone behind her.

"Mark," she said without turning.

"Couldn't leave you alone up here could I," he said as he slowly approached.

"Please don't look at me," she pleaded but Mark continued.

"Why shouldn't I look at you?" he asked as he sat down next to her.

"Haven't you seen me? I look like a monster!"

"No you don't," Mark said reassuringly. "Yes you do look a bit pale and your eyes are a little distinctive but you are still the same person you always have been."

The two sat in silence for a while before Alice spoke again.

"Why did all this happen to us?"

"I don't know; but oddly... I'm glad that it did."

"How can you be glad! We got killed!" she retorted.

"But we came back... and if it hadn't happened then I wouldn't have come to know you."

This admission caught Alice off guard;

"You're telling me that you're glad that you got killed, brought back, imprisoned and nearly killed a few more times so... you could spend time with me?"

"Yes."

"But... how can you want to be with me now. I've got red eyes for God's sake!"

"You're still Alice beneath that."

"Really?" Alice replied, slowly rising up out of her misery.

"Really," he replied as the pair of them looked out across the great city. After a little while Alice slowly leaned over and rested against Mark's shoulder as the two continued to watch the lights twinkling below. However, the moment was suddenly shattered as the unmistakable shape of a helicopter dramatically rose up over the edge of the building.

On board the helicopter an operator slowly swung the chopper's main weapon into position with a joystick. Equipped with an ultra long range taser the man quickly got the target in his sights and pressed the fire button. The two barbs raced towards Alice, leaving her only enough time to push Mark out of the way before they dug into her left arm. The pain was awful but this time it didn't bring her down. Anger once again welled up inside her as she reached out and grasped the cables with her right hand.

The chopper's gunner watched in fascination as Alice stood defiantly and tore the barbs out. Suddenly the operator's screen flashed and lights began to go out throughout the cabin. Alarms sounded and fuses exploded as the electric charge was sent back up the wires and into the helicopter. Frantically the gunner tried to eject the cables but it was too late as the metal panels of the chopper came under attack and began to implode. As a result the helicopter quickly began to spin erratically towards the side of the building; there was nothing they could do except wait for the inevitable crash. The gunner shut his eyes and clenched his teeth expecting it all to be over soon; however to his surprise the swaying soon stopped and the impact never came.

207

As the seconds passed he tentatively opened his eyes to see what had happened. To his utter surprise they hadn't moved since he'd stopped looking. The building's edge was only a few feet away and not getting any closer. But this was impossible! The engine was coming to a stop and the rotors were barely turning. His confusion was only heightened when they slowly began to rise back up to the rooftop and slide over the lip. Gently they were dropped down onto the concrete and to safety.

Mark looked at Alice believing she had done it and Alice looked around knowing she wasn't responsible. Eventually her eyes fixed on a spot a few metres behind where she and Mark had just been sitting. At least her new eyes had some benefits; normally she wouldn't have noticed anything amiss but now she could pick out the faint outline of someone standing there. This was confirmed when the shape slowly moved forwards and with a small flash became a brilliant pure white.

"Quite impressive," Persephone said as she walked the final few steps. "But you really need to control your anger."

"What are you?" Alice asked. "I've seen you in my dreams so many times."

This remark brought forward a stream of images from Alice's visions that allowed Persephone to access them; for a moment she looked at the pair before reaching a decision.

"Come with me."

Chapter 10

High above the city the LAGT silently cut through the dark skies. In the cargo hold, Gallagher sat with his back resting against the army truck as Natasha slept on. During the course of the short flight, colour had gradually returned to her pale skin and her breathing had steadily grown stronger with each passing minute. Kennedy was standing further away looking out of a window in the side of the cavernous cargo hold. The three of them were the only ones present inside the huge space as Apollo and the other Angel had disappeared up a staircase at the far end soon after they boarded the aircraft.

As the minutes ticked by Gallagher couldn't help feeling nervous; he had every confidence that Natasha would wake up but he couldn't help anticipating a host of problems.

"How long did he say it would take?" he called over to Kennedy, his nerves getting the better of him.

"Twenty minutes," Kennedy called back. "You should stop worrying. Anyway I think you might want to see this," he added as he continued to stare out through the glass.

"Why? What is it?" Gallagher enquired.

"There's something really weird going on..."

With that Gallagher quickly got up on his feet and walked over to see what Kennedy was staring at. At first he couldn't see anything as they had just entered a low cloud. The seconds slowly ticked by as Gallagher waited impatiently for a break in the cloud; he didn't want Natasha to wake up alone. Just as he was about to move away from the window a bright blue flash zipped through the clouds which was closely followed by a second.

"That's just lightning," Gallagher commented.

"Yeah, I know its lightning but you haven't seen what else is going on. If only this cloud would clear." Then as if on cue the veils parted and the city became exposed beneath them. For mile after mile diminutive buildings hugged the ground whilst the Spire rose up defiantly, cutting into the wild skies above. As Gallagher's eyes moved up along the length of the needle like structure he quickly noticed how, eerily the clouds had formed a ring encircling the pinnacle.

He was just about to say something when another blue flash of lightening burst from the edges of the ring and arced sideways onto the Spire's golden summit. The scene rapidly grew even stranger when there followed a quick succession of more lightning bolts which struck the upper stories. In the space of a minute Gallagher counted twenty hits on the structure. His eyes drifted down over the gleaming glass of the tower; it had changed a lot since... It was then that something clicked inside his head. Surely it couldn't be; yes it couldn't just be a coincidence. Quickly he looked down at his watch and checked the date. A smile crossed his lips as he saw the digits on the screen. Yes, this was no coincidence...

On the tenth floor of the hospital the police massed for an attack. Many were concerned about what they faced but their sheer weight of numbers gave them confidence. At the front a Captain quietly counted down the seconds before they would charge.

"Three, two, one..." The door was flung open and a deluge of armed officers poured onto the rooftop. It soon became apparent that something was wrong here. Apart from the crew of the downed helicopter there was no one else in sight on the open roof top; it was as if the suspect had never existed.

Thirty metres up and already half a mile away a smaller version of the Legacy skimmed silently over the skyline carrying Persephone, Alice and Mark away from the confused police. They had only been aboard

210

for a few seconds before Persephone abruptly spun round to plant her hand firmly on Alice's forehead. A quick sharp pain surged across Alice's skin and swept into her eyes. Surprised and shocked Alice staggered back before yelling out,

"What did you do that for?"

"I am sorry but I could not look into those red eyes anymore."

The changes were not immediately obvious to Alice but from Marks perspective they were very pronounced. The wispy folds of black robes immediately crumpled away whilst the pale pallor of her skin was replaced by a more natural look. Her eyes however took a little longer to change; slowly moving from a deep red to a red- brown before settling on a shade between brown and gold.

"I am afraid I cannot get them back to their original colour. Eyes tend to reflect the personality behind them; however I think you will agree this is better than red."

Alice turned to one of the windows to see her reflection and couldn't help thinking that they did look very striking.

"What do you think?" she asked whilst turning to face Mark.

"They really suit you," he said as he stared into them. After a few moments of looking into each other's eyes Alice broke off and turned to Persephone.

"Thank you," she said at last.

"The special abilities the Shadow left behind are still intact," Persephone added.

"What abilities?" Alice said sounding a little confused.

"The Shadow had telepathic and telekinetic powers; it appears that you have inherited them."

"Can you remove them?" Alice asked.

"Unfortunately not. I am afraid they are part of you now."

"I don..." Alice began.

"I don't mean to cut across," Mark said as he looked out of the window. "But what's going on over there?" Persephone already knew what he was looking at so didn't turn as the lightning bolts continued to bombard the pinnacle of the Spire.

"What is that?" Alice asked not taking her eyes off the flashing zigzags.

"You will see soon enough."

For over a minute Gallagher was mesmerised by the spectacle of the lightning bolts hammering down with ever increasing ferocity. However, he had to check on Natasha so turned his back on the window and headed over to the tiny vehicle parked in the middle of the cavernous cargo hold. He grew a little concerned at first as there were no signs of further improvement; however his fears were alleviated as she slowly turned her neck to the left.

"Natasha," Gallagher whispered. A deep sense of joy filled his heart as her eyes slowly opened.

"Tom," she said at last as Gallagher squeezed the top part of his body between the seats so she could see him.

"Natasha, I never thought I'd see you again," Gallagher said with relief.

"Was I..."

"Only for a while," Gallagher said guessing what she was going to say.

"Why am I in the back of a truck?" she said as she slowly heaved herself upright. She was stiff and her throat hurt but didn't feel too bad surprisingly. "And where are we for that matter?"

"That's a long story but Kennedy and I... borrowed the truck from the army."

212

"So we..." her sentence trailed off as Apollo re-emerged at the top of the stairs and made his way down towards them.

"There might be a draught," he called. "We are going to open the ramp."

"Why?" Gallagher asked.

Before he could get an answer the rear ramp slowly began to descend revealing a view of the city far below. The wind howled inside of the vast plane and for the first time the massive claps of booming thunder became audible. The disturbance lasted for only a few seconds as with incredible speed and accuracy Persephone's aircraft slipped through a narrow opening into the cargo bay.

The ramp was raised as the small aircraft delicately extended its three legs to rest on the metal surface at the end of the hold. Apollo walked swiftly to meet them just as Persephone exiting the craft.

"Is it true?" she asked as she came to a halt in front of him.

"Yes," Apollo replied. "He has returned."

"Are the others ready?"

"The best that can be expected. Although we still know precious little about the enemy's numbers and their quality," Apollo replied.

Just then Alice and Mark made their way cautiously down the ramp. Swiftly the two Angels began to speak telepathically.

"I knew you were bringing two humans with you but now I see why," Apollo said as he caught sight of Alice's unnatural eyes. *"The Shadows had a hand in this I take it."*

"Yes. It would have been irresponsible of me to have left her like that. She has been given more power than she could possibly imagine and has no idea how to use it."

"She is a danger to those around her," Apollo agreed.

213

"And why did you bring the other humans?" Persephone asked as she watched Gallagher helping Natasha out of the vehicle.

"We found ourselves in a difficult situation; they would have come to harm if I had not acted."

"Are we going to put them down somewhere?"

"That was what Hera initially advised but the Archangel has other ideas. He wants to meet them himself."

"Why?" Persephone asked a little surprised.

"I am unsure; he seemed strangely evasive on the subject. All I know is he wants them to be taken before him in the Ark."

As the city looked on in awe at the Spire the real danger was to be found several miles downriver. High above the gates of Belmarsh, Tartarus stood as the wind screamed around him wildly. He could feel the energy emanating from the Spire and knew that the moment was fast approaching. Slowly he turned from the spectacle that enthralled the city just as two of his oldest Shadows leapt up onto the structure behind him.

"Are we ready?" he asked in his menacingly deep voice.

"Yes my Lord; we are all ready."

Slowly Tartarus walked over to the other side of the rooftop and smiled as he saw the sea of black below him. Three thousand new Shadows; it was a force greater than anything the Angels could muster.

It was then that the rain began to fall; heavy drops suddenly plummeted from the dark skies, pounding the city below. The water trickled off the motionless army's robes as they awaited their orders. After he had finished surveying the ranks of silent Shadows he finally spoke a single sentence that was loud enough to echo round the entire prison.

"Let the good work be done," and with that he shot his hand out towards the now empty tower that housed the gate controls. With a low rumble the two heavy pieces of metal that barred the exit began to slowly slide out of the way. He then turned back to look upon the Spire as the black column silently coursed out of the gates and spread like poison into the heart of the city.

High above, the rain drops pelted the vast wings of the Legacy as it banked slowly to the left and began its descent towards a large run down tower block. The building had once provided a home for hundreds of the city's poorest families but now lay empty and largely forgotten. Silently the huge aircraft came to a gentle stop a few feet above the structure and rotated so its wing tips were over the opposite corners of the building. Once it was in position a series of concealed gears were set in motion. As the huge cogs turned the open expanse of the concrete roof began to split in two. The top of the building opened like a pair of huge jaws as the two halves swung down inside the cavernous depths of the hollowed out building. Without attracting any attention the huge aircraft sank down into the dark void and disappeared from sight. Once it was safely inside, the roof was raised back into place with a hiss and the aircraft might as well have never existed.

Water poured off the wings in great torrents as four huge spotlights flickered on, brightening the stripped out interior of the building. Rapidly the Legacy continued to lose altitude and sank past the level of the ground floor and continued deeper into a shaft carved into the bedrock. The scene was totally new and alien to Gallagher, Kennedy and Natasha who crowded round one of the windows gasping in awe at the scale of what they were seeing. To think that this lay below the city and they had no idea! Alice and Mark were both suitably impressed but knew that something far more spectacular awaited them.

After descending for nearly half a mile, the shaft finally ended in a steep curve that the Legacy smoothly navigated so it was now travelling along a horizontal tunnel made of polished stone. It wasn't long before the spotlights were switched off as the oval tunnel ahead was illuminated by a series of glowing rings set in the cavern walls.

After travelling for what must have been half a mile the passage began to divide up as smaller tunnels fanned out in all directions going to other parts of the subterranean complex. Most of the side tunnels were dark and quiet but occasionally the onlookers would catch glimpses of vast open spaces beyond. As they travelled on, another Legacy soon appeared at a fork in the tunnel; Gallagher couldn't help thinking how unnatural it looked as it hovered motionless as they passed by.

Soon after passing the other craft, the Legacy emerged into an immense open area which stretched out for at least a quarter of a mile on each side of the plane. Below them the onlookers could see long rows of other Legacies and other assorted pieces of strange looking equipment. There were only supposed to be a handful of these rare aircraft in the world but beneath them at least a hundred were arranged in organised rows.

As they continued down the long row of aircraft they began to see signs of activity. Whereas most of the transporters appeared to be unattended, the ones they were now passing had their rear doors open as if they had just been unloaded. Further along it became obvious what the transporters had been carrying as a battle tank slowly crept down its cargo ramp to join a long line of nearly thirty others.

Soon the tanks were left behind as the Legacy slowed to a crawl and turned sharply to the right as it aimed for an empty pad at the far end of the cavernous room. Thirty seconds later the aircraft spun gracefully in the air before it extending its legs to land gently on the polished stone.

"Please follow me," Apollo announced as the ramp clanged down on the floor below.

Alice and Mark hadn't noticed the others present in the cargo hold as the wings of the smaller aircraft blocked their view. It was only when Gallagher and his companions came round the edges of the huge wings that the two groups saw each other. Gallagher immediately recognised them and was pleasantly surprised to see Alice uninjured.

"I see you're up and about again," Gallagher remarked curiously.

"Yes, you could say that," Alice replied.

216

"What happened to your eyes?" Kennedy asked.

"It's a long story..."

Up at the construction site the foreman knew that something was amiss. For the past half an hour the cascade of lightning had pounded the golden blocks on the Spire's summit remorselessly with a sound like an artillery barrage. From the moment the first bolt hit the tower he had wanted to stop construction; he knew this tower had another purpose and he didn't like it at all. However, as much as he wanted to bring a halt to the work he knew that the time for action had gone. The mysterious figures would never allow anything to stand in their way; they now roamed the base of the tower in numbers he had never seen before. Police and members of the public had intermittently tried to approach the tower since the storm began but all had been intercepted and mysteriously sent away after a single touch to their forehead.

As his eyes turned back to the tower the storm entered a new level of ferocity as multiple bolts struck simultaneously. The clouds themselves seemed to be glowing blue with electricity as the lightening continued to bombard the pinnacle. There were only twenty blocks left to install and then, one way or another it would all be over.

Down in the labyrinth beneath the Spire a silver shuttle raced at high speeds through the dark tunnels. In complete silence Apollo and Persephone stood at the front of the pod whilst the rest sat on the various metallic chairs to the rear. There was so much to discuss and so little time; they had barely stopped talking from the moment they boarded the shuttle.

"...but how could they possibly build this place?" Kennedy said in awe. "The size is absolutely staggering."

"I don't know; it would have taken decades with the drilling machines of today," Gallagher remarked.

"It was completed in three years," Apollo remarked unexpectedly.

217

"So how was it done?" Natasha asked.

"You will find out soon enough," Apollo replied as he once more withdrew from the conversation but Alice quickly decided to ask a question of her own.

"What is the blue sphere for?" she asked as she turned to face Apollo. For a while Apollo didn't reply as he began to sift through Alice's memories to find out how much she knew. In the pause Natasha spoke.

"What sphere?"

"Over the past few days I've been having dreams..." Alice began.

"They are not dreams. They are my memories," Apollo cut across.

"But how did your memories get into her head?" Kennedy asked.

"When we restore a life..." Apollo began, "...there is a significant amount of damage that must be repaired. To complete this we break off a small section of ourselves in order to heal the victim. However, in some cases when there is significant brain damage our memories can be left behind. Generally the younger the person the more memories they acquire but the head injury's severity also has an impact."

"I think I have to say thank you then," Alice said after a short pause.

"What for?" Apollo asked curiously.

"For saving me and all the others. You gave us a second chance." For a short while Apollo was at a loss as no one had ever thanked him before. Eventually he answered with;

"You are welcome."

After this he turned back to face the tunnel ahead before announcing.

"We are here."

The others responded eagerly to see the end of the tunnel fast approaching; illuminated by the mysterious blue light. However, before they could take this in, the shuttle had already shot through the opening and into the colossal chamber beyond. High above them the great statue towered imposingly; it was one thing to view it in a dream but seeing it in real life was another thing entirely. Alice marvelled at its beauty and was further delighted to see just how shocked the three detectives appeared.

The shuttle had emerged onto a loop of track that was roughly level with the statue's knees, a good quarter of a mile above the cavern floor. For Gallagher the scene was truly amazing; nothing else on the entire planet could compare to the scale and grandeur of the carved figure. In comparison the Statue of Liberty looked like a toy. For most of the journey Gallagher had remained silent working on a theory in his head but upon seeing the statue he almost discarded it. Discreetly Apollo listened in on Gallagher's thoughts and smiled; the human had nearly pieced it together.

As the onlookers continued to stare in disbelief the shuttle slowly came to a halt alongside a glass station platform. As soon as the pod had stopped moving, the door hissed open allowing the people to step out onto the glass surface beyond. Natasha was the first to disembark and immediately found herself staring at the ghostly lights which flowed only a few inches below the transparent surface. As each person left the pod they all in turn watched the strange fog like substance dance and swirl beneath the glass.

"Do not touch it under any circumstances," Persephone noted as she seemingly brushed the blue fog aside with a sweep of her hand.

"What happens if we do?" Alice asked curiously.

"Nothing would happen to you as you have already been exposed to it," Apollo noted as he gestured for them all to move along.

They did not have far to go as one of the levitating elevators was already waiting at the end of the platform; suspended over the immense chasm below. Apollo and Persephone quickly stepped aboard but the others were not so sure; it was an awfully long way down.

"This is the only way up," Persephone said at last. "Trust us; it is perfectly safe."

219

Eventually they all made it onboard; the two Angels chose to stand perilously close to the edge whilst the others were firmly grouped in the centre. Once they were all in place the disk made a slight whirring noise before it began its ascent into the heights of the cavern above. As they went, Alice felt her curiosity growing and eventually walked away from the others and went over to the edge. She had been terrified of heights her whole life but now as she stood looking down at the immense drop she felt nothing but exhilaration.

The disk soon came to a halt at the base of the statue's right elbow. Apollo and Persephone were the first to step off and the others followed in their wake; thankful to be off the strange disk. Apart from the Angels, Alice was the only one of the group to have seen the walkway and the star like Sphere at its end up close. It had been such a busy place in Alice's dreams but now only a handful of Angels remained.

As they approached the platform one of the Angels broke away from the rest and walked up to the centre of the high platform. Gallagher hadn't seen an Angel like this one; all the others wore robes yet this one had armour. Once in position the Archangel turned slowly and waited to receive them.

Now only a short distance separated them as they came to stop at the base of the high platform under the gaze of the Archangel. His eyes quickly moved over most of the group but paused slightly longer on Gallagher. Apollo had been right, this one was indeed about to piece it all together. Of course he would never have done so if he hadn't been brought into the Ark but on the other hand the Archangel really wanted to see someone solve his little puzzle. He didn't wait much longer before he began to speak.

"Never before have so many humans been in this place at once. You all of course want answers so I feel that I will start at the beginning. Ten years ago I was the most powerful being on this planet but I was alone and without a purpose. However, one dark night on the streets above us I saw an event that changed my life forever. There was a young woman on the far side of the road and a man walking towards her, for a time this was unremarkable but as the man approached he drew a knife and stabbed the woman where she stood before fleeing

220

with her purse. I rushed over but there was nothing I could do as the life slipped from her. I was the most powerful person on the planet yet I was powerless to stop her death. For weeks it tore me apart until I at last understood what I had to do; I knew my purpose... Does this sound familiar to you Detective Gallagher?"

Upon hearing this all of the others turned to face Gallagher as if he had been keeping something from them.

"What does he mean?" Natasha asked also turning to face Gallagher.

"That was one of my first murder investigations after joining the police," Gallagher said whilst looking at Natasha. "And I now know for certain who you are," he added turning back to the Archangel. "You have been called the 'Emperor Industry' and 'The Man Who Made the Modern World' but your real name is Lord Tiberius Aries."

Under his breath the Archangel chuckled slightly.

"Yes, you are of course correct. I am very glad you remembered me," the Archangel replied.

"But... it wasn't just ten years ago," Gallagher added. "It was ten years exactly; tonight is the tenth anniversary of that murder isn't it? And what's more you've built the Spire right on top of where it happened haven't you?"

"You are very astute detective. That incident opened my eyes to the world around me; I saw crime and suffering in the developed world and wars and genocide in the rest. I decreed no more. I searched through all the companies under my control, desperate to find a solution. Soon I had laboratories and institutions across the planet researching different technologies to further my ultimate goal. However, after one year, little progress had been made and many scientists considered my aims to be unachievable. Little did they realise though that a breakthrough was just around the corner; out of great tragedy hope was kindled. One of my laboratories was attacked by an environmental terrorist group who considered our work to be unethical. The laboratory was largely empty that day but even so their bomb left three of my top scientists dead. However, the incident bore miraculous results. The blast ruptured a

221

storage tank which contained a dangerous and untested technology; nanorobots or nanites as we have come to call them. They poured onto the body of my lead scientist and with only their basic programming they did something truly remarkable; they rebuilt her. Cell by cell they repaired the damage until the body was whole once more; the mind however was a different matter..."

"So..." Gallagher cut across, "...they're human?"

"No, not exactly," the Archangel replied. "For two weeks she slept and the nanites remained at work. They were programmed to heal so that is what they did; however they did not know where to stop. They saw all the deficiencies of the body as damage and soon began to manipulate the genetic code itself. In almost every way the new life form proved to be superior to anything that evolution could have produced. Tests showed her to be more intelligent than any human; she was faster, stronger and able to survive incredible levels of damage. But there was a price to pay. The nanites could not restore the memories of the host as they rebuilt her brain to their design before she became conscious. By the end of the fifteenth day they had completed their work and the first Angel, Hera was born. To put it simply the Angels are a cybernetic organism with both organic cells and synthetic nanites working together in a symbiotic relationship."

"That is why we wear robes," Persephone added with a touch of sadness entering her voice. "We hide our faces in shame; because they once belonged to another. We just came into being; we could not stop the nanites from destroying the old consciousness, but we still feel the guilt."

"But why are there so many of you?" Natasha asked.

"Despite the setback we still sought to find a way to restore both the body and the mind without allowing the full conversion to occur. Time after time we tried but on each occasion the nanites went out of control and consumed the host; perceiving faults where there were none. However, we were making progress as the younger Angels started to remember strands of the host's previous life. We knew it was only a matter of time so we initiated the next phase and began to build the Ark. The same nanites that gave the Angels life were now given a design and set work. Over the next six years they devoured the rock beneath the city to form the network of caverns and tunnels around you. The Central Chamber in which you now stand is the oldest section and only took a month and a half to complete. It became the centre of our world and the home for the Sphere," he said as his audience once again looked up at the strange object above them.

"To complete our plan we needed more nanites than you can possibly imagine so the Sphere was created. Beneath your feet molten iron, copper, zinc and gold run in four great pipes before being released into the heart of the Sphere. Inside its depths the elements are fused together and transformed into the seeds of life before being allowed to flow down the cavern walls into our storage cave two miles below."

"But why do you need so much?" Kennedy asked; still awestruck about what he saw around him.

"Bit by bit we managed to refine the process," the Archangel continued. "We moved all of our tests to the Ark and this is where Apollo and Persephone entered the world. In life they were twins; a bond which they continue to share even now. It was with their work and perseverance that five months ago, we finally managed to restore a human to life without any lasting changes. We were overjoyed as you can imagine; we had after all this time managed to do the impossible.

However, our celebrations were not to last as we discovered that the new process only worked fifty percent of the time; some people were restored whilst the others were converted. But then there was another problem... On one of my few trips to the surface, a child ran out in front of an oncoming vehicle. I could not stand back and watch so I leapt out and pushed her to safety at great cost. The doctors at the surface told the press that I had only hours to live as I fell into a deep coma."

"We could never just let our creator die," Persephone said as she took over the story. "He gave us life and cared for us; he deserved so much more. So in the dead of night we smuggled him to safety and made our preparations. We knew it was dangerous but we had to try. It was the first time we had ever attempted the procedure on a living person and we all knew that if it failed we would lose him. However, the results were astounding; the nanites recognised the living mind and changed their own programming to ensure its survival."

"The process worked beautifully," the Archangel continued "The nanites performed perfectly and restored me; however I opted to let them continue the physical conversion. I have worn this armour for many years to protect me. When surrounded by beings with super human strength, even a glancing blow can shatter bones. I was the first Angel to keep my mind."

"Why did you call yourselves Angels," Mark suddenly asked.

"We have... a distinct physical resemblance to them," the Archangel said evasively before he continued. "We had only just refined the nanites when suddenly one hundred and forty three people were killed on our door step. We could not just sit back and watch so Apollo took the new nanites to the surface for our most audacious test so far. When the news came back that it had worked you cannot imagine the sense of joy that filled these halls. We had finally done it..."

On the surface few people dared to venture outside as the storm entered a new level of ferocity. Trees were stripped of their leaves and the rain formed raging rivers that coursed through the streets. However, this was largely overlooked as every eye in the city focused on the spectacle surrounding the Spire. It was also because of this that few noticed as the Shadows advanced along the roof tops towards their target.

Tartarus though was not among the bulk of his forces as he and a small group of his strongest disciples turned out of the rain and into a busy Underground Station. Travellers swarmed the ticket areas but none of the Shadows made any effort to conceal themselves as they marched on. People stared and pointed but the Shadows took no notice until a pair of policemen made to challenge them. Without pausing, Tartarus extended two blades from each hand and simultaneously dealt with both the officers. People screamed and ran as the two men collapsed to the ground but this was of no concern to the Shadows as they advanced into the station beyond.

"I don't understand," Gallagher said at last. "How do the ones with black robes fit into all this?"

"Until recently we had no idea they existed," Apollo replied sourly.

"The Shadows as they call themselves are led by one of our own; an Angel named Tartarus. He was believed to have been killed in an accident several years ago but he survived. Where we seek to heal he only wishes to destroy. We do not know exactly what he plans to do only that he will need the Spire to accomplish it," the Archangel said gravely.

"But what is the Spire?" Gallagher asked.

"The Spire is part of the largest machine ever built," the Archangel explained as he raised a hand towards the screen. Almost instantly a massive three dimensional hologram appeared in the air above the platform; it was so high that the onlookers had to take a few steps back to take it all in. At the top of the image the Spire stood imperiously looking down over all the other buildings surrounding it. The image did not stop there and beneath the Spire the Central Cavern was visible as well as an even larger cave beneath which was large enough to swallow everything above it with ease.

"In the storage cavern beneath us there is nearly a billion tonnes of nanites ready for use. When the command is given the Spire will act like a magnetic rail gun and catapult each and every nanite into the Earth's upper atmosphere. From there they will spread out across the planet to begin their task."

"But what is their task?" Gallagher asked realising just how immense this whole situation was.

"This started as a plan to heal the dead but we have come to realise just how powerful the nanites truly are. They have the ability to rewrite any section of genetic code allowing us to improve on what evolution has left us. Since the beginning of time the smallest life forms have brought down the largest; but no more. The nanites will rewrite the human immune system giving complete protection to every virus and disease from Flu and Chicken Pox to Malaria and HIV. But that is just the start..." the Archangel said riding on his wave of enthusiasm. "Genetic faults that lead to conditions such as Cystic Fibrosis, Huntington's and Downs Syndrome can all be corrected. The blind shall see, the disabled shall walk and the deaf shall hear. Crime rates will fall and wars will end as we correct the errors in the human conscience. People will no longer die of hunger or dirty water and time will no longer ravage the elderly with such ferocity. We will do what evolution could not and end suffering forever."

High in the stormy sky, one of the surveillance drones was being buffeted and pounded in the gale force winds. Its bank of sensors had been scanning the streets for several minutes now and hadn't picked up anything out of the ordinary. The world below seemed to drain of life as the storm raged overhead; so far it had observed just a handful of people as it continued to weave between the city's skyscrapers. Suddenly that all changed when its thermal camera spotted something strange in the distance, instantly it swivelled all of its sensors to face a vast disturbance which was streaming over the buildings to the north; like a tidal wave moving unstoppably towards its goal.

"So why have you brought us here?" Gallagher asked. "It seems you are quite determined to use the Spire and there is no way we could hope to stop you."

"I brought you here because... I want humanity's approval," the Archangel said slowly. In response Persephone and Apollo turned to face him.

"This was never part of the plan my lord," Apollo protested.

"When I began this quest I had a bold dream; bit by bit we have added to it and turned it into a monumental reality but we never sought clarification that this was what humanity wanted," he said as he turned back to his guests. "Now, I give the choice to you; the fate of the world rests in your hands."

"But... that's a monumental decision! How can we possibly decide that..." Gallagher exclaimed. "This is a decision for the whole to make."

"The more people involved the more time that will be wasted. Governments are slow and lumbering entities that would never sanction such a drastic move," the Archangel responded.

"What if we don't reach a decision?" Kennedy asked.

"Then I will take it that the outcome is not important to you and we shall proceed," the Archangel replied as his gaze fell on Kennedy. "You may go first."

"Great," Kennedy murmured as he realised just how enormous this decision was. There had never been a more important answer in the history of mankind. He could see the enormous benefits but also feared the power that this strange technology had. As much as he would like to have said yes he knew that he just couldn't. "I don't think that it is right to do this without proper consent from the people," he said at last.

"Very well," the Archangel said as his gaze fell on Mark.

"I'm also not sure that it's right," he said after a few moments. "I mean the technology is truly amazing and I think it's acceptable for resurrecting people after accidents. But upgrading an entire species is just such a radical step."

The Archangel remained silent as his gaze moved on to Natasha. The other two Angels were growing more concerned with each remark.

However, just as Natasha was about to speak Hermes suddenly rushed over from his screen.

"They are coming my lord," he exclaimed.

"How many?"

"At least two and a half thousand."

227

For a few moments the Archangel was silent as he weighed multiple factors up in his head.

"Impressive," he said at last. "How long do we have?"

"Five minutes, thirty seconds."

"And how long until the system will be ready to fire?"

"One minute, five seconds."

"Now there is a new level to consider," the Archangel remarked whilst turning back to Gallagher. "If the system is activated then it will erase all of the Shadows as we instructed it to earlier. If it is not fired and the Shadows overrun this place then they will use it regardless of any decision you make. However, the choice is still yours."

Gallagher had already made up his mind even before this revelation; looking back towards Natasha he could instantly tell that she had come to the same decision.

"Use it," they both said in unison knowing that it was the right thing to do. They had each joined the police to help make the world a better place to live in; this was an opportunity for mankind which could not be squandered. Yes it was radical but they had each witnessed the evil in this world and knew that this was the best shot they would ever get at defeating it once and for all.

Beneath the Archangel's hood a smile spread across his face.

"Then it appears that we have a tie," the Archangel said as he turned to Alice. "And you have the casting vote. The fate of the world is in your hands..."

On the outskirts of the city a claxon blared mournfully into the night as a long line of Shadows advanced into the high security area beyond. One after another the guards were massacred before the dark procession burst into the main building. Confused workers were mercilessly slain where they stood as the figures marched past the numerous hazard signs

228

on the walls. They had planned this attack days in advance and knew the layout of the huge building in minute detail. It wasn't long before they arrived at the central control room and slaughtered the terrified staff within.

There wasn't a second to waste as the lead Shadow reached out with his warped mind and pushed the master controls into the inactive position. As it clicked into place the room changed surprisingly little; however the effects for the city beyond were far more dramatic. Across London, lights began to flicker and fade whilst televisions quickly died. Entire districts soon fell into darkness as the lack of power instantly paralysed the city.

Just as Alice was about to make her decision a series of alarms suddenly blasted out into the silence. Frantically the few remaining Angels moved between screens trying to work out what had failed however the Archangel already knew.

"Clever, very clever," he said to himself.

"What is that?" Gallagher asked.

"Tartarus has disabled one of the surface power stations," the Archangel said grimly. "We cannot fire the Spire without it."

"You built all this and you rely on mains electric!" Kennedy remarked.

"Not entirely; we produce ninety percent of our own power. You cannot even begin to imagine how much energy is needed for something like this," the Archangel said as he paced back and forth. "Which station has failed?"

"Springvale," Hermes remarked as he analysed the data.

"What about the other plants?"

"Barking Reach and Hackney C are still operating. The National Grid is activating their emergency backups in Wales but they will not be enough," Hermes announced. "The only hope is to restart Springvale's reactors."

To think it has come to this," the Archangel sighed. "Apollo and Persephone it appears that this task has fallen to you; you are the only two I can spare."

"Yes my lord," they both said in unison.

"And take the humans to safety. I should never have brought them here; it appears I have underestimated Tartarus," he said before heading towards one of the elevator disks with Hermes following in his wake.

As the Archangel's platform rapidly ascended out of view, the small group began to move back along the walkway in the direction they had come. Apollo and Persephone stayed at the front with the three detectives close behind. For a little while longer Alice remained, staring up at the Sphere thinking about what she would say if she was given that choice again. To think that for a few seconds the destiny of an entire species lay in her hands.

For Gallagher the whole situation seemed so surreal; he was in the middle of something bigger than anything he could have ever dreamt about. The Spire promised to bring about the birth of a new golden age for humanity; free of disease, suffering and pain. He couldn't just walk away now and let the Angels go on alone.

"I see you want to accompany us," Apollo said, reading Gallagher's mind.

"I've been in the heart of the action for my whole adult life; you can't expect me to just hide."

"Tom, you can't be serious!" Natasha exclaimed.

"I can't just stand back and do nothing," Gallagher remarked. "This tower can change the world either for the better or for the worse; the key is that power station. Without it neither side can use the Spire. I have to help..."

"Fine... I'm going with you," Natasha said defiantly.

"No way..."

"Don't bother trying to stop me; I'm not letting you out of my sight," Natasha remarked. "What about you?" she said turning to Kennedy.

"Well I can hardly stay behind if you're going," Kennedy said whilst turning to Apollo. "Do you want us then?"

For a moment Apollo looked at the three humans in front to him and smiled. None of them knew what dangers lay ahead and still these three volunteered to risk their lives. Normally he would never have taken them into harm's way but this time was different. There was too much at stake.

"Very well."

Chapter 11

Surrounded in a curtain of lightning the final Legacy delicately manoeuvred itself into position above the Spire. Despite the close proximity to the deadly bolts the aircraft remained unaffected as it slowly lowered its cargo ramp for the final time. Ignoring the high winds a lone Angel walked out onto the ramp and carefully guided the aircraft in. The Spire had four small golden pinnacles which extended upwards at an angle above the gaping shaft at the tower's heart. Three of the sections had been completed; now only one remained. Behind the Angel one of the giant crab drones slowly clanked out into the open. In its claws it held the culmination of ten years of work; the final piece of the Spire.

For the drone it was just piece 400900056 but to the Angels it was the most precious object in the world. They watched intently as the piece was swung over the one and a half mile drop and moved into position. With incredible precision the drone slowly slotted it into place and held it as the nanites fused it to the rest of the structure. After all these years, the Spire was complete.

Across the city silence suddenly fell as the lighting barrage abruptly ended and the roar of the thunder was allowed to fade away. The storm may have passed but another was fast approaching. As the dark army moved into place under the cover of the rain, its commander arrived on the battlefield. Tall and unnaturally thin, Thanatos was one of the oldest and cruellest of the Shadows. Although physically weaker than the younger Shadows he was by far one of Tartarus' most trusted disciples.

From a dilapidated church tower he surveyed the enemy's defences and was surprised to see nothing in his way. He had expected all manner of fortifications as well as lines of Angels blocking his advance but instead the road was clear. Seven different roads fed into the area around the Spire and he had planned multiple strikes from the five streets on the north sides. But seeing that the way was clear he quickly changed his plans.

Five hundred metres away, the Spire stood exposed and vulnerable as the Archangel and Hermes watched from the thirtieth floor. Soon after their arrival they caught sight of the dark sea of Shadows advancing across the roof tops towards them. As the seconds passed the enemy hoard had begun to fan out along the length of the main road which ran along the Spire's northern side.

"It appears they are planning to attack using a wide front," Hermes noted grimly.

The Archangel was just about to agree when the Shadows changed direction suddenly and began to move back into one dense group.

"It looks like they are changing their strategy; they are going to try and break through with one almighty blow," the Archangel said as he continued to watch the enemy pour down the road and form a series of long lines. "Send out word to our forces; they are right where we want them."

Thanatos continued to watch as his army advanced unhindered; they were now within a hundred and fifty metres of their target and still nothing challenged them. This was too easy he thought with glee; almost too easy. A dark thought suddenly crossed his mind but it was already too late.

Before Thanatos was even able to form new orders, a blast of blue light discharged out from the Spire's one hundredth floor. The army looked up in terror as the huge dome of light came arcing down towards them. In panic they pushed into one another but there was nowhere to go as the energy shield crashed down onto the road. Many of the

233

Shadows escaped uninjured but there were several that were incinerated on contact with the impassable dome of energy which shone out defiantly into the night.

For a few moments silence hung in the air as the Shadows stared angrily at the shield blocking their advance. From behind it nothing stirred and Thanatos began to try and find a new way round. However, he was suddenly taken by surprise once again as a long line of tarmac fifty metres behind the barrier suddenly collapsed into the Earth. He didn't know what this meant but knew it couldn't be good. Hastily he issued orders to retreat from the street but he was outwitted once again.

From the depths of the trench, the roar of countless heavy duty engines suddenly blasted out into the night as a long line of forty robotic tanks suddenly burst onto the road. The Shadows scattered leaping for the surrounding buildings trying to escape as the lead tank opened fire. There was a blast of fire as the first shot of boiling plasma tore across the battlefield in a streak of white light. The shield allowed the projectile to pass before the shot sliced into the ranks of helpless Shadows beyond. Soon the other tanks began firing as well and the street became a killing field as the barrage of shots effortlessly cut through the dark ranks. From the church steeple Thanatos looked on in disbelief as his army was decimated.

However, as the Shadows moved to a safer position they quickly began to notice something which could tip the balance in their favour; something that the Angels hadn't noticed...

Whilst the battle raged, the city's lights continued to flicker and whole sections remained in complete darkness. From behind one of the gloomy office blocks, a small aircraft lifted up into the air with incredible speed before racing off across the river. In the cockpit Apollo sat controlling the space age craft with Persephone and the three detectives in the small space to the rear; Mark and Alice had been left behind in the safety of the Ark.

As the craft gained altitude Persephone went over to a locker on the wall by the cockpit and swiftly opened the doors. From where he was standing Gallagher couldn't see what lay in the space beyond and he began to grow curious; he tried to get a better look by moving further along but the narrow opening was blocked by Persephone's flowing robes.

"These were designed by one of our companies," she said whilst keeping her back to him. "But we thought they were too dangerous," she added as she turned round holding a strange object in her hands.

The device was totally alien in design but had to be a gun of some description. It was longer than an average pistol and was covered in a curving white shell that glistened like the Angels themselves.

"It fires plasma," she explained. "Only a handful were ever made. Its crude by our standards but they should serve you well," she said as she handed the gun to Gallagher.

As his hands touched it he was amazed by how light it was; it must have been nearly twice as big as his own gun but weighed virtually nothing.

"How do you reload it?" he asked.

"It draws nitrogen from the air and converts it into plasma," she said as she passed another one over to Natasha.

"What will the Shadows be using to defend themselves?" Gallagher asked.

"They will be able to summon daggers and possibly swords or bows if they are exceptionally skilled."

"Those sound rather basic," Natasha remarked as she felt the weight of her weapon.

"We cannot create anything with moving parts; however the nanites themselves make the weapons far more deadly than any you have ever faced," she explained. "I think I should warn you; those guns do have a habit of overheating."

"What happens if they overheat?" Gallagher asked.

235

"Most of the time they will just stop firing; however if they are pushed too far they have been known to explode."

"Oh, great..." Gallagher sighed.

Inside the dome of energy, the Archangel and Hermes looked on as the sea of Shadows began to arc round the side of the tower. Neither could understand why the Shadows were trying to outflank them; the shield enveloped the entire base of the tower.

"What are they trying to accomplish?" Hermes asked as the Archangel walked over to the windows on the corner. From this position he still couldn't see anything so with a flick of his hand he pushed out the entire wall of glass and let it fall down the side of the building below. Quickly he grabbed hold of the now bent metal frame with his right arm and leaned out of the building as the wind howled around him. Almost instantly the Archangel's heart sank as he saw what the Shadows were heading towards.

"Part of the shield is damaged," he said as he pulled himself back in.

"How bad is it?"

"Nearly fifty metres of the road is unprotected. The bomb at New Scotland Yard must have damaged the anchor points," the Archangel replied as he hurried through the building's corridors to reach the other side.

"The tanks will not be able to get round there," Hermes said whilst following in the Archangel's wake.

"Then we will just have to do without them," he said as he rounded the last corner and approached the windows. The gap was even larger than he had at first thought and stretched the entire way across all four lanes of the main road. The only blessing was that the vast crater left behind when New Scotland Yard fell into its underground car park stretched the full width of the road creating a makeshift barrier. Already the Shadows were drawing level with the damage; there was only one thing the Archangel could do now.

236

"Hermes, send forth the Angels."

Down in the eternal dark of the London Underground, Tartarus marched on with his followers close behind in a rigid formation. There was no risk of any trains as these tunnels were part of an extension to the city's incomplete Southern Line. The tracks hadn't even been installed yet and in their place a series of vast bulbous pipes lay motionless.

As they moved on they eventually saw a speck of light in the distance which grew larger as the procession advanced. As they continued it became apparent that the light was fixed to the back of a mammoth machine that sat snugly into the tunnel up ahead.

Soon they arrived at the rear of the machine and with a flick of his hand Tartarus snapped the door off its hinges and sent it crashing to the ground. Quickly the Shadows filed inside and disappeared from view. For a minute or so the tunnel remained silent; until a vast engine roared into life and the machine began to creep down into the Earth.

The aircraft had only been flying for a few minutes before Apollo caught site of the power station which lay cloaked in darkness. The plant was incredibly modern and had only been completed a few years previously. It had three fusion reactors spread out in a line along the Thames Estuary with an assortment of cooling towers and other chimneys sprawling inland.

Slowly Apollo circled the dark facility casting his eyes over the countless buildings; searching for signs of life. At first it appeared that the whole complex had been abandoned but on closer inspection Apollo noticed a pair of feet sticking out grimly from behind a skip. There was no doubt about it; the Shadows were here.

Suddenly there was a flash in the corner of the compound as a jet of fire erupted into the sky. A fraction of a second later an alarm began to wail in the cockpit warning of an impending collision. The power station was equipped with its own air defence missiles in the event of a terrorist attack; one of which was now hurtling straight towards them. Abruptly Apollo swung the craft sharply to the left as the blaze of light drew closer with incredible speed. Apollo continued to bank until the craft finally reached the position he was aiming for and began to fly on its wing tip. The rocket drew ever closer and locked onto the centre of the aircraft's exposed underbelly; astonishingly it never reached its target. As it entered the antigravity field below the hull, the missile began to slow dramatically. For a few moments it seemed to just hang motionless before its motor failed and it was blasted backwards into one of the towering chimneys where it exploded harmlessly.

Apollo flipped the craft back the normal position to the relief of those in the cabin and began a steep descent to the plant below. He had to land quickly as he knew the Shadows wouldn't stop with just one missile. A few moments later his fears were realised as another jet of fire streaked ominously into the sky. The craft dropped quickly below the level of the plant's towering chimneys and began a steep curve to avoid hitting the ground. The missile was only about twenty metres away as the aircraft plunged between a row of cooling towers. The gap was barely wide enough for the plane as each of its wings skimmed along the edges of the concrete structures. The rocket had halved the distance and to make matters worse a large office block obstructed their path. It was a situation that no human pilot could have overcome as danger loomed on both sides. However, Apollo waited calmly until the last possible moment before sharply banking to the right. Such a manoeuvre would have torn any other plane apart but this one held strong as it tipped onto its side and elegantly slipped round the ninety degree bend without even damaging the paint work. The rocket had never been built for such a stunt and as the craft flew off to safety, the missile careered into the building and exploded in a belch of fire.

Free of the rocket, Apollo now searched for somewhere to land and settled on a huge concrete structure at the centre of the plant. Hurriedly he extended the legs and slowed the craft to landing speed as he came in over the building. He just hoped the roof was strong enough.

Unfortunately when the craft came down the legs punctured the thin concrete, descending into the building below. He prepared to take off again but thankfully the hull came to rest on the roof without sinking any lower. After waiting for a moment to see if the structure would hold he hit the ramp release button and clambered from his seat.

"It is time," he said softly.

As stray bits of energy sparked off the edges of the incomplete shield, the Shadows massed for their new attack. There was no sign of any defenders but the Shadows were wary after the massacre that they had just experienced. Before them the road was largely clear except for the enormous crater which stretched across the street where New Scotland Yard had once been.

At the rear of his forces Thanatos stood unsure of what to do; was the gap in the shield another trap or was it simply not working properly? In the end he decided upon a cautious approach by sending a weaker Shadow forwards to assess the situation. Reluctantly the Shadow obeyed its orders and advanced into the unknown. It felt a deep sense of foreboding as it passed through the tear in the shield, hoping none of the stray energy sparks would hit him.

Soon he was through the shield and nearing the chasm which descended twenty metres down into the Earth. Carefully it leapt in and made its way across the contorted mass of steel and concrete to the other side. As the Shadow finally approached the other side it made a series of weak and ungainly bounds to the top where it found nothing that might impede the army's progress.

Eventually it turned slowly and looked back at his brethren; beckoning them on. But then a violent pain exploded in his chest. Staggering back a few steps it slowly looked down and with horror saw a shining white arrow sticking out of its lower torso. The Shadow's strength almost instantly failed as it tipped backwards and disappeared into the gloom of the chasm.

The other Shadows were left in a state of rage as their eyes searched for the culprit. It didn't take them long as a lone Angel stepped out from the dark base of the Spire; clutching a glistening bow in its hand. As the

Shadows roared in anger the archer walked confidently onwards until he reached the edge of the pit and stared out at the opposing army.

"If you want this tower, come and get it," Hades said defiantly as he formed a new arrow in his right hand. From behind him he was soon joined by a procession of shining Angels as they emerged from the Spire and walked boldly over to stand on either side of Hades; each forming a glistening bow in their hands.

Across the other side of the chasm Thanatos made his way to the front to see this act of defiance with his own eyes. There were so few; just as Tartarus had promised. This should not take long.

"A noble gesture," he called out across the chasm. "But I count only a hundred of you and over two thousand of us; we out number you twenty to one."

"Then it is an even fight," Hades called back as he pulled back on the nanite string and took aim.

Thanatos only just had enough time to leap out of the way; letting the arrow bore into the Shadows behind him. As he fled he watched as the hail of arrows peppered the front line causing horrendous casualties. Without delay he gave the order to begin the advance. Already hundreds had been killed but they were expendable; there were so many more to take their place.

From the thirtieth floor the Archangel watched as the wave of Shadows poured into the pit and knew what he had to do. Raising an arm to the window he crumpled the metal frame inwards, sending fragments of glass clattering down the side of the building.

"My lord, we need you here," Hermes insisted. "We need a commander."

"Yes we do need a commander," the Archangel replied. "And I am sure you will do the job well," he added as he stepped out into the dark night.

240

There wasn't a sign of any activity as Gallagher and the others made their way down from the building's damaged roof into the twisting and turning labyrinth of corridors. The entire group were wary of hidden dangers and the three detectives had their guns drawn in readiness. In the gloomy interior every dark silhouette morphed into a knife wielding Shadow and every noise sent them spinning round in search of attackers. Their advance remained unchecked through the deserted passages of the building; maybe the enemy believed they had been shot down by the missile.

Eventually a brighter light became visible at the end of the corridor and the group cautiously headed towards it; but as they reached the corner Apollo abruptly gestured with his hand for them to stop.

"There are at least two occupants in that room; there could be more though as Shadows are hard to detect."

"How far away?" Gallagher whispered.

"Approximately ten metres."

"Ok, let's see what these guns can do then," Gallagher remarked whilst looking at the others. "On my mark... Three... Two... One..."

Kennedy kicked the door in as Gallagher sent a blue burst of energy straight into the nearest Shadow's upper arm; burning a hole clean through. The lack of recoil impressed Gallagher but he didn't have time to dwell on it as the four Shadows swiftly charged towards their attackers. To Gallagher's left, Natasha fired and struck the same Shadow in the centre of the chest. The raw energy instantly burned through its heart with a flash of light, sending it crashing to the ground. Together two shots from Kennedy and Gallagher sent the next Shadow to oblivion and Natasha scored another bull's eye when she took down the third Shadow. The last one was toppled with a volley of shots from all three detectives. Apollo and Persephone stood at the back; they could have defeated the four Shadows easily but had chosen to see how the humans would fare.

241

The small room which they found themselves in appeared to be a control room with a long console that ran the entire length of one wall. Above this was a closed metal shutter which Persephone forced open with a wave of her hand.

From the window a cavernous room extended off into the distance. Looking down on it from their high vantage point they could see vast arrays of pipes and other pieces of machinery snaking off across the floor. It had to be the turbine hall, where the high pressure steam was used to drive the plant's colossal generators. Normally this room was a hive of activity that reverberated with the roar of the turbines spinning thousands of times a minute but now it lay eerily still.

"Are there any down there?" Natasha asked.

"Yes," Apollo answered.

"How many?" Natasha enquired.

"You do not want to know..."

In contrast to the fighting at the surface, the tunnels and caverns of the Ark remained silent and empty. The only life forms in the colossal aircraft hangar were Alice and Mark who were sitting on the wing of one of the equally massive Legacy Transporters. Neither could properly take it all in; a few hours previously the city had been calm and now a horrific battle was raging high above their heads. It felt so odd to be sitting there doing nothing whilst the surface world was thrown into chaos.

"It's too quiet" Alice said at last.

"We are in a cave," Mark replied sarcastically.

"But it seems odd being so close to a battle and not hearing anything at all," she continued.

"I get what you mean. Things have changed so quickly haven't they; I mean yesterday we had no idea just how big this whole thing was."

"You know..." Alice began but abruptly stopped as a loud rumble emanated from the ceiling to the left of them.

"What was that?" Alice asked.

"I don't know. It can't be the battle; we're too far down." Suddenly the noise came again only slightly louder.

"I think we should get down from here," Alice suggested.

"Good idea," Mark murmured as the pair hastily stood up and headed for the hatch that lead into the hull. As they moved, the noise continued to grow in volume and bits of the stone ceiling began to break away, clattering onto the wing around them. Alice quickly scrambled through the hatch, closely followed by Mark just as a massive slab of rock broke free and tore a jagged hole through the wing where they had just been sitting.

As they ran into the cargo hold they could hear the deadly rain intensifying as it pounded the surface above them. Some debris had fallen on the ground beyond the cargo ramp but the two chanced it as they fled the aircraft and dashed towards safety.

They were nearly halfway there when, with the force of a sledge hammer, one of the pieces of rubble struck Alice and instantly shattered her collarbone. Normally this would have been a serious injury but before she even had time to comprehend it, the bones had knitted themselves back together and the pain evaporated.

However, there was no time to marvel at this as ever larger chunks of the ceiling collapsed inwards. As the pair cleared the danger zone, rocks that must have weighed several tonnes were punching holes through the top of the Legacy and crashing into the cargo bay.

"I'm real glad we didn't stay in that thing," Mark said, watching the devastation.

"We've got to get the hell out of here," Alice said as what looked like a laser beam burst through the damaged ceiling.

For a few seconds Mark scanned the area for some method of escape before his eyes settled on a strange eight wheeled lorry which was parked about fifty metres away.

"Over there," he said whilst already running towards the vehicle.

As Alice followed she couldn't help thinking the strange vehicle resembled an insect thanks to its long segmented body. However, there was little time to dwell on this as she scrambled into the cab after Mark. She was immediately stuck by how empty the cab was and the absence of any controls.

"Where's the steering wheel?" Mark called out in exasperation.

Just then the last of the roof gave way over the Legacy and ten revolving laser beams suddenly burst into view, followed by the huge metal body of a tunnel boring machine which came crashing down through the roof of the cavern. Briefly it spun helplessly; clawing its way through the air before slamming down onto a pair of planes which crumpled under the machines massive bulk.

Every fibre in Alice's brain was telling her to move and the vehicle dually obliged! Both Alice and Mark were thrown backwards as the vehicle unexpectedly lurched forwards. Alice quickly realised the vehicle was being controlled by her mind but wasn't fast enough to prevent a collision with a stack of empty metal containers.

For a few moments, the seriously damaged tunnelling machine lay stuck in the ground at a near vertical position before it ominously began to tip over to one side.

"We've got to move; it's coming down," Mark exclaimed as the machine began to lean ever further in their direction.

"I know!" Alice yelled as she managed to reverse the truck and spin it in the right direction.

Behind them, the machine was rapidly picking up speed as it passed the point of no return and thundered down towards the vehicle. However, Alice had other ideas and dramatically skidded the truck into a narrow gap between two of the transport planes. It was a tight fit and

244

she did more than scratch the paintwork but at least they were alive. Behind them, the machine ploughed on and crashed into the ground with a deafening wave of noise which reverberated around the cavernous room.

As the strange vehicle drove away, the clouds of dust were not even given time to settle before the machine's door was explosively thrown outwards. In its place stood the towering figure of Tartarus who stared out and surveyed his surroundings. He had not seen this place for many years and yet it had changed so little.

As he stepped out of the machine and onto the pulverised plane's hull he could not help smiling. He had returned. For a few moments memories flooded his mind until he detected something that was out of place. Why were there humans in this place of salvation? Quickly his eyes turned to see the distant shape of the vehicle as it vanished into the tunnel. For a few moments he just stared before issuing an order to his followers;

"Get them."

The Shadows poured into the pit in ever greater numbers as the arrows rained down on them with near perfect accuracy. The devastated landscape soon became strewn with bodies as the deadly hail killed half the Shadows before they even reached the opposite wall of the pit. Despite the Angels' success though, each time a Shadow made it across the pit, it diverted the Angel's attention, allowing ever more enemies to make it across the chasm.

Soon the numbers reaching the top of the pit became so great that all the Angels' fire became focussed on them. The enemy bodies piled up in ever greater numbers yet the Shadows continued advancing forcing the Angels to gradually retreat towards the Spire.

At the end of the line, the youngest Angel became separated as the enemy drove a wedge between her and the others. There wasn't time to save her as the Shadows swarmed round from all sides. As she slammed the shaft of her bow into one of the Shadows she was grabbed from behind and held in place as another enemy came towards her holding a knife in its hands. Quickly he raised the blade into the air and prepared to strike but he never got the chance as an elegant pure white sword crashed down on him from above. Less than a second later the Archangel landed alongside and quickly freed his blade before turning it on the next attacker as the young Angel threw her assailants to the ground. The time for bows had passed and swiftly the young Angel reshaped her bow into a curved sabre which she used to great effect on a succession of enemies.

Once he was certain that she was safe, the Archangel grasped his sword tightly and carved his way through the Shadows towards the pit. He could see why Tartarus had made so many; the Shadows were so crude and many of them could barely summon a blade, let alone fight. Once the Archangel had made it to the side of the chasm he leapt across in one titanic bound. As he flew through the air he could see his target hiding at the back of the army. It had to be Tartarus he thought as he came crashing down on top of a helpless Shadow.

In the dense blackness that cloaked the ground the Archangel became a small yet powerful beacon of light as he fought relentlessly on; hacking a path through to the other side. Many enemies struck him with daggers and the occasional sword but his armour withstood the blows of such crude weapons. Soon he broke through the rear line of the enemy into the empty street beyond and before him stood a lone Shadow with a sword in hand; but to the Archangel's dismay it was not Tartarus.

As he strode towards the enemy commander, he could sense its defiance as it stood holding the clumsy sword in its hands. Thanatos tried desperately to strike him but the black blade was met by the Archangel's sword which effortlessly cut through the crude metal before slicing into the Shadow's right hand. The Shadow yelled out in pain as the Archangel loomed above him; Thanatos could do nothing as a gauntleted hand came down and picked them up by the neck.

"Where is Tartarus?" the Archangel said menacingly.

"Why should I tell you?" Thanatos sneered as he hung in the air.

The Archangel didn't have time for this so slammed the pathetic being to the ground before ransacking its mind. Thanatos' consciousness was brittle and the information was extracted with ease. Once the process was complete the Archangel yelled out angrily and in a fit of rage grabbed the limp Shadow before throwing them into concrete wall with enough force to send chunks of rubble flying. He had to get back before it was too late...

In the quiet passages of the Ark the strange insect like vehicle charged relentlessly on. Neither Mark nor Alice knew where the tunnel would take them; only that it headed away from danger. Alice had made great progress with the steering but her driving was proving rather erratic. As a result Mark held on for grim death as the vehicle meandered from one side of the tunnel to the other.

"Why couldn't they have put a steering wheel in this thing?" Alice complained as she narrowly avoided another close collision with the tunnel wall. "And I don't want any jokes about women drivers," she added.

"I didn't say anything!" Mark retorted.

"No but you were thinking it," Alice said.

"Were you reading my mind then?" Mark asked curiously.

"No, I just know you were thinking it," Alice replied knowingly.

"I wasn..." Mark began as the vehicle abruptly swung to the left. Frantically Alice tried to maintain control and narrowly missed the tunnel wall.

"What the hell was that?" Mark gasped.

"I don't know but it wasn't me," Alice replied as the vehicle once again veered sharply off course. This time the vehicle struck the wall with great force sending Mark flying across the cab and into Alice. Briefly losing her concentration Alice lost control of the vehicle which rebounded off the wall and hurtled straight to the other side. There was

247

nothing she could do as it rode up the curved sides of the tunnel and slowly tipped onto two wheels. In a shower of sparks and mangled metal the truck passed its tipping point and crashed onto its roof before skidding to an abrupt halt with its wheels spinning wildly.

In the tunnel behind, the Shadows admired their work and closed in on the trapped people inside. There was no escape...

The turbine hall turned out to be infested with Shadows lurking in the room's many dark areas, waiting for the intruders to arrive. Most were unable to create weapons or even use their invisibility but a pair of more adept Shadows had been put among them who were far more skilled. Patiently they waited, staring at the door at the far end, ready to spring their strap.

The silence was suddenly shattered though as a series of unexpected shots burst out from behind the Shadows positions. In confusion the Shadows turned to face this threat leaving the door unguarded as Apollo and Persephone burst out and charged into battle. The Shadow closest to the door only turned back in time to see Apollo's formidable sword baring down on him. A few metres away Persephone leapt into the air and vanished in a flash of light. Before the Shadows had time to react she had already reappeared behind them and swiftly plunged her twin daggers into their backs. Apollo advanced further and finished off another of the hostiles with a slice across its chest before he spotted something on the high gantry. He needed to do something quickly.

On the walkway fifty metres away; Gallagher, Natasha and Kennedy stood firing into the confused rabble below them. The Shadows' carelessness in setting up their ambush had cost them dearly. As Apollo and Persephone advanced through the carnage the shots kept raining down, sowing panic and confusion with each hit. Gallagher was just about to take out yet another helpless Shadow when Kennedy suddenly leapt up and fired back down the length of the gantry. Instinctively Gallagher turned to see what Kennedy had fired at. To his surprise, all that he could see was a scorched hole hovering in the air; he was never going to get used to this invisibility. As Gallagher turned back to the

248

battle below, the black began to slowly pour back into the dead Shadow's robes as it slumped over the edge of the gantry.

"Good shot, how did you know it was there?" Gallagher asked as he continued firing.

"Heard Apollo's warning in my head," Kennedy replied as he dispatched another Shadow with a shot to the chest.

Down on the floor below, Persephone leapt through the air before spinning down between two of her assailants; plunging her twin blades into each simultaneously. Even before the two Shadows fell, she leapt into the air and vanished again in a flash. A few metres away Apollo charged with incredible speed at an enemy wielding an ebony bow. The Shadow just had time to unleash an arrow but with incredible skill Apollo brought his sword up and aligned it so the arrow disintegrated on impact. The Shadow frantically tried to summon another arrow but it was too late as Apollo closed the distance and with a single sweep of his sword ended the Shadow's life.

The enemies' defences were falling into chaos as they were assaulted on two flanks. However, despite their losses most chose to stubbornly stand their ground. It was in this scene of impending defeat that the group's commander, Erebos joined the fray. From the top of one of the huge turbines he surveyed his dwindling forces and cursed at how weak they were. The conversion process was so poor that at least ninety five percent of Shadows were nothing better than cannon fodder. At least he had been one of the lucky ones he thought as he summoned his bow which oozed from his hand like tar before setting into shape. He then formed a jagged arrow in his other hand and lifted it into position.

"Let us see how they deal with this," he hissed.

Several of the remaining Shadows crowded together in one last act of defiance in the middle of the turbine hall. As the shots continued to rain down on them, Persephone landed about fifteen metres in front of them and charged with her blades drawn. She was only a short distance away when the Shadow on the turbine unleashed its arrow. Silently it sailed through the air spinning slightly as it closed in on its target. Effortlessly the arrow passed through her thin robes to tear straight into the side of her chest; puncturing a lung and shattering the spinal column. The blow was agonising and Persephone uncontrollably crashed into the ground only a few metres in front of the waiting group of Shadows. Normally such injuries would be rapidly repaired but the nanites in the arrow had been programmed to resist healing attempts and cause maximum damage.

Apollo hadn't seen Persephone fall so had no idea that a group of Shadows were now charging towards her with knives drawn; her only hope now lay with the three humans up on the gantry who had seen the whole event unfold. Frantically Gallagher and Natasha opened fire but the range was too great and many of their shots missed. They had to get closer and there was only one way they could do that. Quickly Gallagher clambered up over the railings before leaping down onto one of the vast turbines which lay below. As Natasha vaulted over to follow him, Gallagher ran along the top of the huge metal turbine housing to the far side. From the other end, Natasha fired again at the Shadows which were drawing closer to the injured Persephone but her shots only wounded one of the five hostiles.

As the Shadows fell upon Persephone, Gallagher leapt down onto a lower section of the turbine before bounding down onto the ground below. As he ran towards the group he could see little of Persephone as the dark mass crowded around her. Rapidly he closed the distance and brought his gun to bare; taking down two of the Shadows in a blaze of fire. This quickly got the attention of the other three who all withdrew from Persephone and turned to face the new threat. In response, Gallagher kept firing but to his dismay the gun locked up; of all the times for it to overheat! The Shadows were coming closer and Natasha's covering fire only managed to injure one of them. The dark line was drawing ever nearer and still the gun wouldn't fire. Suddenly a flash of white came streaking from the other side of the room as Apollo's sword came sailing through the air. None of them noticed the incoming projectile before it had sliced straight down the black line and imbedded in the turbine housing beyond.

As Apollo ran over to the mortally wounded Persephone, the Shadow on the turbine took aim once more with his bow and smiled. However, just as he was about to release the string, a terrible pain burst through

250

his lower leg and his arrow sailed harmlessly over Apollo's head. Just then another blast of blue tore past him as Kennedy fired once again. Erebos was too exposed so he painfully moved to the edge of the turbine and dropped down into the gloom below.

In addition to the arrow wound Persephone had now also sustained multiple stab wounds across her body. Apollo sat alongside her and quickly grasped the arrow with both hands. As Gallagher and Natasha slowly walked over, he began to pull on the projectile. Inside the wound the arrow had latched itself in place and it took a great deal of Apollo's strength to tear the evil weapon free. As this was done Persephone remained conscious but didn't make a sound. Finally the arrow glided out and Apollo tossed it to the side where the heavily corroded shaft broke apart on contact with the ground.

It was then as the others looked on that Apollo extended his arm and grasped Persephone's hood. Slowly but surely he withdrew the white cloth revealing her face for the first time. Both Gallagher and Natasha had long wondered what lay beneath the shroud of fabric and couldn't help but stare as the cloth was pulled back. Even though they knew what the Angels were; they were still taken aback by what they saw.

Despite being contorted with pain, the face before them looked as if it had been sculpted by the likes of Michelangelo with every feature aligned to perfection. Her skin almost looked like porcelain and was free of any blemishes except for the strange wisps of silver which seemed to ripple and move in a surreal way. At first her eyes were closed but after a few moments the lids opened. Like the rest of her, the eyes resembled those of an ordinary person however the irises were an un-naturally vivid emerald green with a pair of copper rings surrounding them. Despite the gloom they seemed to sparkle as if they were emitting their own light. Her long hair was still largely concealed by the hood but from what Gallagher could see it hung loose and could well have been made of pure gold. Bit by bit the features added up to make a face that looked more elfin than human.

"Will she make it?" Natasha asked tentatively after a few seconds.

251

"Yes, but it will take me time to heal her; time which we do not have. I would never normally ask this of you but you must go on alone from here. If I leave her she will not regenerate in time," Apollo said softly.

"We understand," Natasha said looking again into Persephone's beautiful eyes.

"From the Shadows' memories the control room is at the end of this room; they will not give it up willingly."

On the streets above people ran in terror from the chaos that had engulfed the centre of the city. Suddenly a new wave of screams erupted as a ghostly figure tore down the street at incredible speed wielding a hefty sword. The Archangel ignored the people as he homed in on his destination; a tube station. As he covered the final few metres he noticed the entrance grill was closed and effortlessly tore it apart with his mind, sending chunks of scrap metal flying out in all directions.

In his path stood several terrified members of staff but the Archangel had no time to placate them and simply leapt over their heads. For a few moments he appeared to stand on the ceiling before he pushed off again and cleared the ticket barriers. The whole thing happened in a heartbeat and before anyone could react he had vanished out of sight.

Through the dark and open space of the turbine hall Gallagher and Natasha advanced with their guns drawn. So far they hadn't seen any other signs of life since leaving Apollo but they knew the enemy was there. Every now and then a blast of plasma would fly from the gantry as Kennedy kept level with them. Slowly they rounded one of the vast pieces of machinery only to come face to face with a partially invisible Shadow. Both Gallagher and Natasha fired in unison and the Shadow dropped to the ground.

"I hate these invisible ones!" Gallagher exclaimed.

"Yeah, at least they're not very good at it," Natasha remarked.

252

"Still don't like it," Gallagher murmured.

Up ahead there were only two more turbines to go before the huge metal staircase which lead up to the control room. Suddenly a burst of gunfire erupted from the balcony, aimed behind them. Instantly Gallagher and Natasha spun round to see four Shadows launching a surprise attack. However, the enemy didn't really stand much of a chance against their superior firepower and quickly dropped like flies.

"I'm really starting to like this thing," Natasha remarked as the last Shadow slumped over.

"Don't get too attached; I doubt they'll let you keep it," Gallagher said as he turned back towards the stairs. Silence once again hung over the huge room as they continued on; now only one turbine stood in their path.

Just then there was another shot from above and a Shadow tumbled off the top of the turbine as Kennedy's voice yelled out.

"Watch out; they're coming from both sides!"

Seconds later a group of Shadows burst out from round the back of the turbine and charged forwards. Once again the hail of fire quickly whittled the enemy down but soon they were forced to turn and deal with another advancing hoard that was nearly twice the size. Frantically all three fired as quickly as they were able whilst Gallagher and Natasha edged towards the stairs. Rapidly the piles of dead Shadows accumulated but still they kept coming. The situation was then only made worse when Gallagher's gun once again stopped firing. In desperation he pulled the trigger but nothing happened until suddenly the gun began to make a strange hissing noise and a red light flickered on. Gallagher instantly had a sinking feeling as he guessed what that meant; not daring to have it anywhere near him he threw the gun in the direction of the advancing Shadows.

As soon as the gun struck the ground there was an almighty explosion of blue light as the overheated gun tore itself apart. Both Gallagher and Natasha were catapulted backwards and sent skidding across the floor

253

in a mass of tangled limbs as the Shadows were engulfed in the wave of plasma.

After a few seconds, silence once again fell over the hall and Gallagher groaned; he hadn't expected that. Once he was sure he was still in one piece he heaved himself up off the concrete floor, soon followed by Natasha. Looking back at the scene of the explosion they were surprised to see a sizeable crater sunk deep into the floor and not a trace of the Shadows.

"I can see why only a few of these things were made," Gallagher remarked.

"They're not a gun, they're more of a bomb!" Natasha said as she looked at her own firearm.

"Guys," came Kennedy's voice from above. "There's at least fifty Shadows coming in at the other end of the room so you might want to move it!"

As Hermes watched from his position he could see that the battle was hanging in the balance. The Angels had inflicted horrendous casualties on their opponents but the Shadows showed no signs of retreating. At least a thousand still stood and what's more they had all made it across the pit. Now they formed a vast black column and were using their sheer weight of numbers to drive the Angels back towards the Spire. If they reached the structure then the advantage would be firmly in favour of the Shadows. All the entrances to the Ark had been sealed shut but such barriers would only hold for a limited time.

But then Hermes noticed something that made the situation far worse; at the end of the road a new wave of dark shapes were massing for an attack. There was no way that the others could hold so many at bay. There had to be something he could do to tip the balance; what would the Archangel have done? Then after a few moments an idea came to him.

In the turbine hall the Shadows from all across the power plant were now running as fast as they were able to join the battle and Apollo and Persephone lay right in the path of the oncoming storm. The Shadows' thirst for revenge was insatiable; so many of their brethren had died at the hands of the two Angels and now they would have their vengeance.

Both Angels remained unmoving as the Shadows approached with their daggers drawn. A few moments before they arrived, Persephone whispered something to Apollo and tried to move her hand. Apollo was surprised by what she said and instantly reached down to a concealed pocket in her robes. His hand closed around a small metal sphere which felt unnaturally cold. As he pulled the object free his eyes fell upon the small silver device which closely resembled a gyroscope and glowed with a pale blue light. The Shadows were closing in as he moved his thumb over a button on the top of the device and pressed down.

The flash lit up the entire room and several Shadows instantly disintegrated on contact with the light. For a few moments the rest of them froze as the ball of energy intensified. They were unsure what it was or what to do but as the seconds passed it became clear. Gradually the brightness dimmed and the ball became semi transparent. Inside the blue sphere Apollo looked down at Persephone.

"Where did you get that?" he asked.

Persephone tried to speak but it was too painful so communicated telepathically instead.

"I made it whilst I was working on the Spire's shields," she replied.

"How long does it last?"

"Three minutes."

"Well I had better work quickly then."

As the blast of light was illuminating the room, Natasha and Gallagher were running up the metal staircase as fast as they were able.

255

"Where are they?" Gallagher called up to Kennedy who was on the platform above.

"Most of them stopped after the flash but several are still coming."

"What was the flash?" Natasha shouted whilst panting heavily.

"I couldn't see; but it came from where we left the Angels," Kennedy answered as the others ran up the final few steps to join him.

"Any sign of the control room?" Gallagher asked whilst pulling out his old pistol from its holster.

"Yeah, there's a sign pointing over there," Kennedy replied as the three headed off along the walkway to the left.

Hera stood alone on the control platform. The cavern now seemed so empty as she walked between the different screens trying to keep her mind on the tasks that she had to perform. However, just as she was moving between monitors a noise came from behind her. Like a flash she flew round but at first couldn't see anything. She knew she had heard something so continued to look along the lines of empty work stations until her gaze settled on the main screen by the high platform.

The screen had been switched off but as she looked, the strands of light were already knitting themselves together to form an image. Even before the image was complete she could feel a cold shiver run down her spine as multiple dark shapes appeared. Slowly the picture became more distinct and the dark patches gradually took on humanoid form. Once the image was complete Hera could see a black column of nearly twenty Shadows with the towering figure of Tartarus standing at its head. Hera was so focused on them that it took her a few seconds to recognise the Shadows' surroundings. They were on the other side of the door to the Central Chamber. They had breached the Ark! Frantically Hera reached out with her mind and tried to locate the other Angels but as there were so many in such close proximity she just couldn't make contact.

"Hello Hera," Tartarus said in his unnaturally deep voice as he stared at her through the screen.

"It has been a long time Tartarus," she replied trying to sound braver than she actually felt. "I wish I could say I was pleased to see you."

"Yes, I do so hate making enemies of you all but this is the only way," he said with a touch of mock sadness in his voice. "Now, would you be good enough to open the door for us."

"Do you seriously think I will do as you ask. It was deadlocked for a reason Tartarus; to keep you and your abominations out!"

"Please Hera, it does not have to be this way..." Tartarus began.

"Of course it does! You killed innocent people, raised an army of murderers and seek to steal the Spire from us. There is nothing you can do that will make me unlock the door!"

For a few moments Tartarus remained still before he eventually spoke.

"Hera. You always had a kind heart; you could never stand back whilst there was suffering in the world. The Archangel saw that as your strength whilst I see it as your greatest weakness..." With that he walked slowly to the side revealing a sight that wrenched at Hera's heart.

"Open the door or I kill the humans."

Just as the thousand strong hoard of fresh Shadows began their advance to join the fray, Hermes accessed the construction computer telepathically. The advancing army was nearly halfway to the pit as Hermes overrode the remaining protocols and gave out a series of new instructions.

As the front row of Shadows charged relentlessly on, panic suddenly filled the front ranks as one by one they looked up and saw a looming shape thundering towards them. The Shadows hastily tried to move out of the path of the spinning projectile but there was no room to escape.

257

Frantically they pushed and shoved but it was too late as a five tonne construction lorry struck the ground with incredible speed just in front of the advancing column. The sides of the vehicle crumpled and the cab was flattened as it continued to spin along the ground; carving a gory path in its wake.

In the construction site one of the giant crab robots clanked noisily over to another of the automated lorries and sunk its two giant claws into the weak steel frame. Slowly it lifted it back over its metal body before catapulting it in a high arc towards the Shadows. Alongside it another of the mighty drones moved into position and latched onto a cement mixer. Soon the Shadows were being bombarded with everything from lorries and cranes to diggers and huge lengths of pipe. However, despite the improvised bombardment, the Shadows still advanced. Hermes quickly scanned through the robots under his command; what else could he use? And then he had another ingenious idea...

The Shadows were jostling up the other side of the pit when suddenly something quite small crashed into the top of the chasm before shredding its way down the crumbling sides. At first the Shadows were slow to identify the weapon but then another came to Earth and pieces of rotor blades shot out in all directions, slicing through all before them. Over the Shadows' heads nearly two hundred welding drones were now plummeting downwards in a mass Kamikaze dive. Soon the deadly rain of metal began to pound the enemy army in earnest. The Shadows broke formation and began to run for cover as their comrades were either sliced apart by the rotors or pulverised into the ground. The chaos was increased when one of the crab drones grabbed hold of a large storage tank plastered in hazard symbols. Not knowing what the object contained, it threw it into the air.

In the depths of the chasm the Shadows believed they were safe as they sheltered from the steel rain beneath the detritus from New Scotland Yard. They had no time to move as the storage tank struck a raised pile of rubble and tore open in a cascade of sparks. The effect was dramatic as the highly volatile fuel ignited and exploded in a colossal fireball.

258

From the thirtieth floor Hermes watched as the chasm was engulfed in fire and the remnants of the second wave fled in panic. Now he could turn his attention back to the Angels who were struggling to keep the other Shadows at bay. He was alarmed by what he saw as the Angels had been pushed back further than he would have liked; they were now only ten metres from the Spire and still retreating. He dared not use the drones against these Shadows for fear of hitting the others. There had to be something else he could do and frantically racked his brain until something else came to him.

In response to his new commands, forty heavy duty engines roared into life and the vehicles they powered began to roll towards the Spire.

Hera was thrown into a horrible situation where both possible outcomes were grim. However, despite what her heart told her she knew there was only one choice that she could make.

"I cannot open it," Hera said at last turning away from the screen.

"Very well," Tartarus remarked. "I was curious to see which path you would choose," he added as he extended a hand towards the door. Hera looked on in panic as one by one the locks retracted and the door began to hiss open.

"How are you doing that?" Hera exclaimed turning back to the screen.

"You do not seriously think I would try to attack the Ark if I could not bypass the deadlocks? I helped design this place and I know its every nut and bolt," he said as the door slowly disappeared into its housing. "Now Hera, please step out of the way."

On the floor of the turbine hall Apollo worked swiftly. The arrow had done considerable damage and it took all of his skill to suppress the hostile nanites in the wound. The Shadows remained crowded round the shield braying for blood as he slowly sealed up the wound bit by bit. The time was nearly spent when the damaged backbone finally began to realign itself. Very faintly Apollo could hear Persephone counting down the seconds until the shield would collapsed.

"Nine... eight... seven." The spinal column was repaired.

"Six... five... four." The nervous system was restored.

"Three... two... one." Time up.

As the door disappeared into the wall Hera stood defiantly at the end of the glass walkway. She couldn't defeat them all but she would go down fighting. Like many of her kin before her she summoned her sword which poured from her hand like liquid light. Once the thin curved blade had formed she took a deep breath and began to walk down the glass bridge towards her enemies.

At the door, Tartarus stood watching as Hera slowly approached; then without making a sound he gave his orders. In unison all but the two Shadows holding the prisoners in place marched past their commander. From their position in the clutches of the Shadows, Mark and Alice watched in admiration as Hera continued to advance in the face of far superior numbers.

"Foolish," Tartarus murmured. "So very foolish."

"She's brave!" Alice suddenly exclaimed.

"Yes, but in vain," Tartarus said as he slowly turned round to face them. "Now I would not say anything else or I might just kill you now."

"Why haven't you already then?" Mark asked angrily.

"What is the point in devoting years of your life to a task and having no one there to witness your triumph?" Tartarus said as he turned back to watch the fight unfold.

Halfway along the length of the statue's arms Hera stopped and stood her ground; the Shadows were now only a few metres away as she grasped the sword in both hands. In the last few moments before the impending battle a strange calm fell over her; this was her home and she would never stand aside to let the Shadows take it from her. The front row of enemies were confident as they advanced, clutching all manner of bladed weapons.

Hera stood unmoving until the last possible moment when she suddenly pulled her hands to the side; splitting her sword into two ghostly copies of the original. Elegantly she spun away from the first series of attacks and sent both her swords slicing down the densely packed front row slaying two of the Shadows. The rest hissed in anger as they began to attack from all sides. The odds were against her but Hera deflected each blow and in a great bound she soared above the Shadows. Before the ones at the back could react she had slain four of them before dodging out of the way. However, her luck was not to last; these Shadows were among the best that Tartarus had ever created and were not like the cannon fodder that he had sent into the battle above.

As Hera was skirting round the edge of the group a blade suddenly shot out and sliced along the back of her left hand forcing her to release one of the swords. Despite the wound she still fought on and parried several blows before dispatching another couple of Shadows with savage slices to their chests. She was so engrossed by the battle in front of her though that she failed to see the danger from behind.

As she was leaping out of the way of a swipe towards her throat, a cruel looking sword came in from behind. Hera froze for a moment; almost unable to take it in as the blade erupted out just below her shoulder blade. For a few moments she looked down at it in dismay before collapsing sideways onto the glass floor.

Tartarus ignored the howls of rage from the two humans as he carefully walked around Hera's body looking down upon it. After a few moments he moved on leaving his sword behind and passed through the gap that had formed in the middle of his Shadow's ranks. At last the way was clear and they could begin the final phase...

Gallagher burst into the control room closely followed by Natasha and Kennedy; they held their guns at the ready expecting trouble. However, to their surprise the room seemed to be empty. There was no doubt that

261

they were in the right place as the large room was filled with the control panels and gauges needed to monitor the plant. Keeping their guns at the ready, they ventured into the darkened room whilst trying to avoid the countless dead engineers that littered the floor. Small LED's on the consoles flashed and blipped on and off above the myriad of buttons, switches and other strange instruments.

"Why would they leave this room unguarded?" Natasha asked.

"Perhaps they thought they could stop us before we reached it," Kennedy suggested.

Little did they realise that they were most definitely not alone. At the back of the room Erebos stood in his invisible form waiting to see if the Angels were accompanying the group. He still felt angry at missing Apollo; if it hadn't been for that human then he would have succeeded. As a result he now had extensive damage to his knee and it would take too long to heal.

After a few moments he realised that the Angels were not present and it was just the three weak humans; now he could have his revenge. Silently he crept up behind the nearest of the three and drew his dagger. Just as he was about to bring it down though the words of his master began to flow into his mind. The time had come... Quickly he withdrew the dagger and instead reached out a hand towards the dials.

Gallagher was the first to notice as a series of switches began to move of their own accord.

"They're restarting the plant," he called out as the main lever on the wall began to move into the active position. Quickly he ran for it and grabbed hold but he wasn't strong enough to challenge the elite Shadow as it used its mind to force it into place. Immediately there was a blaring of claxons and the lights began to come on as the turbines one by one spun back into life down in the room below. The station was active and so was the Spire.

As the lights of the city began to flicker, Tartarus took his position on the high platform. Below him his remaining Shadows worked at the consoles as the power bars refilled and the Spire became operational. After all these years the tower was finally complete, all that it required was someone willing to give the nanites their commands.

Gently Tartarus ran his hand over the central console that was positioned just in front of the Sphere. He had once thought that he would never see this place again, but now here he stood at the heart of the greatest structure on Earth. After walking the length of the panel he reached up to the top of his robes and grasped a thin black chain. Carefully he pulled on it and retrieved a large pendant. In almost every respect the medallion was identical to the one worn by the Archangel except that it was entirely black; even down to the gemstones that lined the outer circumference. For a few moments he held it in his hand before turning to look down on the Shadows and his captive audience.

"The time is close at hand; after so much waiting we now stand on the verge of victory. This structure was made to heal the world and that is exactly what it will do."

The immaculate reception area of the Spire sat quiet and empty, untouched by the action. However, the peaceful room was suddenly transformed as one of the lumbering battle tanks ploughed through the glass wall and into the space beyond. Its tracks squealed on the polished marble floor, tearing sections free as it moved on its path of destruction. Another wall soon loomed in its path but it was no match for the ninety tonne juggernaut. Effortlessly the tank tore its way through the thin plaster and continued into an office space beyond just as the next tank rumbled inside. Wall after wall was decimated effortlessly and the once pristine interior was covered in dust and rubble as the convoy forged on.

The Angels were now running out of room as the glass wall of the Spire drew ever closer; if the Shadows made it into the tower then there would be little hope of stopping them reaching the Ark. It was just as the first Angel came into contact with the glass that Hermes sent out a single word to all of the Angels below.

"Duck."

Instinctively all the Angels dropped down just as forty gun barrels burst through the panes of glass above them. For a split second the Shadows stayed rooted to the spot knowing it was too late to move as the tanks fired. Along the line there was one colossal white flash as a single volley smashed into the dark ranks, tearing through everything in their path. In a heartbeat the enemy army was shattered and only a handful of stragglers remained. It appeared that the Angels had won however they were soon to be sorely disappointed.

In the light of the Sphere, Tartarus turned away from the Shadows and expertly slid open a concealed hatch on the control panel with a sweep of his hand. As the two tiny metal doors slid out of the way a circular depression was revealed that lit up with the same blue light as the Sphere above. For a few moments he stood there, holding the medallion in his hand before he slowly and precisely lowered it into position. For a moment the pendant just sat there before it clicked and sank down an inch or so into the console and rotated ninety degrees to the right.

Silence filled the air throughout the cavern for what seemed like an eternity. However, as the seconds ticked by the vivid blue of the Sphere began to falter and fade; almost as if it was dying from within as patches of black began to pollute it and quickly spread like a terrible poison. It wasn't long before the once mystical pure light was replaced by a deathly black which covered the entire Sphere. Then from deep beneath them came a loud clanking noise as the eight vast plates which made up the floor of the cavern slowly began to retract into the walls revealing a sight that would surpass anything else on Earth.

Through the gaps in the floor a sea of swirling and shifting nanites shone brightly up into the now gloomy cavern above. One billion tonnes of un-programmed nanorobots just waiting to be set loose upon the world. As the nanites continued to swirl their entrancing dance a low hum began to reverberate throughout the cavern as the firing sequence was prepared and the nanites began to rise.

It started slowly at first but with each passing second, the nanites began to move towards the centre where they twisted and turned rapidly until they began to break free of the surface and coil themselves into a column. With astonishing speed the column gained altitude as it raced up towards the corrupted Sphere above and when the two met there was a sound like a clap of thunder. The Sphere briefly swelled for a moment and then in an instant it began to spin several times a second; shrieking like a soul in torment. From the top of the Sphere a black tower of unstable and dangerous nanites were catapulted high up into the roof of the cave.

Once they entered the shaft to the Spire there was no stopping them as the powerful electro magnets dragged them upwards at just under the speed of sound. Soon they were approaching the golden pinnacle and spilled out onto the unsuspecting world below.

The Angels who were recovering from the battle looked up in horror as the black torrent explosively blew out of the top of the Spire. Twisting and coiling round each other the nanites began to arc out in all directions like a mass of writhing serpents. People across the city screamed in terror as they stared out of their windows and those on the streets fled in panic as the first column of darkness crashed down upon the London Banking Tower. Windows shattered as the nanites ate their way through the walls and set about devouring all in their path. Everything from computers, books and chairs were rapidly reduced to dust as the nanites fulfilled their programming. It was only a matter of seconds that the superstructure came under assault and soon vast pieces of the building were breaking free and falling down on the city below.

One by one the tallest buildings came under attack as the nanites followed their commands; to heal the Earth.

"Why are you doing this?" Alice shrieked whilst looking at the devastation on the screens around the room. "You are going to kill millions!"

265

"Yes, I once believed that humanity could be saved but now I see the truth. Humanity is by its very nature selfish, violent and seeks to destroy the very worlds it inhabits. I was tasked with making a perfect world and that is what I am achieving here today; through the extermination of mankind!"

"But you were once human," Mark yelled in defiance. "And for all the evil in this world there is so much more that is good..."

"Or have you fallen too far into the dark to see the light?" Alice added.

"Enough! I have spared you long enough. You will be the first of mankind to *fall* this day," Tartarus said sadistically as Alice and Mark were forced over to the edge of the platform. "You two may have come back from the abyss once, but I doubt you will return this time," he added as another Shadow smashed the glass railings in front of the struggling pair.

"Rest in Peace."

Further along the platform Hera just barely clung to life. There was nothing she could do as the two humans were forced ever closer to the edge. To think it had come to this, after all these years of work. But then she felt someone approaching; it had to be another Shadow she thought miserably as it drew closer. But she soon began to wonder; her senses were in turmoil and she couldn't be certain but the presence felt familiar. It was only as they drew alongside her that she recognised who it was and the despair began to ease. Reaching out with an invisible hand the figure grasped the sword and pulled it free, giving Hera a chance to heal her wounds. The figure then lightly tossed the sword in his hand to gauge its weight before he drew it back behind his head and threw it with all his might.

The dark blade sailed through the air towards the group gathered at the edge of the platform. Spinning end over end as it flew, the blade tore straight through the closest Shadow before continuing on towards Tartarus. On contact with the target, the blade ripped through his robes and sunk deep inside. However, unlike the Shadow, Tartarus simply re-absorbed his own sword and recreated it out of his right hand in one fluid motion.

"So, you saw through my little deception, old friend," Tartarus said whilst turning to look at the walkway.

"Yes," the Archangel said as he reappeared at the entrance to the platform. One of the Shadows instinctively lunged for him but without even turning his gaze, the Archangel recreated his sword to swiftly dispatch them with a sideways stab.

"I see you left your humanity behind," Tartarus remarked.

"In some ways," the Archangel said slowly as he walked among the Shadows. "And I see you became a monster at the same time."

"I am fulfilling our purpose!"

"You have forgotten yourself! I am going to give you one last chance at redemption. Deactivate the Spire and release your prisoners."

"Or what?" Tartarus remarked.

"Or I will have to stop you," the Archangel said as he paused in front of Tartarus. "And now I will say it one last time; release them."

For a few moments Tartarus remained silent and stared back at his former friend in silence. Then in one deft movement he lunged sideways and before either Mark or Alice could react, the glass floor of the platform had slipped away and they were plunging down into the void below.

Rapidly gaining speed Alice and Mark tumbled in horror down towards the sea of nanites beneath them. After all they'd been through Alice really hadn't thought it would end like this. She had heard that in situations like this your life was supposed to flash before your eyes but the only thing she felt was pure and unrestrained terror.

However, as the two gained speed, a strange sensation distracted Alice from their impending doom. As they continued to fall, the feeling grew steadily worse and seemed like someone had sunk their nails deep into her back and was viciously tearing into the skin.

267

"You said release them and so I did," Tartarus cruelly remarked as he raised his sword and walked over to the centre of the platform. Slowly the two adversaries began to circle each other as the other Shadows looked on, not daring to get in the way of two such powerful beings.

"I had hoped there was some good left in you but deep down I knew that you had fallen too far," the Archangel responded.

"So you let your precious humans die then."

"No, you have forgotten one thing Tartarus..." the Archangel said defiantly. "Angels have wings." And with that the Archangel dived forwards and in a shower of sparks the two swords clashed.

As the pair continued to fall, Mark's attention was suddenly caught by a glint of white off to the side of him. Turning his head, he was startled to see that the top section of Alice's jacket seemed to be burning. Given the circumstances he wasn't sure what to do so he continued to watch as two long slits formed behind the shoulder blades. From the slits two narrow projections of pure white nanites began to emerge. Rapidly they spread out several metres in each direction before they began to unfold into the shape that was required.

It was at this stage that Alice finally realised what was happening to her and what the nanites were trying to accomplish. Their purpose was to preserve life and the only way to achieve this demanded drastic action; they were building her wings. Steadily the bird like wings unfolded until her descent began to slow. Mark however, continued to race on and almost immediately slammed into her right wing sending both of them careering to the ground once again.

High on the platform the two sparring immortals clashed swords as the black and white sparks flew again. As the hand guards collided Tartarus aggressively spun his blade free and brought it back in a vicious swipe at his former friend's exposed neck. The Archangel only just had time to lean back, letting the blade skim within a hairs breadth of his throat.

Tartarus then tried the same manoeuvre again from the opposite direction but this time the Archangel parried the blow and spun into Tartarus knocking him backwards against one of the consoles.

Seizing the opportunity two of the Shadows leapt over to their master's aid with their swords drawn. As the Archangel was about to strike Tartarus in the chest, the voice of Hera screamed in his mind to watch out. Instinctively he shot over to the side letting the two Shadow's blades slice down into empty air. In a state of fury Tartarus pushed himself upright before in one colossal flourish, sliced straight through both of his surprised creations as he advanced on the Archangel.

Frantically Gallagher tried to pull the lever back down but it was no use. There had to be a Shadow in the room with them; he quickly surveyed the area once again searching for it. In the dark it had been impossible to see but now as the lights came back on a small area of black just to the side of Natasha's knee caught Gallagher's attention. Instantly he let go of the lever and raised his old pistol. He doubted his shots would have much of an effect but he had to do something.

Erebos' concentration was broken as the bullets struck in a wide spread across his chest. Searing pain coursed through him and he lashed out sending Natasha flying towards Gallagher. Kennedy immediately opened fire but the Shadow was too quick and even with its wounded leg managed to dive behind one of the consoles as it reappeared.

Natasha and Gallagher frantically tried to get back to their feet. Both of their guns had been sent flying in the impact and Gallagher quickly scoured the ground for his pistol. He soon spotted it under a table and was just reaching for it when it abruptly sped across the floor towards the Shadow.

Alice and Mark continued to plummet at great speed as Alice tried to right herself after the collision. Beneath them one of the partially retracted sections of the floor was looming ever nearer and Alice only

269

just managed to swing off to the side to avoid it. Beneath them the cavern widened dramatically and the sea of blue seemed to go on for an eternity. However, there was no time to consider this as Alice finally managed to stop her erratic spiral.

Time was almost out as the seething nanites drew ever closer. Gently and with as much precision as she could muster she moved over sideways towards Mark with her wings trailing in an upright position. She was drawing nearer and was almost within touching distance when she over shot him and drifted off to the left. Frantically she regained control, narrowly avoiding the blue column blasting up into the cavern above.

For a second time she drifted over towards Mark with her arms outstretched. The eerie blue nanites were getting so close and Mark tried to wave her away but she had come too far to abandon him now. At the last second, Alice reached out and grasped Mark's wrist. In a flash of white her wings extended and rapidly began to slow the descent; but it wasn't fast enough. Still heading downwards at over fifty miles an hour there was almost no hope of stopping in time as the nanites rushed up to meet them.

The Archangel parried blow after blow at such speed that the movements blended together into a blur of intense motion. The few remaining Shadows had by now moved as far as they could from the deadly dance, fearing the wrath of either of the participants. It was then in the flurry of movement as the swords were once again set to collide that Tartarus changed direction at the last possible moment. The end of his blade tore through the Archangel's armour and gouged a wound diagonally across his chest.

Clamping his teeth down hard, the Archangel staggered for a moment as Tartarus watched his pain triumphantly.

"You have lost, admit it," Tartarus sneered. The Archangel said nothing; for a few moments he just stood there before he slowly raised his hands up to his head and withdrew his hood. In the dim light of the cavern Tartarus stared into the face of his creator; a face he had not

270

seen in such a very long time. In many ways it had changed little despite his conversion; the most obvious difference though was the colour of his hair which now looked to be made of red gold. His eyes were also different as the iris' had become a deep purple with a pair of gold halos that encircled them.

"Lost?" he said at last; panting from the battle. "Never," and in an almighty leap he shot into the air. As he rose, two panels broke free from the back of his armour allowing his wings to rapidly unfold, keeping him suspended in the air. He did not need to flap the wings as the nanites were able to exert a small anti gravity field which kept him airborne. Looking down on the others he hovered motionless waiting for Tartarus to follow.

Down on the platform Tartarus laughed as he unfolded his own wings which had turned as black as his soul. He then soared into the air as the Archangel knew he would and the battle continued.

Reaching out, Erebos took the gun as it flew towards them. In its wounded state, forming a weapon was too tiring so they opted to use something a little more primitive. Quickly it checked to see if it was still loaded before leaping from cover and taking aim. As it happened the gun only had one shot remaining which sped across the room before sinking into Kennedy's right hand.

In agony Kennedy dropped the gun just as the Shadow leapt forwards and tried to close the distance to the humans. However, before it could reach them Natasha had retrieved her gun and opened fire. Once again Erebos was forced to dive for cover but this time they landed behind a metal cabinet and quickly formed a new plan of attack. Using its pent up anger it grasped the object with its mind and catapulted it forwards straight at Natasha.

Natasha saw the improvised projectile just in time and dived out of the way as it sailed past her and ploughed into the wall. However, the Shadow wasn't done and in a clumsy forward roll it dived for Kennedy's fallen gun. Its hand quickly grasped the plasma weapon's handle and raised it towards Natasha as she tried to aim her own weapon. The Shadow got its gun into position first but was caught completely by surprise as Gallagher took a running leap and came down on top of it.

The force of the impact and its damaged knee conspired together and the pair came crashing to the ground. The impact stunned both of them but Erebos quickly recovered and lashed out with a series of powerful blows before pushing Gallagher away with enough force to send him flying. The Shadow took aim again but this time Natasha was quicker and her shot bored straight through Erebos' left shoulder.

Once again the Shadow refused to submit and rolled out of the way of Natasha's next shot before taking one of their own. The blast discharged from the barrel and raced directly to its target; striking the top of Natasha's gun and instantly disintegrated the firing mechanism. Without their precious weapons they were helpless.

Apart from the column of nanites, little stirred down in the depths of the statue cavern. All eyes were on the duel that raged overhead so no one saw the pair of exhausted humans as they crashed down on top of a ledge in a state of exhaustion.

"I never want to do that again," Mark said rubbing his wrist.

"Me neither..." Alice replied. "But how else are we going to get back up there?"

On the statue's shoulder, chips of stone exploded outwards as Tartarus narrowly missed the Archangel who had just evaded the blow. Despite his skilful dodge the Archangel was weakening from the infected wound he had been dealt. Constantly he parried the blows as they came but he was now on the defensive as he backed steadily further up the shoulder towards the colossal carved hood. He had led Tartarus away from the control panel but he needed help and fast.

In the power plant's control room Erebos aimed the gun at Natasha and slowly squeezed the trigger. However, just before the Shadow could fire, a blade of glistening white streaked out from the doorway and imbedded deep in its throat. Shocked by what had happened, Erebos let the gun fall which clattered noisily to the ground. Slowly it slumped down onto its knees just as the glowing robes of an Angel entered the room. The Shadow knew it was finished but it took some satisfaction in that there was only one Angel present; the other must have been slain. However, this hope was dashed when another entered the room; their robes heavily torn from an intense battle. As the end drew near, Erebos' mind began to unravel and pieces of the person they had once been rose to the surface. An early birthday party, his first bike, his twin brother and the hundreds of dead at the Square all drifted past until Erebos and what was left of Brian Gorse finally collapsed sideways and moved no more.

Just then a wave of Shadows appeared in the doorway as Apollo tried to push it closed. Reaching out a hand in the other direction he quickly disabled the plant; but for how long he could not be certain.

From the base of the statue's neck both Tartarus and the Archangel felt the change as the black jet of nanites flickered and narrowed. For a few moments too long Tartarus let his focus shift and failed to counter the blow that was heading straight towards him. He realised at just the last second and tried to dodge the blow; but in the process he lost his footing and fell backwards onto the smooth stone work and immediately began to slide backwards down towards the edge. Frantically he began to unfold his wings and only just got them open in time to avoid tumbling downwards.

He turned to see where the Archangel was and to his alarm found he had disappeared. He looked around wildly, searching for his opponent. The Archangel couldn't be cloaked as he would still be able to see him so where had he gone? It was after a few moments that Tartarus had a sudden wave of realisation and looked up only to see the Archangel thundering down towards him. Tartarus just had time to raise his sword but wasn't able to deflect the blow which slipped off his blade and

273

plunged down into his left shoulder. The injury didn't stop there as the Archangel's momentum carried the sword onwards, tearing a horrific gash across the top half of his torso.

Tartarus clenched his teeth in agony and sprang upwards, in an effort to get as much distance between him and the Archangel as he could. By the time he reached the summit of the statue the wound was almost healed; the Archangel's sword was a dangerous weapon but unlike his own blade, it didn't infect a wound as effectively. It had still been a close thing though and Tartarus didn't want to risk it happening again so began to summon his followers.

Down on the platform the remaining Shadows heard their master's call and unfurled their wings to join the battle. As the bulk of them flew away the four who were not able to fly remained to monitor the controls.

As one of them checked the power fluctuations, a sudden flash of white caught their attention. Quickly it looked up from the console and stared out at the cave around them. That couldn't be good... Then in the corner of their vision they spotted it again, disappearing beneath the walkway. They were just about to warn the others when a vicious kick from behind sent them reeling over the top of the railings. The Shadow wailed in terror and tried to create a set of wings but quickly toppled over the edge and plummeted out of sight.

The other Shadows spun round but failed to see anything other than an empty console. It was then that the mystery attacker struck again and touched down behind the rearmost Shadow and grabbed them by the head. The Shadow writhed and squirmed but was unable to do anything as it was catapulted upwards towards the corrupted sphere. It had no time to do anything as it was slammed into the poisoned object's outer surface and reduced to a dark cloud of atoms.

The two remaining enemies were trying to understand what was happening when a voice called out from the walkway.

"You're not so tough without your boss around!"

274

Instantly the two Shadows spotted Alice standing by herself in the middle of the walkway.

"What are you waiting for? Come and get me!"

The Shadows were uncertain of what to do; Alice looked perfectly normal and incapable of dispatching two of their number. What was going on? Eventually though, the two Shadows crept forwards; eager for blood. It was a mistake they would live to regret...

In the control room of the power plant the mass of Shadows continued to try and force their way inside. The room only had one entrance, through a thin metal door but this wouldn't provide protection for long. As Gallagher reached down to retrieve Kennedy's pistol from the dead Shadow's cold hands the door began to open. As the lock failed Apollo threw his weight against it slamming it shut once more and crushing several pale hands in the process. The Shadows shrieked and wailed as they continued to pound against the door until the hinges collapsed. Persephone was forced to leap over and help keep the barricade in place.

"How many are there?" Gallagher asked.

"Nearly forty," Persephone replied.

"Great," Gallagher muttered as a pale hand punched through the wall.

Alice dashed back over to Mark who she had left on the other side of the Sphere's circular walkway. High above the pair could see the battle raging on the very brim of the statue's hood. The Archangel and Tartarus had so far been relatively evenly matched, except now the Shadows had joined the fray. Forming a dark circle they tried to harass the Archangel at any possible opportunity; diverting his attention away from Tartarus.

"We have to help him," Alice said as she stared up at the distant fight.

"We have to shut this thing down!" Mark responded.

"If we turn this off, they will soon be down here," Alice pointed out.

"But the world will be safe!" Mark retorted.

"No they'll just restart it again and what of the nanites that are already devouring the city?"

It was then that a weak voice entered both their minds; in the space of a few words it told them what they had to do.

The Archangel dodged yet another lunge from behind as the Shadows exploited any opportunity to weaken him. So far they had lost several of their number in these attacks but had successfully inflicted multiple small stab wounds through the Archangel's armour. Diving to the side he avoided a swing from Tartarus but went straight into the path of a Shadow who struck out wildly towards him. Raising his sword he only just managed to block the blow.

Time was fast running out as the Shadows closed in. But then as he evaded yet another blow Hera's frail voice entered his mind and spoke to him. As he fought on, her words filled him with new strength as he realised what she was planning. Quickly he vaulted out of the circle and spun round so the Shadows couldn't see what he was doing. In a split second he tore the medallion free from his neck and let it drop to the floor where it slid down the right hand side of the statue's hood. The Shadows didn't seem to notice as the piece of metal disappeared and the fight continued as before.

The pendant slowly picked up speed as gravity took hold; it wasn't long before the medallion was skidding down the near vertical sides of the hood and tumbled into seeming nothingness. Spinning several times it fell with the light glinting through its crystals as the shoulders seemed to race up towards it. Just before the impact though, a hand reached out and snatched it from destruction.

As the pendant fell into Alice's hands, Tartarus seemed to realise something was wrong. The Archangel seemed to be fighting back with

276

renewed vigour as if he was expecting victory. It was then that Tartarus noticed the absence of the medallion and a feeling of dread entered his mind. In response he sent the Shadows up into the air and back towards the control platform. They were not going to steal victory from him now!

As Gallagher opened fire on the first writhing hand which had breached the wall, a wave of others smashed through in quick succession sending pieces of masonry clattering to the floor. There were too many of them to target as they tore at the wall, ripping open ever larger holes; soon the gaps would be big enough to climb through. It wasn't long before a large section of plaster fell away and the brim of a hood became visible before a shot of seething plasma checked its progress. However, as this Shadow fell another almost instantly took its place.

Over to his right, Gallagher could hear a shriek from behind and turned for a fraction of a second to see Apollo plunging his sword through the thin door to drive off the hoard beyond. Gallagher then turned back to see a Shadow attempting to scramble through a tiny hole on the far side of the room. In response a succession of normal gunshots came from beside him as Natasha opened fire with her old pistol. Despite the use of regular bullets the gun still had the desired effect on the weak Shadow and it soon toppled backwards and out of sight. However, it was only a small victory against a vast number of hostiles. Huge gaps were forming all along the wall and the door was already disintegrating; it was only a matter of time.

Alice only realised she was being pursued when an arrow skimmed within a hair's breadth of her ear. She took a quick look behind her and was alarmed to see all five of the remaining Shadows hurtling towards her with their bows at the ready. Immediately she banked to the left, only just missing the deluge of arrows which sailed off passed her right wing.

277

As the enemies reloaded their bows she suddenly had an idea and darted off to the left heading straight for the side of the walkway. The walkway loomed ominously in front of her and as she shot over the top of the glass structure she reached out and grasped the railings, letting her momentum do the rest. Pivoting on the thick glass bar she performed a drastic change in direction and shot off downwards at incredible speed. The Shadows who were not expecting such a stunt and desperately pulled up to avoid striking the stone arms. However, in their haste, two of them collided straight into each other. Alice swerved back round the base of the statue's arms just as a section of the walkway shattered and the two of them slammed into the stonework beneath.

Corkscrewing round the arms she thought she had left the other assailants behind until they suddenly appeared from behind the walkway and fired. Diving to the left she was a fraction too slow as one of the arrows punched through her right wing and out the other side. The wound stung a little but was not serious so Alice charged on, straight for the control platform.

The glass platform was coming closer but she was too scared of being hit to slow down. Suddenly the platform seemed to rise up to meet her as she crashed down hard onto its surface. Her legs buckled and she found herself rolling across the glass until she came to a halt at the base of the steps. As she performed her ungainly landing Mark quickly performed his part. Gingerly he reached down into the recess in the panel and grasped the black medallion. Briefly he wondered how he had come to be in this mess as he tugged at the unnaturally cold object and tried to pull it free. At first the metal disk seemed as if it wasn't going to budge. However, Mark persevered and after considerable effort it finally flew free of the console.

High up on the statue's hood the two combatants turned in unison as the black pillar of nanites faltered and died.

"It appears you have lost," the Archangel announced.

"You think that little show of defiance will stop me?" Tartarus laughed. "My Shadows will soon kill your friends and restart the beam. And even if they do not then the nanites at the surface have been given their commands and will continue multiplying. A new black death will pour across this world one way or another."

"And that is why you must die," the Archangel replied simply as he leapt forwards once again.

Slowly Alice staggered back to her feet, using the steps to lever herself upright. The way to the control panel was clear so she quickly scaled the short flight of stairs with the medallion held tightly in her grasp. However, just before she reached the steps, the three Shadows suddenly swooped down and landed in her path with their bows trained on her.

"So close and yet so far," one of the Shadows sneered.

"You have cheated death a surprising number of times young human; but this time it is the end," the lead Shadow remarked as it pulled back on the string.

At the power plant the situation was deteriorating rapidly as the door finally shattered and both Apollo and Persephone were forced to leap deeper into the room; weapons at the ready. As the final pieces of the door were pushed aside a large group of hostiles all tried to force themselves in at once causing them to temporarily jam in the narrow frame. Seizing the opportunity Apollo was able to dispatch many of them before they were even able to get free. However, the situation deteriorated again as a large section of the wall collapsed in a cloud of dust and another wave of enemies poured in. A volley of arrows and plasma rounds was only just enough to hold them off. There were just too many Shadows and as they advanced the Angels and their allies were forced deeper into the room.

It was then at this critical moment that Apollo felt something in his mind; the presence was weak but it could only be Hera.

279

"Apollo; you must reactivate the station," she said slowly.

"We have just lost control of the console," he replied as he thrust his sword straight through and a nearby Shadow.

"We are running out of time. Tartarus is attempting to destroy the world; it has to fire now!" she said as she withdrew; her strength spent.

Apollo quickly relayed this to Persephone; the controls were now behind the advancing Shadows and they would have to fight even harder to recover the lost ground.

As the three Shadows sent their arrows sailing towards the target, Alice reacted with incredible speed. She had seen the Angels form bows, daggers and swords so she knew they were possible but what about something a little larger... Raising her left arm she formed an image in her head and instantly the nanites responded. Racing out from her arm they formed a shining tear drop shaped shield which shone out into the gloom. The arrows were no match for Alice's handiwork and shattered upon impact.

Alice didn't just leave it there and before the Shadows could react she had launched herself towards her attackers and slammed the shield down onto the first Shadow. The hostile to her left suddenly seized the opportunity to lunge towards her but Alice was too fast and swung the shield round; smashing it across the Shadow's head with enough force to cave its skull in. Continuing the sweeping movement she spun around one hundred and eighty degrees before releasing the shield. It revolved a couple of times as it sliced through the air before crashing into the final Shadow to send it tumbling to the ground.

Swords danced as the duel entered its final phase. Blurring together the two combatants circled each other as they countered each other's blows with neither able to achieve a victory. Yet another swipe skimmed past the Archangel's neck and Tartarus blocked another flourish. However, the duel was abruptly ended as Tartarus moved his sword in from the right and summoned a dagger to his left. As the Archangel moved to deal with the first attack he didn't see the dagger until it was too late.

As the blade punched through his armour and deep into his chest the Archangel stood looking at the blade; defiance still burning in his eyes before he slowly sank down onto his knees.

"You fought well old friend but it seems that I have won," Tartarus remarked as he stared down at his creator.

"No... Not exactly," the Archangel gasped as he knelt there.

"How can you still not admit that you have lost!" Tartarus yelled. "My Shadows' control the Spire, the Angels are too far away to reach us and only one of our kind can use the activation key. Where exactly is my disadvantage?"

"Do you really want to know?" the Archangel asked in a weak voice; despite the pain a smile still spread across his face. "Your Shadows are dead." In response Tartarus looked down at the platform and was stunned to see the limp remains of his creations. How could the humans have possibly defeated them? The balance of power was shifting too much for his liking; in a split second he made a decision and reached out with his mind towards the surface to give the corrupted nanites their final orders.

"So you have had your little victory," Tartarus snarled. "Enough nanites have already been released to fulfil my plan and I no longer need the Spire. By the time Hera makes it to the controls it will be too late..."

Across the city the highest buildings had been worn down to only a shadow of their former glory. One by one the tendrils of darkness wrapped around ever more structures consuming them with terrifying speed. People looked on in terror as judgment beckoned and debris rained from above. Thousands had already fled their homes as they ran from their impending doom.

281

The Spire had by this point stopped emitting fresh nanites but a black swarm of them still hung above the tower. However, upon receiving their new orders the nanorobots quickly began to take shape as dozens of inky tentacles extended downwards towards the Spire. Coiling and writhing they twisted around one another as they rapidly approached the smooth glass walls of the tower and smashed their way inside, devouring all in their path. As they latched onto the load bearing columns and began to eat ravenously, time began to run out for the Spire.

As Apollo and Persephone continued to slash away at the Shadows, Gallagher and Natasha continued to fire as quickly as they were able; knocking out many of the dark beings before they reached the two Angels. Step by step they drove the enemy back until at last the lever was within reach.

"Push the lever up," Apollo called out to the humans behind him. "End this!"

Quickly Natasha and Kennedy rushed over to the lever and began to slide it into place. However, the Shadows soon saw what they were doing and began to mentally move the metal object in the other direction. Natasha pushed with all her might as did Kennedy with his one good hand however all they could achieve was a kind of stalemate where the lever remained stuck between the two positions. Assessing the situation Gallagher fired a few more times before he broke from his position and ran over to join the other two. With his added strength the lever slowly but surely began to move into place.

On the platform, the last Shadow lay mortally wounded as it watched Alice raise the medallion over the console and slowly lower it into place. Sinking down into the machine an array of sensors scanned the device extracting the correct programming from the tiny carvings around the edges of the metal disk. The Spire now had its orders but didn't have the power to fulfil them until the combined strength of Gallagher, Natasha and Kennedy eventually forced the lever back into

282

place. As the dying Shadow continued to watch, the first glimmers of white began to break through the corruption that filled the Sphere. It knew that they had lost and strangely it couldn't help feeling that it was right.

Whilst the Shadow breathed its last breath, the light inside the Sphere exploded outwards consuming the darkness that had poisoned it. Like a white sun the Sphere shone out bathing the cavern in its brilliance. Up on the statue's hood Tartarus felt the light upon the back of his robes and turned away from the wounded Archangel in surprise. No! They were ruining everything; he had to stop them!

Completely forgetting the Archangel he ran towards the void unfolding his wings as he went. Behind him though, the Archangel quickly tore the dagger from his chest and in a wave of awful pain staggered to his feet, charging forwards. Tartarus soon reached the edge and took off with his wings fully extended. However, the Archangel closed the distance and leapt over the edge grabbing hold of his former friend. Tartarus panicked trying to gain altitude but powerful hands tightly grasped hold of his wings and were pulling them out of alignment. Unable to fly Tartarus rapidly lost control and spun chaotically as the two of them plummeted towards the walkway. At the last moment though he was able to free one of his wings and managed to avoid a collision but the Archangel would not let go of the other wing and the pair plunged in a deadly embrace.

Girders groaned and concrete shattered as the nanites tore into the fabric of the great tower. Rivers of the corrupted nanorobots poured through the floors collapsing each one in turn. It wasn't long before they had eaten through the casing of the firing shaft and began to pour downwards towards a strange pale white light far below.

Alice and Mark watched in awe as the Sphere continued to shine with a light that seemed to represent everything pure in this world. Below them the column of blue un-programmed nanites were fast approaching the base of the Sphere. This had to work!

283

Apollo swung his sword out, slaying yet another Shadow but the torrent of enemies was ever increasing. Turning briefly, he reached out and crushed the activation switch with his mind leaving it jammed in the on position. From there they began to retreat deeper into the room; time was running out for them...

The blue pillar of nanites made contact with the Sphere which once again began to swell and rotate rapidly as it prepared to fire...

Persephone ducked under a crude sword which cut through the air above her head and she stabbed the assailant in the ribs whilst another enemy leapt past her heading for Apollo. There wasn't time to stop him as he plunged the knife down into Apollo's shoulder blade. A shot from Gallagher swiftly dealt with the Shadow but the damage was done and Apollo's sword fell from his grasp. There was no way they could hold out now. Only a miracle could save them...

In the depths of the cavern the dream the Archangel had worked towards for ten long years was about to be realised as with a thunderous roar a jet of shining nanites blasted up into the roof of the cavern. Rapidly they entered the shaft to the surface and raced on erasing their corrupted counterparts as they went.

From several hundred metres away the other Angels turned back to watch as the Spire creaked and groaned. They had received no news from the Ark and many wept beneath their hoods. But then suddenly a flash of white burst out of the fiftieth floor through a gaping hole in the structure. Immediately the Angels turned to look just as another cloud of nanites shot out through a crack in the one hundredth floor. The Angels almost dared not to breathe as every few floors the nanites exploded outwards in a brilliant jet; there were so many gaps in the structure, would they reach the pinnacle?

Tartarus and the Archangel corkscrewed through the air as they plummeted downwards. Tartarus frantically clawed at his rival trying to make him release his hold but to no avail. Tartarus desperately tried to summon his sword but upon its completion the Archangel forced it from his grasp. They were going to slam into the ground and there was nothing Tartarus could do about it.

Less than a few seconds after the firing sequence began and to the jubilation of the Angels, the white column finally erupted out of the Spire high into the night sky. In unison the Angels cheered with delight, hugging each other in mid air joyously. They had finally done it! However, the celebrations stopped abruptly as a terrible groan came from the Spire as several floors collapsed. Could the Spire hold out long enough to complete the process?

In the Ark multiple alarms blared out and the hologram of the Spire automatically appeared with large vast sections highlighted in red.

"What do you think it means?" Mark asked.

"The Spire is failing," a voice came from behind them.

Both Alice and Mark turned to see Hera walking painfully towards them.

"Will it last long enough?" Alice asked but got no reply as Hera unexpectedly turned away.

"*You know what you have to do Hera,*" the Archangel said softly at the back of her mind.

"*But what about you?*" she replied.

285

"*I do not matter. Fulfil the dream and begin the new age,*" the Archangel replied with a strange calmness as the ground thundered towards him and Tartarus with incredible speed. "*Goodbye my little Angel.*"

Tears flowed down Hera's concealed face as she made her way over to one of the consoles. She had to do this; it was the only way. Swiftly she pulled open a panel and placed her hand upon a scanner. Instantly the hologram of the Spire vanished and in its place a countdown appeared showing 00:29.

"What are you doing?" Alice gasped.

"Ending this."

For half a mile the glistening pillar of nanites rose into the night sky. Upon reaching the correct altitude it quickly began to change shape as its upper most reaches began to fan out and spill over into a great glowing ball which hung motionless in the air. With every passing second the pillar fed it with more nanites allowing it to rapidly swell in size. In the space of ten seconds it was already half a kilometre across and still growing although it was still far too small.

Far below, one of the Spire's main columns suddenly cracked and the tower shifted a half a degree to the south west; however the beam kept going strong. Around the Spire, debris fell burying the construction site but still the tower held; it had come too far to fall now.

It was at this moment that the thousands of fleeing people all slowed in unison and turned to gaze upwards at the amazing brilliance which shone down through the clouds turning night into day. Despite the devastation that they had just witnessed no one wanted to run or hide; the light seemed so perfect and pure. Why would they want to run from it and then suddenly, the sphere exploded.

Like a star in a supernova, the giant sphere suddenly swelled in size and raced outwards in a brilliant flash of light. As the nanites surged downwards towards the ground, the onlookers still did not move as the

Spire vanished into the light. As if in a trance they continued to look on at the amazing beauty before them as the sphere swelled to over four miles in diameter and made contact with the ground. Still the sphere continued to expand and in the wave of light, engulfed every building in its path. Still the people did not move as the wave surged forwards and fell upon them.

At the power station, the three humans and two Angels had been forced back to the rear wall of the control room. Shadows were now streaming into the room from all sides and were preparing for an attack. So many of their number had fallen that they now massed into a dark wall and, slowly but surely, constricted the space available to their enemies.

Inside the trap Persephone and Gallagher continued to fire however it seemed to make no impact on the vast hoard in front of them. Apollo had tried to break through the wall behind them but it was made of thick concrete and he had little impact. The only way through seemed to be three slit like windows five metres above them however they were just too small for them to escape.

The enemy was now only a few metres away, braying for blood when suddenly a light began to shine through the windows. Gallagher wasn't sure what it meant but instantly the Shadows halted and looked around nervously. With every passing second the light grew brighter and in unison the enemy began to back away shuffling and tripping over each other in blind panic but it was no use. The wave of nanites burst in through the windows and swept over all in their path.

Inside the light Gallagher could hear the Shadows wailing in despair before their voices were silenced. All around him the light raced by; beautiful, pure and dazzling. The effect was strange as if it was passing straight through him and reaching every cell in his body. But then almost as soon as it had begun it was over and the light moved on. Before them the control room lay dark and empty except for a large pile of ash.

The sphere had been transformed into a halo of light which now raced with increasing speed out across the surface of the Earth. People have dreamt of a perfect world for as long as humanity has existed; now as the light circumnavigated the globe this dream was made a reality. The blind could see, the crippled could walk and the deaf could hear. The planet was healed.

However, a great vision cannot be completed without great sacrifice and as the nanites raced off, the Spire gave one final agonising groan and began to disintegrate. The one and a half mile structure was damaged beyond repair and would cause untold devastation if its three million tonne bulk were to fall onto the city. A new era was dawning but thousands would not even live to see it.

However, this eventuality had been foreseen long ago and as the countdown in the Ark reached zero over four thousand demolition charges buried in the rock at the tower's base detonated. The explosion was muffled by the millions of tonnes of rock above but its effects were dramatic as a circular crack tore open around the base of the tower and began to sink downwards into the chasm below. For a few moments the great Spire seemed to stand proud one last time before it succumbed to gravity and began to plummet down into the void.

Half a mile below, the ceiling of the Central Cavern thundered downwards shattering the great statue into millions of jagged fragments. Under the immense strain the arms tore free from the shoulders allowing molten metal to spurt out into the abyss. Disconnected from its controls and no longer being fed with materials, the Sphere's light finally died as it exploded outwards into a shower of particles; its task completed. For what seemed like an eternity the Spire continued its descent into the chasm with the faint beam of nanites still streaming from its battered summit.

Just as the light began to fail, two small specks of white burst free of the pinnacle. It had been a close run thing but as the tower slipped into the underworld, first Hera and then Alice emerged through the disintegrating shaft holding Mark in their arms. Beneath them, they watched as the tip of the Spire struck the outer edge of the chasm and

288

tore apart in a shower of gold before it was engulfed in the dark abyss. It was over...

Epilogue

In the hours after the collapse of the Spire, the halo like wave of nanites completed their journey across the planet and converged in the heart of the Australian Outback. Little more than a metre or so high the halo collapsed in on itself and fell to Earth as a fine white powder; its job completed. As the last nanites floated to Earth they left the planet in a frenzy. Governments, the media and the general public clamoured for answers which they could not find. All around them miracles were happening which they could not explain as the world was remade anew.

The blind could see, the lame could walk and the sick were healed. Hospitals emptied of people and care homes were filled with laughter as the burdens of old age were lifted. Almost instantly crime rates plunged as thieves found they no longer wanted to steal and murderers could no longer kill. Out in Africa two civil wars immediately ended as the two sides embraced each other as friends and in the Middle East, corrupt dictators found they no longer had the strength to oppress their people. The faults of the old Earth had been fixed and a new era had dawned.

The effects of the Spire soon became known in every corner of the planet but as to how it had happened remained a mystery. It wasn't long before attention focused on the Spire and drones were sent down into the immense chasm to search for answers. However, after venturing nearly three miles down all they found was an immense debris pile; the wonders of the Ark had vanished without a trace along with the Spire.

People eventually filled in the blanks and the rumours soon spread like wildfire. Strange reports from unknown sources only added to speculation as they confirmed the involvement of Lord Aries and his subsequent demise. In life he had never been quiet about his faith in technology; in fact he had said many times to the press that it would overcome any obstacle and revolutionise mankind's existence. It wasn't long before he acquired an almost mythical status.

Rapidly the world's governments tried to condemn the actions of an *insane billionaire* but the majority of people would have none of it. He had saved millions worldwide from suffering and rapidly became a hero for people to aspire to be. When it became clear that no official ceremony was to be held for him the people took matters into their own hands...

Three weeks after the collapse of the Spire over five million people descended on the city and crowded together on the edges of the chasm. It was the largest gathering the city had ever seen as people came solemnly to pay their respects to a man they had never known but who had given his life to end suffering.

One by one the mass of people slowly moved to the front and stood at the edge for a few moments before releasing a handful of flower petals into the chasm which were allowed to flutter down into the void below. As the mourners one by one repeated this gesture the jagged edges of the pit slowly became smothered in a carpet of stray petals.

It was a half an hour into the ceremony that Alice and Mark eventually reached the edge of the pit and gazed down into the blackness. For a few moments they just stood there reliving that night when the world changed forever and remembering the person who had made it all possible.

"Thank you," Alice whispered beneath her breath as she released her own handful of petals to join the thousands of others falling into the depths below.

"We knew him for such a short space of time and yet the world doesn't seem right without him now," Mark said as they continued to stare downwards.

"Yes," a voice said behind them. Both Alice and Mark turned to see Gallagher, Natasha and Kennedy who had appeared behind them.

"London doesn't seem right without the Spire anymore; looming down on us from above," Gallagher remarked.

"The city seems all the poorer without it," Mark agreed as the detectives dropped two handfuls of blue petals into the abyss.

"How are you doing at the police?" Alice asked as the five of them turned back into the crowd.

"It's a lot quieter," Kennedy remarked. "There's still petty crime but the murder rate has fallen to zero."

"Does that mean you're out of a job?" Mark asked.

"Not just yet. Anyway we joined the police to make a difference and that is exactly what we've done," Gallagher remarked.

For a while they walked in silence through the crowd until Mark eventually asked.

"I wonder where the Angels are now? It seems odd how they left so suddenly without even saying goodbye."

"They're probably here now?" Natasha remarked. "I mean this is a ceremony for their creator I'd guess they were here somewhere."

"Yeah... see that building over there," Alice said pointing as her eyes focused on something. "There's a concealed figure standing on the edge."

"Just one of them?" Gallagher asked.

"Yes," Alice said before adding. "They're beckoning us over."

It took five minutes to move through the crowd over to the base of the three story building in question where they found the door unlocked for them. Quickly they made their way up through the corridors and staircases until only the final flight to the roof remained.

Almost apprehensively they opened the door to see a lone Angel standing on the edge of the building looking down on the ceremony below. They may have all looked identical but Alice somehow felt that it was Hera.

"We have been waiting for you," she said slowly turning to face them.

"We?" Gallagher said as he turned to see over a hundred Angels materialising in quick succession. The vast majority stood in a dense group however Apollo and Persephone stood slightly further forwards than the rest.

"We have fulfilled our purpose and now it is time for us to leave," Hera said calmly as she stepped down from the ledge and walked around the group to stand in between Apollo and Persephone.

"You're leaving," Alice repeated. "But where will you go?"

"Where we are needed," Hera replied. "But before we go we have one final thing that we must do..." For a few moments she just stared at them before unexpectedly she bowed her head. The five of them were unsure what to do as all of the other Angels did the same.

"We would like to say thank you. Your courage and determination saved us and all of humanity. You have our everlasting gratitude and respect."

Then as the Angels raised their heads they began to slowly fade away one by one leaving the four of them alone on the rooftop. However, just before they completely vanished a solitary figure lingered for a few seconds longer. Like the others the hood was worn low over their face but beneath that, the heavily damaged armour glinted in the sunlight. In response the stunned spectators couldn't help smiling in delight as the Archangel silently nodded towards them in gratitude before he too vanished into nothingness.

And so this chapter of mankind was concluded; but this is a story that never ends...

293

Other Titles by the Author

Coming soon...

A Tale of Three Empires: Burning Giants

In a world where three great empires teeter on the verge of war, small events have great consequences...

When two zeppelins of the Imperial and Alliance navies collide with each other and explode over a remote chain of islands it sets a series of events in motion that risk plunging the whole world into war. It falls to an unlikely pair of survivors to try and overt the conflict and discover the island's mysterious secret.

That is of course if they don't kill each other along the way...

Picture Books for Children

Tales from the Forest

1 Badger's Holiday

2 Fire Breath

3 Finding the Sun

4 A Touch of Magic

5 A Spooky Night